A Season of Love

A Season of Love

CARLA KELLY

SWEETWATER
BOOKS

An Imprint of Cedar Fort, Inc.
Springville, Utah

Other Books by Carla Kelly

FICTION

Daughter of Fortune

Miss Charley's Guided Tour

Marian's Christmas Wish

Mrs. McVinnie's London Season

Libby's London Merchant

Miss Grimsley's Oxford Career

Miss Billings Treads the Boards

Mrs. Drew Plays Her Hand

Summer Campaign

Miss Whittier Makes a List

The Lady's Companion

With This Ring

Miss Milton Speaks Her Mind

One Good Turn

The Wedding Journey

Here's to the Ladies: Stories of the Frontier Army

Beau Crusoe

Marrying the Captain

The Surgeon's Lady

Marrying the Royal Marine

The Admiral's Penniless Bride

Borrowed Light

For This We Are Soldiers

Coming Home for Christmas: Three Holiday Stories

Enduring Light

Marriage of Mercy

My Loving Vigil Keeping

Her Hesitant Heart

The Double Cross

Safe Passage

Carla Kelly's Christmas Collection

In Love and War

A Timeless Romance Anthology: Old West Collection

Marco and the Devil's Bargain

Softly Falling

Paloma and the Horse Traders

Reforming Lord Ragsdale

Enduring Light

Summer Campaign

Doing No Harm

A Timeless Romance Anthology: A Country Christmas

A Timeless Romance Anthology: All Regency Collection

The Star in the Meadow

Courting Carrie in Wonderland

NONFICTION

On the Upper Missouri: The Journal of Rudolph
Friedrich Kurz

Ford Buford: Sentinel at the Confluence

Stop Me If You've Read This One

This is a work of fiction. The characters, names, incidents, places, and dialogue are products of the author's imagination and are not to be construed as real. The opinions and views expressed herein belong solely to the author and do not necessarily represent the opinions or views of Cedar Fort, Inc. Permission for the use of sources, graphics, and photos is also solely the responsibility of the author.

ISBN 13: 978-1-4621-1982-0

Published by Sweetwater Books, an imprint of Cedar Fort, Inc.
2373 W. 700 S., Springville, UT 84663
Distributed by Cedar Fort, Inc., www.cedarfort.com

Library of Congress Control Number: 2017950957

Cover design by Katie Payne
Cover design © 2017 by Cedar Fort, Inc.
Edited and typeset by Jessica Romrell and Nicole Terry

Printed in the United States of America

10 9 8 7 6 5 4 3 2 1

Printed on acid-free paper

Contents

SEASON'S REGENCY GREETINGS

Let Nothing You Dismay

It was obvious to Lord Trevor Chase, his solicitor, and their clerk that all the other legal minds at Lincoln's Inn had been celebrating the approach of Christmas for some hours. The early closing of King's Bench, Common Pleas, Chancery Court, and Magistrate's Court until the break of the new year was the signal for general merrymaking among the legal houses lining Chancery Lane. He had already sent his clerk home with a hefty bonus.

Trevor had never felt inclined to celebrate the year's cases, won or lost. He seldom triumphed at court because his clients were generally all guilty. True, their crimes were among the more petty in English law, but English law always came down hard against miscreants who meddled with another's property, be it land, gold bullion, a loaf of bread, or a pot of porridge. A good day for Lord Trevor was one where he wheedled a reprieve from the drop and saw his client transported to Australia instead. He knew that most Englishmen in 1810 would not consider enforced passage to the Antipodes any sort of victory. Because of this, a celebration, even for the birth of Christ, always felt vaguely hypocritical to him. Besides that, he knew his solicitor was in a hurry to be on his way to Tunbridge Wells.

But not without a protestation, because the solicitor, an earnest young man, name of George Dawkins, was almost as devoted to his young charges as he was. "Trevor, you know it is my turn to take that deposition," the good man said, even as he pulled on his coat and looked about for his hat. "And when was the last time you spent more than a day or two home at Chase Hall?"

"You, sir, have a family," Trevor reminded him firmly. "And a wife eager to see her parents in Kent."

Dawkins must have been thinking about the events of last Christmas. "Yes, but I could return for the deposition. I would rather not . . ." he paused, his embarrassment obvious.

". . . leave me alone here, eh? Is that it?" Trevor finished his solicitor's thought.

The man knew better than to bamboozle. "Yes, that's it. I don't want to return to . . . Well, you know. You were lucky last time."

Not lucky, Trevor thought. I thought I was home free. Darn those interfering barristers in the next chamber. "I suppose. I suppose," he said. "I promise to be good this year."

His solicitor went so far as to take his arm. "You'll do nothing besides take that deposition? You'll give me no cause for alarm?"

"Certainly not," Trevor lied. He shrugged off his solicitor's arm (even as he was touched by his concern), and pulled on his overcoat. He looked around the chamber, and put on his hat. Nothing here would he miss.

He and his solicitor went downstairs together and stood at the Chancery Lane entrance to the Inn. He looked up at the evening sky—surprisingly clear for London in winter— and observed the stars. "A rare sight, Dawkins," he said to his employee.

As they both looked upward, a little shard of light seemed to separate itself from a larger brightness, rather like shavings from some celestial woodcarver. Enchanted, he watched as it dropped quickly, blazed briefly, then puffed out.

Dawkins chuckled. "We should each make a wish, Trevor," he said, amusement high in his voice. "Me, I wish I could be more than five minutes on our way and not have one of my children ask, 'How much farther, Papa?'" He turned to Trevor. "What do you wish?"

"I don't hold with wishing on stars," he replied.

"Not even Christmas stars?"

"Especially not those."

But he did. Long after his solicitor had bade him good night and happy Christmas, and was whistling his way down the lane, Trevor stood there, hesitating like a fool, and unable to stop from staring into the heavens. He closed his eyes.

"I wish, I wish someone would help me."

"Miss Ambrose, do you think we will arrive in time for me to prevent my sister from making this Tragic Mistake that will blight her life and doom her to misery? I *wish* the coachman would pick up speed!"

Cecilia Ambrose—luckily for her—had been hiding behind a good book when her pupil burst out with that bit of moral indignation. She raised the book a little higher to make sure that Lady Lucinda Chase would not see her smile.

"My dear Lady Lucinda, I have not met her, but from what I know of your family, I suspect she is in control of her situation. Is it not possible that your sister welcomes her coming nuptials? Stranger things have happened."

Her young pupil rolled her eyes tragically, and pressed the back of her hand to her cheek. "Miss Ambrose, in her last letter to me she actually admitted that Sir Lysander kissed her! Can you imagine anything more distasteful? Oh, woe!"

Cecilia abandoned her attempt at solemnity, put down the book after marking her place, and laughed. When she could speak, she did so in rounder tones. "My dear little scholar, I think you are lacing this up a bit tight. If the wicked stage were not such a pit of evil and degradation, you would probably be anointed a worthy successor to Siddons! It is, um, possible that your sister doesn't consider kissing to be distasteful. You might even be inclined to try it yourself someday."

The look of horror that Lucinda Chase cast in her direction assured Cecilia that the time was not quite ripe for such a radical comment. And just as well, she thought as she put her arm around her twelve-year-old charge. "It is merely a suggestion, my dear. Perhaps when you are eighteen, you will feel that way, too." It seemed the teacherly thing to say, especially for someone into her fifth year as instructor of drawing and pianoforte at Miss Dupree's Select Academy for Young Ladies.

Her young charge was silent for a long moment. She sighed. "Miss Ambrose, I suppose you are right. I do not know that Janet would listen to me, anyway. Since her come out she has changed, and it makes me a little sad."

Ah, the crux of the matter, Cecilia thought as the post chaise bowled along toward York. She remembered Miss Dupree's admonition about maintaining a firm separation between teacher and pupil and—not for the first time—discarded it without a qualm. She touched Lucy's cheek. "You're concerned, aren't you, that Janet is going to grow up and leave you behind?" she asked, her voice soft. "Oh, my dear, she will not! You will always be sisters, and someday you, too, will understand what is going on with her right now. Do trust me on this. Perhaps things are not as bad as you think."

Her conclusion was firm, and precisely in keeping with her profession. Lucy sighed again, but to Cecilia's ears, always quite in tune with the nuances of the young, it was not a despairing sigh.

"Very well, Miss Ambrose," her charge said. "I will trust you. But it makes me sad," she added. She looked up at her teacher. "Do you think I will survive the ordeal of this most trying age?"

Cecilia laughed out loud. "Wherever did you hear that phrase?"

It was Lucy's turn to grin. "I overheard Miss Dupree talking to my mama, last time she visited."

"You will survive," Cecilia assured her. "I mean, I did." Lucy stared at her. "Really, Lucy, I *was* young once!"

"Oh! I didn't mean that you are precisely old, Miss Ambrose," Lucy burst out. "It's just that I didn't . . ." Her voice trailed away, but she tried to recover. "I don't know what I meant."

I do, Cecilia thought. Don't worry, my dear. You're not the first, and probably not the last. She smiled at her charge to put her at ease, and returned to her book. Lucy settled down quietly and soon slept. Cecilia put the book down then and glanced out the window on the snowy day. She could see her reflection in the glass. Not for the first time, she wondered what other people thought when they looked at her.

She knew she was nice-looking, and that her figure was trim. In Egypt, where her foster parents had labored for many years—Papa studying ancient Coptic Christian texts, and Mama doing good in many venues—her appearance excited no interest. In England, she was an exotic, Egyptian-looking. Or as her dear foster brother liked to tease her, "Ceely the Gift of the Nile." Cecilia looked at Lucinda again and smiled. And heaven knows I am old, in the bargain, she thought, all of eight and twenty. I doubt Lucinda knows which is worst.

She knew that her foster brother would find this exchange amusing, and she resolved to write him that night, when they stopped. It was her turn to sigh, knowing that a letter to William would languish three months in the hold of an East India merchant vessel bound for Calcutta, where he labored as a missionary with his parents now, who had been forced to abandon Egypt when Napoleon decided to invade. She looked out the window at the bare branches, wishing that her dear ones were not all so far away, especially at Christmas.

She had been quite content at the thought of spending Christmas in Bath at the Select Academy. Miss Dupree was engaged to visit her family in London, and the other teachers had made similar arrangements. She had remained at the Academy last year, and found the solitude to her liking, except for Christmas Day. Except for that one day, when it was too quiet, it was the perfect time to catch up on reading, grade papers, take walks without students tagging along, and write letters. That one day she had stood at the window, wanting to graft herself onto families hurrying to dinner engagements or visiting relatives. But the feeling passed, and soon the pupils and teachers returned.

Lady Maria Chase, Marchioness of Falstoke, had written to Cecilia a month ago, asking if she could escort Lucinda home to Chase Hall, on the great plain of York. *I cannot depend upon my brother-in-law, Lord Trevor Chase, to escort her because that dear man is woefully ramshackle. Do help us out, Miss Ambrose,* she had written.

At the time, Cecilia saw no reason to decline the invitation, which came with instructions about securing a post chaise, and the list of which inns would be expecting them. Miss Dupree had raised her eyebrows over the choice of inns, commenting that Cecilia would be in the lap of luxury, something out of the ordinary for a teacher, even a good one at a choice school. "I doubt you will suffer from damp sheets or underdone beef," had been her comment.

No, she did not wish to visit in Yorkshire. Lucinda had not meant to be rude, but there it was. I *am* different here in England, Cecilia thought. I might make my hosts uncomfortable. As they traveled over good roads and under a cold but bright sky, Cecilia resolved to remain at Chase Hall only long enough to express her concerns to her pupil's mother, and catch a mail coach south. It was too much to consider that the marquis would furnish her with a post chaise for the return trip.

Always observant of her students, especially the more promising ones, Cecilia had watched Lucy mope her way through the fall term. Her pupil, a budding artist, completed the required sketches and watercolors, but without enthusiasm. As she gave the matter serious consideration, Cecilia thought that the bloom left the rose with the letter from home in which Janet announced her engagement to Sir Lysander Polk of the Northumberland Polks, a dour collection of thin-lipped landowners—according to Lucinda, who already had an artist's eye for caricature—who had somehow begotten a thoroughly charming son. Not only was Lysander charming; he was handsome in the extreme, and rich enough in the bargain to make Lord Falstoke, a careful parent, smile. Or so Lucy had declared, when she shared the letter with Cecilia.

The actualities were confirmed a short time later, when Lord and Lady Falstoke and the betrothed pair stopped at the Select Academy on their way to London's modistes, cobblers, and milliners. On acquaintance with Sir Lysander, who did prove to be charming and handsome, Cecilia began to see the difficulty. She watched how Lady Janet hung on his every word, and found herself unable to tear herself from his side during the entire evening. Cecilia could not overlook the fact that the more Janet clung, the quieter Lucinda became.

Cecilia looked down at her sleeping charge. It *is* a most trying age, my dear, she thought. Hopefully a visit home would prove the antidote. At least Cecilia could lay the matter before Lady Falstoke, and get help from that quarter.

They arrived at Falstoke in the middle of the next afternoon, and the view, even in December, did not disappoint. Cecilia listened with a smile on her face as Lucy, more excited as the miles passed, pointed out favorite places. Her smile deepened as Lucy took hold of her arm and leaned forward.

"Oh, Miss Ambrose, just around this bend!"

She knew that Hugo Chase, Marquis of Falstoke, was a wealthy man, but the estate that met her eyes surprised her a little. Chase Hall was smaller than she would have imagined, but discreet, tasteful, and totally in harmony with the setting of trees, meadow, and stream. She could see a small lake in the near distance.

"Oh, Lucinda!" she exclaimed.

"I love coming home," her pupil said softly.

They traveled the tree-lined lane to the circle drive and wide front steps, Lucy on the edge of the seat. When they came to a stop, Lucy remained where she was. "This is strange," she murmured. "No one is here to meet us." She frowned. "Usually the servants are lined up and Mama and Papa are standing on the steps." She took Cecilia's hand. "Can something be wrong?"

"Oh, surely not," Cecilia replied. "We would have heard." But we've been on the road, she added silently to herself. "Let us go inside." She patted Lucy's hand. "My dear, it is Christmastime and everyone is busy!" She saw the door open. "There, now. Uh, is that your butler? He is somewhat casual, is he not?"

Lucy looked up, her eyes even wider. "Something has happened! It is my uncle Trevor."

The man came down the steps as Lucy came up, and caught her in his arms. Cecilia was relieved to see the smile on his face; surely that did not signal bad news. It was a nice smile, she decided, even if the man behind it was as casually dressed as an out of work road mender. She couldn't really tell his age. She assumed that Lord Falstoke was in his middling forties. This uncle of Lucy's had to be a younger brother. How curious then, for his hair was already gray. She smiled to herself. And had not seen a comb or brush yet that day, even though it was late afternoon.

He was a tall man who, despite his disheveled appearance, managed to look quite graceful, even as he hugged his niece, then kissed the top of her head. No, graceful was not the precise word, she decided. He is dignified. I doubt anyone ever argues with him. I know I would not.

She left the post chaise herself, content to stand on the lowest step quite unnoticed, as a young boy hurtled out of the open door and into his sister's arms. The three of them—niece, nephew, and uncle—stood on the steps with their arms around one another. She came closer, feeling almost shy, and Lucy remembered her manners. "Miss Ambrose, I am sorry! Allow me . . . This is my uncle, Trevor Chase, Papa's only brother. Uncle, this is my teacher, Miss Cecilia Ambrose."

Cecilia didn't see how he did it, not with children on both sides of him, but he managed an elegant bow. You are well trained enough, she thought as she curtsied back, even if you do look like a refugee from Bedlam. "Delighted to meet you," she said.

"I doubt it," he replied, and there was no mistaking the good humor in his wonderful voice. "You are probably wondering what lunatic asylum I escaped from."

It was not the comment she expected, and certainly not the appraisal she was used to: one glance, and then another, when the person did not think she was looking. Cecilia could see nothing but goodwill on his face, rather than suspicion.

"My uncle is a barrister," the young boy said. He tugged on the man's sleeve. "I shall go find Janet," he said, and went into the house.

"You are . . . you are a barrister?" she asked. The name was familiar to her. Was he a father of a student in her advanced watercolor class? No, that was not it. It will come to me, she thought.

"Miss Ambrose, he is the best barrister in the City," Lucinda assured her. She leaned against him, and Cecilia could tell that in the short space of a few minutes, all of Miss Dupree's deportment lessons had flown away on little wings. "Papa says he likes to right wrongs, and that is why he almost never comes here. There are more wrongs in London, apparently."

The man laughed. "You're too polite, dear Lucy," he replied, and gave his niece a squeeze before he released her. "He refers to me as the patron saint of lost causes." He gestured toward Cecilia. "Come indoors, Miss Ambrose. You're looking a little chilly."

The foyer was as beautiful as she had thought it would be, soft color on the walls, delicate plasterwork above, and intricate parquetry underfoot. "What a wonderful place," she said.

"It is, indeed," Lord Trevor agreed. "I know there are many country seats larger than this one, but none more lovely, to my way of thinking." He rubbed his hands and looked around. "I love to come home, now and then."

"Where is Mama?" Lucy asked as a footman silently approached and divested her of her traveling cloak.

"Lucy! Thank God you have come! This family is beset with Trying Events!"

Well, I suppose I can safely say that others in this family besides Lucy tend to speak in capital letters, Cecilia thought as she allowed Lord Trevor to help in the removal of her cloak. Lucy ran to her sister Janet, who stood with her arms outstretched dramatically.

"I do believe the most trying event is Janet's propensity to be Yorkshire's premier actress of melodrama and melancholy," Lord

Trevor murmured to her as he handed her cloak to the footman. "I have only been here three days myself, and already I want to strangle her."

She looked at him in surprise, then put her lips together so she would not laugh.

Lord Trevor only grinned at her, which made the matter worse. "Such forbearance, Miss Ambrose," he said. "You have my permission to laugh! If you can withstand this, then you must be the lady who teaches deportment at Miss Dupree's Whatchamacallit."

"Far from it," she replied. "I teach drawing and the pianoforte."

He took her arm through his and walked her down the hall toward the two young ladies. "My dear Janet, wouldn't this be a good time to tell your sister what is going on, before she thinks that pirates from the Barbary Coast have abducted your parents?"

"Lucy would never think such a thing!" Janet declared, looking at him earnestly. "I doubt there have ever been any pirates in Yorkshire."

Lord Trevor only sighed. Forcing down her laughter, Cecilia spoke up in what she hoped were her best educator's tones. "Lady Janet, perhaps you can tell us where your parents are? Your sister is concerned."

Janet looked at her, a tragic expression on her lovely face. "Oh, Miss . . . Miss Ambrose, is it? My parents have bravely gone into a charnel house of pestilence and disease."

Lord Trevor glowered at his older niece. "Cut line, Janet," he said. He put his arm around Lucy. "Amelia's brood came down with the measles three days ago, and your parents have gone to York to help. I expect them home tomorrow. Amelia is the oldest of my nieces," he explained to Cecilia over his shoulder. "It's just the dratted measles."

"Only this afternoon I wrote to my dear Lysander, who will drop everything to hurry to this beleaguered household and give us the benefit of his wisdom," Janet said.

"Janet, we can depend upon Uncle Trevor to look out for us," Lucy said shyly.

"Uncle Trevor is far too busy to worry about us, Lucy," her sister replied, dismissing her sister with a wave of her handkerchief. "And didn't he say over breakfast this morning that he must return to London immediately after our parents are restored to us? Depend upon it; Lysander will hurry to my side, and all will be well." She nodded to Cecilia. "Come, Lucinda. I have much to tell you about my dear Lysander."

"But shouldn't I show Miss Ambrose to her room?" Lucy asked.

"That is what servants are for, Lucy. Come along."

After a backward glance at Cecilia, Lucinda trailed upstairs after her sister. Cecilia's face burned with the snub. Lord Trevor regarded her with sympathy.

"What do you say, Miss Ambrose? Should we wait until Lysander arrives, tie him up with Janet, and throw them both in the river? It's too late to drown them at birth. Ah, that is better," he said when she laughed. "Do excuse my niece's manners. If I ever fall in love—and the prospect seems remote—I promise not to be so rude." He indicated the sitting room, with its open door and fire crackling in the grate. "Come sit down, and let me take a moment to reassure you that we are not all denatured, drooling simpletons."

She needed no proof of that, but was happy to accompany him into the sitting room. He saw that she was seated close to the fire, a hassock under her feet, and then spoke to the footman.

"Tea or coffee, Miss Ambrose?" he asked. "I know coffee isn't ordinarily served in the afternoon, but I am partial to it, and don't have a second's patience with what I should and should not do."

"Coffee, if you please," she answered, amused out of her embarrassment. She removed her gloves, and fluffed her hair, trapped too long by her bonnet.

The footman left, and Lord Trevor stood by the fireplace. She regarded him with some interest, because she remembered now who he was. Miss Dupree, considered a radical by some, subscribed to two London newspapers, even going so far as to encourage her employees to read them. The other female teachers seldom ventured beyond the first page. The Select Academy's two male instructors read the papers during the day while they drank tea between classes. When class was over, and if the downstairs maid hadn't made her circuit, Cecilia gathered up the papers from the commons room. She took them to her room to pore over in the evening hours, after she had finished grading papers, and when it was not her turn to be on duty in the sitting room when the young ladies were allowed visitors.

She knew next to nothing of the British criminal trial system, but could not resist reading about the cases that even Mrs. Dupree, for all her radical views, must have considered sordid and sensational. No matter; Cecilia read the papers, and here was a barrister well known to her from criminal trials, written up in the florid style of the London dailies.

I should say nothing, she told herself as she sat with her hands folded politely, her ankles together. *He will think I am vulgar. Besides, I am leaving as soon as I can.*

He cleared his throat and she looked up.

"Miss Ambrose, I am sorry for this disorder in which you find us."

He is self-conscious about this, she thought. *I think he even wishes he had combed his hair. Look how he is running his fingers through it.* She smiled. *I suppose even brilliant barristers sometimes are caught up short. Well, join the human race, sir.*

"Oh, please don't apologize, Lord Trevor," she said. She hesitated, then gave herself a mental shrug. *This is a man I do admire,* she thought. *What can it hurt if I say something? I will be gone tomorrow.* "Lord Trevor, I . . . I sometimes read in the newspaper of your legal work."

"What?"

She winced inwardly. How could one man invest so much weight in a single word? Was this part of his training? Oh, Lord, I am glad I will never, ever have to face this man in the docket, she thought. Or over a breakfast table.

She opened her eyes wider, wondering at the origin of that impish thought. She reminded herself that she was a teacher, and dedicated to the edification of her pupils. Breakfast table, indeed!

She dared to glance at him, and saw, to her temporary relief at least, he had not turned from the fireplace, where he warmed his hands.

"I beg your pardon, Miss Ambrose," he was saying, "I must have misheard. Do forgive me. Did you say that you *read the newspaper*?"

"I do," she replied simply. She discovered that she could no more lie to this man than sprout wings and fly across the plain of York. In for a penny, she thought grimly. "And . . . and I am a great admirer of your work."

It must have been the wrong thing to say, she decided. Why on earth did I admit that I read the paper? she asked herself in misery as he slowly turned around from his hand warming. As he raised his eyebrows, she wished she could vanish without a trace and suddenly materialize in her Bath sitting room, grading papers and waiting for the dinner bell. "Well, I am," she said.

He smiled at her. "Why, thank you, Miss Ambrose." He seated himself beside her. "Do you pass on what you learn to your students?"

She listened hard for any sarcasm in his voice, but she could detect none. She also did not see any disparagement or condescension in his face, which gave her heart. "No, I don't pass it on," she said quietly, then took a deep breath. "I only wish that I could." She sat a little straighter then, suddenly feeling herself very much the child of crusading evangelists. "I believe you should receive great credit for what you do, rather than derision, Lord Trevor. Didn't I read only last week that you had been denied a position of Master of the Bench at Lincoln's Inn?"

"You did, indeed," he replied. "Sometimes I imagine that the Benchers wish I had been called from another Inn." He shrugged. "Even my brother Hugo calls this my 'deranged hobby.'"

The maid came in with coffee, which Cecilia poured. "You are going back to London tomorrow?" she asked.

"I am, as soon as Hugo and Maria arrive. Lowly Magistrate's Court does not sit during the holiday, but I have depositions to take." He took a sip and then sat back. "I know my solicitor could do that, but he wanted to spend the week with his family in Kent. I am, as you might suppose, a soft touch for a bare pleading."

"I am delighted to have met you, Lord Trevor," she told him.

The housekeeper stood at the door to the sitting room. Lord Trevor rose, cup in hand, and indicated that Cecilia follow her. "She'll show you to your room. We keep country hours here, so we will eat in an hour." He winked at the housekeeper, who blushed, but made no attempt to hide the smile in her eyes. "As you can also imagine, there's no need to dress up!"

Smiling now, the housekeeper led her upstairs. "He's a great one, is Lord Trevor," she said to Cecilia. "We only wish he came around more often."

"I suppose he is quite busy in London," Cecilia said. "Indeed he is," the woman replied, "even though I sometimes wonder at the low company he keeps." She stopped then, remembering her position. "Miss Ambrose, your pupil is across the hall. You'll hear the bell for dinner."

Cecilia decided before dinner that it would be easy to make her excuses the next day when Lord and Lady Falstoke returned, and take the mail coach back to Bath. She would express her concerns about Lucy to the marchioness before she left.

To her consternation, David looked as glum as his sister when he came into the dining room with Lord Trevor, who carried a letter. The man seated himself and looked at his nieces. "I received a post not twenty minutes ago from your parents," he said.

"They're not coming home tomorrow," David said. He looked down at his plate.

"Why ever not?" Janet asked, indignant. "Don't they know we need them? I mean, really, they took Chambliss with them, and Cook!"

"Chambliss is our butler," Lucy whispered to Cecilia.

"It seems that your older sister needs them more," Lord Trevor replied, his voice firm. "Do have a little compassion, Janet. They have promised to be here for Christmas. I'll be staying until they return."

Janet turned stricken eyes upon her uncle. "But they are to host Lysander!"

"Perhaps the earth will continue to orbit the sun if he has to postpone his arrival for a few days," Lord Trevor remarked dryly. "David, eat your soup."

They ate in silence, Lord Trevor obviously reviewing in his mind how this news would change his own plans. Cecilia glanced at Lucy, who whispered, "I will hardly have any time to be with her, before we must return to Bath."

"Then the time will be all the more precious, when it comes, my dear," Cecilia said, thinking of her dear ones in India.

David began to cry. Head down, he tried to choke back his tears, but they flowed anyway. Lord Trevor looked at him in dismay, then at Cecilia. As sorry as she felt for the little boy, she almost smiled at the desperation on the barrister's face. You can argue cases for the lowliest in the dockets, she thought, but your nephew's tears are another matter. She rose from the table. I have absolutely nothing to lose here, she thought. No one should be crying at Christmastime.

She walked over to David's chair and knelt at his side. "This is difficult, isn't it?" she asked him quietly. "I know your mama wishes she were here, too."

"She's only twenty miles away!" Lord Trevor exclaimed, exasperated.

"It's a long way, when you're only—are you six, my dear?" she asked the little boy, who had stopped crying to listen to her. She handed him her napkin.

"Seven," he mumbled into the cloth. "I am small for my age."

"You know, perhaps we could go belowstairs and ask the cook for . . ."

"Mama never coddles him like that," Janet said.

"I would," Cecilia answered. She looked at Lord Trevor, who was watching her with a smile of appreciation. "Do you mind, sir?"

"I don't mind at all," he replied. "Miss Ambrose, do as you see fit."

17

Cecilia took David downstairs. The second cook beamed at the boy, and suggested a bowl of the rabbit fricassee left from luncheon. In another minute, he was eating. Cecilia sat beside him, and Cook placed a bowl of stew before her, too. "If you don't mind leftovers," he said in apology. "I know Lord Trevor don't mind, but there are them above stairs who are a little too high in the instep these days."

"Janet makes us eat in the dining room," David said when he stopped to wipe his mouth. "We always eat in the breakfast room when Mama is here." He glared at the ceiling. "*She* thinks it is not grand enough."

"I think Janet is going through a trying time," Cecilia said, attempting to keep her face serious.

He shook his head. "Grown-ups do not have trying times."

They do, she thought. "Perhaps now and then."

She sat there, content in her surroundings, as David finished the stew. He pushed away the bowl when the cook brought in a tray of gingersnaps with a flourish, and remembered his manners to offer her one.

"Any left for me?"

You're a quiet man, Cecilia thought as she looked over to see Lord Trevor standing beside his nephew. David made room for his uncle on the bench. He passed the biscuits, even as the cook set a glass of milk in front of Lord Trevor. He dipped a biscuit in the milk and ate it, then looked at her. "Try it, Miss Ambrose. Anyone who reads newspapers can't mind dipping gingersnaps."

"Will I never be able to live that down?" she said as she dipped a gingersnap.

He touched David's shoulder. "It is safe to go above stairs now. Your sisters have retired to their room, where Janet, I fear, will continue to brag about darling Lysander."

"Oh, dear," Cecilia murmured. "I have to speak to Lady Falstoke about that."

"Then you must remain here through the week," Lord Trevor told her.

"I couldn't possibly do that," she replied as he gestured for her to proceed them up the stairs. "I will write her a letter from Bath."

The three of them walked down the hall together, uncle and nephew hand in hand. They paused at the foot of the stairs. "David and I will say good night here," Lord Trevor told her. "I brought my files with me from Lincoln's Inn, and he is helping arrange my 1808 cases alphabetically."

"But it is 1810," she reminded him. "Nearly 1811."

"I'm behind." He ran his long fingers through his hair, a gesture she was coming to recognize. "Not all of us were kissed by the fairy of efficiency at birth, madam!"

She laughed, enjoying that visual picture. He smiled at her, then spoke to David, who went on down the hall.

"I can't get you to change your mind?" he asked, keeping his voice down. "You can see from my ham handling of David at the dinner table that I need help." He hesitated. "I seldom stay here until Christmas. Well, I never do."

"I am certain you will manage until your brother and sister-in-law return." Cecilia curtsied to him. "Thank you, Lord Trevor, for your hospitality. If you can arrange for a gig to take me tomorrow to the mail coach stop, I will be on my way to Bath."

He bowed. "Stubborn woman," he scolded. "What is the big attraction in Bath?"

There is no big attraction in Bath, she thought. "I . . . It's where I live."

He took her hand. "That is almost as illogical as some of the courtroom arguments I must endure! Good night, Miss Ambrose. We will see you on your way to Bath tomorrow, since you are determined to abandon us."

"You are as dramatic as your nieces," she chided him.

"I know," he said cheerfully. "Ain't it a shame?"

She wasn't certain what woke her, hours later. Her first inclination was to roll over and go back to sleep. All was quiet. She sat up and allowed her eyes to focus on the gloom around her. Nothing. She debated whether to get up and look in the hall, but decided against it. That would mean searching for her robe, which she hadn't bothered to unpack, considering the brevity of her visit.

Then she heard it: someone pounding up the stairs and banging on a door down the hall. She leaped out of bed, ran to her door, and opened it at the same time she smelled smoke. Her hand to her throat now, she stepped into the hall. She thought she recognized the footman, even though he was wearing his nightshirt. "My lord! My lord!" he yelled as he banged on the door.

The door opened, and Lord Trevor stepped barefoot into the hall. "Fire, my lord," the footman said, breathless from dashing up the stairs. "The central chimney!"

Cecilia hurried back into her room, grabbed her traveling case, and threw it out the window. She snatched her cloak, stepped into her shoes, and turned around to see Lord Trevor right behind her. He grabbed her arm and pulled her into the hall. "Stay here," he ordered. "You don't know this manor." Smoke wafted up the stairs like her vision of the last plague of Egypt. She pulled a corner of her cloak across her face to cover her nose, and watched Lord Trevor go in the bedchambers and awaken his nieces and nephew.

He pulled David out first, and thrust him at her. She locked her arms tight around the sleepy child. "We'll wait right here for your uncle," she whispered into his hair.

Lucinda came next, her eyes wide with fear, and Janet followed, wailing about her clothes. "Shut up, Janet," her uncle ordered. "Take Lucy's hand and hold mine."

With his free hand he grabbed Cecilia around the waist and started down the stairs. David coughed and tried to pull away, but she clutched his hand. She put her other arm around Lord Trevor and turned her face into his nightshirt so she could breathe. No one said anything as they groped down the stairs and across the foyer. In another blessed moment the footman, who must have been in front of them in the smoky darkness,

A SEASON OF LOVE

flung open the front door. They hurried down the steps into the cold.

Still he did not release her. She kept her face tight against his chest, shivering from fright. If anything, he tightened his grip on her until his fingers were digging into the flesh of her waist. He must have realized then what he was doing, because he opened his hand, even though he did not let go of her.

She forced herself to remain calm, if not for herself, then for the children, and perhaps for Lord Trevor, who surely had more to do now than hold her so tight on the front lawn. She released her grip on his waist then, and stepped back slightly, so he had no choice but to let go.

Before he did, he leaned forward and kissed the top of her head. Because he offered no explanation for his curious act, and no apology, she decided that emergencies did strange things to people who were otherwise rational.

"Keep everyone here, Cecilia. No one goes back for anything." He turned and hurried up the steps again.

What about you? she wanted to call after him as he disappeared inside. She gathered his nieces and nephew around her. "We'll be fine, my dears," she told them, reaching out her arms to embrace them all. They stood together and watched the manor. Although smoke seeped from the front door, she saw no flames.

They endured several more minutes of discomfort, then Lord Trevor and the household staff came around the building from the back. The footman, more dignified with trousers now, carried the grip she had thrown out the window. Lord Trevor had also taken the time to find his own pants and shoes, although he still wore his nightshirt. To her amusement, the housekeeper was fully dressed. I'll wager you would rather have burned to a crisp before leaving your room in a state of semi-dress, she thought.

Lord Trevor hurried to her, the housekeeper and footman following. "Mrs. Grey will escort you and the children to the dower house for the night. It's in that little copse."

"Can you save our home, Uncle?" Janet asked, clutching his arm.

He kissed her cheek. "I rather think so. The servants are inside the kitchen now, where the fire appears to have originated. We'll know more in the morning, when it's light." He looked over Janet's shoulder at Cecilia. "If you can keep things organized, I'll be forever in your debt."

They followed Mrs. Grey to the dower house, which she hadn't even noticed yesterday when they arrived at Chase Hall. All the furniture was shrouded in holland covers, which made David cling even tighter to her. He relaxed a little when the footman flung away the covers, and then dumped coal in the grates and started fires.

She decided that the dower house gave new meaning to the word cozy. A trip upstairs revealed only two bedchambers, one with a small dressing room. Since it was so late, Cecilia directed Mrs. Grey to pull out blankets. "I think proper sheets and coverlets can wait for morning," she explained as she handed each girl a blanket. "You girls take the chamber with the dressing room, and I will put David in the other one. Come, Davy," she said, resting her hand on his shoulder, "I think that you and your uncle will have to share."

"He snores."

Cecilia laughed. "Then you will have to get to sleep before he does, won't you?"

Below stairs, Mrs. Grey had already made room for herself. "I'll send the footman to the manor for food, and you'll have a good breakfast in the morning," she assured Cecilia. "Where are you planning to sleep, Miss Ambrose?"

She took the blanket Mrs. Grey held out. "I will wait up for Lord Trevor in the sitting room. Perhaps tomorrow we can find a cot for the dressing room." She looked around, already anticipating a busy day of cleaning ahead. If Janet keeps busy, she won't have time to complain, Cecilia thought. If Lucinda keeps busy with her sister, they might even remember all those things they have in common. If Davy keeps busy, he won't have so much time to miss his mother. She wrapped the blanket around her shoulders, savoring the heavy warmth. She thought at first that she might sit up on the sofa, but surely it wouldn't hurt to lie down just until Lord Trevor returned. She closed her eyes.

When she woke, the room was full of light. Lord Trevor sat in the chair across from her. She sat up quickly, then tugged the blanket down around her bare feet.

"I thought about covering them, but reckoned that would wake you." He coughed. "Lord, no wonder chimney sweeps seldom live past fifteen," he said when he finished coughing into his handkerchief that was already quite black.

"Let me get you something to drink," she told him, acutely aware that she was still in her nightgown, her favorite flannel monstrosity that was thin from washing.

"Mrs. Grey is bringing in coffee, and probably her latest harangue about the way I take care of myself." He sighed, then gave her a rueful look. "Lord spare us from lifelong retainers, Miss Ambrose! They must be worse than nagging wives."

She laughed, and pulled the blanket around her shoulders. If ever a man looked exhausted, she thought, it is you. He was filthy, too, his nightshirt gray with grime, and his hair black. Bloodshot eyes looked back at her. When he smiled, his teeth were a contrast in his face.

He held up his hand. "No harangue from you, Miss Ambrose, if you please."

"I wouldn't dream of it," she replied serenely. "I don't know you well enough to nag you." She paused and thought a moment. "And even if I did know you better, I do not think I would scold."

"Then you are rare, indeed."

She shook her head. "Just practical, sir! Don't we all pursue our own course, no matter what people who care about us say?"

She could tell that her words startled him; they startled her. "I mean . . ." she began, then stopped. "No, that was exactly what I meant. Anyone who does what you do in London's courts doesn't need advice from a teacher."

He sat back then, his legs out in front of him, in that familiar posture of men who feel entirely at home. "Miss Ambrose, you are wise, as well as clean," he teased.

"And you, sir, are dirty," she pointed out. "Mrs. Grey can arrange a bath for you."

She wrapped her blanket around her and started for the door. As she passed his chair, he put out his hand and took hold of hers. "That I will appreciate, Miss A. Do one thing more for me, please."

He did not release her hand, and she felt no inclination to remind him. His touch was warm and dry, and standing there in the parlor, she realized that she was still shivering inside from last night. "And that would be . . ."

"Reconsider your resolve to leave us on the morning coach, Miss A," he said, and gave her hand a squeeze before he released it. "I need help."

"Indeed you do, my lord," she replied quietly. She left him, spoke to the housekeeper, then returned to the parlor.

She thought he might be asleep, but he remained as she had left him, leaning his chin on his hand, his eyes half closed. He had tried to dab some of the soot from his eyes, because the area under them was smudged. Without comment, she took his handkerchief from him and wiped his face carefully. He watched her the whole time, but for some unaccountable reason, she did not feel shy.

When she finished, she sat down again. "How bad is the damage to the house?"

"Bad enough, I think," he said with a grimace. "When the Rumford was installed, the place where the pipe runs into the chimney must have settled. Ashes have been gathering behind it for some time now, I would imagine. It's not really something a sweep would have noticed." He shook his head. "That portion of the house is three hundred years old, so I can not involve the builder in any litigation."

She smiled at him. "I'm glad you can joke about it, Lord Trevor. It didn't seem so funny last night, standing on the lawn."

"No, it wasn't." His face grew serious. "Miss Ambrose, I'm a little embarrassed to ask you, but I hope I did not leave bruises on your waist."

"You did," she replied, feeling warmth on her own face. "I put it down to your determination to get me down the stairs in a strange house."

He sat back. "This isn't shaping up to be much of a Christmas, is it?"

It seemed a strange remark, one that required a light reply. "No, indeed," she said. "I mean, you were planning to spend it in the City, weren't you, going over legal briefs, or . . ."

"Depositions, my dear, depositions," he corrected. "And now we have cranky children on our hands, and a broken house."

How quickly he seemed to have included her in the family. "You needn't try to appeal to my better nature," she teased. "I will stay for the duration, bruises or not. Only give me my orders and tell me what you want done here today."

"That is more like it!" he said. He stood up and stretched. "Let Mrs. Grey be your guide. I am certain there is enough cleaning here to keep the children busy. If they complain, remind them that the servants are involved at the hall."

"Very well." Cecilia stood next to him, noting that she came up only to his shoulder. "Perhaps you could take David with you to York, Lord Trevor," she suggested. "He so misses his mother, and he told me that he has already had the measles."

Lord Trevor shook his head. "I dare not, Miss Ambrose. What I did not tell anyone last night was that the letter was from their mother, and not my brother Hugo, who is ill from the measles himself. I am riding to York most specifically to see how he does."

"Oh, my!" Cecilia exclaimed. "Is his life in danger?"

Lord Trevor shrugged. "That is the principal reason I'm leaving here as soon as possible, and without the encumbrance of a little boy, who would only be anxious."

"I promise to keep everyone quite busy here," she assured him.

"Excellent!" He stretched again, and then placed his hand briefly upon her shoulder. "Don't allow any of the children near the manor, either, if you please," he said, his voice quite serious. "I do not trust the timbers in that old place yet, not without an engineer to check it for soundness. The servants will bring over whatever clothing and books are needed." He wrinkled his nose. "And it will all smell of smoke."

He stopped in the doorway, and put his hand to his forehead. "Hell's bells, Miss Ambrose! Do excuse that . . . I don't see how we can possibly have that annual dinner and dance on Christmas Eve."

"A dinner!" she exclaimed.

"It is the neighborhood's crowning event, which I have managed to avoid for years." He rubbed his eye. "My sister-in-law used to trot out all the local beauties and try to convince them that I was a worthy catch." He shuddered elaborately, to her amusement. "Maybe that is why I have never stayed for Christmas. No, the dinner must be cancelled. I will retrieve the guest list from the manor, and you can assign the imperious Janet the task of written apology to all concerned." He started for the door.

"Or I can go get the list while you bathe."

"No!"

His vehemence startled her. Before she could assure him that she didn't mind a return to the manor, he stood in front of the parlor door, as though to bar her way. "Miss Ambrose, I'd really rather no one from this house went to the manor. The soot is a trial, and the smoke quite clogs the throat."

"Very well, then," she agreed, gratified not a little by his concern. "I'm hardly a shrinking violet, my lord," she murmured.

He smiled at her, and she could have laughed at the effect of very white teeth in a black face. "Well, then, you may get your list, once you have bathed," she said, acutely aware that she had no business telling the second son of a marquis what to do.

"What a nag you are, Miss Ambrose," he told her. He turned toward the hall. "I will wash and then get the list. If that does not meet with your whole approval, let me know now."

She laughed, quite at ease again. "And comb your hair, too! My father used to tell me that if you can't be a good example, you can always be a bad one." Lord, what am I saying? she asked herself.

Lord Trevor seemed to think it completely normal. He nodded to her, and winked. In another moment she heard him whistling on the stairs.

She was finishing her eggs and toast in the breakfast room when Lord Trevor came into the room. He lofted the guest list at her, and it glided to her plate. He then leaned against the sideboard with the bacon platter in his hand and ate from it.

"You have rag manners," she scolded, "or is this a typical breakfast in the City?"

"No, indeed," he assured her. He finished the bacon, and looked at the baked eggs, then back at her. She raised her eyebrows and handed him a plate. "Breakfast is usually a sausage roll from a vendor's stall in front of Old Bailey." He put two eggs on his plate and sat beside her. "*This* is Elysian Fields, Miss Ambrose. I should visit my dear brother more often. Not only is the food free, it is well cooked and must be eaten sitting down."

He finished his eggs, then tipped back in his chair and reached for a piece of toast from the sideboard. "Do I dare wipe up this plate with toast?" he asked.

"Would it matter what I said?" she countered, amused. He was the antithesis of everything that Miss Dupree attempted to teach her select females, and quite the last man on earth for any lady of quality. Why that should be a concern for her, she had no clue. The idea came unbidden out of some little closet in her mind. "Do you really care?"

"Nope." He wiped up the plate. "I did ask, though," he said, before finishing the toast. "I probably ought to get a proper cook in my house, and maybe even a butler," he said, as though he spoke more to himself.

She thought he was going to leave then, but he turned slightly in his chair to face her. "Since we have already decided that I have no manners, would you mind my comment, Miss Ambrose, that you really don't look English?"

Her face felt warm again. When the embarrassment passed, she decided that she did not mind his question. "People usually just stare, my lord," she told him. "Politely, of course. My parents went to Egypt to study old documents, and do good. Perhaps you have heard of philanthropists like them. They found me on the steps of Alexandria's oldest archive. They could only assume that whoever left me there had seen them coming and going." She smiled. "They suspect that an erring Englishwoman from Alexandria's foreign community became too involved with an Egyptian of unexalted parentage."

"How diverting to be found, and at a dusty old archive," he said, without even batting an eye. "Much more interesting than the usual garden patch, or 'tucked up under mama's heart' entrance."

Is there *anything* you won't say? she thought in delight. "It's better. There was a note pinned to my rather expensive blanket, declaring I was a half-English love child."

He threw back his head and laughed. "That certainly trumps being a duty!"

"Yes, certainly," she agreed, trying not to laugh. "My foster mother named me Cecilia because she is a romantic doing *homage* to the patron saint of music." She looked at him, waiting for him to draw back a little or change the subject. To her delight, he did neither.

"Which means, as far as I can tell, that you will always look better in bright colors than nine-tenths of the population, and you probably will never burn in the sun, and should curly hair be in vogue, you are in the vanguard of fashion." He stood up. "Miss Cecilia Ambrose, you are quite the most exotic guest ever to visit this boring old manor. Do whip my nieces and nephew in line, and render a thorough report this evening! Good day to you, kind lady. Thank you for rescuing me from utter boredom this Christmas."

He left the room as quickly as he had entered it. For the tiniest minute, it seemed as though he had sucked all the air out with him. She was still smiling when she heard the front door close behind him. *My lord, you are the exotic,* she thought, *not me.* She took a final sip of her tea. *I think it is time I woke the sleeping darlings in this lovely little house and put them all to work.*

She got off to a rocky start. Lady Janet had no intention of turning a hand to dust or sweep the floors after the footman removed the elegant carpets to beat out the dust. "Lysander would be aghast," she declared. "I shan't, and you can't compel me."

Lucy gasped at her sister's rudeness. "I *always* do what Miss Ambrose says."

"You're supposed to," her sister sniffed. "You're still in school." She glared at Cecilia. "I have a grievance about this, and I will speak to my uncle when he returns. I will remind him that I Have Come Out."

"From under a rock," David muttered. He looked at Cecilia. "I do not know why my Uncle Trevor did not let me accompany him."

"Nor I," replied Lady Janet with a sniff. "Then we would be rid of a nasty little brother who would try a saint. I am going to write to Lysander this instant! I know my darling will rescue me from this . . . this . . ."

"Your home?" Cecilia asked quietly. "Very well. Do write to him. Lucinda and I will dust, and then we will make beds." She noted the triumphant look that Janet gave her younger sister. "Lady Janet, when you have posted your letter to your fiancé, your uncle specifically asked me to have you write to your family's guests and tell them the Christmas dinner is canceled."

"No party?" Janet shrieked, her voice reaching the upper registers.

You could use a week or two at Miss Dupree's, Cecilia thought as she tried not to wince. "Not unless you think there is room for one hundred in the front parlor here, Lady Janet. Just give them the reason why, and offer your parents' apologies," she replied. "Your uncle has also gone to York, not only to see your parents and sister, but to procure workmen enough to put this place to rights again. Apparently there was considerable smoke damage, and the floor downstairs suffered."

Lady Janet's offended silence almost made the air hum. Cecilia touched Davy on the shoulder. "If you could help Lucinda and me, I'm certain we could ask the footman to fetch your uncle's briefs from the manor, and you could continue alphabetizing them."

"I can do that." Davy looked at his older sister, who had devoted all her attention to the still life over the sideboard. He glared at her rigid back, shrugged, and gestured to his other sister. "C'mon, Lucinda. I'll wager that I can dust the bookroom before you're halfway through the first bedchamber!"

So it went. Lord Trevor returned after dinner, when the fragrance of roasted meat and gravy had settled in the rooms like a benevolent spirit. They had finished eating before he began. Her voice firm, Cecilia told them to wait in the sitting room and allow him to eat in peace before they pounced on him. She held her breath, but Lady Janet only gave her a withering look before flouncing into the sitting room.

When the children were seated, Cecilia excused herself and went to the breakfast room, where Lord Trevor, leaning his hand on his chin, was finishing the last of the rice pudding. He looked up and smiled when she sat down.

"Was it the mutiny on the *Bounty*, Captain Bligh?" he teased.

"Very nearly," she replied. "Lady Janet wrote what I must imagine was an impassioned letter, begging for release, then condescended to write letters of apology to the guests. We tossed bread and water into the room. At least she did not have to gnaw her leg out of a trap to escape."

Lord Trevor laughed. "God help you, Miss Ambrose! Whenever I am tempted to marry and breed, I only have to think of Janet, and temptation recedes. Was Lucinda biddable?"

"Very much so, although she remains ill-used because her sister barely acknowledges her. Davy alphabetized your 1808 cases, and I started him on 1809."

"You are excellent," he said. He drained his teacup and stood up. "Let me brave the sitting room now, and listen to my ill-used, much-abused relatives."

She held out a hand to stop him. "Lord Trevor, how is your brother?"

Lord Trevor frowned. "He is better, but really can't leave before Christmas, no matter how I pleaded and groveled!" He leaned toward her. "He wants you to continue whatever it is you're doing, and not abandon his children to my ramshackle care."

She opened her eyes wider at that artless declaration. "Surely neither he nor Lady Falstoke have any qualms about you."

"They have many," he assured her. He bowed slightly, and indicated that she precede him through the door. "Miss Ambrose, whether you realize it or not, we are an odd pair. You were found on the steps of an archive—still quite romantical, to my way of thinking—and I am the black sheep."

He nudged her forward with a laugh. "When the little darlings in the sitting room have spilled out all their umbrage and ill-usage and flounced off to bed, I will fill you in on my dark career." He took her by the arm in the hall. "But you have already agreed to help me, and I know you would never go back on your word and abandon this household, however sorely you are tried, eh?"

If she had thought to bring along her sketchbook, Cecilia would have had three studies in contrast in the sitting room: Janet looked like a storm was about to break over her head. Lucinda picked at a loose thread in her dress and seemed to swell with questions. Davy, on the other hand, smiled at his uncle.

When Trevor entered the room and sat himself by the fire, they all began at once, Janet springing up to proclaim her ill-usage; Lucinda worried about her parents and whether Christmas would come with them so far removed; and Davy eager to tell his uncle that 1808 was safely filed. Lord Trevor held up his hand. "One moment, my dears," he said, and there was enough edge in his voice to encourage Janet to resume her seat. He looked at his eldest niece. "I am certain that your first concern is for your older

31

sister and her family in York. All are much improved. I knew you wanted to know that." He turned to his nephew, and held out his hand to him. Davy did not hesitate to sit on his lap. Trevor ruffled his hair and kissed his cheek. "That is from your mother! She misses you."

Oh, you do have the touch, Cecilia thought as Davy relaxed against his uncle. "And I hear that you have finished my 1808 cases and started on 1809." Trevor put his arms around his nephew. "Do you think your mama would let me take you back to the City with me and become my secretary?"

"She would miss me," Davy said solemnly. "P'rhaps in a year or two."

"I shall look forward to it." Trevor smiled at Lucinda. "I hear that you have been helping all day to make this little place presentable. My thanks, Lucy."

Lucinda blushed and smiled at Cecilia. "Miss Ambrose says I will someday be able to command an entire household." She looked at her teacher, and her eyes were shy. "A duke's, even."

Janet laughed, but there was no humor in it. "Possibly when pigs fly, Lucinda," she snapped. "Uncle, I . . ."

"What you should do is apologize to your sister," Trevor said. "Your statement was somewhat graceless."

Lucinda was on her feet then, her face even redder, her eyes filled with tears. "I . . . I think I will go to bed now, Uncle Trevor. It's been a long day. Davy?" He followed her from the room. With a look at Lord Trevor, Cecilia rose quietly and joined them in the hall. She closed the door behind her, but not quick enough to escape Janet's words.

"I hope you do not expect us to take orders from that foreign woman, Uncle. That is outside of enough, and not to be tolerated. *Who* on earth is *she*?"

Cecilia closed the door as quietly as she could, her face hot. It's not the first insult, she reminded herself, and surely won't be the last. She turned to the children, who looked at her with stricken expressions, and put her finger to her lips. "Let's just go upstairs, my dears," she told them. "I do believe your uncle has his hands full now."

Even through the closed door, they could hear Janet's voice rising. Cecilia hurried up the stairs to escape the sound of it, with the children right behind. At the top of the stairs, Davy took her hand. "Miss Ambrose, I don't feel that way," he told her, his voice as earnest as his expression.

She hugged him. "I know you don't, my dear. Your sister is just upset with this turn of events. I am certain she did not mean what she said."

"You're too kind, Miss Ambrose," Lucinda said.

I'm nothing of the sort, Cecilia thought later after she closed the door to her pupil's room, after helping her into a nightgown, and listening to her prayers for her older sister's family and her parents, marooned in York with the measles.

"No, I am not kind, Lucy dear," she said softly. "I am fearful." She thought she had learned years ago to disregard the sidelong glances and the boorish questions, because to take offense at each one would be a fruitless venture. As much as she loved England now, after a lifetime spent in Egypt, it took little personal persuasion to keep her at Madame Dupree's safe haven. She doubted that she ever went beyond a three-block radius in Bath. I have made myself a prisoner, she thought, and the idea startled her so much that she could only stand there and wonder at her own cowardice.

Reluctant to go downstairs again, she knocked softly on the door of the room that Davy was sharing with his uncle. Better to be in there, she thought, than to have to run into Lady Janet and her spite on the stairs. Davy lay quietly as she had left him, reading in bed, his knees propped up to hold the book. She looked closer, and smiled. He was also fast asleep. She carefully took the book from him, marked the place, and set it on the bedside table. She watched him a moment, enjoying the way his face relaxed in slumber.

I would like to have a boy like you someday, she thought, and the very idea surprised her, because she had never considered it before. I wonder why ever not, she asked herself, then knew the answer before any further reflection. Even though her foster parents had endowed her with a respectable dowry, she had no expectations, not in a country whose people did not particularly relish the exotics among them.

To keep her thoughts at bay, she went around the room quickly, folding Davy's clothes that had been brought over from the manor and placing them in the bureau. He shared the room with his uncle, whose own clothes were jumbled on top of the bureau. Several legal-sized briefs rested precariously on his clothes, along with a pair of spectacles. She wondered if he even had a tailor, and decided that he did not, considering that his public appearances probably found him in a curled peruke and a black robe, which could easily hide a multitude of fashion sins.

She heard light feet on the stairs, and remained where she was until they receded down the short hall to Lucinda's room. The door slammed, and Davy sighed and turned onto his side. She left the room, but it occurred to her that she did not know where to go. She had arranged to sleep on a cot in the little dressing room, but wild horses could not drag her in there now. To go downstairs would mean having to face further embarrassment from Lord Trevor. She knew he would be well meaning, but that would only add to the humiliation. Perhaps I can go below stairs, she thought, then reconsidered. All the servants' rooms in this small dower house were probably full, too, considering that things were a mess at the manor. She also reckoned that a descent below stairs would only confirm Lady Janet's opinion of her.

Cecilia sat on the stairs and leaned against the banister, wishing herself away from the turmoil, uncertain what to do. Probably Lord Trevor would understand now if she wanted to leave in the morning, even if she had promised she would stay. It was safe in Bath. She shook her head, uneasy with the truthfulness of it.

"Is this seat taken?"

She looked up in surprise, shy again, but amused in spite of herself. "No. There are plenty of steps. You need only choose."

Lord Trevor climbed the stairs and sat on the step below her. He yawned, then rested his back against the banister. She didn't want him to say anything, because she didn't want his pity, but she was too timid to begin the conversation. When, after a lengthy silence, he did speak, he surprised her.

"Miss Ambrose, I wish you had slapped my wretched niece silly, instead of just closed the door on her. You have oceans more forbearance than I will ever possess."

"I doubt that, sir," she said, and chose her own words carefully, since he was doing the same. "I've learned that protestation is rarely effective."

"Not the first time, eh?" he asked, his voice casual.

"And probably not the last." She rose to go—where she did not know—but Lord Trevor took her hand and kept her where she was. "I . . . I do hope you were not too harsh with her."

He released his hold on her. "Just stay put a while, Miss Ambrose, if you will," he told her. "I was all ready to haul her over my knee and give her a smack." He chuckled. "That probably would have earned me a chapter in the tome she is undoubtedly going to write to her precious Lysander in the morning."

"But you didn't."

"No, indeed. I merely employed that tactic I learned years ago from watching some of the other barristers who plead in court, and looked her up and down until her knees knocked. Then I told her I was ashamed of her." He leaned his elbow on the tread above and looked at her. "And I am, Miss Ambrose. Believe me, I am."

The look that he gave her was so contrite that she felt tears behind her eyelids. I had better make light of this, she thought. I'm sure he wants me to assure him that it is all right, and that I didn't mind. She forced herself to look him in the eye. Even in the gloom of the stairwell, she could tell that nothing of the sort was on his mind. She had never seen a more honest gaze.

"I won't deny that it hurt, Lord Trevor," she replied, her voice quiet, "but do you know, I've been sitting here and thinking that it's been pretty easy the last few holidays to hide myself in Bath. And . . . and I really have nothing to hide, do I?"

There. She had told a near stranger something that she could not even write to her mother, when that dear woman had written many times from India to ask her how she really did, on her own and without the protection of her distinguished missionary family.

Again he surprised her. He took her hand and held it. "Nothing to hide at all, my dear Miss Ambrose. Would it surprise you that I have been doing that very thing? I have been confining myself to the area of my rooms near Lincoln's Inn and Old Bailey for nearly eleven years. We are more alike than my silly niece would credit."

Her bewilderment must have shown on her face, because he stood up and pulled her up, too. "If you're not too tired, or too irritated at the ignorance and ill-will in one little dower house, I believe I want to explain myself. Do join me in the sitting room, Miss Ambrose."

She didn't really have a choice, because he never released her hand. Mystified rather than embarrassed now, she followed him into the sitting room. He let go of her hand to pull another chair close to the fireplace, and indicated that she sit. She did, with a sigh. The fire was just warm enough, and the pillow he had placed behind her back just the right touch. He sat in the other chair and propped his feet on the fender.

"I told you I am the black sheep, didn't I?"

She had to laugh. "And I am, well, a little colorful, too." He joined in her laughter, not the least self-conscious, which warmed her heart. He surprised her by quickly leaning forward to touch her cheek. "Your skin is the most amazing shade of olive. Ah, is that the Egyptian in you? How fine! And brown eyes that are probably the envy of nations." He chuckled. "I don't mean to sound like a rakehell, Miss A." He looked at the far wall. "I suppose I am used to speaking my mind."

"I suppose that's your privilege," she said.

"I do say what I please. I doubt anyone in the *ton* thinks I am a gentleman."

"You're the brother of a marquis," she reminded him. "Surely that counts for . . ."

"It counts for nothing," he interrupted, finishing her thought. "I am not playing the game I was born to play, Miss Ambrose, and some take offense."

She sat up straight and turned to face him impulsively. "How can you say that? I have been reading of the good you have done!"

"You are too kind, my dear. When I was in York today, I spoke to the warden at the Abbey. You're from a crusading family, yourself, aren't you?"

She nodded. "Papa and Mama lived in Egypt for nearly twenty years. I am not their only 'extra child,' as Papa puts it."

"The warden was sufficiently impressed when I mentioned that a member of the Ambrose family was visiting the Marquis of Falstoke."

Cecilia smiled. "And now they are doing good in India, and plumbing the depths of Sanskrit." She looked up, pleased to see Lord Trevor smiling at her, for no particular reason that she could discern. At least he does not look so tired, she thought. "We came to England in 1798, when I was sixteen. I went four years to Miss Dupree's Select Academy, and now I teach drawing and pianoforte."

"You weren't tempted to go to India with them?"

"No, I was not," she said. He was still smiling at her, and she decided he was a most attractive man, even with his untidy hair and rumpled clothing. "I like it right here, even with . . . with its occasional difficulties. And that is all I am going to say now. It is your turn to tell me why someone of your rank and quality thinks he is a black sheep."

"It's a sordid tale," he warned her.

"I doubt that. Slide the hassock over, please. Thank you."

He made himself comfortable, too. "Miss Ambrose, the fun of being a younger son cannot be underrated. I did a double first at Oxford, contemplated taking Holy Orders, considered buying a pair of colors, and even thought I would travel to the Caribbean and invest in sugar cane and slaves."

She relaxed, completely at ease. "That sounds sufficiently energetic."

"I didn't have to *do* anything. Some younger sons must scramble about, I suppose, but our father was a wealthy man, and our mother equally endowed. She willed me her fortune. I am better provided for than most small countries."

"My congratulations," she murmured. "You know, so far this is not sordid. I have confiscated more daring stories from my students late at night, when they were supposed to be studying."

"Let me begin the dread tale of my downfall from polite society before you fall asleep and start to snore," he told her.

"You're the one who snores, according to Davy," she reminded him.

"And you must be a sore trial to the decorum of Miss Deprave's Select Academy," he teased.

"*Dupree*," she said, trying not to laugh.

"If you insist," he teased, then settled back. "I suppose I was running the usual course for second sons, engaging in one silly spree after another. It changed one evening at White's, while I was listening to my friends argue heatedly for an hour about whether to wear white or red roses in their lapels. It was an epiphany, Miss Ambrose."

"I don't suppose there are too many epiphanies in White's," she said.

"That may have been the first! I decided the very next morning, after my head cleared, to toddle over to Lincoln's Inn and see about the law. My friends were aghast, and concerned for my sanity, but do you know, Miss A, it suited me right down to the ground. I sat for law through several years, ate my required number of dinners at the Inn, and was called to the Bar."

"My congratulations. I would say that makes you stodgy rather than sordid."

He smiled at her, real appreciation in his eyes. "Miss Ambrose, you are a witty lady with a sharp tongue! Should I pity poor Janet if she actually tries your kindness beyond belief and you give her what she deserves?"

She was serious then. "She is young, and doesn't know what she says."

"Spoken like the daughter of the well churched!" He leaned across the table and touched her arm. "Here comes the sordid part. Miss A." And then his face was more serious than hers.

"I went to Old Bailey one cold morning to shift some toff's heir from a cell where he'd languished—the three D's, m'dear: drunk, disorderly, and disturbing the peace. It was a matter of fifteen minutes, a plea to the magistrate, and a whopping fine for Papa to pay. Just fifteen minutes." He stood up, went to the fireplace, and stared into the flames. "There was a little boy in the docket ahead of my client. I could have bumped him and gone ahead. I had done it before, and no magistrate ever objected."

Cecilia tucked her legs under her. Have you ever told anyone this before? she wanted to ask. Something in his tone suggested that he had not, and she wondered why he was speaking to her. Of course, Mrs. Dupree always did say that people liked to confide in her. "It's your special gift, dearie," her employer had told her on more than one occasion.

"There he stood, not more than seven years old, I think, with only rags to cover him, and it was a frosty morning. It was all he could do to hold himself upright, so frightened was he."

She must have made some sound, because Lord Trevor looked at her. He sat down on the hassock. "Did he . . . was he represented?" she asked.

He nodded, his face a study in contempt. "They all are. We call ourselves a law-abiding nation, Miss A, don't we? His rep was one of the second year boys at Gray's Inn, getting a practice in. Getting a practice in! My God!"

Impulsively she leaned forward and touched his arm. He took her hand and held it. Something in her heart told her not to pull away. "He had copped two loaves of bread and, of all things, a pomegranate." Lord Trevor passed his free hand in front of his eyes. "The magistrate boomed at him, 'Why the pomegranate, you miscreant?'" He put her hand to his cheek. "The boy said, 'Because it's Christmas, your worship.'"

Cecilia felt the tears start in her eyes. She patted his cheek, and he released her hand, an apologetic look in his eyes. "Miss A, you'll think I'm the most forward rake who ever walked the planet. I don't know what I was thinking."

"*I* am thinking that you need to talk to people now and then," she told him.

He tried to smile, and failed. "His sentence was transportation to Van Diemen's Land. Some call it Tasmania. It is an entire island devoted to criminals, south of Australia. Poor little tyke fainted on the spot, and everyone in the courtroom laughed, my client loudest of all."

"You didn't laugh."

"No. All I saw was a little boy soiling his pants from fear, with not an advocate in the world, not a mother or father in sight, sentenced to a living death." He looked at her, and she saw the tears on his face. "And this is English justice," he concluded quietly.

She could think of nothing to say, beyond the fact that she knew it was better to be silent than to let some inanity tumble out of her face, after his narrative. She glanced at him, and his own gaze was unwavering upon her. She realized he was seeking permission from her to continue. "There must be more," she said finally. "Tell me."

He seemed to relax a little with the knowledge that she was not too repulsed to hear the rest. "Is it warm in here?" he asked, running his finger around his frayed collar.

"Yes, and isn't that delightful? I never can get really *warm* in this country!" she countered. "Don't stall me, sir. You have my entire attention."

He continued. "I could not get that child out of my mind. In the afternoon I went back to Old Bailey, found the magistrate—he was so bored—and went to Newgate."

Cecilia shivered. Lord Trevor nodded. "You're right to feel a little frisson, Miss A. It's a terrible place." He grimaced. "I know it must be obvious to you that I am no Brummel. Nowadays, when I know I'm going to Newgate, I wear my Newgate clothes. I keep them in a room off the scullery at my house because I cannot get the smell out." He sighed. "Well, that was blunt, eh? I found Jimmy Daw—that was his name—in a cell with a score of older criminals. I gave him an old coat of mine."

Lord Trevor hung his head down. Cecilia had an almost overwhelming urge to touch his hair. She kept her hands clenched in her lap.

"My God, Miss A, he thanked me and wished me a happy Christmas!"

"Oh, dear," she breathed. She got up then and walked to the window and back again, because she knew she did not wish to hear the rest of his story. He stood, too, his lips tight together. He went to the fireplace again and rested his arm on the mantel.

"You know where this is going, don't you?" he asked, surprised.

She nodded. "I have lived a little in the world, my lord. I'm also no child."

"The magistrate met me in my chambers the next morning—it was Christmas Day—to tell me that those murderers, cutpurses, and thieves had tortured and killed Jimmy for the coat that I left for him, in my naïveté."

She could tell by looking at his eyes that the event might have happened yesterday. "That is hard, indeed, sir," she murmured, and sat down again, mainly because her legs would not hold her. She took a deep breath, and another, until her head did not feel so detached. "I did not know about Jimmy," she said softly, "but I told you that I have read about your work—or some of it—in the papers. I know you have made amends."

"With a vengeance, Miss A, with a vengeance," he assured her. "That frivolous fop I bailed out the day before had the distinction of being my last client among the titled and wealthy. I am a children's advocate now. When they come in the docket, I represent as many as I can. Yes, some are transported—I cannot stop the workings of justice—but they are *not* incarcerated with men old enough to do them evil, and they go to Australia, instead of Van Diemen's Land. It is but a small improvement, but the best I can do."

"How did . . . how did you manage that?"

He smiled for the first time in a long while. "Like all good barristers, I know the value of blackmail, Miss A! Let us just say that I lawyered away a juicy bit of scandal for our dear Prinny, and he owed me massively. God knows he has no interest in anyone's welfare but his own, but even he has a small bit of influence."

It was her turn to relax a little, relieved that his tone was lighter. She could not imagine the conditions under which he labored, and she had the oddest wish to hold him close and comfort him as a mother would a child. "Lord Trevor, I think what you are doing is noble. Why do you say that you are the family's black sheep?"

He sat down again and looked at her. "It is your turn to be naïve. What I do, and where and how I do it, has cut me off completely from my peers. It is as though I wear my Newgate clothes everywhere. No one extends invitations to me, and I am the answer to no maiden's prayer."

"And people of your class are a little embarrassed to be seen with you, and you don't really have a niche," she said, understanding him perfectly, because she understood herself. "That life has made you bold and outspoken, and it has made me shy."

She looked at him with perfect understanding, and he smiled back. "We are both black sheep, Miss Ambrose," he said.

"How odd." Another thought occurred to her. "Why are you here?"

To answer her, he reached in his vest pocket and pulled out a folded sheet. "You may not be aware that my niece Lucinda has been writing to me."

"She did mention you in sketching class once," Cecilia said, and her comprehension grew. She put her hand to her mouth. "Oh! She said you worked with children, and several of the other pupils started to laugh! Their parents must have . . ."

"I told you I am a hiss and a byword in some circles. I sometimes keep stray children at my house until I can find situations for them." He hesitated.

"Go on," she told him. "I doubt there is anything you can say now that would surprise me."

"There might be," he replied. "Well! Some of my peers think I am a sodomite. These things are whispered about. Who knows what parents tell their children."

"Really, Lord Trevor," she said. "It *is* warm in here."

He crossed the room, and threw up the window sash. "I assure you I do *not* practice buggery, Miss A! What I do have

42

are enlightened friends who are willing to take these children to agricultural settings and employ them gainfully."

"Bravo, sir," she said softly.

"I do it for Jimmy Daw." He tapped the letter. "Lucinda tells me how unhappy she is, and darn it, I've been neglecting my own family."

"She is sad and uncomfortable to see her sister growing away from her," Cecilia agreed. "I had wanted to talk to Lady Falstoke about that very thing. I suppose that is why I came."

He folded the letter and put it back in his waistcoat. "I came here with the intention of giving them a prosy lecture about gratitude, well larded with examples of children who have so much less than they do." He rubbed his hands together. "Thank God for a fire in the chimney! Now we are thrown together in close quarters to get reacquainted. Do you think there is silver to polish below stairs?"

She laughed. "If there is not, you will find it!" She grew serious again. "There is more to this than a prosy lecture, isn't there? Lord Trevor, when did Jimmy Daw . . ."

"Eleven years ago on Christmas Eve," he answered. "Miss Ambrose, for all that time I have thrown myself into my work, and ignored my own relations." He shook his head. "I see them so seldom."

She went to the window and closed it, now that the room was cooler, or at least she was not feeling so embarrassed by this singular man's blunt plain speaking. "I must own to a little sympathy for them, Lord Trevor. Here they are, stuck in close quarters with two people that they don't know well. It is nearly Christmas, and their parents are away."

He winked at her. "Should we go easy on the little blokes?"

"Lord Trevor, *where* do you get your language?" she said in exasperation.

"From the streets, ma'am," he told her, not a bit ruffled. "I feel as though I have been living on them for the past eleven years."

"That may be something that must change, sir," she replied.

He laughed and opened the window again. "Too warm for me, Miss Ambrose! You are an educator *and* a manager? Did one of your ancestors use a lash on those poor Israelites in Egypt?"

"Stuff and nonsense!" She went to the door. "And now I am going to bed." She stopped, and she frowned. "Except that . . ." Be a little braver, she ordered herself, if you think to be fit company this week for a man ten times braver than you. "I have no intention of sleeping on that servant's cot in the girls' chamber, not after the snippy way Lady Janet treated me! She already thinks of me as a servant, and I have no intention of encouraging that tendency. Is the sofa in the book room comfortable, sir?"

"I don't know. Seems as though we ought to do better for you than a couch in the office, Miss A," he told her as he joined her at the door.

"Are all dower houses this small?"

"I rather doubt it. Some of my ancestors must have been vastly frugal! What say you brave the sofa tonight, and we'll see if we can find you a closet under the stairs, or a secret room behind some paneling off the kitchen where the Chase family used to hide Royalists."

He tagged along while she went downstairs to the linen closet and selected a sheet and blanket. He found a pillow on a shelf. "You could sleep in here," he told her. "You're small enough to crawl onto that lower shelf."

She laughed out loud, then held out her hand to him. "I am going upstairs now. What plans do you have, if Sir Lysander whisks Janet away from this?"

He was still holding her hand. He released it, and handed her the pillow. "I happen to know Lysander's parents." They left the linen closet. "He is an only child, and my stars, Miss A, they are careful with him." He looked toward the ceiling. "Do you happen to know if she mentioned measles in her letter?"

"You can be certain I was not allowed to look at the letter." They started for the stairs. "Besides, the contagion is in York, and not here."

He only smiled. "Did I mention they are careful parents? Good night, m'dear."

The sofa in the book room realized her worst fears, but Cecilia was so tired that she slept anyway. When she finally woke, it was to a bright morning. She sat up, stretched, then went to the window. Lord Trevor had spent his time well in York, she decided. A veritable army of house menders had turned into the family property and were heading in carts toward the manor.

Someone knocked. She put her robe on over her nightgown and opened the door upon Lord Trevor. "Good morning, sir," she told him.

"It is, isn't it?" He grinned at her. "Miss A, what a picture you are!"

Her hands went to her hair. "I can never do anything with it in the morning. You are a beast to mention it."

He stepped back as if she had stabbed him. "Miss A! I was going to tell you how much I like short, curly hair! No lady wears it these days, and more's the pity." He winked at her. "Is it hard to drag a comb through such a superabundance of curls?"

"A perfect purgatory," she assured him. "I used a comb with very wide teeth." She felt her face go red. Mrs. Dupree would be shocked at this conversation. "Enough about my toilette, sir! What are your plans?"

"I am off to the manor to get the renovation started. Mrs. Grey will accompany me. She has set breakfast, and left one servant, should you need to send a message."

"And did she locate a plethora of silver begging for polish?"

"Indeed she did! There is more than enough to keep my relatives in cozy proximity with each other."

"If they choose to be so," she reminded him. "Sir Lysander . . ."

He put a finger to her lips. "Miss A, trust me there." He took his hand away, and she watched in unholy glee as his face reddened. "Sorry! And Janet is to apologize."

"Only if she means it," Cecilia said softly.

"She will," he told her, then leaned closer. "I am not her favorite uncle, at the moment, however." He straightened up. "I'll be back as soon as I can. Do carry on."

He left, and she suffered another moment of indecision before straightening her back and mounting the stairs to the room where the girls slept. They were awake and sitting up when she came in the room and pulled back the draperies. She took a deep breath, not wanting to look at Lady Janet and see the scorn in her eyes.

"Good morning, ladies," she said, her voice quiet but firm. "Your uncle has gone to the manor to direct the work there, and breakfast is ready." She took another deep breath. "Lady Janet, there are letters to finish. Lady Lucinda, you and your brother may wish to begin polishing some silver below stairs. Excuse me please while I dress."

It took all the dignity she could muster to retreat to the dressing room, throw on her clothes, and then pull that comb through her recalcitrant curls. When she came into the chamber again, Lucinda and Janet were making the bed. She almost smiled. The pupils at Mrs. Dupree's all did their own tidying, but Janet was obviously not acquainted with such hard service. Her eyes downcast, her lips tight together, she thumped her pillow down and yanked up the coverlet on her side of the bed. Lucy took a look at her sister and scurried into the dressing room. Cecilia stood by the door, not ready to face Janet, either. Her hand was on the knob when the young lady spoke.

"I am sorry, Miss Ambrose."

She turned around, wishing that her stomach did not churn at the words that sounded as if they were pulled from Janet's throat with tongs. "I know your uncle Trevor meant well, Lady Janet, but I know I am a stranger to you, and perhaps someone you are not accustomed to seeing."

"That doesn't mean I should be rude," Janet said, her voice quiet. "It seems like there is so much to think of right now, so many plans to make . . ." She looked up then, and her expression was shy, almost tentative. "Lucy tells me you are a wonderful artist."

"She is the one with great talent," Cecilia replied, happy to turn the compliment. She returned Janet's glance. "I hope Lord Trevor was not too hard on you."

Janet turned to the bed and smoothed out a nonexistent wrinkle. She shook her head. "I know I will feel better when Lysander arrives."

Well, that is hopeful, Cecilia thought as she went to the next room, woke Davy, then went to the breakfast room. By the time the children came into the room, chose their food, and sat down, her equilibrium had righted itself. Janet said nothing, but Lucinda, after several glances at her sister, began a conversation.

It was interrupted by the housekeeper, who brought a letter on a silver platter. Janet's eyes lighted up. She took it, cast a triumphant glance at the other diners, excused herself, and left the room, her head up.

"I hope Sir Lysander swoops down and carries her away," Davy said.

"Do you not call him just Lysander?" Cecilia asked, curious. "He is going to be your brother in February, is he not?"

Davy rolled his eyes, and Lucinda giggled. "Miss Ambrose, we have been informed that he is *Sir* Lysander to us," Lucinda said. She sighed then. "I hope she stays, Davy."

"Then you are probably the only one at the table with that wish!" her brother retorted. He blushed, and looked at his plate. "I don't mean to embarrass you, Miss Ambrose."

"You don't," she said, and touched his arm. "In fact, I think—"

What she thought left her head before the words were out. A loud scream came from the sitting room, and then noisy tears bordering on the hysterical. Lucinda's eyes opened wide, and Davy lay back in his chair and lolled his head, as though all hope was gone.

"Oh, dear," Cecilia whispered. "I fear that Sir Lysander did not meet Lady Janet's expectations. She's your sister, and you know her well. Should we *do* anything?"

"I could prop a chair under the door, so she can't get in here," Davy suggested helpfully.

"David, you know that is *not* what Miss Ambrose means!" Lucinda scolded. She looked at Cecilia. "Usually we make ourselves scarce when Janet is in full feather." She stood up. "Davy, I have a craving to go tramping over to the south orchard. There is holly there, and greenery that would look good on the mantelpiece. Would you like to join us, Miss Ambrose?" She had to raise her voice to compete with the storm of tears from the sitting room across the hall, which was now accompanied by what sounded like someone drumming her feet on the floor.

"I think not," Cecilia said. She finished her now-cold tea. "Bundle up warm, children, and take the footman along. You might ask him to stop at the manor and inform your uncle."

Lucinda nodded. She opened the breakfast room door and peeked into the hall. "We don't really want to leave you here alone, Miss Ambrose."

"It is only just a temper tantrum, my dear," Cecilia said, using her most firm educator's voice. "I can manage." I think I can manage, she told herself as the children gave her doubtful glances, then scurried up the stairs to get their coats and mittens. She sat at the table until they left the dower house with the footman. The last person Janet wants to see is me, especially when we have just begun to be on speaking terms, she thought.

"Miss?"

Cecilia looked up to see the housekeeper in the doorway, holding a tray.

"Please come in, Mrs. Grey," she said, managing a half smile. "We seem to be in a storm of truly awesome dimensions."

Mrs. Grey frowned at the sitting-room door, then came to the table, where she set down the tray. "Between you and me, Miss Ambrose, I think that Sir Lysander is in for the surprise of his life, the first time she does *that* across the breakfast table!"

"Oh, my," Cecilia said faintly. "That will be a cold bath over baked eggs and bacon, will it not!"

Mrs. Grey smiled at her, in perfect agreement. "I am suggesting that you not go in there until she is a little quieter." She indicated the tray. "Lady Falstoke sometimes waves burnt feathers under her nose, and then puts cucumbers on her eyes to cut the swelling." She frowned. "What she really needs is a spoonful of cod-liver oil, and the admonition to act her age but . . ." She hesitated.

". . . but Lady Falstoke is an indulgent mother," Cecilia continued. "I will give her a few minutes more, then go in there, Mrs. Grey, and be the perfect listener."

The look the housekeeper gave her was as doubtful as the one that Davy and Lucinda left the room with. "I could summon her uncle, except . . ."

". . . this is a woman's work," Cecilia said. "Perhaps a little sympathy is in order."

"Can you do that? She has been less than polite to you." Mrs. Grey's face was beet red.

"She just doesn't know me," she said, and felt only the slightest twinge of conscience, considering how quick she had been ready to bolt from the place as recently as last night.

Her quietly spoken words seemed to satisfy Mrs. Grey, who nodded and left the room, but not without a backward glance of concern and sympathy as eloquent as speech. She considered Lord Trevor's words of last night, and the kind way he looked at her. If he can manage eleven years of what must be the worst work in the world, she could surely coddle one spoiled niece into a better humor.

She waited until the raging tears had degenerated into sobs and hiccups, and then silence, before she entered the sitting room. Janet had thrown herself facedown on the sofa. A broken vase against the wall, with succession-house flowers crumbled and twisted around it, offered further testimony of the girl's rage. Janet is one of those people who needs an audience, Cecilia thought. Well, here I am. She set the tray on a small table just out of Janet's reach, and sat down, holding herself very still.

After several minutes, Janet opened her swollen eyes and regarded Cecilia with real suspicion. Cecilia gritted her teeth and smiled back, hoping for a good mix of sympathy and comfort.

"I want my mother," Janet said finally. She sat up and blew her nose vigorously on a handkerchief already waterlogged. "I want her now!"

"I'm certain you do," Cecilia replied. "A young lady needs her mother at a time like this." She held her breath, hoping it was the right thing to say.

"But she is not here!" Janet burst out, and began to sob again. "Was there ever a more wretched person than I!"

I think an hour of horror stories in your uncle's company might suggest to you that perhaps one or two people have suffered just a smidgeon, Cecilia thought. She sat still a moment longer, and then her heart spoke to her head. She got up from her chair, and sat down next to Janet, not knowing what she would do, but calm in the knowledge that the girl was in real agony. After another hesitation, she touched Janet's arm. "I know I am only a poor substitute, but I will listen to you, my lady," she said.

Janet turned her head slowly. The suspicion in her eyes began to fade. Suddenly she looked very young, and quite disappointed. She put a trembling hand to her mouth. "Oh, Miss Ambrose, he doesn't love me anymore!" she whispered.

With a sigh more of relief than empathy, Cecilia put her arm around the girl. "My, but this is a dilemma!" she exclaimed. She gestured toward the letter crumpled in Janet's hand. "He said *that* in your letter?"

"He might as well have said it!" Janet said with a sob. She smoothed open the message and handed it to Cecilia. "Read it!"

Cecilia took the letter and read of Sir Lysander's regrets, and his fear of contracting any dread diseases.

Janet had been looking at the letter, too. "Miss Ambrose, I wrote most specifically that the measles were confined to my sister's house in York. He seems to think that he will come here and . . . and die!"

She could not argue with Janet's conclusion. The letter was a recitation of its writer's fear of contagion, putrid sore throat, consumption, and other maladies both foreign and domestic. "Look here," she said, pointing. "He writes here that he will fly to your side, the moment all danger is past."

"He should fly here now! At once!"

Lord Trevor Chase would, Cecilia thought suddenly. If the woman he loved was ill, or in distress, he would leap up from the breakfast table and fork the nearest horse in his rush to be by her side. Nothing would stop him. She sat back, as amazed at her thoughts as she was certain of them. But he was a rare man, she decided. This knowledge that had come to her unbidden warmed her. She tightened her grip on Janet. "My dear, didn't your uncle tell me that Sir Lysander is an only child?"

Janet nodded. She stared sorrowfully at the letter.

"I think we can safely conclude that his parents are overly concerned, and that is the source of this letter." She scanned the letter quickly, hoping that the timid Sir Lysander would not fail her. She sighed with relief; he did not. "And see here, my dear, how he has signed the letter!"

"'You have my devoted, eternal love,'" Janet read. She sniffed. "But not including measles, Miss Ambrose."

"No, not including measles," she echoed. "Surely we can allow him one small fault, Lady Janet, don't you think?" Lady Janet thought. "Well, perhaps." She raised her handkerchief, and looked at it with faint disgust.

Cecilia pulled her own handkerchief out of her sleeve. "Here, my dear. This one is quite dry."

Janet took it gratefully and blew her nose. "You don't ever cry, Miss Ambrose?"

It was the smallest of jokes, but Cecilia felt the weight of the world melting from her own shoulders. "I wouldn't dare, Lady Janet!" she declared with a laugh. "Only think how that would ruin my credit at Mrs. Dupree's Select Academy." She touched Janet's shoulder. "This can be our secret." She stood up. "I recommend that you recline here again. Mrs. Grey has brought over a cucumber from the succession house. A couple of these slices on your eyes will quite remove all the swelling."

Janet did as she said. Cecilia tucked a light throw around her, then applied the cucumbers. "I would give the cucumber about fifteen minutes. Perhaps then you might finish the rest of those letters."

"I will do that," Janet agreed. The cucumber slices covered her eyes, but she pointed to the letter. "Do you think I should reply to Lysander's sorry letter, Miss Ambrose? I could tell him what I think and make him squirm."

"You could, I suppose, but wouldn't it be more noble of you to assure him that you understand, and look forward to seeing him in a week or so?" Janet's mulish expression, obvious even with the cucumbers, suggested to Cecilia that the milk of human kindness wasn't precisely flowing through Janet's veins yet. "I think it is what your dear mother would do," Cecilia continued, appealing to that higher power.

"I suppose you are right," Janet said reluctantly, after lengthy consideration. "But I will write him *only* after I have finished all the other letters!"

"That will show him!" Cecilia said, grateful that the cucumbers hid her smile from Janet's eyes. "My dear, Christmas can be such a trying time for some people."

"I should say. I do not know when I have suffered more."

Cecilia regarded Janet, who had settled herself quite comfortably into the sofa, cucumber slices and all. My credit seems to be on the rise, she thought. I wonder . . . "Lady Janet, perhaps you could help me with something that perplexes me."

The young lady raised one cucumber. "Perhaps. By the time I finish writing lists for wedding plans, I am usually quite fatigued at close of day."

No wonder Lord Trevor remains put off by the topic of reproduction, Cecilia thought. Even on this side of her better nature, Lady Janet is enough to make anyone think twice about producing children. "It is a small thing, truly it is," she said. "Your younger sister seems to have taken the nonsensical notion into her head that you are too busy with wedding plans to even remember that you are sisters."

"Impossible!" Janet declared.

"I agree, Lady Janet, but she is at that trying age of twelve, and feels that you haven't time for her."

"Of course I . . . well, there may be some truth to that," Janet said. "H'mm."

She was silent then, and it occurred to Cecilia that this was probably more introspection than Janet had ever waded in before. "Something to think about, Lady Janet," she said.

She was in the book room, folding her blanket and wondering where to stash it, when Lady Janet came in. She smiled to see that the cucumbers had done their duty. "Ready to tackle the letters again, my lady?" she asked.

Janet shook her head, then looked at Cecilia shyly. "Not now. I think I will go find Lucinda and David. Did they mention where they were headed?"

"Your sister said something about the south orchard."

"Oh, yes! There is wonderful holly near the fence." She left the room as quickly as she had come into it.

"Someone needs to do these letters," Cecilia told herself when the house was quiet. She sat down at the desk and looked at the last one Janet had written. She picked up the pen to continue, then set it down, with no more desire to do the job than Lady Janet, evidently. She decided to go below stairs, and see if Lord Trevor had carried out his threat to find silver to polish.

She laughed out loud when she entered the servants' dining room to see Lord Trevor, an apron around his waist, sleeves rolled up, rubbing polish on an epergne that was breathtaking in its ugliness. He looked up and grinned at her. "Did ye ever see such a monstrosity?" He looked around her. "And where are my nieces and nephew? Isn't this supposed to be the time I have ordained for my prosy talk on gratitude and sibling affection?" He put down the cloth, and leaned across the table toward her. "Or is this the time when you scold me roundly for abandoning you to the lions upstairs?"

"I should," she told him as she found an apron on a hook and put it around her middle. "Now don't bamboozle me. Did you leave me to face Lady Janet alone when that letter came from her dearly beloved?"

"I cannot lie," he began.

"Of course you can," she said, interrupting him. "You are a barrister, after all."

He slapped his forehead. "I suppose I deserved that."

"You did," she agreed, picking up a cloth. "For a man who fearlessly stalks the halls of Old Bailey, defending London's most vulnerable, you're remarkably cowardly."

"Guilty as charged, mum," he replied cheerfully. "I could never have soothed those ruffled feathers, but it appears that you did." He turned serious then. "And did my graceless niece apologize, too?"

"She is not so graceless, sir!" Cecilia chided. "Some people are more tried and sorely vexed by holidays and coming events than others. We did conclude that Sir Lysander is still the best of men, even though he dares not brave epidemics. We have also resolved to make some amends to Lucinda." She dipped the knife she had been polishing into the water bath. "I, sir, have freed you from the necessity of a prosy lecture! May I return to Bath?"

"No. You promised to stay," he reminded her, and handed her a spoon.

"I'm not needed now," she pointed out, even as she began to polish it. "Hopefully, Lord and Lady Falstoke will be here at Christmas, which will make the dower house decidedly crowded, unless the repairs at the manor can be finished by then. You will have ample time to get to know your nieces and nephew better, and do you know, I think they might not be as ungrateful as you seem to think."

He nodded, and concentrated on the epergne again. She watched his face, and wondered why he seemed to become more serious. Isn't family good cheer what you want? she asked herself.

It was a question she asked herself all that afternoon as she watched him grow quieter and more withdrawn. When the children came back—snow-covered, shivering, but cheerful—from gathering greenery, she watched uneasily how he had to force himself to smile at them. All through dinner, while Davy outlined his plans for the holly, and his sister planned an expedition to the kitchen in the morning to make Christmas sweets, he sat silent, staring at nothing in particular.

He is a man of action, she decided, and unaccustomed to the slower pace of events in country living. He must chafe to return to London. She stared down at her own dinner as though it writhed, then gave herself a mental shake. That couldn't be it. Hadn't he told her earlier that both King's Bench and Common Pleas were not in session? He had also declared that was true of Magistrate's Court, where most of his clients ended. Why could he not relax and enjoy the season, especially since he had come so far, and met with pleasant results so easily? Even after she told him before dinner that Janet had seemed genuinely contrite and willing to listen, he hadn't received the news with any enthusiasm. It was as though he was gearing himself up for a larger struggle. She wished she knew what it was.

Once the children were in bed, she wanted to ask him, but she knew she would never work up the nerve. Instead, she went into the sitting room to read. He joined her eventually, carrying a letter. He sat down and read through the closely written page again. "Maria writes to say that my brother is much better now, and will be home on Christmas Day," he told her.

"And your niece Amelia's brood?"

"Maria says they are all scratching and complaining, which certainly trumps the fever and vacant stare," he told her. He sat back in the chair and stared into the flames.

Now or never, she thought. "Lord Trevor, is there something the matter?"

He looked up quickly from his contemplation of the flames. "No, of course not." He smiled, but the smile didn't even approach his eyes. "Thanks to your help, I think my nieces and nephew will be charting a more even course."

Chilled by the bleakness on his face, she tried to make light of the moment: anything to see the same animation in his face that had been there when she arrived only a few days ago, or even just that morning. "We can really thank Sir Lysander and his fastidious parents."

"Oh? What? Oh, yes, I'm certain you are right," he said. She might as well not have been in the room at all. His mind was miles away, oceans distant. "Well, I think it is time for me to go strangle four or five chickens," she said softly. "And then I will rob the mail coach in my shimmy."

"Ah, yes," he said, all affability. "Good night, Miss Ambrose."

She was a long time getting to sleep that night.

The next day, Christmas Eve, was the same. She woke, feeling decidedly unrested, and sat up on her cot in the dressing room, where the girls had cajoled her to return. Certainly it was better than the book room, and the reasons for avoiding the dressing room seemed to have vanished. Quietly she went into the girls' chamber and looked out the window. Although it was nearly eight o'clock, the sky was only beginning to lighten. The workers from York, who were staying at an inn in the village, were starting to arrive, their wagons and gigs lit with lanterns.

I wonder how much work is left to do there, she thought. If the marquis and marchioness are to return tomorrow, then they must be in a pelter to finish. She stood at the window until her bare feet were cold, then turned toward the dressing room. She moved as quietly as she could, but Janet sat up. "Good morning, Miss Ambrose," she said as she yawned. "Do you want to help Lucinda and me in the kitchen? Mrs. Grey has said we may make however many Christmas treats we want. Think what a welcome that will be for my parents."

Cecilia sat down on the bed beside her, and Janet obligingly shifted her legs. "You'll be glad to see them, won't you, my dear?" Cecilia asked.

"Oh, yes!" Janet touched her arm. "I can only wish they had been here for all of the season, but Amelia needed them." She sighed. "This is my last Christmas at Chase Hall, you know."

Cecilia smiled. "You'll be returning with a husband this time next year."

Janet drew up her legs and rested her chin on her knees. When Lucinda moved, she smoothed the coverlet over her sister's back. "Oh, I know that," she whispered, "but it is never the same, is it?"

"No, it is not," Cecilia agreed. "When my parents return from India, I wonder how we all will have changed."

"Does it make you sad, even a little?"

Cecilia was not certain she had ever considered the matter in that light. "I suppose it does, Lady Janet," she replied after a moment's thought. "Perhaps this is a lesson to us both: not to dwell in the past and wish for those times again, but to move on and change."

"It's a sobering consideration," Janet said. "Do you ever wish you could do something over?"

"Not really. I like to look ahead." She stood up. "My goodness, you have so much to look forward to!"

"Yes, indeed," Janet said, and Cecilia could hear the amusement in her voice. "Shortbread, drop cakes, and wafers below stairs!"

They smiled at each other with perfect understanding. "Lady Janet, you are going to make Sir Lysander a happy man," she said, keeping her voice low.

"I intend to," Janet replied, "even if he is not as brave as I would like. I love him." She said it softly, with so much tenderness that Cecilia almost felt her breath leave her body. Unable to meet Janet's eyes, because her own were filling with tears, she looked at Lucinda, sleeping so peacefully beside her sister. You are all so fine, she thought. Lord Trevor has no need of a prosy scold; nothing is broken here, not really. He was so wrong.

"Lady Janet," she began carefully, not even sure what she wanted to ask. "Do you . . . has Lord Trevor ever kept Christmas here with you?"

Janet thought a moment, a frown on her face. "Not that I recall. No. Never. I wonder what it is that he does?"

"I wish I knew."

Breakfast was a quiet affair. Lord Trevor ate quickly and retreated to the book room, saying something about reviewing his cases. David had to ask him twice if he could join him and continue alphabetizing the files. They left the room together. Lucinda and Janet hurried below stairs, and Cecilia found herself staring out the window toward the manor. She had tried to ask Mrs. Grey casually how the work was going, but the housekeeper just looked away and changed the subject. She had tried again after breakfast, with the same response. She found herself growing more uneasy as the morning passed, and she didn't really know why.

"Miss Ambrose?"

Startled out of her disquietude, she turned around to see Davy standing there. "Davy! Are you thinking it would be good to go below stairs and check on your sisters' progress? It already smells wonderful, doesn't it?"

To her surprise, he shook his head. To her amazement, he came closer and rested his head against her waist. In a moment she was on her knees before him, her arms tight around him. "My dear, you're missing your mother, aren't you? She'll be here tomorrow."

Davy burrowed as close to her as he could, and she tightened her grip. "Davy, what is it?"

She pulled him away a little so she could see his face, took a deep breath, then pulled him close again. "What's wrong?" she whispered in his ear, trying to sound firm without frightening him.

"It's my uncle," he said finally, the words almost forced out between his tight lips. "I'm afraid."

Cecilia sank down to the floor and pulled him onto her lap. "Oh, Davy, tell me," she ordered, fighting against her own rising tide of panic.

Davy shivered. "Miss Ambrose, he just sits and stares at the case files! I . . . I tried to talk to him, but he doesn't seem to hear me! It's as though there is a wall . . ." His voice trailed away.

Cecilia ran her hands over his arms, and rubbed his back as he clung to her. "Tell me, my dear," she urged.

He turned his face into her breast, and his words were muffled. "He told me not to look into the files, and I didn't, until this morning." He looked up at her, his eyes huge in his face. "Miss Ambrose, I have never read such things before!" He started to cry.

She held him close, murmuring nonsensicals, humming to him, until his tears subsided. "My dear, you don't know what he does, do you?"

Davy shook his head. "No, but I think it really bothers him."

"I think you are right, Davy." She put her hands on each side of his face and looked into his eyes. "Can you get your coat and mittens?"

He nodded, a question in his eyes.

"We're going outside to get some fresh air." She stood up, keeping Davy close. "Perhaps we can figure out what to do with all that holly you collected yesterday."

The coats were in a closet off the front entrance. She helped Davy with his muffler and made sure his shoes were well buckled, then got into her coat. Mrs. Grey and the cook were below stairs with the girls. She could hear laughter from the kitchen now and then. She tiptoed down the hall to the book room and pressed her ear against the door panel. Nothing.

They left through a side door out of sight of the book-room windows. She did not have a long stride herself, but she had to remind herself to slow down anyway, so Davy could keep up.

"We're not supposed to go to the manor," he reminded her as they hurried along. "Uncle Trevor is afraid we will be hurt while the repairs are going on." He stopped on the path. "He might be angry, Miss Ambrose!"

"I don't know what he will be, Davy, but I want to see the renovations." If a judge and jury had demanded to know why she was so determined, she could not have told them. Some alarm was clanging in her brain. She did not understand it, but she was not about to ignore it one more minute.

On Davy's advice, they approached the manor from the garden terrace. There was only a skiff of snow on the flower beds, which had been cleaned, raked, and prepared for a long Yorkshire winter. All was tidy and organized.

Her parents had done extensive renovations once on their Egyptian villa. She remembered the disorder, the dust, the smell of paint, the sound of saw and hammer. When she opened the door off the terrace and stepped inside with Davy, there was none of that confusion. Nothing. The house was completely silent. Nothing was out of place. She sniffed the air. Only the faintest smell of smoke remained; she couldn't be sure it wasn't just the ordinary smell of a household heated with coal.

Davy stared around him, and took her hand again. "There's nothing wrong."

"No, there isn't," she said, keeping her voice calm, especially when she saw the question in his eyes. "Where are the workers?"

They walked down the hall, holding tight to each other, until they came to the door that led belowstairs. Cecilia took a deep breath and opened it. As soon as she did, they heard voices, the soft slap of cards, and some laughter. She took a firmer grip on the boy's hand, and they walked down the stairs together.

The workers sitting around the table in the servants' hall looked up when she came into the room. The oldest man—he must have been the foreman—smiled at her. "G'day, miss!" he called, the voice of good cheer. "Are you from that dower house?"

She smiled back, even though she wanted to turn and run. "Yes, indeed. I am a teacher for one of the young ladies, and this is David Chase, Viscount Goodhue."

The men put down their cards and got to their feet.

"Is my uncle Trevor playing a joke on us?" Davy asked her.

"Let's ask these men," she said. "Sir, have you been repairing any damage at all?"

The foreman shrugged. "After Lord Trevor sent all the servants off on holiday, we opened up the windows and aired out the place. Watts, over there—perk up, Watts!—cleaned out the pipe behind the Rumford and seated it again, but that's all the place really needed." He scratched his head. "His lordship's a good man, he is. Said he just wanted us to stay here all week, and get paid regular wages."

"Did he . . . did he tell you why, precisely?" Cecilia asked.

"I don't usually ask questions like that of the gentry, miss, but he did say something about wanting to keep everyone close together."

He said as much to me, she thought, hoping that his young relatives would discover each other again, if they were in close quarters. "I can understand that," she said.

"Yes, mum, that's what he said," the foreman told her. "This is our last day on the job." He laughed and poked the cardplayer sitting next to him. "Guess we'll have to earn an honest wage next week again!"

The men laughed. The man called Watts spoke up shyly. "'E's made it a happy Christmas for all of us, miss. You, too, I hope."

"Oh, yes," Cecilia said, wishing she were a better actress. "Lord Trevor is a regular eccentric who likes a good quiz! Good day to you all, and happy Christmas."

They were both quiet on the walk back to the dower house, until Davy finally stopped. "Why would he want us to keep close together?"

"He told me that first night, after you were all in bed, that he was worried that you were all growing apart, and were ungrateful for what you had," she explained. "He had a notion that if you were all together, he could give you what he called a 'prosy lecture' about gratitude." She took his hand, and set him in motion again. "Davy, the people he works with—his clients—are young, and have so little. He helps them all he can, but . . ." But I don't quite understand this, she thought to herself. He does so much good! *Why* is he so unhappy?

The dower house was still silent when they came inside, but the odors from the kitchen were not to be ignored. Without waiting to stamp off the snow upstairs, she and Davy went down to the kitchen, where his sisters were rolling dough on the marble slab. She watched them a moment, their heads together, laughing. Nothing wrong here, she thought. She looked at Davy, who was reaching for a buttery shortbread.

She noticed that Mrs. Grey was watching her, and she took the housekeeper aside. "Mrs. Grey, there's nothing going on at the manor. Do you know why Lord Trevor is doing this?"

"You weren't to know," the woman declared.

The room was quiet, and she knew the children were listening. The frown was back on Davy's face, and his sisters just looked mystified. "Uncle Trevor's been fooling us," Davy said. "There's nothing wrong with our home."

It took a moment to sink in, then Lady Janet sat down suddenly. "We . . . we could have had the Christmas entertainment? And Lysander could have come?"

"I think so, Lady Janet," Cecilia said. "He said he wanted everyone here in close quarters so you could all appreciate each other again." She reached out and touched Lucinda's arm. "But I don't think there ever really was a problem."

She smiled at Janet. "Well, maybe a word or two in the right ear was necessary, but that was a small thing."

"I know I'm glad to be here now," Lucinda said. She put her arm around her sister, then tightened her grip as her face grew serious. "I told Uncle Trevor that very thing this morning, but I'm not sure he heard me."

"I did the same thing in the book room," Davy said. "Told him I missed Mama, but it was all right. He didn't seem to be paying attention."

Davy looked at Cecilia, his eyes filled with sudden knowledge. "Miss Ambrose, he was trying to *fix* us, wasn't he? We're fine, so why isn't he happy?"

It was as though his question were a match struck in a dark room. Cecilia sucked in her breath and sat down on the bench, because her legs felt suddenly like pudding. She pulled Davy close to her. "Oh, my dear, I think he is trying to fix himself."

She knew they would not understand. She also knew she would have to tell them. "Mrs. Grey, would you please leave us and shut the door?"

The housekeeper put her hands on her hips. "I don't take orders from houseguests," she said.

Janet leaped to her feet. "Then you'll take them from me! Do as Miss Ambrose says, and . . . and not a word to my uncle!"

Bravo, Janet, Cecilia thought, feeling warmer. When the door closed with a decisive click, she motioned the children closer. "Do you know what your uncle really does? No? I didn't think so." She touched Davy's face. "You have some idea."

He shuddered. "Those files . . ."

"Your uncle is an advocate for children facing sentencing, deportation, and death."

Janet nodded, and pulled Lucinda closer to her. "We do know a little of that, but not much." She sighed. "I own it has embarrassed me, at times, but I am also proud of him." She looked at her sister. "I think we all are."

"And rightly so, my dear," Cecilia said. "It is hard, ugly work, among those who have no hope." She took a deep breath. "Let me tell you about Jimmy Daw."

She tried to keep the emotion from her voice, but there were tears on her cheeks when she finished. Janet sobbed openly, and Lucinda had turned her face into her sister's sleeve.

Davy spoke first. "Uncle Trevor didn't mean any harm to come to Jimmy Daw."

"Oh, no, no," Cecilia murmured. "He thought he was doing something kind."

"Is Jimmy Daw why he works so hard now?" Lucinda asked, her voice muffled in her sister's dress.

"I am certain of it," she said, with all the conviction of her heart.

"Then why isn't he *happy*?" Davy asked, through his tears. "He does so much good!"

Cecilia stood up, because the question demanded action from her. "Davy, I fear he has never been able to forgive himself for Jimmy's death, in spite of the enormous good he has done since." She perched on the edge of the table and looked at the three upturned faces, each so serious and full of questions. "He probably works hard all year, works constantly, so he can fall asleep and never dream. He probably has no time for anything except his desperate children."

"Father does say that when he and Mama go to London, they can never find a minute of time with Uncle Trevor," Janet said.

"Does he come here for Christmas?"

"Hardly ever," Lucinda replied. She stopped; her eyes grew wider. "He might stay a day or two, but he is always gone well before Christmas Eve. You said Jimmy died on Christmas Eve."

"He did." Cecilia got up again, too restless to sit. "I don't know what your uncle usually does on Christmas Eve, but somehow he must punish himself." She started to stride about the room again, then stopped. "I doubt he was planning to stay, in spite about what he said of his 'prosy lecture,' that he could have delivered and left."

"He was forced to, wasn't he?" Janet said slowly. "When Mama and Papa went to be with Amelia, he had no choice!"

"No, he didn't," Cecilia replied. "I think he used the excuse of the fire to keep everyone close. My dears, I think he *wants* to change now—if not, he would have bolted as soon as I got here— but I think he is afraid to be alone. And that is really why we are crammed so close here." She sat down again, dumbfounded at the burden that one good man could force upon himself.

They were all silent for a long moment. Janet looked at her finally, and Cecilia saw all the pride in her eyes, as well as the fear. "I love my uncle," she said, her voice low but intense. "There is not a better man anywhere, even if people of our rank make fun of him." She smiled, but there was no humor in it. "Even Lysander thinks him a fool for—oh, how did he put it?—'wallowing in scummy waters with the dregs.' My uncle is no fool." Her eyes filled with tears again. "Miss Ambrose, how can we help him?"

She mulled over the question, and then spoke carefully. "I think first that he would be furious if he knew I had told you all this."

"Why did he tell you?" Davy asked.

It was a question she had been asking herself for several days now. She shook her head, and started to say something, when Janet interrupted.

"Because he is in love with Miss Ambrose, you silly nod," she told her brother, her voice as matter-of-fact as though she asked the time of day.

Cecilia stared at her in amazement. "How on earth . . ." Janet shrugged, and then looked at Lucinda, as if seeking confirmation. "We both notice how his eyes follow you around the room, and the way he smiles when he looks at you." She grew serious, but there was still that lurking smile that made her so attractive. "Trust me, Miss Ambrose, I am an expert on these matters."

Cecilia laughed, in spite of herself. "My goodness."

"Do you mind the idea?" Lucinda asked, doubt perfectly visible in her eyes.

Did she mind? Cecilia sat down again and considered the matter, putting it to that scrutiny she usually reserved for scholarship. Did she mind being thought well of by a man whose exploits had been known to her for some time, and whom she had admired for several years, without even knowing him? Her face grew warm as she thought of his grip on her waist as they left the smoky manor in the middle of the night. "He doesn't even know me," she protested weakly.

"As to that, Miss Ambrose, I have been writing him about you," Lucinda said.

"You have *what*?" she asked in amazement.

Her pupil shrugged. "He wanted to know if there was anyone interesting in my school, and I told him about you." She hesitated. "I even painted him a little picture."

"Of me?" she asked quietly. Me with my olive skin and slanted eyes, she thought.

"Of you, my most interesting teacher ever," was Lucinda's equally dignified reply. "He's no ordinary man."

And I am certainly no ordinary English woman, she thought. She reached across the table, took Lucinda's hand, and squeezed it briefly. "You are the most wonderful children."

Janet laughed. "No, we're not! We probably are as selfish and ungrateful as Uncle Trevor imagines. But do you know, we aim to be better." She grew serious and asked again, "How can we help our uncle?"

"Leave him to me," Cecilia said. "I know he does not want you to know about Jimmy Daw, or he would have told you long before now, Janet. How can I get time alone with him?"

Davy was on his feet then. "Lucinda, do you remember how fun it was last Christmas to spend it in the stable?"

"What?" Cecilia asked. "You probably needn't be *that* drastic!"

"You know, Miss Ambrose," Janet said. "There is that legend that on the night of Christ's birth, the animals start to speak." She nudged her brother. "What did Davy do last year but insist that he be allowed to spend the night in the stable! Mama was shocked, but Papa enjoyed the whole thing." She looked at her younger brother and sister. "We will be in the stable. The footman can light a good fire, and we have plenty of blankets."

The other children nodded, and Cecilia could almost touch the relief in the room. Precious ones, she thought, you will do anything to help your uncle, won't you? No, you most certainly do not require fixing. "Very well," she said. "Janet . . ." She stopped. "Oh, I should be calling you Lady Janet."

"I don't think that matters . . . Cecilia," the young woman replied. "I will make arrangements with Mrs. Grey, and we will go to the stables after dinner." She looked at her siblings. "Cecilia, we love him. We hope you can help him because I do believe you love him, too."

They were all quiet that afternoon, soberly putting Christmas treats and cakes into boxes for delivery to other great houses in the neighborhood on Boxing Day, arranging holly on mantelpieces, and getting ready for their parents' return on Christmas. After an hour's fruitless attempt to read in the sitting room, Cecilia went for a walk instead. How sterile the landscape was, with everything shut tight for a long winter. Little snow had fallen yet, but as she started back toward the dower house, it began, small flakes at first and then larger ones. Soon the late afternoon sky was filled with miniature jewels, set to transform the land and send it to sleep under a blanket of white. She stood in the modest driveway of the dower house and watched the workers leave the manor for the final time. Some of them called happy Christmas to her. She looked at the house again, wondering why it was that the most joyous season of the year should cause such pain in some. With a start, she realized that her preoccupation with Lord Trevor and his personal nightmare had quite driven out her own longing for her family in far-off India. "Tonight, I hope I remember all the wonderful things you taught me," she said out loud. "Especially that God is good and Christmas is more than sweets and gifts."

Before dinner, she went to the book room, squared her shoulders, and knocked on the door. When Lord Trevor did not answer, she opened the door.

He sat probably as he had sat all day, staring at his case files, which Davy had alphabetized and chronologized. Everything was tidy, except for his disordered mind. When she had been standing in the doorway for some time, he looked at her as though for one brief moment he did not recognize her. She thought she saw relief in his eyes, or maybe she only hoped she did.

"Dinner is ready, Lord Trevor," she said quietly. "We hope you will join us."

He shook his head, then deliberately turned around in his chair to face the window. She closed the door, chilled right down to the marrow in her bones.

Dinner was quiet, eaten quickly with small talk that trailed off into long pauses. A letter had come that afternoon from York with the good news that the marquis and marchioness would arrive at Chase Hall in time for dinner tomorrow. "I wish they were here right now," Davy said finally, making no attempt to disguise his fear.

"They'll be here tomorrow," she soothed. "Davy, I promise to take very good care of your uncle."

Her words seemed to reassure them all, and she could only applaud her acting ability, a talent she had not been aware of before this night. After a sweet course that no one ate, Janet rose from the table and calmly invited her younger brother and sister to follow her. Cecilia followed them into the hall, and waited there until they returned from their rooms bundled against the cold.

Janet looked almost cheerful. She tucked her arm through Lucinda's and reached for Davy. "Do you know, this is my last Christmas to be a child," she said to Cecilia. "I will be married in February, and this part of my life will be over." She looked at her siblings. "Lucinda, you will marry someday, and even you, Davy!" He made a face at her, and she laughed softly. "I am lucky, Miss Ambrose, and I *did* need reminding."

"We all do, now and then," Cecilia replied. She opened the door, and kissed each of them as they passed through. "If you get cold, come back inside, of course, but do leave me alone in the book room with your uncle."

'Take good care of him," Lucinda begged.

"I will," she said. "I promise you."

Easier said than done. When the house was quiet, she found a shawl, wrapped it tight around her for courage, and went to the book room. She knocked. When he did not answer, she let herself into the room.

He sat at the desk still. This time there was only one file in front of him. He looked at her and his eyes were dark and troubled. "What are you doing here?" he asked, his voice harsh.

"The children wanted to spend Christmas in the stable," she said. "It's a silly thing."

"I remember when they did that, years ago," he said. "I remember . . ." Then he looked at the file before him, and he was silent.

Her heart in her throat, she came into the room and around the desk to stand beside him. "Is that Jimmy Daw's file?" she asked.

He put his hand over the name, as though to protect it. She wanted to touch him, to put her arms around his shoulders and press her cheek against his, all the while murmuring something in his ear that he might interpret as comfort. Instead, she moved to the front of the desk again and pulled up a chair.

"He died eleven years ago this night, didn't he?" She kept her voice normal, conversational.

Lord Trevor narrowed his eyes and glared at her. "You know he did. I told you."

"What is it you do on Christmas Eve to remember him?" There.

Silence. "Shouldn't you be in bed, Miss Ambrose?" he asked finally, in a most dismissive tone.

She smiled and leaned forward. "No. It's Christmas Eve, and the children are busy. I think I will just stay here with you, and see what you do to remember Jimmy Daw, because that's what you do, isn't it? You probably plan this all year."

More silence.

"Do you go to church? Read from the Bible? Work on some-one else's charts? Visit old friends in the City? Have dinner out with your fellow barristers? Sing Christmas carols? Squeeze in another good work or two?" She stopped, hating the sound of her own rising voice and its relentless questions. She looked him straight in the eye. "Or do you just sit at your desk all day, alone and depressed?"

He leaped to his feet, fire in his eyes, and slammed the file onto the table like a truncheon. "I don't need this!"

She looked away, frightened, but held herself completely still in the chair. She studied his face, his empty eyes. With courage she knew she did not possess, she stood in front of him until they were practically toe to toe. "Do you hate yourself, apathetic about your own life, because you failed one little boy?"

He raised his hand and she steadied herself, because she knew it was going to hurt, considering his size and the look in his eyes. Almost without thinking, she grabbed him around the waist and pulled him close to her in a fierce grip. She closed her eyes and waited for him to send her flying across the room. She tightened her grip on the ties on his waistcoat. All right, she thought, you'll have to pry me off to hurt me.

To her unspeakable relief, the file dropped to the floor and his arms went around her. She released her grip and began to run her hands along his back instead. 'Trevor, it's going to be all right. Really it is," she murmured.

He began to sob then as he rested his chin on her hair. "All through Christmas Eve, Christmas, and Boxing Day, Cecilia," he said, when he could speak, "I can't do anything. I can't eat, can't sleep. If one of the other barristers at the Inn didn't come and force me to take care of myself last Christmas, I would have wasted away." He leaned against her until his weight almost top-pled her. "Please stop me! I don't want to die!"

Holding him so close that she could feel his waistcoat but-tons against her, she understood the enormity of his guilt, as irrational as it seemed to her logical mind. She moved him toward the sofa and sat down. He released her only to sink down beside her and lay his head in her lap. She twitched her shawl off her shoulders, spread it over him, and rested her hand on his hair— did he never comb it, ever?—as he cried. Sitting back, she felt his exhaustion and remorse seeping into her very skin. As he cried and agonized, she had the tiniest inkling of the Gethsemane that her dear foster father spoke of from the pulpit, upon occasion. "Bless your heart," she whispered, "you're atoning for the sins of the world. My dear, no mortal can do that! What's more, it's been done, and you don't have to."

"That's your theology," he managed to gasp, before agony engulfed him again.

"And I am utterly convinced of it, dear sir," she said. Cecilia pushed on his shoulder until he was forced to raise himself and look at her. She kissed his forehead. "Even someone as young as Davy understands that we celebrate Christmas because Christ gave us *hope!* Dear man, you're dragging around chains that He took care of long ago." She kissed him again, even though his face was wet and slimy now. "I really think it's time you stopped."

"But Jimmy's dead!"

It was a lament for the ages, and she felt suddenly as old and tired as he, as though he had communicated the matter into her in a way that was almost intimate. She considered it, and understood her own faith, perhaps for the first time. "Yes, Jimmy Daw is dead," she whispered finally as he lowered himself back to her lap, his arm around her this time. "And you have done more to honor his memory than any other human being. Every child you save is a testimony to your goodness, and a memorial to Jimmy Daw. I know it is. I believe it."

He didn't say anything, but he had stopped crying. She knew he was listening this time. She cleared her throat, and wiped her own eyes with a hand that shook. "May I tell you how we are going to celebrate Christmas Eve next year? We are going to remember all the children you have *saved*. We are going to thank Kind Providence that you have the health and wealth to do this desperately hard work."

"We are?" he asked, his voice no more than a whisper.

"We are," she replied firmly. "You are not going to do it alone ever again."

What am I saying? she asked herself, waiting for the utter foolishness of her declaration to overtake her. When nothing of the kind happened, she bowed her head over his, then rested her cheek against his hair. "You're a good man, Trevor Chase. I even think I love you."

"Cecilia," was all he said, and she smiled, thinking how tired he must be. She could feel his whole body relaxing. After a long time of silence, she moved her legs, and he sat up.

"I believe I will go to bed now," she told him. "Or should I stay?"

He shook his head, and reached for a handkerchief. He blew his nose vigorously. "No, it's fine. You can go."

She gathered up her shawl and went to the door. "Good night, and happy Christmas, Trevor," she said, and blew him a kiss.

The house was so quiet. She pulled herself up the stairs, practically hand over hand, and went into the girls' room. The bed looked far more inviting than her own little cot. Since they were in the stable, she shucked off her clothing down to her shimmy and crawled in.

She was nearly asleep when Lord Trevor opened the door, came to the bed, and stood there. "I threw the file on the fire," he said, his voice sounding as uncertain as a small child's.

"Good," she told him, and after only the slightest hesitation, pulled back the blankets.

"Are you certain?" he asked.

"Never more so."

"I don't want to be alone tonight," he told her as he took off his shoes, then started on his waistcoat. "I'm so tired."

"I know you are, but I have to know one more thing. I think you know what it is."

He sat down on the bed, and rested his head in his hands. "I do. I was going to go back to my chambers this year, lock the door, and stay in there until . . ." He stopped, unable to speak.

Cecilia sat up and leaned her head against his back. "My goodness, Trevor, my goodness," she whispered. "What . . . what changed your mind?"

"Well, I had to stay here with the children when Hugo and Maria bolted, but even then . . ." He turned around and put his arm around her. "Then you came, and I had second thoughts. I didn't plan on falling in love."

"Just like that?"

"Just like that. Are you as skeptical as I am?"

"Probably. But, you looked so defeated in the book room tonight."

"I don't know what would have happened, considering how matters had changed. I suppose I'll never know," he told her as she put her arms around him. "I think I was counting on you to stop me. Thank you from the bottom of my heart, Cecilia."

He lay down beside her and gathered her close. With a sigh, she threw her arm over his chest and rested her head in that nice spot below his collarbone. His hand was warm against her back. Her feet were cold and he flinched a little when she put them on his legs, but then he kissed her neck, and she fell asleep.

He was gone in the morning. She got up and dressed quickly, then hurried downstairs. She heard laughter from the breakfast room, his laughter. She opened the door.

"Lucy, you are telling me that your graceless scamp of a little brother actually stood over by the horses and began to *talk*?" asked Lord Trevor. The picture of relaxation, he slouched negligently in his chair, with his arm along the back of Lucinda's chair.

Janet giggled. "He scared Lucy so bad that she jumped up and stepped in the water bucket the footman had left by the lantern!"

"Did not!"

"Oh, we both saw it!"

Lord Trevor held up both hands. "I've never met more disgraceful children," he scolded, but anyone with even the slightest hearing could have picked out the amusement in his voice.

"It's never too late for my prosy lecture. Good morning, Miss Ambrose, how do you do?"

I know my face is red, she thought. "I do well," she replied. "Happy Christmas to you all."

Lord Trevor pushed out a chair with his foot. "Have a seat, my dear Miss Ambrose. I've told my long-suffering relatives all about my silliness next door at the manor. They have agreed that a week in the dower house was not too unpleasant." He smiled at them all. "And now they will move their belongings back, with some help from Mrs. Grey and the footman."

"Mama is coming home today," Davy said.

"I received a letter from Lysander only a few minutes ago," Janet said, holding out a piece of paper. She smiled at Cecilia. "He promises to come as soon as all contagion is gone."

Cecilia poured a cup of tea and sat down, just as the children rose and left the room. Davy even looked back and winked. "Scamp," she murmured under her breath, trying to concentrate on the tea before her, and not on Lord Trevor, who had decided to put his arm on her chair now. In another moment his hand rested on her shoulder, and then his fingers outlined her ear.

"You're making this tea hard to drink," she commented.

"It isn't very good tea, anyway," he told her as he took the cup from her hand and pushed it away. He cleared his throat. "Cecilia—Miss Ambrose—it has certainly come to my attention that I . . . er . . . uh . . . may have compromised you last night."

I love him, she thought, looking at him in his rumpled clothes, with his hair in need of cutting. I wonder why he does not stand closer to his razor, she thought. His eyes were tired, to be sure, but the hopeless look that had been increasing hour by hour on Christmas Eve was gone. She turned in her chair to face him.

"I would say that you certainly did compromise me. How loud you snore! What do you intend to do about it?"

"What, my snoring?"

She laughed and leaned toward him. He put his hand around her neck, drew her closer, and kissed her forehead.

"I suppose I must make you an offer now, eh?" he asked, the grin not gone from his face.

"I would like that," she told him. "We'll be an odd couple, don't you think?"

"Most certainly. I'm positive there will be doors that will never open to either of us," he replied, without the blink of an eye. "People of my sort will wonder if I have taken leave of my senses to marry Cleopatra herself, and those evangelizing, missionary friends of your parents will assume that you have taken pity on a man desperate for redemption." He kissed her again, his lips lingering this time. "Oh, my goodness. Cecilia, I will be bringing home scum, riffraff, and strays."

"Of course. I'm going to insist that you close your chambers at the Inn and move me into a house on a quiet street where the neighbors are kind and don't mind children," she said, reaching for him this time and rubbing her cheek against his. She felt the tears on his face.

"Miss Deprave is going to be awfully upset when you give your notice," he warned.

She giggled. "Your brother and sister-in-law will probably have a fit when you tell them this afternoon."

He laughed and pulled her onto his lap. "There you are wrong. They'll be so relieved to find a lady in my life that they won't even squeak!"

She tightened her arm around his neck as the fears returned momentarily. "I hope they are not disappointed."

"No one will be disappointed about this except Miss Deprave. Trust me, Cecilia."

"Trust a barrister?" she teased, putting her hands on both sides of his face and kissing him.

"Yes, indeed." His expression was serious then. "Trust me. I trusted you when I told you about Jimmy that second night." He took her hand. "I looked at your lovely face, and some intuition told me I could *say* something finally." He shook his head.

She knew she did not know him well yet, but she could tell he wanted to say something more. "What is it?" she prodded him. "I hardly think, at this point, that there is anything you might be embarrassed to tell me."

He looked at the closed door, then pulled her onto his lap. She sighed and felt completely at home there.

"Before I left London, I made a wish on a star. Is that beyond absurd?"

Resting there with her head against his chest and listening to the regular beating of his heart, she considered the matter. "Teachers are interested in results, dear sir, not absurdities. Did it come true?"

"Oh, my, in spades."

She went to kiss his cheek, but he turned his head and she found his lips instead. "Then I would say your wish came true," she murmured, once she could speak again.

He smiled. "I'm a skeptic still, but I like it."

"I like it, too," she admitted.

"D'ye think you'll still like it thirty or forty years from now?" he asked.

"Only if you're with me." She kissed him again. "Promise?"

"Promise."

No Room at the Inn

"Mama, are we there yet?"

Mary McIntyre smiled, and added another entry to her growing list of what was going to make the single life so comfortable.

"I told you less than fifteen minutes ago that the snow is slowing our progress."

Mary glanced at Agatha Shepard, her seat companion, who was doing her best not to glare at her offspring. I understand totally, Mary thought. She was no more inclined than a child to enjoy creeping along at a snail's pace, through a rapidly developing storm.

She had left Coventry two days earlier, joining the travel of Thomas and Agatha Shepard and their two children from London, who were to spend Christmas in York with Agatha's parents. The elder Shepards—he was a solicitor with Hailey and Tighe—already appeared somewhat tight around the lips when they stopped at her parents' estate. In a whispered aside, Agatha said that Thomas had not made the trip any easier with his deep sighs each time the children insisted upon acting their age.

Mary understood perfectly; she had known Thomas for years. What was it that his younger brother Joe told her once? "If people could select their relatives, Thomas would be an orphan."

As much as she liked Agatha, Mary never would have chosen the Shepards' company for anything of greater length than an afternoon's tour of Coventry's wonderful cathedral. The fates had intervened, and dictated that she be on her way to Yorkshire. Two weeks ago, her station in life had changed drastically enough to amuse even the most hardened Greek god devoted to the workings of fate.

She wished she could pace around the confining carriage and contemplate the folly of an impulsive gesture, but such exercise would have to wait. Tommy and Clarice quarreled with each other, their invective having reached the dreary stages of "Did not! Did, too!" My head aches, she thought.

They should have stopped for the night in Leeds, even though they had scarcely passed the noon hour. Agatha's timid "Thomas, dear, don't you think . . ." had been quelled by a fierce glance from her lord and master.

"My dear Agatha, I pay our coachman an outrageous sum to be highly proficient," he said. He glared around the carriage, his eyes resting finally on his squabbling olive branches. "Agatha, can you not do something about *your* children?" he asked, before returning to the legal brief in his lap.

We could dangle *you* outside the carriage until you turn blue, Mary thought. "Thomas, don't you think it odd that we have not observed a single wheeled vehicle coming from the other direction in quite some time?" It's worth a try, she thought. Let us see if I have any credit left with the family solicitor.

She discovered, to her chagrin, that she did not. Not even bothering to reply, the family solicitor stared at her. She sat back in embarrassment.

I suppose it is good to know where one stands in the greater scheme of events, she told herself later, when she felt like philosophizing. There was a time, Thomas Shepard, when you would have been nodding and bobbing at my least pronouncement, she thought. You would have at least considered my request to stop, and there would have been no withering looks. I think I liked you better when you were obsequious. And *that* is a sad reflection upon me, she decided.

She thought about Colonel Sir Harold Fox, Chief of Commissary Supply, currently serving occupation duty in Belgium. His last letter to her had indicated a season of celebration, now that the Monster was on his way to a seaside location somewhere apart from shipping lanes in the South Atlantic. "My dear, you dance divinely," he had written. "I wish you were here, as we endure no end of balls and routs."

I doubt you wish that now, she told herself. When her father—no, Lord Davy—broke the news to her, she had calmly retreated upstairs and wrote to Sir Harry. He had made her no declaration, but in his last letter, he had hinted broadly that he would be asking her a significant question during his visit home at Christmas. It seemed only fair to alert him that he might not wish to make her an offer.

She sighed, then hoped that Agatha was engaged with her children, and not paying attention. Should I be angry at life's unfairness? she asked herself, then shook her head. Here she sat, fur-lined cloak around her, in a comfortable coach, going to spend Christmas with . . . She faltered. With a grandmother I do not even know, who lives on a *farm*, God help me.

They continued another two hours beyond Leeds, with the coachman stopping again and again for no reason that Mary could discern beyond trying to see if he was still on the highway. She knew Agatha was alarmed; even the children were silent, sitting close together now.

Another stop, and then a knock on the carriage door. Thomas pulled his overcoat up around his ears and left the vehicle to stand on the roadway with the coachman, their backs to the carriage. Young Tommy looked at Mary. "I have a pocketful of raisins, and Clarice has a muffin she didn't eat from breakfast this morning," he told her seriously.

Mary reached over to touch his cheek. "I think you are wonderful children," she told him. "How relieved I am to know that because of your providence, we won't starve." He smiled back, at ease now.

Thomas the elder climbed back in the carriage a few minutes later, bringing with him a gust of snow. He took a deep breath. "The coachman advises me that we must seek shelter," he said. "Thank God we are near Edgerly. If the inn there is already full, we will be forced to throw ourselves on my brother's mercy."

Tommy clapped his hands. "Clarice, did you hear that? Uncle Joe!"

"I didn't know Joe lived around here," Mary said.

A long silence followed. When Thomas finally spoke, there was an added formality to his careful choosing of words. "He purchased what I can only, with charity, describe as a real bargain, Miss McIntyre. I tried to make him reconsider, but Joe has ever been stubborn and inconsiderate of the needs of others."

And *you* are not? she thought.

The discussion animated Agatha. "Oh, my dear, it is a wreck!" she confided. "A monstrosity! He bought it for practically pence from a really vulgar mill owner who thought to retire there." She giggled, their plight momentarily forgotten. "I believe the man died of apoplexy after taking possession of the place. Thomas thinks the shock carried him away. The place was too much, even for him!"

A smile played around Thomas's lips. "I told him he'd regret the purchase." He shrugged. "That was four years ago. We haven't heard much from Joe since."

She tried to remember Joseph Shepard, the second son of her father's—no, Lord Davy's—estate steward, which wasn't difficult. She couldn't help smiling at the memory of a tall, handsome man who spent a lot of time in the fields, who was cheerful to a fault, and who seemed not to mind when both she and her little sister Sara fell in love with him. Edgar followed him everywhere, and there was never a cross word. Of course, he was a family servant, she reminded herself. He must be nearly thirty-three or so now, she thought.

The inn at Edgerly proved to be suffering from the same problem experienced many Christmases ago. The innkeeper came out to their carriage to say that he had no room for anyone more. "Of course, you could sit in the taproom," he suggested.

"We would never do that," Thomas snapped.

I wish your father could hear you now, Mary thought, and felt no regret at her own small-mindedness. Funny, but if my choice was for my family to freeze in a carriage, or sit among less renowned folk in a taproom, I would choose the taproom. She smiled. Perhaps I *am* better suited to the common life.

"Well, then," said the innkeeper. "I won't keep you from . . . uh . . . whatever it is you think you can do now."

"One thing more," Thomas said. Mary felt her toes curl at his imperious tone. "Are you acquainted with Joseph Shepard?"

"We all know Joe! Are you a friend of his?"

"I am his brother."

"Who would have thought it?" the keep said. "Planning to drop in on him now?"

Thomas glared at him. "My arrangements are my business. Give me directions."

The innkeeper looked inside the carriage, and Mary realized exactly what he was thinking. She had no doubt that if Tom had been unaccompanied, he would have been given directions that would ultimately have landed him somewhere north of St. Petersburg. Mary couldn't resist a smile at the keep, and was rewarded with a wink.

Practically feeling his way like a blind man, the coachman finally stopped before a large house, just as the winter night settled in. The carriage shifted slightly as the coachman left his box and walked around to the door. Thomas stepped down after the coachman dropped the steps. "Agatha, I predict that Joe will open the door. He has probably sent his servants home during the Christmas season. Providing he has any to send home!"

The Shepards chuckled as Mary watched thoughtfully. "I suppose you have retained your regular household in London this week, even though you are not there?" she asked, hoping that the question sounded innocent.

"Of course!" Agatha exclaimed. "The housekeeper will release them for a half day on Christmas. Only think what an excellent time this is for them to clean and scrub."

"Of course," Mary murmured. "Whatever was I thinking?"

The house was close to the gate. Peering through the darkness, Mary could discern no vulgar gargoyles or statues. It appeared to be of ordinary brick, with a magnificent cornice over the door, which even now was opening.

"It *is* Joe himself," Agatha said. "There is probably not a servant on the place."

The carriage door opened, and Joseph Shepard looked around at them, his eyes bright with merriment. "Can it be? Lord bless me, do I see Tommy the Stalwart, and Clarice the Candid? Welcome to Edgerly, my dears."

It felt like a rescue, especially when he held out his arms and his niece and nephew practically leaped into them. Agatha's feeble effort at control—"Children, have you no manners?"— dissolved quickly when he beamed at her, too. "Oh, Joe, thank goodness you're here! I do not know what we would have done."

He only smiled, and then looked at her. "Lady Mary? What a pleasure."

His arms were full of children so he could not help her down. Instead of retreating to the house with his burden, he stood by the carriage while Thomas helped Agatha and then Mary from the vehicle. He brushed off Agatha's apologies with a shake of his head, then led the group of them to his house. Mary still stood by the carriage as the others started up the narrow walk. The coachman closed the carriage door. "Things are always a little better when Joe is around," he said, more to himself than to her.

She started up the walk after the others, when Joe came toward her. He had deposited the children inside, and he hurried down the steps to assist her. She did not think she had seen him in at least eight years, when she was fifteen or so, but she would have recognized him anywhere. He bore a great resemblance to his brother; both were taller than average, but not towering, with dark hair and light eyes. There was one thing about him that she remembered quite well. She peered closer, hoping she was not being too obvious, to see if that great quality remained. To her delight, it did, and she smiled at him and spoke without thinking. "I was hoping you had not lost that trick of smiling with your eyes," she said, and held out her hand.

"It's no trick, Lady Mary," he replied, and he shook her hand. "It just happens miraculously, especially when I see a lovely lady. Welcome to my house."

He ushered her in and took her cloak. She looked around in appreciation, and not a little curiosity. He must have noticed the look, because he glanced at Thomas and his family toward the other end of the spacious hallway. "Did Thomas tell you I was living in a vulgar barn I bought for ten pence to the pound from a bankrupt mill owner?"

She nodded, shy then.

"All true," he told her. "I wonder why it is he seems faintly disappointed that the scandalous statues and the red wallpaper are gone?" He touched her arm. "Perhaps he will be less disappointed if I tell him that the restoration is only half complete, and he will be quite inconvenienced in the unfinished bedchambers. Do you think he will prefer the jade green wallpaper, or the room where Joshua and I have already stripped the paper?"

She laughed, in spite of herself. "Joshua?" she asked.

"My son. I believe he is belowstairs helping our scullery maid, Abby, cook the sausages." Joe looked at his brother. "Thomas, I trust you have not eaten yet?"

"And where would that have happened?" Thomas asked in irritation. "Even the most miserable inn from Leeds on is full of travelers! Surely you have something less plebian than sausages, brother," Tom continued.

"We were going to cook eggs, too," Joe offered, with no evident apology.

"And toast," Thomas said with sarcasm. Her face red, Agatha tugged at his arm.

"Certainly. What else?"

"Brother, did you dismiss your staff?"

"I did, for a fact," Joe stated. "My housekeeper has a sister in Waverly, and she enjoys her company around the holiday. Ditto for my cook, of course. The two maids—they are sisters—informed me that their older brother is home from the war. I couldn't turn them down."

"I call it amazingly thoughtless of you!"

Mary stared at Thomas and curled her hand into a fist. Surprised at herself, she looked down, then hoped that no one had noticed. She was almost afraid to look at the brothers. The angry words seemed to hang in the air between them. "Thomas, I am certain your brother had no any idea that we were all going to descend on him," she said.

Thomas turned to glare at her. "*Miss* McIntyre, this is a matter between me and my brother," he snapped. "I'll thank you to stay out of it."

Joseph Shepard spoke quickly. "Thomas, have some charity. It's Christmas." He smiled at Mary. "Lady Mary, if you don't mind what I am certain amounts to delving deeper into low company than you ever intended, you might want to help Joshua belowstairs. I know that you are a game goer, and we need more sausages." He gestured down the hall. "It's through that door. I'll sort out some sleeping arrangements."

"Certainly," she said, grateful to flee the scene.

The servants' hall was empty, so she followed her nose into the kitchen, where two children stood by a modern Rumford stove. The little boy with the apron about his middle who poked at sausages sizzling in the pan was obviously Joshua. The young girl who cracked eggs into a bowl must be Abby. She felt their scrutiny, but also felt it was unencumbered by the tension that was so heavy upstairs.

"Hello, my dears," she said. "My name is Mary McIntyre. I think I'm going to be a Christmas guest. Joshua, your uncle Thomas and his family are upstairs. Your father says there will be a few more people for dinner."

"Good," he replied. "We like company." He smiled at her. It was Joe Shepard's slow smile, but without any other resemblance to the originator of it. As the boy put more sausages in the pan, she wished his uncle Thomas could have appeared belowstairs to witness real courtesy.

Mary rolled up her sleeves and placed herself at the service of the scullery maid, who shyly asked for more eggs, and showed her how to crack them. When she admired the way Abby whisked the eggs around in the bowl and told her so, the child

83

blushed and ducked her head. "She's a little shy, Miss McIntyre," Joshua said.

Joe Shepard came downstairs when the next batch of sausages was cooking. He helped Abby pour the eggs into a pan. "You see what good hands I am in, Miss McIntyre," he said, "even if my own brother thinks I am a barbarian without redemption." He leaned against the table. "I think I offended Agatha's maid."

"Never a difficult task," Mary murmured. "Did you dare suggest that if she wanted a can of hot water that she come belowstairs to get it?"

"How did you know?" he asked. "She insists that the 'tween stairs maid bring it up to her." He looked at his son. "Josh, do we need a 'tween stairs maid?"

"I could take her a can," he suggested.

"No, no. Let's see if she comes for one. Some tea, Miss McIntyre?"

"Delighted." She accepted the cup from him. "It appears that your brother has told you of my fall from grace, since you are no longer calling me Lady Mary." He nodded, and took a sip from his own cup. "I don't understand it, though." He glanced at the children. "Lord and Lady Davy took you in when you were a baby, and only decided just before Christmas to tell you that it was all a *mistake*? My Lord, that's gruesome." He took another sip. "I could almost think it cruel."

He was saying exactly what she felt, and until that moment, had refused to acknowledge. He must have noticed the tears in her eyes, because he gave her his handkerchief. "I didn't mean to make you do that," he told her. "Just another example of my barbarism, I suppose. Forgive me, Miss McIntyre. You can explain this a little later, if you wish. I don't want to pry, but I'm used to thinking of you as Lady Mary."

"I'm used to hearing it," she said. She had to change the subject. "Is Joshua's mother away?"

"Farther than any of us like. She died three years ago," he said. "I don't know if you even knew I had married, but she was a fine woman, a widow with a little boy."

"Josh?"

"Yes." She could see nothing but pride in his eyes as he regarded the boy at the Rumford. "Isn't he a fine one? I'm a lucky man, despite it all."

She looked at Joshua, and back at Joe Shepard. I think I have stumbled onto quite a family, she thought. "He's certainly good with sausages." It wasn't what she wanted to say, but it seemed the right thing, particularly since Agatha's maid was stomping down the stairs now. Joe got up to help her.

As the maid, her back rigid, snatched the can from Joe and started for the door, he called after her, "Miss, could you tell the others that dinner will be ready soon?"

She turned around, her expression awful. "I do not announce meals!"

"Good Lord, what was I thinking?" Joe said.

"Papa, why is she so unpleasant?" Joshua asked when the maid slammed the door.

"Happen someone forgot to tell her it was Christmas," he replied. He bowed elaborately to Abby. "My dear Miss Abigail, if you and Miss McIntyre will go upstairs and lay the table, we will bring up dinner. Do I ask too much?"

Abby laughed out loud. As Mary got up to follow her, she noticed the look that Joe and Joshua exchanged.

"She came to us from a workhouse in September," Joe explained. "I do believe this is the first time she has laughed, isn't it, Josh?"

The boy nodded. "Maybe she finds the maid amusing."

"I know I do," Joe said.

"Come, miss," Abby called from the top of the stairs.

"Right away, my dear!" She turned to Joe. "Did she stay here with you this Christmas because she has nowhere else to go?"

"Precisely."

I have nowhere to go, either, Mary thought as she went upstairs. And then surprisingly, may I stay here, too?

The thought persisted through dinner, even as she carried on a perfectly amiable conversation with Agatha, and everyone tried to ignore Thomas's elaborate, rude silence. His eye on his father, Tommy began a cautious conversation with Joshua, which quickly flourished into a real discussion about the merits of good English marbles over the multicolored ones from Poland.

Joe had placed Abby next to him. He kept his arm along the back of her chair in a protective gesture that Mary found gratifying. Joe carried on a light conversation about the changes underway in his house, but offered no apologies for the inconvenience.

"Did you construct that beautiful cornice over the front door?" Mary asked.

"I designed it, but I hired a stonemason for the work." He beamed at her in the way that she remembered. "Familiar to you, Miss McIntyre?"

"Indeed, yes," she replied. "I seem to recall a similar cornice over the door that leads onto the terrace at Denton."

"I always liked it," he said. He looked at his brother. "Tom, d'ye remember when we weeded the flower beds below the terrace?"

Thomas turned red in the face. "I see no point in remembering those days."

"Pity, considering what an enjoyable childhood we had," Joseph said. He turned his attention to Mary. "I remember a time you and Lady Sara got in trouble for coming to help us weed. How is she, by the way? And Lord Milthorpe?"

"Really, Joseph," Thomas said in a low voice. "I already told you that Miss McIntyre has had a change in her circumstances."

"True, brother. What I know of Miss McIntyre, unless she has changed drastically, is that she couldn't possibly forget the people she was raised with, unlike some," Joseph replied, his voice calm, but full of steel. "I trust they are well?"

Oh, bravo, Mary thought. "Lady Sara has got herself engaged to a marquess from Kent. Our . . . her parents have gone there this Christmas to renew their acquaintance with the family. Edgar—Lord Milthorpe—is desperately disappointed that the wars are over and he cannot pester Papa . . . Lord Davy . . . to purchase a commission."

"Do give Lady Sara my congratulations when next you see her," Joseph said as his brother rose. "Thomas, I can offer you no inducement to stay at table. Agatha, I do not even have a whist table."

"That's all right," she replied. "I believe I will see the children to bed now."

"Oh, Mama!" Tommy protested. "I would very much like to see Joshua's marbles. Oh, please, Papa. It is nearly Christmas!"

Thomas opened his mouth and closed it again. He sighed and went to the door of the breakfast room.

Joseph looked at his brother. "Is that someone at the door? Could it be Father Christmas, or is someone else lost? Tom, could you answer the door?"

"I do not answer doors in strange establishments," Tom snapped. In another moment they heard him on the stairs.

"I doubt he would carry hot water, either," Abby said. She gasped, and stared at Agatha Shepard. "Begging your pardon, ma'am."

Agatha rose to the occasion, to Mary's relief. "I believe you are right, child."

Mary followed Joseph into the main hall and stood watching as he opened the door on a couple considerably shorter than he was, and older by several decades. "Frank! We are saved!" cried the woman.

Mary turned away so no one would hear her laugh.

They were Frank and Myrtle King of Sheffield, and the driver of their hired post chaise, with a tale to tell of crowded inns, surly keeps, full houses along the route, and snow with no end in sight. "I can pay you for yer hospitality, sir," Mr. King declared as Joe tried to help him with his overcoat. "Nothing cheap about me! I'm assistant manager at the Butler Ironworks in Sheffield."

His eyes bright, Joseph turned to Mary. "Miss McIntyre, meet the Kings. I do believe we are all going to spend Christmas together."

The Kings had no objections to going belowstairs; Mary could see how uncomfortable they seemed, just standing in the hallway of Joe's magnificent bargain house. Frank repeated his earnest desire to pay for their accommodations, and Myrtle just looked worried and chewed on her lip.

While Mary stirred the eggs this time, and Joseph cooked more sausage, the coachman led his team around behind the house to unhitch them, and came inside again to report that he was going to be fine in the stables with the Shepards' coachman. He tucked away the first order of sausage and eggs, and assured them that they would both come inside for breakfast, come morning.

Provided there is anything left to eat, Mary thought as she poured more eggs into the pan on the Rumford. To her amusement, Joe nudged her shoulder. "We have a full pantry, Miss McIntyre," he told her. "Too bad there is not a cook among us."

"There is, sir," Myrtle declared. "There's nothing I can't cook."

"Then you are an angel sent from heaven, Mrs. King," Joseph declared.

She giggled. "It appears to me that you and your missus shouldn't have dismissed your entire staff for the holiday. Were you planning to go away, too, but for the snow?"

"I did dismiss my staff, Mrs. King," Joseph said. "As for going away, no. Miss McIntyre is an old acquaintance, and she and my brother and his family were stranded by the weather, too." He turned back to the stove long enough to fork the sausages around and allow his own high color to diminish, to Mary's glee.

"Orphans in the storm, eh?" Mrs. King said.

"Precisely. We will be in your debt, madam, if you would cook for the duration of this unpleasant weather. I have a scullery maid, and Mary here is a willing accomplice." He laughed. "Did I say accomplice? Did I mean apprentice?"

"I think you meant accomplice, Joe," Mary said, without a qualm that their relationship seemed to have changed with the use of her first name. "Mrs. King, I do hope you like your eggs scrambled. It is my sole accomplishment. Mr. King?"

She made no objection to Joe's suggestion, an hour later, that they adjourn to the bookroom upstairs together. The Kings were safely tucked in belowstairs in the housekeeper's room. Abby had retired to the room that she shared belowstairs with the absent maids, and Mary promised to join her there later.

"Of course, more properly you should be upstairs, but the only room left unoccupied has two sawhorses and everything else draped in Holland covers. Joshua thinks it is spooky, and so do I."

"I am certain I will be quite comfortable in the maids' room." She propped her feet up on the hassock between the chairs.

Joe leaned back. "I'll tell you my troubles, but you first, Mary, unless it makes you desperately unhappy. I want to know what happened to you. It's not every day that an earl's daughter turns into plain Mary McIntyre."

She settled herself comfortably into the chair, wondering if the late Mrs. Shepard had used the chair before her. If that was the case, Joe's wife must have been about her size, because it suited her own frame. "I don't suppose it is, Joe," she agreed. "My mother—oh, I know she is Lady Davy, but please, you won't mind if I call her my mother, will you? She still feels amazingly like my mother."

Joe was silent. She looked at him, startled to see tears in his eyes. She touched his arm. "Joe, don't feel sorry for me."

"Call me a fool, then."

"Never," she declared. "Mama never let me read those ladies' novels. You know, the ones where the scullery maid turns out to be an earl's daughter? Isn't that what happens in those dreadful books? Who can believe such nonsense?"

"I can assure you that *my* scullery maid isn't an earl's daughter. Where do authors get those stupid notions?"

"My case is the precise opposite of a bad novel. Papa and Mama had been married for several years, with no issue in sight, apparently."

"It happens. I know."

"Mama had a modiste who called herself Clare La Salle, and claimed to be a French émigrée."

"That's glamorous enough for a bad novel," Joseph said. "I take it that Clare was not her real name."

"No, indeed. Apparently Clare found herself in an interesting condition."

"Any idea who the father was?"

"I don't think he was a marquess or a viscount," she said. "Clare came to Mama in desperation, and she and my parents hatched a scheme. You can imagine the rest."

"What happened to Clare?"

"She was so obliging as to die when I was born, apparently. Mama had retired to Denton, so no one knew I wasn't really hers," Mary said. "What could interfere now? Mama found herself in an interesting condition later, and Sara was born. And then Edgar."

Joe settled lower in his chair. "So Lady Mary, daughter of the Earl of Denton, spent a blissful childhood of privilege, completely ignorant of her actual origins." He looked at her. "Do you think it was just two weeks ago that they had second thoughts about their philanthropy?"

She shook her head. "As I reflect on it now, I think not."

"You never had a come-out, did you?"

My stars, she thought, *you were mindful of such a thing?* "No, I never did. I am surprised that you were ever aware of it, though."

"Don't think me presumptuous when I say this, but your family was a choice topic of conversation in our cottage." He shrugged. "I expect this is true of any large estate."

She digested what he said, and could not deny the probable truth of it. The reverse gave her some pause; at no point in her life had she ever been interested in those belowstairs. "We never spoke of you, sir," she said honestly.

"A candid statement," he said. "I appreciate your honesty. I wager that you do not remember the first time I could have come to your attention."

"You would lose, sir. I remember it quite well."

"What?"

"Let me tell you here that Sara and I both fell in love with you when we were little. We decided you were quite the nicest person on the whole estate."

"My blushes."

"You rescued me from an apple tree when I was five," she said, enjoying the embarrassment on his face. "As I recall, Thomas put me there on a dare from the goose girl."

"That was it," he said. "I trust you and Lady Sara survived your infatuation?"

"I think we did. But you know, I never thanked you for rescuing me."

"You weren't supposed to."

"Then I thank you now."

They were both quiet. Mary smiled and looked into the flames. "Now that I think of it, by the time for my come-out, my parents were likely coming to realize the deception they were practicing on those of their rank regarding my . . . my unsuitability."

"I say, sod'um all, Mary."

She gasped. "Joe, your language!"

He leaned across the space between them, his eyes merry. "Sod them, I say. You always were the most interesting of the lot, Mary McIntyre. Did you want a come-out?"

"No. I like to dance, but I have no patience for fashion— can you imagine how my real mother is spinning in her grave? Idle chat bores me." She rested her chin on her hand. "Joe, I'm going to miss Denton." The tears slid down her face then. She wasn't sure how she had gotten into this state, but she decided to blame her tiredness.

Joe seemed not to mind. He didn't harrumph and walk around in great agitation, as Lord Davy had when she cried after his terrible news to her. He regarded her for a moment. "What finally brought the matter to a head? Who connected the McIntyres with Clare La Salle?"

"It was a Bow Street Runner, of all things. Mrs. McIntyre— she would be my real grandmother—had long mourned that

91

wayward daughter. After some years, she contacted the Bow Street Runners. After considerable time and much perseverance, they connected her missing daughter to Clare La Salle through one of London's houses of fashion. They found me less than a month ago," she concluded simply.

She took a deep breath. "Mama couldn't face me. Papa told me the whole story. He offered me an annuity that Hailey and Tighe drew up. I . . . I signed it and left the room Mary McIntyre."

"Darn them all, Mary."

"No," she said quickly, startled at his vehemence. "I have an income that most of England would envy, and all my faculties. It could have been much worse." The silence from the other chair told her quite eloquently that Joseph Shepard did not agree. She folded her hands in her lap and felt greatly tired. "I will miss them all. Lord Davy thinks it best that I quietly fade from the scene. No family needs scandal. I have . . . had a suitor, Colonel Sir Harold Fox. Perhaps you remember him?"

"Yes, indeed. A tall fellow who rides his horses too hard."

"Does he? I have written him a letter laying the whole matter before him. We shall see what he chooses to do. Rides his horses too hard, eh?"

Joe laughed. "Sod him, too, Mary."

She joined in his laughter, feeling immeasurably better. "Your turn, Joe," she said when she quit laughing. "Why are you and Tom so out of sorts?"

She thought he was disinclined to reply at all, considering the lengthy silence. Or it may have been only a few moments. Her state of exhaustion either shut out time, or let it through in odd spurts.

"I hope this won't offend you," he began finally.

"No one else has been concerned about offending me lately," she reminded him.

"Your father—well, Lord Davy—is a misguided philan-thropist, I do believe."

Two weeks ago she would have disputed with him, but not now. "My father was his estate steward, as you know," he went on. "One day he told my father that he wanted to educate Tom and me. You know, send us to university, give us a leg up. Lord Davy paid Tom's charges at the University of London, and he became a solicitor."

"But not a barrister? Does that bother him?"

He looked at her with some appreciation. "Bravo, Mary! Poor Tom. No matter how fine his patronage, no one would ever call Tom, the son of a steward, to the bar."

She thought a minute. "I really don't recall seeing Thomas much at Denton, after he went to university."

"Try never. We weren't good enough," he said. "He never came around. Think of it, Mary: he was too good to visit the steward's cottage, and will never be good enough for an invitation to Denton Hall. Poor man, poor man."

She mulled it over. "There is a certain irony to this conversation, Joe," she said after some thought. "Tom goes up in society, but never quite high enough. I go down . . ."

". . . but you will always be a lady, no matter what your former relatives do to you. He may just resent you, too, Mary." He was starting to mumble now. "You're in good company, because he resents me, too."

"Because you didn't go to university? Obviously you turned down the same offer from Lord Davy."

"Oh, but I did go to university. I did well, even though it bored me beyond belief. It is . . . It is worse than that."

She closed her eyes, and after a moment, the matter became quite clear. She laughed.

Joe watched appreciatively. "Figure it out?"

"Joe, you'll have to tell me what you do for a living, I suppose," she said.

"I am a lowly grain broker, but I am certainly an excellent businessman." He smiled. "Despite my lofty education!" He started to laugh again. "I decided to do what I like. Every spring I visit farms and estates in Yorkshire, make predictions, and give them an offer on their crops. It is called dealing in futures, and I am good."

She clapped her hands, delighted at his good fortune. "I can hardly imagine more lowly commerce."

"Thank you! I have considered developing a side line in the bone and hide business, just to spite Thomas." He grinned. "Imagine how I would stink! If I were to turn up at his London house, Thomas would probably fall on his knife."

She watched him, not flinching at his scrutiny, even as she felt her whole body grow warm. Sir Harry never looked at me like that, she thought. I should go to bed. But she remembered there was one more matter. "Let us see how this tallies: Thomas is unhappy because he will never scale the heights he feels he deserves, and he resents your success. I have seen my hopes of a lifetime dashed. What about you? You said earlier that you spend too much time doing just this."

It sounded so blunt that she wished she had not spoken, especially when he avoided her gaze. "I miss my wife," he said, just as bluntly. "She was a grand woman, although I daresay Tom would have thought her common, had he ever met her."

"Would *I* have liked her?" Mary asked.

"You would have loved her," he replied promptly. "You remind me of her a little: same dark hair, eyes almost black, quiet, capable. Tall, for a woman. I like looking women in the eye." He reached out to touch her leg, then pulled his hand back. She held her breath, not moving, not wanting to break whatever spell he was under. He took one deep breath and then another, and she could tell he was as tired as she was. "Maybe I was even thinking of you when I met her, Lady Mary. Or maybe I am thinking of her now when I see you. Or maybe I am exhausted beyond redemption tonight." He shook his head. "I will regret this conversation in the morning."

"I do hope not, Joe," she said quietly. She was silent then, as spent as he was. After a moment, she moved her legs away from the hassock, then gathered herself together enough to stand.

He chuckled, and struggled to his feet. "Let me help you down those stairs, Mary McIntyre. I would feel wretched if you landed in a heap in the servants' hall."

She could think of no objection as he put his arm around her waist and pulled her arm around his. By hanging onto the wall, then clutching the banister, he got her to the door of the maids' room.

"Are you all right now?" he whispered. He turned his head. "My goodness, can Frank King ever snore. Unless that is Myrtle."

They laughed softly together, his head close to hers. He leaned on her, and she thought for a moment that he was asleep. For no discernible reason, she thought of Christmas. "Joe," she whispered. "Do you and Joshua not really celebrate the season?"

"I never quite know what to do," he replied.

"Have you any holiday decorations?"

"Melissa had quite a few, but I do not know that either of us are up to those yet."

"Any others?" He was leaning on her quite heavily now.

"There may be a box belonging to the defunct owner of this palace," he said. "Probably vulgar and destined to set off Thomas. Oh, do find them!" He laughed.

She put her hand over his mouth to silence him, and he kissed her palm, his eyes closed, then it was her wrist. His head was so close that she couldn't think of a reason not to kiss his cheek. "I think I will see what Mrs. King and I can do about Christmas," she murmured, "considering that we are snowbound."

He pulled her very close then. They were about the same height. When she turned her face to look at him—so close he was out of focus—kissing him seemed the only thing to do that made any sense.

He must have been of similar mind. He kissed her back, one hand tugging insistently at her hair, the other caressing her back in a way that made her sigh through his kiss.

Mr. King stopped snoring. Joe released his grip on her hair when she pulled away, and regarded her sleepily, but with no apology.

"Do you think we woke him up?" Joe asked quietly, his voice a little strange.

"I don't know," she whispered back. "Goodness, I hope not."

Joe touched his forehead to hers. "Good night, Mary," he said.

She went quietly into the maids' room, closed the door, and leaned against it. She laughed when she heard him stumble on the steps, then held her breath, hoping he would not plunge to the bottom.

She woke to the sound of someone screaming in her ear. Someone well schooled in torture must have placed weights on her eyes, because they refused to respond. She managed to open one eye.

Mrs. King, her eyes kindly, stood beside her bed. She held a tall glass.

"Someone was screaming," Mary gasped.

"Oh, no, dearie," she said. "I just said good morning." She lowered her voice when Mary winced. "Abby was concerned about you, but I told her you didn't get enough sleep last night, Miss McIntyre."

"Thank you, Mrs. King," she said. "I believe I will never stay awake that late with Mr. Shepard again."

The older woman put her hand to her mouth. "He said exactly the same thing this morning, my dear, when he prepared this little concoction for you."

"Do sit down, Mrs. King," she said, and pressed both hands to her head. "If I told you that I rarely stay up that late, you would probably call me a liar."

Mrs. King did laugh then. "Of course I would not! My dear, I rather think that we shall lay the blame at Mr. Shepard's door. He *is* a persuasive gentleman, isn't he?" She leaned forward and held out the glass. "Do you wish this, my dear?"

Mary eyed the glass with disfavor. "It's so . . . black," she said. "What is in it?"

"He made me promise not to look, but he left the treacle can on the table."

"Oh, Lord, I am being punished for all my sins," Mary said with a sigh and reached for the glass. Her stomach heaved at the first tentative sip. She took a deep breath and drank the brew, then slowly slid back into the mattress.

"He said I was to wait a half hour and then bring you porridge, well sugared."

"I will be dead before then!"

To her amazement, she was not. She lay as still as she could, wondering at the sounds around her. After a moment, she understood why everything sounded strange: she had never heard a house at work from the ground up. In the world she had just left, servants were silent and invisible, the kitchen far away. She listened to Mr. King talking, and heard Joe Shepard laugh at something he said. Chairs scraped against the floor, pans rattled. Mrs. King must have opened the oven door, because the fragrance of cinnamon drifted right under the door.

She looked around. The maids' room was tidy and attractive, with lace curtains, a substantial bureau, and a smaller bed for Abby. The furniture was old and shabby. She knew it must have come belowstairs after its usefulness ended abovestairs, but it was polished and clean. I wonder if servants' quarters are this nice at Denton, she mused.

She thought then about her own establishment. Lord Davy had promised to provide her with a house anywhere she chose to live. Although he had not stated the obvious, she knew he would be more comfortable if she were far away. "After a while, people will forget," he had told her. To her enduring sorrow, he had not even flinched as he threw away her entire life. *And your questionable background will not be an embarrassment* was unspoken but real.

I wonder if Canada would be far enough for Papa, she thought, or even the United States. I am an educated lady of comfortable means, but what am I to *do* with myself? I need never work. If Sir Harry does not choose to pursue his interest in me, I am unlikely to marry within that sphere I thought I was born to inhabit. And who of another class would have me? Joe Shepard, you are right: Lord Davy was a misguided philanthropist.

When the snow stopped, they would continue their journey, and she would be deposited at the home of her real grandmother, the woman who had begun the search that ruined her life. "A farm in Yorkshire," she said out loud. Joe, you may be at home on the farms, but I am not, she concluded. I have nothing in common with anyone on a farm.

She got out of bed slowly. Dressing taxed her sorely. Her own lady's maid had left her employ a week ago when the gory news of her mistress's changed social status filtered down to the servants at Denton. When Genevieve had approached her, eyes downcast, and said that she had found a position on a neighboring estate, she learned another bitter lesson: servants cared about social niceties. Genevieve knew that working for the illegitimate daughter of a modiste was not a stepping-stone to advancement.

She took only a few minutes with her hair. Brushing it made her wince, but it was an easy matter to twist it into a knot and know she did not have to worry overmuch that it was tidy. In a rare burst of candor—he was a reticent man—Sir Harry had told her once that he liked her hair *en deshabille*. Well, you should see me today, Harry, she thought.

What she saw in the mirror surprised her. Her cheeks were rosy, and her eyes even seemed to smile back at her, despite the late night. Suspecting that her lot today was to scrabble among boxes for holiday decorations, she had put on her simplest dress, a dark green wool with nothing to recommend it beyond the elegant way it hung. At least I won't frighten small children, she told herself as she left the room.

She had hoped that Joe would not be belowstairs, but there he still sat, chopping nut meats on a cutting board. Please don't apologize to me for last night, she thought suddenly, and felt the color rise to her face. Let me think that you enjoyed the kiss as much as I did, and that you wanted to tell me your story, as you wanted to hear mine.

She held her breath as he tipped the knife at her. "Good morning, Mary McIntyre," he said. "Did the magic potion work?"

"I am ambulatory," she said, "That, of itself, is a prodigious feat."

He nodded and returned to the work at hand. "I believe Mrs. King has some porridge for you. Do take these nut meats to her, and then come back, will you? I have all manner of schemes, and you have agreed to be an accomplice, as I recall." He funneled the chopped nuts into a bowl and handed it to her. "If she has any cinnamon buns left, could you bring me another one?"

She smiled at him and went into the kitchen, where Mrs. King presided at the table, rolling out dough while Abby stood by with a cookie cutter and a look of deep concentration on her face. Clarice hovered close by the bowls of sugar colored green, red, and yellow. "We are making stars, Miss McIntyre," she announced. "And then ivy leaves?" she asked, looking at Mrs. King, who nodded.

"Mrs. King, I believe you are a gift from heaven," Mary said. She set down the bowl of nut meats. "I believe I am to find a bowl of porridge, and there is a request for another cinnamon bun, if such a thing is available."

Mrs. King took the porridge from the warming shelf. "It already has plenty of sugar, and here is the cream, dearie." She touched Mary's cheek. "You look fit enough."

"I feel delicate," Mary said with a laugh. "Only think: I already know what my New Year's resolution will be!"

Mrs. King leaned toward her, and looked at the little girls before she spoke in a conspiratorial whisper. "You have to beware of even the best men, Miss McIntyre." She straightened up. "Not but what your own mother has not already told you that."

No, she did not, Mary thought. If someone had given my mother that warning, or at least, if she had heeded it, perhaps I would not be here at all. Then she thought of Lady Davy, and her cautions about fortune hunters, which was hardly a concern now. "She warned me, Mrs. King," Mary said. "I intend to be extremely prudent in the new year!"

She handed Joe his cinnamon bun, sat down at the table, and stared at the porridge for a long enough moment to feel Joe's eyes on her. She picked up the spoon, frowned at it, then took a bite.

She felt nearly human by the time she finished. She pushed back the bowl, and looked at Mr. King, who had been watching her with a twinkle in his eye. I am in excellent company, she thought suddenly, and the feeling was warm. "Mr. King, I know that Joe and I are both feeling some remorse at chaining your sweet wife to the Rumford, and here you are, orphans of the storm."

She stopped, embarrassed with herself, wondering why she had impulsively included herself with Joe Shepard so brashly, as though they had conferred on the matter, as though they were closer than mere acquaintances. She looked down in confusion, and up into Joe's eyes.

"That is precisely what I have been saying to Frank," he said. "We should be ashamed of ourselves for kidnapping the Kings, and setting you at hard labor in the kitchen." He looked at his half-finished cinnamon bun. "Yet I must temper my remorse with vast appreciation of your wife's culinary abilities." He picked up the bun. "You have fallen among thieves, but we are benevolent thieves, eh, Mary?"

And there he was, continuing her own odd fiction. Do we want to belong together? she asked herself. Is there something about this season that demands that we gather our dear ones close, even if we must invent them? She knew without any question that she wanted to continue the deception, if that was what it was; more than that, she *needed* to.

"I agree completely, Joe," she said quietly. "Mr. King, we are in your debt."

To her complete and utter astonishment—and to Joe's, too, apparently, because his stare was as astounded as hers—Mr. King began to cry. As she sat paralyzed, unsure of what to do, tears rolled down the little man's face.

"I'm sure we did not wish to . . ." Joe began, and stopped, obviously at a loss.

Mr. King fumbled in his waistcoat for a handkerchief and blew his nose into it vigorously, even as the tears continued to course down his cheeks. "What you must think of me . . ." he said, but could not continue.

Mary sat in stupefied silence for a moment, then reached across the table to Mr. King. "Sir, please tell us what we have done! We would not for the world upset you."

Her words seemed to gather him together. He looked at the kitchen door. "It's not you two," he managed to say finally. "I have to tell you. You have to know." He gestured toward the door that led to the stairs. "Myrtle mustn't see me like this."

Without a word, they rose to follow him across the room, moving quietly because he was on tiptoe. As she looked at Joe, her eyes filled with questions; he took her hand, then tucked her close to him.

With the door shut, the three of them sat on the stairs leading to the main floor. It was a narrow space. Mr. King filled one of the lower steps, and she and Joe sat close together above him, their legs touching. Joe put his arm around her to give himself room.

Mr. King wiped his eyes again. "I'm an old fool," he said apologetically. "I want you to know that in ten years, this is my happiest Christmas."

"But, sir . . ." Mary said. "We don't understand."

He kept his voice low. "Fifteen years ago, our only child ran away. Myrtle had many plans for him, but they quarreled, and he left home at Christmastime." He tucked his handkerchief in his waistcoat. "We looked everywhere, sent out the Runners, even, put advertisements in every broadside and newspaper in England. Nothing." He shrugged. "We thought maybe he shipped out on an East India merchant vessel, or took the king's shilling." He looked away. "We followed every possible lead to its source."

"Nothing?" Joe asked. "You never heard of him again?"

Mr. King shook his head. "Not a line, not a visit. I thought Myrtle would run mad from it all, and truth to tell, she did for a while."

"Poor woman," Mary said, and felt her own tears prickle her eyelids. Joe tightened his arm around her, and she gradually relaxed into his embrace.

"Those were hard years," Mr. King said. "After five or six years, Myrtle seemed to come back to herself again." He sighed, as though the memory still carried too much weight. "Except for this: every year near Christmas, she looks at me and says, 'Frank, it's time to seek David.' " He spread out his hands. "And

CARLA KELLY

we do. For nearly ten years we've done just that. We set out from Sheffield with a post chaise and driver."

"What . . . what do you do?" Mary asked.

"We pick a route and drive from place to place, spend the night in various inns, ask if anyone has seen David King. Myrtle has a miniature, but it is fifteen years old now. One inn after another, until finally she looks at me and says, 'Frank, take me home.' " He shook his head. "He would be thirty-five now, but I don't even know what he looks like anymore, or even if he is alive."

Mary felt her throat constrict. What a fool I am for imagining that I have been given the cruelest load to carry, she thought. "Where were you going this year?"

"Myrtle got it in her head that we should go to Scarborough and drive along the coast up to the Tyne. 'Maybe he's on one of them coal lighters what ships from Newcastle,' she's thinking, and who am I to tell her 'No, dear woman'?"

"You're a good man, Mr. King," Joe said, his voice soft.

"I love Myrtle," he replied simply. "We're all we have."

Mary took a deep breath. "You're stranded here now, and this is better?"

She was relieved to see the pleasure come into his eyes again. Mr. King pocketed his handkerchief this time. "It is, by a long chalk, miss! You see how busy she is. She's going to make Christmas biscuits and buns with the little girls. There will be a whacking great roast going in the oven as soon as I get back in the kitchen to help her lift it. Wait until you taste her Yorkshire pudding!" He reached up to take Joe's hand. "Thank'ee, sir, for giving us a room when there was no room anywhere else."

It was Joe's turn to be silent. Mary leaned forward. "Oh, Mr. King, he's pleased to do it. I think Joe is a great host."

Mr. King laughed softly. "I have to tell you, Mr. Shepard, Myrtle was nearly in a rare state, thinking that you and little Josh were doomed to eat sausage and eggs all through the holidays. 'It's not fitting, Mr. King,' she told me, 'especially since his cook left this full larder. Thank God we have come to the rescue.' " He held out his hand. "Do you understand my debt now?"

102

"I do," Joe said. "And you understand mine, as well." He smiled. "Mr. King, you had better help your charming wife with that roast. I like to eat at six o'clock. Does she stir in all those little bits of burned meat and fat into her gravy?"

"She does, indeed!" Mr. King declared. He stood up. "I do not know when she will tell me it's time to go home, but I know you will keep her busy until then."

"You can depend upon it, sir."

With a nod in her direction, Mr. King left the stairs and went into the servants' hall again, closing the door quietly behind him. Joe stayed where he was, his arm around Mary. He tightened his grip on her. When he spoke, she could tell how carefully he was choosing his words. "Do you know, sometimes I feel sorry for myself."

"You, too?"

They looked at each other. "Did you ever see two more certifiable idiots?" he asked her.

"Not to my knowledge, Joe," she replied, and let him pull her to her feet on the narrow stairs. She dusted off her skirts. "Did you find me some garish decorations?"

"I did, indeed." He started up the stairs. "They proved to be a major disappointment in one respect."

"Oh?"

"They are not nearly as vulgar as I had hoped. I do not think they will cause my dear brother any distress at all."

"That *is* a disappointment. By the way, where is your brother?"

Joe sighed. "He asked me where the mail coach stops, and walked there to see if the road is open. He says he is expecting correspondence from his firm." He shook his head. "Too bad that a man cannot just enjoy a hiatus from work. I always do."

He took her down the hall to what was eventually going to become the library, when the plastering on the ceiling was finished. When she stopped, he looked up at the ceiling with her. "The former owner had several well-bosomed nymphs doing scurrilous things around that central curlicue," Joe said, pointing up to the bare spot. "I didn't want questions from Joshua, so I am replacing them with more acceptable fruit and leaves."

"Coward," she teased.

"Wait until you are the parent of an inquisitive eight-year-old, my dear," he said.

"That is unlikely in the extreme," she told him as she opened up one of the boxes and pulled out a red silk garland.

"Oh? Your children are going to go from age seven to nine, and skip eight altogether?" he asked, pulling out another garland.

She laughed. "Joe, you don't seriously think any men of my acquaintance are going to queue up to marry a woman of such questionable background. Even one with two thousand a year?"

He surprised her by touching her cheek. "I will tell you what I think, Mary McIntyre. I think you need to enlarge your circle of friends."

"You are probably right." What had seemed just right last night seemed too close this morning, but she made no move to back away from him. *You would think you wanted him to kiss you again*, she scolded herself.

She wasn't sure if she was relieved or chagrined when he patted her cheek and went to the door. "I'm off to find my son and nephew and go hunt for the wild greenery. Can you decorate a wreath or two? I'll ask Mr. King to put a discreet nail over the mantel in the sitting room and another on the front door." He stood in the doorway a moment. "It may be time for Joe and his boy to consider Christmas again."

"A capital notion, sir," she told him. A few moments later, she heard him calling the boys. *Why is it that more than one boy sounds like a* herd, she thought. There was laughter, and then a door slammed. A few minutes later, Agatha Shepard stood in the library doorway, smiling at her. "Could you use some help, Mary?"

More than you know, she thought. *Please take my mind off the molehills I am rapidly turning into mountains.* "I am under orders from your brother-in-law to create some Christmas." She knew her face was rosy, so she looked into the box of decorations. "What a relief to know this is not a forlorn hope, my dear.

I do believe our late mill owner had some notions of a proper Christmas. Look at this beautiful garland."

By the time the boys returned, red-cheeked and shedding snow, Agatha was positioning the last star burst on the window while Mary observed its hanging from the arm of the sofa. "Mama!" Tommy shouted. "Look! Joe says we are holly experts!"

The boys carried a holly wreath between them. "Father tied it for us, but we arranged the holly," Josh said. He looked at Mary. "He said you were to be the final arbiter, whatever that is."

Mary helped the boys carry the wreath to the box of decorations. "It's marvelous, Joshua. If we tie this red bow to the top, it will answer perfectly here over the fireplace."

"See there, Josh, I knew she would know just what else it needed."

She hung the wreath, then turned around to smile at Joe, who held a larger wreath shaped from pine boughs. "And this for the front door?" she asked.

"Yes, indeed, after you and Agatha give it the magic touch." He looked at the room. "Boys, I believe the ladies were busy while we stalked the greenery." He touched his son's shoulder. "Perhaps you and Thomas can convince Mrs. King that you are in the final stages of starvation. She seems like a humane woman." He looked at Agatha, and must have noticed something in her expression. "Do let Tommy have lunch belowstairs. I would not feel right in asking Mrs. King to serve us upstairs. She is my guest, too."

"Mama, please!" Tommy begged. "I know Clarice has been belowstairs making Christmas treats. We could smell them the moment we opened the front door!"

"You may go belowstairs, Tommy," Agatha said quietly. "These are special circumstances." She turned to her brother-in-law. "Thank you for asking, Joe."

He hugged her, and waved the boys off. "My dear sister, loan your shawl to Mary. I need someone to make certain I do not hang this wreath cockeyed."

Mary stopped him long enough to twine a gilt cord through the boughs and tie it in a bow at the bottom. Agatha secured some smaller star bursts scavenged from the bits and pieces remaining in the box, then threw her shawl around Mary's shoulders. "I will go belowstairs and see what wonders Mrs. King has created."

He was still chuckling when he hung the wreath on the front door. "Mary, you must feel sorry for Thomas. He thought he was marrying a proper lady, only to find that she enjoys putting up her own decorations and will probably be rolling out dough when we go belowstairs. He will accuse me of ruining his efforts to be what he is not. Too bad there was no room for *him* at the inn. All right, Mary, what do you think?"

I think that sometimes philanthropy is sadly misdirected, she told herself as she walked backward toward the front gate, her eyes on the wreath. "Move the wreath a little to the left. A little more. There. Excellent."

To her gratification, Joe walked down the path toward her, then turned around for his own look. "You didn't trust me?" she teased.

"I trust you completely," he replied. "I am just wondering what you would think if we painted the trim white. Would that look right against the brick?"

She glanced sideways at him, but his attention was on the façade of his house. You are doing it again, she thought. You are including me in your decisions, as though I were in residence at this place. Dear, lonely man, are you even aware of it? "Yes, by all means," she said firmly. "And if you can arrange for a cat to nap in one of those windows this summer, that would be the final touch. Oh, flower boxes, too."

"Consider it done, madam. Pansies or roses?"

"Joe, you don't put roses in flower boxes!"

"Pansies, then."

She looked around her at all the snow. Mr. King had shoveled the walks earlier, but there was no getting away from winter's cold and stark trees and branches, with only the idle leaf still clinging. Not a bird flew overhead. "Joe, you speak of pansies and cats in windows," she said softly, "and here we are in December."

He took her arm through his. "I told you last night that I deal in futures, Mary. And excuse me, but you're the one who mentioned the cat. Do you deal in futures, too?"

"Perhaps it's time I did," she replied, her voice soft. How do I do it? I wish I were not afraid, she thought. She wanted to ask Joe about the courage to carry on when things didn't turn out as planned, but there was Thomas walking up the middle of the road, which had been cleared by a crew from the workhouse.

"Tom, the roads are still open behind us, I gather," he said. "Is that a newspaper?"

Tom held it out to him. "There will be a road crew through here by nightfall. Apparently the road to York will be cleared by tomorrow afternoon, or sooner."

"Any mail for you?"

Tom shook his head, but handed a letter to Mary. "It appears that Colonel Sir Harry Fox is in the country. Let us hope this is good news."

She took the letter, which had been addressed several times, as it went from Denton, then to Haverford, Kent, where Lord and Lady Davy had gone for Christmas, to her as-yet unknown grandmother's farm. "I assured the coach driver that I was your solicitor, and would see that you got your letter," Tom said. "I thought I would need to give a blood oath. What a suspicious man!"

"Just doing his job, brother," Joe said serenely. "Perhaps you and I can go to the house and wrangle over whether you must have luncheon upstairs or downstairs, and leave Mary to her correspondence. You are welcome to use my bookroom."

She watched them walk away, already in lively conversation. Poor Joe! Here he had thought to spend a quiet holiday with his son, eating eggs and sausage. The only guests with any merit at all are the Kings, she thought. His own brother is too proud to eat belowstairs. Thank goodness we can at least choose our friends.

Sir Harry had posted the letter from London, probably from the family town residence, a particularly magnificent row house in the best square. She had been there on several occasions, the last during a celebration of Wellington's victory in Belgium, when he had danced more than three dances with her, and, face red enough to match his uniform, had declared that she was the finest lady present. After asking Lord Davy's permission, he had corresponded with her through the fall, telling her nothing of interest, because she did not find troop movements or glum Frenchmen to her taste.

In the bookroom, she opened the letter, took a deep breath, and starting reading. When she was finished, she was too astounded to do anything but stare into the fire, ashamed that she had ever written Sir Harry Fox.

She looked up. Someone knocked on the door, but she made no motion to speak or rise to open the door.

"Dearie, don't you want something to eat?"

It was Mrs. King. She got up quickly and opened the door. "Mrs. King, you did not need to do this," she protested as the woman came into the bookroom with a tray.

"That's precisely what Joe said, but I told him I wanted to, and was he going to stop an old woman?"

Mary made herself smile.

"Now, sit back down there and I will set this tray beside you. There, now. May I pour you some tea?"

She started to cry, unable to help herself, helpless to do anything except hold out the letter. Mrs. King's face filled with concern. She closed the door, poured a cup of tea, and sat down, then handed Mary her handkerchief. "You cry until you feel better, dearie, and then you will drink this," she ordered.

Mary sobbed into the handkerchief. Mrs. King settled herself on the arm of the chair and rested her hand on Mary's back. Mary wiped her eyes, blew her nose, and leaned against the other woman, grateful for the comfort, but missing Lady Davy—the woman she would always think of as her mother—with every fiber of her heart.

"Joe told me about your difficulties, dearie," Mrs. King said.

"I think the entire world must know of them, Mrs. King," she said. "I am glad he told you. I would not have you think I am a habitual watering pot."

"I think you're rather a charming lady, and I know that Joe agrees with me," Mrs. King said firmly. "But this is bad news, isn't it? Mr. Shepard—Thomas—is even downstairs walking up and down, hoping that you have good news."

Mary looked down at the letter that she still held. "I suppose he would call this good news, then. Sir Harry has agreed to pay his addresses to me." She thought of Mrs. King's own trials, and tried to hide the bitterness in her words, even as she knew she failed. "He claims that he will not reproach me with my ignominious birth, should we decide to form an alliance." She held out the letter again. "Mrs. King, he has asked all his relatives what they think, and they are united in their opposition to me!" She leaned back and closed her eyes as shame washed over her. "There are probably men taking wagers at White's on what will be the outcome of this sorry tale!"

"And still Sir Harry persists?" Mrs. King asked.

"I suppose he does," Mary said quietly. "Mrs. King, I do not love him. I never have." She turned in her chair for a better look at the woman. "I have come with the Shepards this Christmas because they are to leave me with a grandmother I have never met . . . on a farm! Sir Harry is my last chance to remain in the social circle in which I was raised." She rested her cheek against Mrs. King's comforting bulk. "Am I too proud?"

Mrs. King's answer was not slow in coming. "P'raps a little, my dear, but if you do not love this fellow, marrying him would be a worse folly than pride." She laughed softly. "I think there are worse fates than farms. Didn't Joe say you had enough income to do what you want, should the farm prove unsatisfactory?"

"It's true," she agreed. She folded the letter, then looked at Mrs. King, who was regarding her with warmth and surprising affection, considering the shortness of their acquaintance. She took her hand. "It's hard to change, isn't it? I mean, I could have gone along all my life as the daughter of Lord Davy, but now the matter is different, and I must change, whether I wish it or not. Mrs. King, I do not know if I am brave enough."

She stopped then, noting the faraway look in the woman's eyes, and the sorrow she saw there. "Here I am complaining about what must seem to be a small matter to you," she said. "Do forgive me."

Mrs. King gave her a little shake. "It is not a small matter! It is your life."

She considered that, and in another moment took a sip of tea. "This will upset Thomas more than you can imagine. He places such emphasis on class and quality." She stood up. "You say everyone is belowstairs?"

Mrs. King nodded. "Thomas is there on sufferance, but Mrs. Shepard seems content to decorate Abby's batch of Christmas stars."

"And Joe?"

"He and Mr. King are playing backgammon."

"Are we a strange gathering, Mrs. King?" she asked. "I suppose that other than Joe and Joshua, none of us are where we really want to be."

Mrs. King rose. "I am not so certain about that, my dear. Are you?"

She could think of no reply that would not involve a blush.

The two of them went down the stairs. Mrs. King gave her a little push when she reached the bottom and stood there, the letter in her hand. Thomas's eyes lighted up. "Do you have good news, Mary?" he asked.

"That may depend on what you consider good news," she replied, and handed him the letter. "Here. I wish you and Joe would read it."

With a nod to Mr. King, Joe got up from the game-board and sat beside his brother, who had spread out the letter on the table. She watched them both as they read, Thomas becoming more animated by the paragraph, and Joseph more subdued. How different they are, she thought, but how different they had always been.

When he finished reading, Thomas looked at her in triumph. "There you are, Mary!" He smiled at his wife, who was dusting the last of the cookie dough with sugar. "She need not leave her sphere, Agatha." He shrugged. "It may take a year or two before you are received in the best houses again, Mary, but what is that? People forget."

Mary looked at Joe, who finished reading and sat back, his face a perfect blank. He stared at the letter, then picked it up. "'. . . no matter how disgusting the whole affair is to sensible people, the sort I wish to associate with, I will never reproach you with your ignominious birth,'" he read out loud. "Mary, he is irresistible."

Ignoring his brother, Thomas took her hand. "Mary, you are most fortunate. The road is clear south of us. Any letter you write will reach Sir Harry in a mere day or two."

Joe grabbed the letter. Without a word he crumbled it into a tight ball. "Thomas, I am not sure I even know you anymore," he said, his voice filled with emotion. "You would have Mary McIntyre, this little lady we watched grow up at Denton, pawn her dignity for a crumb or two? I am surprised at you."

Thomas stared at him and his face grew red. Mouths open, Tommy and Joshua had stopped their game of jackstraws. Abby held the rolling pin suspended over another wad of dough. Agatha dabbled her fingers nervously in the sugar. On the other hand, Frank King appeared to be enjoying the drama before him. His eyes were bright as he looked from one to another.

"Joseph, Mary is no lady anymore," Thomas said. "But you are no gentleman."

Oh, God, Mary thought, and felt her face grow white. The brothers glared at each other. Clarice was already in tears, her face pressed against her mother. What has happened here, Mary thought in the silence that seemed to grow more huge by the second. If ever there were unwanted guests, we have met and exceeded the criteria. She knew that she could not please both men. No matter what she said, it would be wrong to someone, and she would offend people she never wished ill.

Her footsteps seemed so loud as she walked the length of the room and stood between the brothers. "You are probably right, Tom. I will write Sir Harry immediately."

"Thank God," Thomas said, his relief nearly palpable.

"I will assure him that even though I am grateful for the honor I *think* he is doing me, I chose not to further the alliance," she concluded.

"My God, Mary, do you *know* what you are saying?" Thomas gasped. "Do you seriously believe you will ever get another offer as good as Sir Harry?"

For the first time that day, or maybe even since Lord Davy had ruined her hopes two weeks ago, she felt curiously free. "Thomas, Sir Harry is a boring windbag. You can't honestly think he would ever let me forget my origin."

"But he is so magnanimous!" Thomas exclaimed.

"To trample my feelings?" she asked. "I think not. Honestly, Thomas, I believe I would rather . . . rather . . . slop hogs and . . . and . . . oh, heavens . . . milk cows at Muncie Farm than endure life with a man who thought I was common!" She gave him a little push. "How unkind you are to call me common! A woman is only common when the people around her tell her that she is. And I am not."

Mary looked around her, noting the expressions of wounded reproach on Agatha's and Tom's faces. Mr. King winked at her, and she smiled back. To her confusion, Joseph was regarding her with what appeared to be amusement. *I should be grateful someone considers this imbroglio humorous*, she thought with some asperity. *In fairness, he is entitled to think what he chooses. Imagine how glad he will be when the road is open.*

"Joe, may I use your bookroom again to write that letter?" she asked.

"Of course." His expression had not changed. "Did you say Muncie Farm?"

"I did."

"But your name is McIntyre."

"Yes. From what I gather, the modiste's mother was widowed not long after her daughter ran away and later remarried. I gather I am still a McIntyre, though. You have heard of Muncie Farm?"

"I have. In fact, Thomas, rather than be any hindrance to you when you are able to bolt my vulgar establishment, I can transport Mary to Muncie Farm. I could give you directions, but I can easily take her there." He bowed to them all. "And now, I have some work to do in my shop. Josh? You may come, and Tommy, too. Use my bookroom as long as you need it, Mary." He bowed again. "Mrs. King, I look forward to dinner at six o'clock."

Mary returned to the bookroom with an appetite. Mrs. King's meal, though cold now, took the edge off her hunger quite nicely. She thought she would have to use up reams of paper to find the right words of regret for Sir Harry, but one draft sufficed. After all, Lady Davy had taught her to regard brevity as the best antidote for unreturned love, and quite the safest route. *Poor Sir Harry*, she thought. *You will miss me for a while, perhaps, but I suspect that your paramount emotion will resolve itself into vast relief.* Humming to herself, she sealed the letter and set it aside for a brisk walk tomorrow to the inn to mail it.

"Silly," she said out loud. "Tomorrow is Christmas. It can wait for the day after."

After a little more thought, and a long time gazing out the window, she took out another sheet of paper and wrote a letter to Lady Davy. It proved more difficult to write, because she found herself flooded with wonderful memories of her childhood. She knew down to her stockings that she would miss Denton, and her brother and sister, and even more, the quiet, lovely woman who had chosen to take her in, keep her from an orphanage or workhouse, and raise her. If events had not fallen out as Mary desired, it was not a matter to cause great distress now. She chose to remember the best parts. She decided then that she would write Lady Davy at least once each year, whether Lord Davy wanted her to, or not. Perhaps a time would come when she would be invited home.

She did feel tears well in her eyes as she remembered how many of her mother's acquaintances had called her the very image of Lady Davy. *I suppose we see what we choose to see*, she thought, then rested her chin in her hand. *I hope Thomas can see that someday. Joe already seems to understand.*

By dinner, the workhouse road crew was shoveling in front of the house. Thomas and Agatha had decided to take dinner upstairs, to Mary's chagrin and Joe's irritation. Mrs. King only laughed and assured him that the entertainment the Shepards had provided far outweighed any inconvenience. "Abby and I will take them food. If it is cold, well, that's the price for being better than the rest of us." She put her arm around Mary. "If they want seconds, they can come downstairs. It is Christmas Eve, after all, and Mr. King and I are on holiday. Dearie, you lay the table here."

Mrs. King's roast beef was the perfect combination of exterior crust and interior pink tenderness. Abby glowed with pleasure when Mrs. King pointed out that the scullery maid had made the Yorkshire pudding. "I may have directed it, dearies, but I think the secret is in the touch, and not the telling. Mr. King, don't be hoarding the gravy at your end of the table!"

The coachmen joined them, coming into the servants hall snow-covered from helping the road crew. "We met a mail coach coming from York, so the highway is open now," the Shepards' coachman told them as he reached for the roast beef. He jostled the King's driver. "We can all be on our way."

Mary could not help noticing the worried look that Mr. King directed at his wife, who was helping Abby with the gravy. Her heart went out to him as she imagined what it must be like to wonder every Christmas when the melancholy would strike her, and how long she would struggle with it. She leaned toward Joe, and spoke softly. "I wonder, do you suppose a parent ever recovers from the loss of a child through an angry word, or a thoughtless statement?"

He shook his head, and rested his hand on Joshua's head. "It doesn't even have to be your own child, Mary, to fear such a disaster. I pray it never happens to me."

She sat there in the warm dining hall, surrounded by people talking, spoons clinking on dishes, wonderful kitchen smells, and fully realized what he was saying to her. I have a grandmother at a place called Muncie Farm, she thought with an emotion akin to wonder. She has been looking for me. Me! Not to shame me with my shaky background, but to *find* me, because I am all that remains of her daughter. I have been dreading this, when I should be welcoming the chance to put someone's mind at rest. It is a blessing ever to be denied the Kings, I fear, and I nearly passed it by. God forgive me.

"You know where Muncie Farm is?" she asked Joe.

He nodded and ruffled Joshua's hair. "We could take you there tomorrow."

"Then you may do it," she said, and took the bowl of gravy from the Kings' coachman, "*after* we have Christmas dinner here with the Kings."

Thomas and Agatha did not invite her to attend Christmas Eve services with them at St. Boniface, which troubled her not at all. There would have been nothing comfortable or even remotely rejuvenating in celebrating the birth of a Peacemaker with people who chose so deliberately to divide. When Joe told the Kings that indeed there was a Methodist establishment in town—although not the better part of town, and certainly not close to St. Boniface—she demurred again. She had heard much about Methodism and the enthusiastic choirs that it seemed to produce, but Abby was accompanying the Kings. She wanted that kindly couple to give the scullery maid their undivided attention.

"What do you generally do on Christmas Eve?" she asked Joe, while they were washing dishes. (Joe had insisted that Mrs. King did not need to do dishes, and Mrs. King had not objected too long.)

"What do we do, Josh?" he asked his son, who sat on a stool, drying plates.

"We read Luke Two, because it talks about shepherds, I think," Josh said. "Then we watch for the carolers." He looked at his father. "Will there be carolers this year?"

"I rather doubt it, son, considering the depth of the snow."

"Do you feed them sausage and eggs after they sing?" Mary teased.

"I will have you know, I make an excellent wassail," Joe replied. He laughed and flipped his son with the drying towel. "The secret to living here is to maintain low expectations."

When the other guests had left the house—the Shepards by carriage and the Kings on foot—Joe and Joshua made wassail. They carried it outside to the road crew, which was beginning work now on the side streets of the village, now that the main thoroughfare was open for travel. As she watched from the sitting room window, a steady flow of traffic worked its way in both directions, coaches full of travelers anxious to be home by Christmas, or failing that, Boxing Day.

She thought she would find the house lonely, but she did not. She took her copy of *Pamela* into the bookroom, made herself comfortable in the chair where she already fit, and began to read.

As she read, she gradually realized that she was waiting for the sound of Joe returning with Joshua, and then the Kings coming back, probably to sit belowstairs, drink tea, and chat. At peace with herself, she understood the gift of small pleasures. It warmed her heart as no other gift possibly could, during this season of anxiety for her. She smiled when she heard them finally, realizing with a quick intake of breath that she was as guilty as Joe of thinking and speaking as though she were part of the family. We have to belong to someone, don't we? she asked herself. If we don't, then life is just days on a calendar.

She closed the novel when they came into the bookroom, bringing with them a rush of cold, and the fragrance of butter and spices. Joe carried a pitcher and a plate, and Josh dangled the cups by their handles. "We had a little wassail left, and Father purloined the biscuits from belowstairs," Josh said as he sat down beside her on the hassock. He held out a cup while Joseph poured, and handed it to her. "Father says I am to read Luke Two all by myself this year, but if I get stopped on a word or two, he will help me."

Joe handed him the Bible and opened it to the Book of St. Luke before he sat down with a sigh and stretched his long legs toward the fire. He closed his eyes while Joshua read about governors, and taxes, and travelers, and no room. Mary watched his handsome profile and felt some slight envy at the length of his eyelashes. This is a restful man, she thought, not someone tightly wound who is never satisfied. She wondered what he was like in spring and summer, when his life in the fields and among the grain brokers probably kept him in motion from early light until after dark. Did he become irritable then, restless like his brother? She decided no, that Joseph Shepard was too wise for that.

"'And there were in the same country shepherds abiding in the field, keeping watch over their flock by night.'" Joshua had moved closer to the fire to see better, his finger pointing out the line. He leaned against his father's legs.

As she watched him, Joe opened his eyes and looked at her. He smiled and reached across the space between them to take her hand and hold it firmly, his fingers intertwined in hers. She almost had to remind herself to breathe. You keep watch over your own little flock, don't you, sir, she thought. You even care about your unexpected guests. It was a wild notion, but she even dared to think that he had been caring for her for years, in his own way. She tried to dismiss the notion as patently ridiculous, but as he continued to hold her hand, she found herself unable to believe otherwise.

He released her hand when Joshua finished, and took his dead wife's son on his lap, holding him close. "Well, Josh, we have almost rubbed through another year," he said, his voice low and soothing. "What do you say we go for another one?"

Joshua nodded. Mary had to smile as she realized this must be a tradition with them.

"What about you, Mary? Will you go for another one?" Joe asked her suddenly.

"I . . . I do believe I will," she said. Even if it means things do not turn out as we wish, some hopes are dashed, and the future looks a bit uncertain, she added to herself. "We are all dealing in futures, eh?" she asked.

He reached for her hand again. He held it until he heard the Kings returning, when he got up to become the perfect host, and carry his son to bed. When he returned to the bookroom, she was standing by the window, admiring the snow that the moonlight had turned into a crystal path. He stood beside her, not touching her in any way, but somehow filling her completely with his presence. When he spoke, it was not what she expected; it was more.

"I loved Melissa," he told her, his eyes on the snow. "I have to tell you that in some measure, I think I loved her because she reminded me of you." He glanced at her quickly, then looked outside again. "I'm not completely sure, but it is my suspicion. I . . . I've never admitted this to myself, so you are the first to hear it."

He took her hand, raised it to his lips, and kissed it. "I am quite sober tonight, Mary McIntyre, so I will say Happy Christmas to you, and let it go at that for now." He shook his head and laughed softly. "Oh, bother it, I would be a fool to waste such a celebratory occasion." He kissed her cheek, gave her a wink, and left the room. In a moment she heard him whistling in the hall.

The Shepards left as early as they could in the morning, Thomas just happy to be away, and Agatha shaking her head and apologizing for the rush, but wouldn't it be grand to be in York with grandparents before the day was entirely gone? Of the two, Mary had to admit that Thomas's attitude, though more overt, at least had the virtue of honesty. Joe must have felt the same way. As they stood in the driveway and saw the Shepards off, he turned to Mary. "My brother is honest, even when he says nothing."

Joe declared that his Christmas gift to the Kings was breakfast. "Mary and I will cook eggs and sausage for *you*, my dears." He winked at Mary. "And do I see some presents on the table? That will be the reward for eating my cooking."

By keeping back two presents she had ordained earlier for Thomas and Clarice, Mary had gifts for the children: a sewing basket with a small hoop and embroidery thread for Abby, and a book with blank pages for Joshua. "This is your journal for 1816," she told him. "And let us pray it is a more peaceful year than 1815."

"It usually is in Edgerly," he assured her, which made Joseph look away and cough into his napkin.

Mr. and Mrs. King presented both children with aprons, Abby's of pale pink muslin that had probably been cut down from one of Mrs. King's traveling dresses, and Josh's of canvas, which turned out to be a prelude for his present from his father of carpenter tools. "I saw what 'e was giving you yesterday, lad. Every man needs his own carpenter's apron," Mr. King said.

Nothing would do then but they must all troop out to Joseph's workshop to see the bench Joe had made for Joshua that did not require a box to reach, and the tidy row of tools with smooth grips right for an eight-year-old's hand. While they were there, Joe pointed to a hinged box held tight in a vice. "That is for you, Mary," he told her, and his face reddened a little when he glanced at the Kings. "I will have it done by Twelfth Night and bring it to you at Muncie Farm." He smiled at her. "Provided you are still there. I was thinking of painting it pale green, with a brass lock, unless you have a better idea."

She shook her head, unable to trust her voice. She thought of the presents she had received from Lord and Lady Davy through the years, not one of which had been made by hand. "I . . . I . . . wish I had something for you," she stammered when she could talk.

Mrs. King was merciful enough to distract them all by throwing up her hands and admonishing Abby because she was faster on her feet to rush back to the kitchen and remove the sponge cake from the Rumford before it turned into char. Mary followed quickly enough herself, happy to leave the men in the workshop, comparing notes on the construction of a miter box.

When crisis, agony, and certain doom had been averted belowstairs, Mary went to the maids' room to pack, a simple task, considering that she had worn her plainest dresses of the entire Christmas season. The coachman had removed her luggage from the old carriage that traveled with the Shepards, and the sheer magnitude of it caused her to blink and wonder what her grandmother at Muncie Farm would think of such extravagance. Does a woman really need all this? she asked herself, wondering why she had ever thought it so important. I should have left some of my hats at Denton with Sara.

They ate Christmas dinner when the noon bells tolled in Edgerly, a charming tradition reserved for Christmas and Easter. Mr. King had been pleased to offer grace, and did his Methodist best with enough enthusiasm and longevity to make Joshua begin to squirm, and Mrs. King finally whisper to him that the food was getting cold, and what was worse than a shivering Christmas goose?

Mary knew she had never eaten a better meal anywhere. She was asking for Joe to pass the stuffing when Mrs. King suddenly set down her fork and stood up. "Mr. King, I think it is time for us to go," she announced, her face calm, but her eyes tormented. "Don't we have to look for David? Won't he wonder where we are?"

"I am certain of it, my dear," her husband said. He rose and gently pressed her back down to her seat. "We will finish this wonderful dinner that you have made, and then we will be on our way to Scarborough."

To Mary's amazement, Abby burst into loud sobs. She covered her face with her Christmas apron and cried into it. "I don't want you to go, Mrs. King," she cried, getting up from the table to run from the room.

Before she could leave, Mrs. King was on her feet and clutching the child to her ample belly. There was nothing vague in her eyes now, nothing tentative in her gesture. She hugged the sobbing girl, crooning something soft. Mr. King seemed to be transfixed by this unexpected turn of events. He looked at Joe; the glance that passed between them was as easy to read as headlines on a broadside.

"I just had a thought, Mrs. King," Joe began. "Tell me how you feel about it. Hush, now, Abby! You may want to hear this, too." He propped his elbows on the table and rested his chin in his hands. "Abby's a grand girl in the kitchen with the pots and pans, but did you see how she handled that rolling pin yesterday?" He shook his head. "I'm not entirely certain, but it is possible that when my cook returns tomorrow, she just might be jealous of Abby. Where will I be then?"

"These are weighty problems, Joe," Mr. King said, and there was no disguising the twinkle in his eyes. "You could find yourself without a cook, and forced to live on sausage and eggs."

". . . and wassail . . ." Josh interjected.

". . . for a long time." Mr. King cleared his throat. "Would you be willing to part with Abby?"

"Well, this is a consideration," Joe said.

Mary looked from Joe to Mrs. King, whose eyes were alert now.

"We would give her such a home, Mr. Shepard," the woman said. "I could certainly use the help, but more than that . . ." She stopped, unable to continue.

Joe didn't seem to trust his voice, either, because he waited a long moment to continue. When he did, his voice sounded altered. "We could ask Abby what she thinks. Abby? Would you be willing to go home with the Kings?"

"You wouldn't be angry with me, would you?" Abby asked.

"Not a bit! We would miss you, but I look on this as an opportunity for you." Joe smiled at her. "I think you should do it."

Mr. King looked at his wife. "Myrtle?"

"Oh, yes, let us do this," Mrs. King said, her voice breathless, as if someone were hugging her tight. Her eyes clouded over for a moment. "Mr. King, I think we should return to Sheffield now, and forget Scarborough this year. I hope this does not disappoint you, but Abby must come first."

"I agree, Mrs. K," he replied. There was no disguising the relief in his voice, or the optimism.

Joe stood up. "I do have one condition: the three of you must return here for Christmas next year. I think we should make a tradition of it. What do you think, Mary?"

There he was, including her again. "I think it is a capital notion," she said.

"Then we all agree," Joe said. "Abby, Happy Christmas."

The Kings and Abby left when the dishes were done, their driver smiling so broadly that Mary thought his face would surely split. Abby hugged Joe for a long moment then whispered, "Mr. Shepard, I think you should go to the workhouse and ask for Sally Bawn. She cried and cried when you picked me in September."

"Sally Bawn, it is," he said. "I will tell her she comes highly recommended." He kissed her cheek and gave her a pat in the direction of the Kings. "That may be the wisest thing anyone ever did," he said to no one in particular as the post chaise rolled south. "Mary, it's your turn. Joshua, shall we take her to Muncie Farm?"

She blushed over the amount of luggage she had, but Joe got what he could into the spring wagon and assured her he would bring the rest tomorrow. Joshua climbed into the back, and he gave her a hand up onto the high seat. "Not exactly posh transportation," he said in apology. "I could probably hire a post chaise, but I'd rather not trouble the innkeeper on Christmas."

"I wouldn't have wanted that, either," she said, while he arranged a carriage robe over both of them. She knew she should keep it light, even though the familiar dread was returning. "After all, I am destined for a farm, and this will, in all likelihood, be the mode of transportation, will it not?"

Joe only smiled and spoke to the horses. She looked back at Joshua. "Are you entirely warm enough, my dear?" she asked.

He nodded, his eyes bright.

"I think it is awfully nice of Joshua to come along, especially when I suspect he wants to get back in your workshop," she told Joe.

"He likes Muncie Farm," Joe replied. The road was open, but narrow still with snow, and he concentrated on his driving.

Likes Muncie Farm? she asked herself. "He has been there before?" she asked.

"A time or two."

He was grinning now, and she wanted to ask him more, to pelt him with questions, but he appeared to be more interested in staying on his side of the road than talking. I will keep my counsel, she thought. He has been so obliging to put up with a houseful of unwanted guests, and I should not pester him.

They had traveled on the road to York not more than an hour, when he turned the horses west onto a lane that had been shoveled quite efficiently. "Do the road crews come out here, too?" she asked, surprised to see the road cleared.

"No. Muncie Farm is rather well organized."

She touched his shoulder and made him look at her when he started to chuckle. "Joe, are you practicing some great deception on me?"

He laughed out loud. "Just a little one, Mary, just a little one." He pointed with his whip. "There. Take a look at your grandmother's home." He grinned at her. "And resist the urge to smite me, please."

She looked; more than that, she stared, her mouth open. Located at the end of what by summer would probably be a handsome arch of trees, the farmhouse was a sturdy, three-storied manor of the fight gray stone common in the shire. The white shutters gleamed, and at each window she could see a flower box. The stone cornice over the double doors was even more imposing than the one Joe had commissioned for his house in Edgerly.

Barely able to contain himself, Joe pointed with his whip again. "See? Flower boxes already." He dodged when she made a motion to strike him with her reticule. "Be careful, Mary. I am the only parent Joshua has!"

"You are a scoundrel," she said with feeling. "You let me wallow in self-pity and . . . and . . . talk about learning to slop hogs and milk cows!"

He ducked again. "Do you have rocks in that reticule, my dear? I am certain that if you wished to slop the hogs, your grandmother would let you, although she might wonder why. Ow! Joshua, you could quit laughing and come to my defense!"

"You don't deserve any such consideration, sir!" she said, then stopped when the door opened. "Oh, my."

An older woman stood in the doorway. From her lace cap, to the Norwich shawl about her shoulders, to the cut of her dark dress, she was neat as a pin. Her back was straight, and she did not look much over sixty, if that. Mary looked closer, and then could not stop the tears that welled in her eyes. "Oh, Joe, I think I look a little like her," she whispered.

"You look a great deal like her," he whispered back, "but do you know, I didn't really see it until you mentioned Muncie Farm yesterday. Strange how that is."

Joe stopped the wagon in the well-graveled drive in front of the manor, leaped down, and held out his arms for her, his eyes bright with amusement. She sat there a moment more, watching as Joshua jumped from the back of the wagon and ran up the front steps. The woman hugged him, then kissed him and wished him Happy Christmas. "Your present is inside in the usual place, my dear," she told him, and stepped aside as he hurried into the house.

"I really don't understand what is going on," Mary said, completely mystified.

"I think we can make this clearer, if you will let me help you down, Mary," he said. This time there was compassion in his eyes. "Don't be afraid."

She did as he said. If she stood for a moment longer than necessary in the circle of his arms, she did not think he minded. He offered her his arm then, and they started up the short walk. "Mrs. Muncie, Happy Christmas to you!" he called. "I told you last week I would bring Josh over after Christmas dinner, but I have another guest. She was stranded at my house in all that snow, imagine that!" He stopped with her at the bottom of the steps. "May I introduce your granddaughter, Mary McIntyre?"

As Mary watched through a fog of her own, the woman began to cry. Mary released her death grip on Joe and ran up the steps. When the woman held out her arms, she rushed into them with a cry of her own. Mrs. Muncie's grip was surprisingly strong. As Mary clung to her, she saw in her mind's eye Abby clutched close to Mrs. King. Her heart spilled over with the sheer delight of coming home.

In another moment, Joe had his arms around both of them. "Ladies, do take your sensibilities inside. You know that Mr. Muncie would be growling about warming up the Great Plain of York, if he were still here." He shepherded them inside. In another moment, a maid had Mary's cloak in hand. Her bonnet already dangled down her back, relegated there by the tumult of her grandmother's greeting. She stood still, sniffing back her tears as Joseph untied the ribbon from her neck and handed the bonnet to the maid, who curtsied and rushed off, probably to spread the news that something amazing was happening in the sitting room.

The sitting room was as elegant as her own favorite morning room at Denton. Mary looked around in great appreciation, and then at Joe, who continued to grin at her. She sat next to her grandmother on the sofa and reached for her hand again. "Mrs. Muncie, he let me believe that Muncie Farm was on the outer edges of barbarism. What a deceiver!"

"Yes, that is Joe," she agreed. She laughed, and then dabbed at her eyes with a lace handkerchief. "I tried to warn Melissa six years ago, but she thought he would do." She smiled at Joe, and blew him a kiss. "And he did."

Mary looked from one to the other. "I am beginning to suspect that an even greater deception has been practiced on me than I imagined! Will someone please tell me what is going on? Joshua, does your father run mad on a regular basis?"

From his spot on the floor where he had already opened his present—which looked like more tools—Joshua grinned at her. She felt her heart nearly stop as she took a closer look at him. "Oh, God," she whispered, and reached for Joe's hand, too. "Joe, don't tease me anymore. Is Josh . . . oh, my stars . . . is he my *nephew*?"

He squeezed her hand, then put his arm around her. "That he is, Mary. Melissa's first husband was Michael McIntyre, your mother's younger brother." He held up his free hand. "Don't look at me like that! I didn't know about the McIntyre name when I courted Melissa. It's common enough in these parts, and I didn't give it a thought when you were introduced to me as McIntyre." He touched her forehead with his own. "There were hard feelings about your mother running away, and Michael had told Melissa next to nothing." He looked at Mrs. Muncie. "He was younger, and he may not have known much. I never put your mother together with you until you mentioned Muncie Farm. And I can tell you don't believe me. Help me, Mrs. Muncie!"

The woman laughed and touched Mary's face. "Oh, my dear, he is a little innocent, or at least not as guilty as you would think. Yes, your name is McIntyre. I was married to Edward McIntyre, and had two children by him, Michael and Cynthia."

"Cynthia," Mary said. "In all this, no one ever told me her real name."

Mrs. Muncie closed her eyes for a moment. "Oh, my dear, all these years, all this sadness." She opened her eyes. "Cynthia was a lovely girl, and such a brilliant seamstress. I suppose there was something in her that none of us truly understood." She inclined her head toward Mary. "At any rate, when she was eighteen, and resisting a perfectly good marriage to a farmer, she and her father quarreled and she ran away." She held her handkerchief to her eyes again. "I cannot tell you how I grieved, but there was never a word from her."

"It is hard to take back harsh words," Mary murmured.

"It is," her grandmother agreed. "Edward McIntyre died two years after Cynthia . . . left us. I ran the farm by myself for a while, and two years later married a neighbor, Stephen Muncie, who owned this wonderful place. He absorbed the McIntyre farm, and adopted Michael, because he had no children of his own."

"I only came into this district nine years ago, Mary, and I never knew Michael as a McIntyre," Joe said. "He was killed in a farming accident, and after a few years, I married his widow." He smiled. "And acquired Joshua, Melissa's son. Lord, this is strange! Mary, you have a grandmother and a nephew, which makes you Joshua's aunt, a closer relationship than I can claim with this lad I consider my own son." He shook his head. "We'll have to write the Kings and tell them about this."

And there you are, including me, Mary thought. I like it. Overwhelmed by the sheer pleasure of it all, she looked from Joe, to her grandmother, to Joshua, who had turned his attention back to his present. She released her grip on Joe and took Mrs. Muncie by the hand. "Grandmama, may I stay here with you?" she asked. "I do not think now that I would be happy anywhere else."

Mrs. Muncie embraced her. "This is your home." She held herself off from Mary to look at her. "In fact, it probably will belong to you and Joshua some day, considering that you are my heirs."

"I could even teach you how to milk," Joe teased. "Used to do a lot of that at Denton. Lord, wouldn't Thomas suffer palpitations if I actually mentioned that to anyone of his acquaintance!"

"What I expect you to do, dear sir, is find a way to come to terms with him," Mary said. She looked at Mrs. Muncie. "Let us here be your cautionary tale. Life is too short to foul it with petty discord."

"Your point is well taken," he admitted. He rose then, and motioned to Joshua. "Son, we had better go home before it gets too dark and the wolves start howling."

"Joe! Really!" Mrs. Muncie said. "Do you ever have a serious moment?"

"Plenty of them, madam," he replied, "but maybe not on Christmas. Mary, I promise to bring the rest of your numerous trunks tomorrow." He looked at Mrs. Muncie. "Do you want Joshua here for a couple of days?"

"Any time is fine with me . . . with us . . . Mrs. Muncie replied. She touched Mary's hand. "My dear, you will see much of Joshua in the spring, when his father makes the rounds of his clients in the shire. Josh always stays with me then."

As Mrs. Muncie summoned the housekeeper to make arrangements for Mary's room, Mary walked Joseph and Joshua to the door. "What can I say?" she asked as Joshua scrambled up into the high seat of the wagon.

Joseph hugged her. "Just forgive me for not spilling out my suspicions and realizations sooner, Mary."

"Sooner? Sooner?" she exclaimed. "You played that hand awfully close to your vest!"

He laughed and joined her nephew in the wagon. In another moment, they started down the lane. He looked back when they were near the end of the trees. On impulse, she blew him a kiss, then went up the steps and into the house again.

Mrs. Muncie was motioning to her on the stairs. She put her arm around her grandmother and walked up the steps with her, and into a room easily as beautiful as her old room at Denton.

Mrs. Muncie touched the bedspread. "I made this for your mother when she was five years old," she said softly. She patted the pillow, then leaned against the mattress as though all her strength had left her. "When I first contacted Bow Street and told them to search for Cynthia McIntyre, I put this back on the bed. Oh, Mary, welcome home."

Her heart full, Mary hugged her grandmother. "Happy Christmas, my dear," she whispered.

She didn't want the embrace to end, but her grandmother started to chuckle. "Oh, my dear," she said finally, "you should be looking out the window right now from my vantage point. Better still, I think you should hurry down the stairs."

Mary opened her eyes and turned around to see what was causing Mrs. Muncie so much amusement. "Why is he coming back?" she asked, and then she knew with all her heart just why. "Oh, excuse me," she said as she started for the door.

"Here. Take my shawl. It's December, remember, my dear?"

She snatched up her grandmother's shawl and swirled it around her shoulders as she hurried down the stairs. She flung open the door, then closed it quickly, remembering the late Mr. Muncie's admonition about heating all of Yorkshire. Joe was out of the wagon seat, and she was in his arms before she had time to clear the last step. With a shaky laugh, he took her down the last step and held her off from him for a moment.

"I'm perfectly sober, Mary McIntyre," he warned her. "I'm really going to mean it this time. Did you just blow me a kiss?"

"Only because you were too far away," she replied. It must have been the right answer, because he kissed her soundly, thoroughly, and completely at her grandmother's front door. He held her close then, and she wrapped Mrs. Muncie's shawl around both of them.

"Poor Mrs. Muncie," he murmured in her ear. "I mean, what kind of a common scoundrel and skirt raiser would take away her granddaughter so soon?"

"You would, my love," she whispered.

REGENCY
CHRISTMAS
GIFTS

The Lasting Gift

PROLOGUE

"Suzie, I am bored."

There. He'd admitted it. Maybe if the house Thomas Jenkins had purchased here in Plymouth, England, had been in dire need of renovation, it would have kept him busy for a year. But no, the prospect of moving into a wreck had no appeal. Besides, Thomas could afford to be overcharged for a pastel-blue row house with white shutters located north of the Barbican on Notte Street. Once the carter had delivered Suzie's furniture all the way from Cardiff, Wales, and he had added his paltry bed and favorite chair, what else was there to do?

Convincing his sister to quit Cardiff had taken up several months of his time and involved diplomacy worthy of Talleyrand at the Congress of Vienna. As little brother, Thomas Jenkins (sailing master retired, Royal Navy) had no bargaining chips except one, which he hated to play. He had played it at last, when the matter seemed in some doubt and he had no choice.

He even remembered the date: November 4, 1816. For six months he had been cooling his heels at the Drake in Plymouth, sending his widowed sister letter after letter, cajoling her to leave her little place in Cardiff and move in with him in the house he was about to purchase. He wheedled; she wavered. He put down his foot; she played the older sister card and ignored him. There seemed to be no end to her evasion.

As did many things in life, the matter came down to money. Bluntly, he had it and she didn't. A visit to Cardiff in September had found him sitting across the desk from Susan Jenkins Davis in her closet of a bookroom, staring at her banking statements showing a paltry balance, thanks to the tiny pension from her late husband.

"Suzie, you're at your last prayers and I won't have you living here in genteel poverty," he said, through with dodging and weaving the issue like Gentleman Jackson.

Ah, but she was still a Jenkins, so she gave the matter one last stab. "Tommy, you could move back here to Cardiff."

"I think not, Sister," he replied, but gently. "I'm fond of Plymouth, and I have bought a lovely place with a view of Sutton Harbor. You'll have your bedchamber and your own sitting room." He took both her hands in his. "And I will not have to worry about you, dear heart. Humor me and manage my domestic affairs. What do I know about living in a house?"

She finally agreed, probably because each foray through her tattered accounts was more frightening than the one before. She certainly did not need to oversee the little brother who had fought for years at sea and who could take care of himself.

A month later, she'd moved into his new house. Her last feeble attempt to dissuade him only made him laugh.

"Me, marry? Suzie, who in the world wants a sailing master set in his ways?"

"Bored, Tommy? Do this little thing: I have wrapped the brush and comb set that the former owner left here. Either deliver it in person—it is a mere four miles to Haven—or take it round to the posting house. Mrs. Poole can afford whatever the charge will be."

Packaged addressed, he wrapped his boat cloak tighter and braved the treachery of slick streets in autumn rain. If he mailed the package, time would remain for a walk to Devonport to observe good ships being dismasted and placed in ordinary, now that Napoleon was far away and peace reigned. Of course, such a sight wasn't one to foster a cheerful mood.

The rain let up after the package was safely on its way. He stared at the ships long enough to mangle his heart, the one that still wanted to be at sea.

"Peace is a humbug," he announced to a seagull eyeing him from the mainmast of a frigate—gadfreys, it was the HMS *Thunderer*—doomed to lose its masts in a day or two.

He sighed. "I am still bored."

CHAPTER ONE

"There must be some mistake. How in the world am I to pay for this package?" Mary Ann Poole asked herself in dismay as she stared at the note her landlord had tacked to her front door.

Since yr were at worke, I paid ta man, he had written—dear Mr. Laidlaw, whose grasp of English was a loose hold, indeed. *We can sittle up this evling.*

She hadn't ordered anything. Any extravagance through the post was far beyond her means.

Such news was the last straw in a week of last straws. Mary Ann wanted to plop herself down on the bench by her home, drum her feet on the pavement, and throw a royal tantrum, such as she had seen today at the home of Lady Naismith, where she worked. True, she was Lady N's secretary and in the bookroom with the door closed, but the argument was loud and long. She was too frightened by all the noise to open the door even a crack to see if Lady's Naismith's spoiled daughter threw the fit or if her little boy did the honors. Thank goodness her own daughter Beth had better manners.

"My head aches," Mary Ann said as she stood up, removed the note, and entered her home.

Beth looked up when Mary Ann came inside. She held the open package in her hands, and Mary Ann saw what looked like a carved ivory brush and comb set.

Mary Ann kissed the top of her daughter's head. "Did school dismiss early, or am I late again?"

"Late again, Mama," Beth said. "Is Lady Naismith being unreasonable?"

More than unreasonable, Mary Ann thought, *but you don't need to know that*. The subject was easy enough to change. "'Unreasonable'? Is that a new spelling word for this week?"

Beth nodded. "So are 'quality' and 'inestimable,' but unreasonable seemed to fit. After all, I am only seven," she concluded, satisfied she had made her point and logic was on her side.

The unwanted brush and comb forgotten a moment, Mary Ann wished with all her heart that her late husband were there to enjoy Beth and her wit, which reminded her of his own. *Drat you for dying, my dear*, she thought for the umpteenth time.

"So you are only seven," she said. "I don't doubt that before bedtime, you will find a way to use both words in a sentence."

She sat down beside her daughter, because she couldn't continue to ignore the expensive-looking comb and brush. She picked up the brush from Beth's lap, turning it over to admire the delicate filigree. Her own hairbrush was serviceable beech, with boar bristles, left behind by her husband when he left for Spain with Sir John Moore's army.

Beth held the ivory comb, equally carved along the top. "Mama, does this belong to a princess? Ha!" She held it high in triumph. "It is of *inestimable quality*. I did it!" She leaned against her mother and giggled.

"I predict you will someday be the first woman admitted to the Royal Academy for. . . for. . . something or other."

Mary Ann set down the brush and picked up the box that the set had arrived in. She looked at the brown paper, putting two torn edges together. "Mrs. M. Poole, plain as day. I am certainly M. Poole," she said. "I can see why you opened it, Bethie, but this can't be ours." She looked closer at the address itself, squinting, because the hour was late and Beth had been taught not to lay a fire without her mama or Mr. Laidlaw present. Coal was dear, after all. "Fifty-two Dinwoody Street. Oh dear. That is the error." She held it up so Beth could read it. "I suppose Dinwoody looks like Carmoody at least a little. Maybe they were rushed at the posting office."

"Should we take it 'round to Dinwoody Street?" Beth asked. She avoided Mary Ann's gaze and spoke in a small voice. "I should have looked carefully, but Mama, I have never opened a package before and I wanted to."

"I suppose you have not," she said, wondering just how many prosaic events Elizabeth Poole would be denied because of their poverty. She could be philosophical as she pulled her daughter closer. "Did you enjoy opening it?"

Beth leaned back against her. "I *anticipated* something wonderful," she said solemnly, rolling that wonderful word from last week's spelling list around on her tongue. "It was a mystery, all wrapped in tissue and brown paper."

She turned around in Mary Ann's lap to look at her. "Can we put it back in the box and take it to that address?"

Mary Ann tightened her arms around the only blessing that Second Lieutenant Bartimus Poole had been able to give her. "If it is supposed to be a surprise to this Mrs. Poole, we had probably better return it to the original owner so he or she can rewrap it." She squinted at the return address. "S.M. Thomas Jenkins, 34 Notte Street, Plymouth, Devon. That's a relief. We're only a few miles from Plymouth. We'll take it to . . . what on earth is S.M.?"

"Sadly Maintained?" Beth teased, and cuddled closer.

Mary Ann laughed. "I prefer Strangely Morbid." Sitting so close, she heard her little daughter's stomach growl. "But now I suggest supper."

Mary Ann waited until after supper and put Beth to copying her letters on her slate before taking a look in the tin box where she kept her monthly funds. The postal stamp on the gift clearly indicated five pence that she now owed her landlord. She took out the coins, thinking of the vicar's sermon on loaves and fishes. That was well and good for sermons, but only left her wishing she could turn even one pence into a handful of them. Well, the package had to be paid for no matter what.

She left her daughter busy with the week's spelling words and went next door to the Laidlaw residence, no more grand than her own three rooms. There was a time when she would have laughed behind her hand at such a humble row of houses, but that was back when she was newly married, with Bart's promising career dangling before them like a carrot before a horse—but no, more like Aesop's goose, whose golden eggs would keep coming, providing no one killed her.

"Think of it, Mary A," he had told her before the transport bearing the Fifth Northumberland Foot sailed for Lisbon. "If the late Lord Nelson, son of a vicar like me, can climb to the top, why not I? I aim to come home a general."

He came home a second lieutenant still, dead at Corunna defending the British army backed up against the ocean by the French. Her share of his battle glory was a tiny pension to support her and their daughter, born a month after his death in Spain.

As she stood in front of Mr. Laidlaw's modest row of four houses, she envied the kind old fellow the income of three of those, and the living in one of them. In her present state of penury, that income sounded munificent.

If she had once been too proud and notably lacking in humility, those days were gone. *Let this be a lesson to you, Mary Ann Poole*, she thought now, and not without some humor. She was, despite everything, an optimist still.

Mr. Laidlaw had been kind, but he still needed the pence, which she gave him, after assuring him that she would return the package to the owner and no doubt receive reimbursement. Besides, it would never do for her landlord to know how close she skated to ruin, since he expected three shillings monthly rent.

As Mary Ann lay in bed that night, Beth snuggled close, she wondered just how she was going to tell her child the bad news. Lady Naismith had informed her today that as of Christmas Eve, her services were no longer required.

When Mary Ann, shocked, had asked why, the woman had shrugged her shoulders. "My children think I can find a cheaper secretary," she said.

"Will you at least provide me with a good character?" Mary Ann asked. "I've done all that you required, and done it well."

The baronet's widow agreed. She promised to provide just such a letter at the end of the week.

Happy Christmas to us, Mary Ann thought, as she closed her eyes. She tried to remember what it felt like to have her husband's arms around her. It was years ago now, and even the best of memories begins to fade. It saddened her to think that soon she would have to refer to the miniature of him, proud in his regimentals, to call to mind the lovely man who had married her and promised great things, before Mars the God of War worked his own will.

Mary Ann glanced at the ivory brush and comb set on her bureau, idly wondering what they might bring if she took them to a pawn shop. The notion passed quickly, but not as fast as her conscience wanted. Her father might have been just a clerk in a cloth factory and not a vicar like her father-in-law, but she had learned from an early age that stealing was sinful.

Beth stirred and whimpered in her sleep. Mary Ann kissed her daughter. She thought about the approaching holiday and had only the smallest wish. *Please, please let S[trangely] M[orbid] Jenkins pay me back my five pence.*

CHAPTER TWO

Mary Ann couldn't return the brush and comb to Mr. Jenkins in Plymouth any sooner than Saturday, when she had her half-day off. To her relief, the weather was precisely right—cool but no rain in sight.

Mary Ann bundled the box and its lovely gifts into a satchel. After a check of Beth's muffler and coat, they started off. She would like to have had sandwiches with her daughter in Plymouth at a tearoom, but if they hoped to take a hired conveyance home, it was better to eat their bread and butter before they left.

For December, the day was surprisingly mild. Careful to remain close to the road's edge, Mary Ann matched her steps to Beth's. As they walked, she reminded her daughter that her father had been part of the Fifth Foot from Northumberland, and he was a champion walker.

"Didn't Papa ride a horse?" Beth asked as they swung along.

"Aye, he did, but he told me in one letter that he liked to march on foot with his men, too," she replied. "He would be proud of us."

And he would, too, Mary Ann decided, as she admired her daughter's auburn curls, so like her father's. If there was some moment in the celestial realms when a heavenly curtain ever parted, she hoped Bart knew that their child was well cared for, and that she was doing her best—no matter how paltry it seemed at times. It wouldn't be too much to ask that he be allowed a glimpse of their daughter.

But what did she know of heaven? She hadn't the money to have her husband's body returned to Blyth, Northumberland, or herself and their infant daughter, for that matter. The vicar, overworked because of so many burials in a common grave that day, hadn't time to answer questions about what happened to a good soldier after death. She had decided by herself that God was merciful and surely allowed glimpses below for residents in His heavenly kingdom. It was serviceable theology and gave her enough comfort to keep going when times were tough. Lately, they were always tough.

But she could worry about hard times later. Today it was enough to be free from that bookroom where she handled Lady Naismith's financial affairs, wrote her letters because the woman could barely compose a sentence, and wished herself elsewhere. Soon she would be elsewhere, as a matter of fact. *But I will not think about that today*, she told herself.

Hand in hand, they walked the few miles to Plymouth, past country houses and long lanes with larger manors at the end of them. Road traffic increased the nearer they came to Plymouth, and eventually there were sidewalks.

"Do you know where Notte Street is, Mama?" Beth asked, when they reached that lovely height where Plymouth stretched below, a busy seaport still, even with the war over.

"Not a clue, my dear, but we shall find someone honest-looking and ask."

Even that could wait. The busy highway turned into a street and then another, until they were in the bustling labyrinth called the Barbican, the old city. Beth looked around, her eyes wide at the sight of buildings three stories high and shop windows with toys and books and ready-made coats and hats.

"That's it," Beth said, pointing to a fur muff. "That is what I would like for Christmas this year."

"You wanted one last year, too, as I recall," Mary Ann said. She reached in her reticule and handed her daughter a small tablet and a pencil. "Better draw it."

While Beth sketched the fur muff, Mary Ann wandered next door to a lending library and bookstore. There it was in the window: a copy of *Emma*, out only a year, cozied up next to *Guy Mannering*, and the scandalous *Glenarvon*, by Lady Caroline Lamb, who dampened her petticoats to make them cling and carried on a torrid romance with Lord Byron. Mary Ann had learned a lot by listening to Lady Naismith's low-brow daughters.

"Mama? Is it to be a book for you this Christmas?" Beth asked. She held out her drawing of the muff, which Mary Ann tucked into her reticule.

"I believe so, dearest." Mary Ann pointed to *Emma*. "That one. I should find employment in a bookstore. I could read a book overnight and return it the next day, no one the wiser."

They laughed together at such nonsense. Mary Ann drew the book cover and added it to Beth's sketch in her reticule.

For good measure, Beth drew a pair of kid gloves, dyed a gorgeous lavender, declaring, "I will give these to you, Mama," which meant that Mary Ann had to draw a darling chip straw bonnet for Beth.

They exchanged glances, and Mary Ann was glad for the package that went astray, so they could have a half-day like this in Plymouth. *We need to do this more*, she thought, which yanked her back to earth and the reality that in a week she would be unemployed, with empty hours on her hands.

But now it was time to smile and hold out her hand for Beth, so they could cross the busy road and find 34 Notte Street.

And there it was, a pastel-blue house, part of a row of houses but nothing like their modest dwelling in Haven. These were two-story symphonies in stone, probably built to mimic Bath's Crescent Row. Each bore a different pastel shade, with shallow steps leading up to a door under an equally stylish cornice.

"My stars," Mary Ann said. "Perhaps the S.M. stands for Stunningly Magnificent." Her reward was a giggle from Beth.

They had found the house, but the issue became which entrance to use. Beside the front steps ran a wrought-iron fence, behind which were more steps leading down to the servant entrance.

"We're not servants or staff, but we certainly weren't invited and aren't expected," Mary Ann said, eyeing the distance to the front door and a brass knocker. *What do I feel like today?* she asked herself. *A secretary in Lady Naismith's house, or a widow touring Plymouth with her daughter?*

She decided she felt like a tourist. Maybe, on that short trip from the street to the front door, she could pretend it was her house. Those few seconds of dreaming would be enough, even if the footman who answered the door shooed them downstairs.

Her hand in Beth's, Mary Ann took her time mounting the steps. Beth wanted to use the knocker, so Mary Ann let her.

An older woman opened the door. She was neat as a pin, with a serviceable apron about her middle. Perhaps Stunningly Magnificent Thomas Jenkins employed a housekeeper rather than a butler or footman. *Never mind*, Mary Ann decided. He was evidently wealthy and could be eccentric if he chose.

"I am Mrs. Poole, and this is my daughter, Elizabeth," Mary Ann said. She held out the opened package. "This was delivered to our address in Haven, but I'm not *that* Mrs. Poole."

She remembered to dip a small curtsey, hoping the housekeeper would invite them in for a glimpse of grandeur within, although it certainly wasn't necessary. She did want that five pence.

She could see that the woman was mulling over exactly that: whether to just take the package and thank them for their honesty or usher them inside. As it turned out, Beth decided the issue.

"I like your house," she told the woman, who started to smile.

"Between you and me, you'd get tired of dusting it," the woman said.

"I wouldn't mind," Beth said, then shyness took over. She turned her face into Mary Ann's skirts.

Another moment, and the door opened wider. "Come inside then," the woman said. "Your mama can talk to Master Jenkins while I find a biscuit or two. Would you please wait in the sitting room while I rummage about for Master Jenkins?"

"Master Jenkins. Master of what? I believe this day just became an adventure, Mary Ann thought. She smiled and let the kind woman usher them in. *We've been lean on adventures lately. What can it hurt?*

CHAPTER THREE

Thomas looked up when Suzie knocked on the bookroom door. *You've rescued me,* he thought, as he told her to come in. *Give me geometry any day, but don't give me counting house statements.*

Not that he couldn't figure them out; far from it. What he wanted more than anything was to be back on deck again, at sea. Sitting behind a desk was anathema and he wanted no more of it.

"I don't like retirement," he said to his sister, before she could get a word out. "Please tell me something interesting that doesn't involve counting house statements."

"There is a quite pretty lady and her daughter in the sitting room wishing to speak to you," she said. "Is that interesting enough?"

"Anyone you know?" he asked, getting up. He put his hands up to straighten his neckcloth and then remembered not bothering to put one on this morning. *I am going to rack and ruin,* he thought. "I don't look like much of a gentleman," he said.

"You never were one, except by virtue of the Navy Board," she replied cheerfully. "Who needs a gentleman anyway? Don't let it go to your head, but I always thought you handsome enough for general purposes."

"You flatter me, Sis," he told her. "I think."

"Only a little," she teased back. "And now I believe I will see if Mrs. Williams has some tea and biscuits."

"That kind of a visit?" he asked, as he started down the hall with her.

Outside the sitting room door, she said, "They look genteel, if a little shabby." She gave him a push. "Go find out."

His sister was quite right on both counts. A lovely lady rose gracefully to her feet when he opened the sitting room door. What hair he could see under her dark bonnet looked blond. He thought her eyes were brown. She wore a cloak as serviceable-looking as her hat. He smiled inwardly to see mismatched gloves, which made him feel slightly less self conscious about his neck-cloth that was missing in action.

"I am Mrs. Poole," she said, and dipped a curtsy. "This is my daughter Elizabeth."

"Beth, sir," said the child, and followed her pronouncement with a curtsy of her own. "I like your house."

Who could resist that? He smiled back, noting that she had a tooth missing. "I'm still getting used to living on land," a glance at her mother, "Beth." Then, remembering his manners, he added, "Let me take your cloaks. "We do have a maid around here somewhere, except that she has scarpered off."

Beth grinned at that, which told Thomas that she was a girl who herself liked to scarper on occasion.

Mrs. Poole was going to give him a hard time. "That isn't really necessary," she told him, and held out a package. "We won't occupy much of your time. It's this package."

He took it from her and recognized the ivory hairbrush and comb set. Mrs. Poole came a little closer and he took an appreciative sniff of a familiar fragrance. Was it vanilla?

"I am Mrs. Poole, but not this one," she said, pointing to the address. "We live at Carmoody Street and not Dinwoody. I think the posting house clerks are overly busy this time of year."

By gadfreys, she had a pleasant voice. The almost-burr to her Rs placed her almost in Scotland but not quite.

"I shouldn't have opened it," Beth said, coming closer. "Mama wasn't yet home from work and I hadn't ever opened a package before." She hung her head. "I couldn't resist."

She was honest little minx, not looking a great deal like her mother, with hair auburn and curly and eyes so blue. He had no doubt she would be a beauty some day, but her mother already was. *Who are these people?*

The missing maid came into the room first, followed by Suzie, who gave him *such* a look. "Thomas, you're supposed to take their cloaks," she said in that forthright, big sister way.

"I tried."

"We're just returning a package," Mrs. Poole said. "We don't wish to take up your time."

"Please do." Suzie held out her hands for their cloaks. "My brother was saying just this morning how bored he is."

Mrs. Poole surrendered her cloak and muffler to his sister, even as he introduced them.

"This is my sister, Mrs. Davis," he told his impromptu guests. "She was kind enough to leave Wales and tend house for me. Suzie, this is Mrs. Poole and Beth."

Once the tea tray was on the table in front of the sofa and the cloaks in the maid's hands, Suzie gestured for them to sit down.

"I truly don't want to be a bother," Mrs. Poole said, even as she saw her cloak carried from the room.

"You're no bother," Thomas assured her again. "Is there a carriage and driver that my all-purpose handyman should see to?"

"We walked from Haven," Mrs. Poole said as she accepted a cup of tea from his sister.

He glanced down at her shoes, which appeared to be as sturdy as her cloak and hat. Still, dusk was nearly upon them this December afternoon. "I trust you are not walking home."

"Oh, no," Beth said. "We could afford to walk one way and ride the other. That is our plan. Thank you." She accepted a macaroon from Suzie.

There was no overlooking the blush that rose to Mrs. Poole's cheeks, making her even more attractive. With a pang, he knew he was looking at poverty, the genteel sort, the quiet kind that hid itself in hundreds, maybe thousands, of British households, most recently where death had come to soldiers and seamen.

Maybe his manners were atrocious, but he had to know. "Mrs. Poole, do you have a . . . is your—"

"He was a second lieutenant, Fifth Northumberland Foot, and he died on the beach at Corunna," she said, her voice so soft. "They were the forlorn hope, holding back the French so others could live, and waiting for the frigates to arrive."

"I'm so sorry," he said. "We came up too slow because of contrary winds. I was there."

Oh, he had been. In thirty years of stress and war, the beach head at Corunna stood out, giving him nightmares for years. In his dream, the fleet moved with dream-like slowness, and he was the only one who appeared interested in the proper use of sail. More than one night, he had wakened himself, calling "Listen to me!" over and over. Now he just muttered it and went back to sleep, thanks to the distance of seven years.

He had to share what he knew with Mrs. Poole. Something in her eyes told him that she wanted to know even the tiniest scrap about a good man gone. "We watched that rearguard, Mrs. Poole. You have ample reason to be proud of your late husband."

"Thank you for telling me, sir," she said. "Bart was always a brave man."

It was simply said, but told him worlds about this woman he had only just met and probably would never see again. Funny how such a thought could make him uneasy. *Never see her again? Impossible.*

She was a lady of great presence, probably earned in the fiery furnace of war, the kind of war that comes flapping home to roost among widows and children. "It could have been worse, I suppose. His body was recovered and he is buried here in Plymouth." She gave her daughter a look of great affection. "Beth was born a month later. I was here in Plymouth, and what with one thing and another, we never left."

He thought about the probable pension for a second lieutenant—a rating little higher than that of an earthworm—and suspected there was no money for her to return north.

He discovered she was also a practical woman. "We are taking up entirely too much of your time, Mr. Jenkins." She stopped then, and he could tell she had a question. From the way she shook her head first, as though trying to stop herself, he found himself diverted for the first time in months.

"It can't be any more rude than my question, Mrs. Poole," he broke in, encouraging her. "Can it?"

"Well, no," she agreed, then blushed again. "But your question wasn't rude. Beth and I . . . we were wondering . . . what does S.M. stand for? It's here on the return address." She pointed to the little scrap. "And you just said you were . . . were there at Corunna."

"S.M. Did I write that?" he asked. "Old habits die hard. Mrs. Poole and Beth, it stands for Sailing Master, nothing more. I'm retired now, but I evidently have to remind myself."

She gave him a sympathetic look, as if his face had betrayed him, or if she simply understood that he did not want to be retired.

"You miss the ocean," she said and it was a statement.

"Beyond everything."

They were both silent, missing people and places, apparently. Thank the Almighty that his sister had some social skills, at least—those skills he had never learned because he was always at sea.

"Tom, you try me," Suzie said, then directed her attention to the widow. "Mrs. Poole, I am his older sister and I can talk to him like that."

Both women laughed, which relieved Thomas, grateful his clumsy reminder of a difficult time had not chased away Mrs. Poole's sense of humor.

"Seriously, my dear, do have a macaroon or two, before Beth and I devour them all. And would you like tea?"

She would, and took a macaroon while Susan poured and Beth asked, "Mr. Jenkins, what does a sailing master do?"

"Most nearly everything," he told her, then sat back and noted her skepticism. This was not a child easily bamboozled. "It's true. Come here."

With no hesitation, she sat beside him, her mother moving over a little. Thomas glanced at Mrs. Poole, pleased to see her savoring her macaroon. A slight nod of his head to Suzie made his sister slide the plate of macaroons closer to the widow.

"I was the frigate's senior warrant officer, which means I had a specialty. My job involved everything related to a ship's trim and sailing."

"Trim?"

"How it sits in the water and sails," he said. "I was the one, my mate and I, who decided where every keg, box, and ballast must be placed in the hold. Tedious work, but everything must balance. Do you follow me?"

"Oh, yes," the child replied with admirable aplomb. "Mama tells me I am quite bright."

Thomas threw back his head and laughed. "And none too shy about it, either, eh?"

A glance at Beth's mother told him she was enjoying the conversation hugely. "Perhaps I have read my daughter that chapter in St. Matthew too many times about the inadvisability of hiding's one candle under a bushel," she joked, which made him laugh some more.

"If it didn't balance, your ship might sink in a storm," Beth said, with some dignity.

"Aye to that, Miss Poole," he said. "For the sake of simplification, I also set the navigational course, made sure the sails were also in proper trim, and the rigging true. I taught young boys not terribly older than you. You . . . you are . . ."

". . . seven."

"Five years older than you, how to navigate. Many of them hated it, but—"

"I would never hate it," she interrupted, her eyes intense. "Mama, he probably knows more about . . . about . . . planes and angles . . ."

"Geometry," he filled in, fascinated by this little girl.

". . . than the vicar knows," she finished. "I go to a church school that the vicar runs." She opened her mouth, glanced at her mother, and closed it again. "But I am not to complain." That wasn't enough. "Mr. Pettigrew does not precisely shine in math."

Thomas wanted to laugh and then laugh some more, delighted by the company he was keeping that had just dropped in unannounced. He used considerable discipline to limit himself to a smile at Mrs. Poole, who to his further amusement had pressed her lips tight together to keep from laughter, too.

"Beth, you would have been welcome in my quarterdeck lessons," he told her. "What else? I also keep—kept—the ship's official log." He waved his hand. "I was all the time signing documents and doing boring stuff."

"You kept the log?"

Mrs. Poole's interest equaled her daughter's, to his further delight. She put down her cup and given him her full attention. "I had thought the captain did that."

"A ship's captain keeps a personal log. Mine is—was—the official log. At the end of each voyage, I took it to the Navy Board as the full and official record of all that happened during a single cruise."

"Mama could do that," Beth supplied. "She likes to write and draw and she doesn't mind tedious things."

"Then I should turn her loose in my bookroom to balance accounts and keep records," he told Beth.

"She would never disappoint you," the child replied.

Mother and daughter looked at each other, and Thomas saw a comradeship that touched his heart. From the few things she had said, it was evident to him that it was Life versus Mrs. Poole and Beth, with no buffer. They were all they had.

"And now we truly must conclude this delightful visit," Mrs. Poole said, with what Thomas hoped was real regret.

"We've been charmed," Suzie said. "Let me put those macaroons in a parcel for you to take along." She rose and left the room even as Mrs. Poole opened her mouth, probably to object.

"So we leave you the brush and comb to rewrap and send to another Mrs. Poole," the widow said. "I hope it was not to have been delivered in timely fashion."

"Oh no," he assured her. "*That* Mrs. Poole is an old dear who sold me this house and most of its contents. Suzie found the set in the back of a drawer. We thought she might want it."

CARLA KELLY

She paused and took a deep breath, and he witnessed the regrettable look of a woman forced to pawn her dignity. Her shoulders drooped and her eyes wouldn't meet his as she said in a small voice, "I must trouble you for that five pence I paid to claim the package."

He felt his heart break a little. Five pence was such a small sum, but he had already deduced that there was little between survival and ruin for Mrs. Poole and her daughter. Her head went up then and she squared her shoulders, a sight he knew he would never forget. He doubted that Beth's father, holding off the French Army at Corunna, was any more gallant than his wife.

Don't cry, you idiot, he told himself, as he reached into his waistcoat pocket and pulled out a shilling. "It's the smallest coin I have." He saw her open her mouth to object and he overrode it with his senior-warrant officer voice. "The other seven pence will be recompense for your efforts in returning this parcel to me, and I will not have an argument, Mrs. Poole."

She took the coin, and her expression told him she knew exactly what he was doing. "You are so peremptory! You must have been a trial to the midshipmen and subordinates, Mister . . . no . . . *Master* Jenkins."

"Fearsomely so, madam," he told her, pleased to hear the word 'master' applied to his name again. "Turn it over to Beth. What would you do with seven pence?"

Beth didn't even have to think about it. "I would buy water-colors," she said promptly.

You were born to command, he thought, amused. *No hesitating there.* "What would you draw?"

"Not here, Beth," her mother said quietly, then turned away because Suzie and maid had come into the sitting room with parceled macaroons and cloaks. In another minute she was drawn into a conversation with his sister.

"What would you draw?" he whispered to Beth.

"I don't know why she doesn't want you to know," the child whispered back. "We look in store windows and decide what we want for Christmas. We draw little pictures and give them to

152

each other for Christmas." She clapped her hands. "Think how wonderful our pictures will look if we can color them! I hope she will let me spend a few pence on that."

It was a good thing that Mrs. Poole called her daughter over to help her into her cloak, because Thomas Jenkins, sailing master hardened through years of war, suddenly found himself close to tears. A few deep breaths and a surreptitious dab with his fingers tamped them down, and he was able to walk with Suzie to the door and wish them Happy Christmas.

When the door closed on their unexpected guests, he leaned against the panel, trying to control himself.

Suzie touched his back. "Tom! What on earth is the matter?"

He took her hand and walked her to the stairs, where he sat down with a thump. Mystified, she sat beside him. When he told her what Beth had said, she dissolved in tears. He put his arm around her and they sat together until the maid returned to light the lamps.

"We have to do something to help them," he said finally, when he could speak.

Suzie nodded. She blew her nose. "We have to do it without rousing any suspicions."

"How in the world can we do that?"

"You're the smart one," Suzie told him, her words ragged. "You had better think of something."

"I will," he said and tugged her to her feet. He gave her a little squeeze. "Suzie, I am not bored now."

CHAPTER FOUR

Mary Ann could think of at least fifty ways to spend an unexpected seven pence, but she had no trouble leading Beth by the hand right up to a Plymouth stationer's shop.

Beth got no farther than a small set of watercolors in miniature metal pans. "Mama, you used to paint with these, didn't you?"

"I did. I am surprised you remember," she replied. "What I would give . . ."

She picked up the tin box with wells of powdered colors in red, yellow, and blue and set them on the counter, while the old man minding the store watched them with interest. She selected two brushes, one for her and one for Beth, and two black pencils, and added those to the pile. Finally she stepped back, afraid to ask the price, prepared to be disappointed, and not so certain just what she would do if he named a huge sum. She had schooled herself not to cry over fate, but something inside her wanted to paint, wanted a tiny pleasure, even though she was about to lose her job, and so far, no other employment had wafted down from heaven above on angels' wings.

Trust Beth. "This really mustn't be more than a shilling," her daughter told the shop owner, her eyes anxious, too.

"No, no, seven pence, my dear," Mary Ann said, unmindful of the man who watched them with such interest. "Five will get us back to Haven on the conveyance. Remember? That was our plan."

154

"I can walk, Mama. It isn't that far, and it isn't too dark yet. Besides, what road agent is going to accost *us*?" Beth assured her. "We need this. It would be nice if we had paper, too."

They both looked at the stationer. Mary Ann felt Beth's fingers seeking hers and they held hands. She was loath to pray about something so unimportant to the Lord Omnipotent, who had far bigger fish to fry, but she hadn't asked for anything in ever so long. *Please, Father*, she prayed silently. *Just a little diversion for a change. It's Christmas.*

"I won't sell it to you without paper, because you need the right kind of rough texture for the colors to stick," the owner said. He looked from one to the other.

"My father died in the war," Beth announced all of a sudden. "He never saw my face."

Mary Ann felt her own face go hot. "Beth, we don't do that," she said quietly. She raised Beth's hand, kissed it and turned toward the door. "We don't have enough money, but we aren't pitiful yet."

"I'm sorry, Mama," Beth whispered as she opened the door.

"My dears, you haven't even heard my offer," the shop owner said. "Come back here, please."

Too embarrassed to turn around, Mary Ann stood where she was and took a deep breath. "We didn't mean to trouble you," she told the half-open door.

"You haven't. Come, come. Let us consider this."

As one, they returned to the counter. The man stared hard at the colors, then shook his head. "I could sell you the colors alone for a shilling. They came from Conté in Paris. That is the best I can do." He brightened. "I can set aside the rest for you and you could pay me next week."

Next week there wouldn't be a spare shilling, not with Lady Naismith ready to cut her loose. "We will just take the pencils then," she said.

"No," said Beth. "I want it all."

"So do I," Mary Ann said, wanting the whole day to be over. Somehow, their visit to Thomas Jenkins and Suzie Davis had raised her expectations, never high in the first place, and certainly not after Bart's death in battle.

She thought the unthinkable and touched the necklace her mother had given her so many years ago. It was nothing but a simple gold chain, but she had never removed it.

She removed it now. Beth gasped as she laid it on the counter, along with the shilling. Mary Ann said nothing. It took all her courage, but she looked the shop keeper in the eye.

Silence. Somewhere a clock ticked.

"Done, madam," the man said as he scooped up the necklace. "This will buy you a lot of paper, and . . . and," he handed back the shilling, "your change." He leaned closer, his eyes merry. "I wouldn't want you walking back to Haven with all of this. You might drop it."

Thomas watched Mary Ann and Beth through the front window after they left, a frown on his face. "They didn't turn toward the conveyance stop, Suzie. Do you suppose they are going to find a stationers and buy those colors and pencils and walk home? It's dark out."

He felt Suzie's fingers in the small of his back. "Follow them, or I will," she ordered and gave him a push. "I don't care what you have to do, but get them on that carriage."

He needed no further insistence to fling his boat cloak around his shoulders, grab his low-crowned beaver hat—criminy, but he hated the thing, after years of wearing that intimidating bicorn—and set off into the Barbican.

He stopped as he saw them enter the only stationers' shop he knew of and blended into the shadow as much as a fairly tall man could blend anywhere. They were in there a long time. At one point he saw them turn around and head to the door, but no, they returned to the counter. He saw Mary Ann lift her arms to her neck.

"You're giving him a treasure," he whispered, which made a passing sailor step back in surprise then hurry around him.

Impatient now, he waited until they came out of the shop, Mary Ann carrying something bulky that must be paper, and Beth holding a smaller parcel. This time, they hurried toward the carriage stand in the next block, heads together, laughing. For one terrible moment, he felt as though a cosmic hand smacked him with the sorrow of knowing that but for war and Napoleon, Bart Poole would have walked alongside his girls. He closed his eyes, thinking of his own lost opportunities, and decided to make the most of this holiday season for a widow and a child he had only met today.

When no one was in sight, he crossed the street and went into the stationers' shop. "That lady and child," he began, without any prologue, "what did they buy and could they afford it?"

The old fellow gave Thomas a wary stare, and he certainly deserved one. "I am Thomas Jenkins of Notte Street. Mrs. Poole and her daughter recently visited my sister and me. I am hoping they did not spend their carriage money."

The man shook his head, the wary look gone. "The little minx even told me that her father died in battle! Oh my, I would hate to have been the recipient of that look her mam gave her!" He turned serious quickly. "She took off a necklace, this necklace, and asked if that would do." He rummaged under the counter and held out a gold necklace, the modest sort that a woman of simple means might receive as a wedding gift. "I was able to give her the watercolors, brushes, and lots of paper, plus return their shilling."

He leaned closer, looking most benevolent and like the grandfather he probably was. "I would never have let them walk back to Haven in the dark." He straightened up. "I suppose they are drawing something grand for someone for Christmas."

"Actually, no," Thomas said. "They are barely getting by. What they do is draw a picture of something they know the other one wants Father Christmas to give them, then present the picture because they cannot afford the actual gift." He wasn't sure how he managed to say that without his lips trembling, but he was made of stern stuff himself.

The stationer was silent a long time. He tried to speak, failed, then tried again. "At least they are not walking to Haven tonight." He turned away to collect himself.

"Bless you, sir," Thomas said. He reached for his wallet. "Let me pay you for the necklace, and I will see that it is returned." How, he had no idea, because whatever he did would brand him as a meddler. He knew he would think of something, because he was a resourceful man.

Necklace in his pocket, Thomas Jenkins walked slowly home, planning his next maneuver in what he already thought of as the Second Battle for Corunna.

CHAPTER FIVE

The next day was Sunday. Accompanying his sister, Thomas twiddled and fumed his way through a boring sermon about loving his neighbors and remembering to be charitable at Christmas. He wanted to stand up and ask the vicar what would be the harm in being charitable all year.

He must have made a motion to get to his feet, because Suzie grabbed his arm and hissed in his ear that if he didn't behave himself she would confine him to his room and feed him bread and water. That made him smile and settle down, but still he wondered, he who knew better, why the world was so unfair.

He spent the afternoon just standing at the window, hands in his pockets, rocking back and forth on his heels. He longed to be at sea so much that it was almost a physical ache. Suzie finally threw up her hands and told him in pithy Welsh that he was behaving worse than a small boy, and would he grow up?

Such admonition always sounded worse in Welsh, so he stomped off to his bookroom and took down his well-worn Euclid. He reread favorite portions until he felt better, then stared at his battered sextant, reduced to hanging on the wall now, until his shoulders relaxed.

Thomas slept the troubled sleep of the worried, because he had stayed awake far too long, pacing the floor in his room until he had a serviceable idea. It would involve a bit of snooping worthy of a secret agent, but needs must, as his mother would have said.

I don't look like a secret agent, he thought as he shaved and stared back into his mirror at a man tallish for a Welshman, but with the requisite dark hair and eyes that branded his race. He was common as kelp and nothing more than an able-bodied seaman who had risen to senior warrant officer because of true facility with numbers.

One of his lowly tasks at the age of fourteen aboard the mighty *Agamemnon* had been swabbing decks, of which that ship of the line had plenty. Topside, he always seemed to find his way to that corner of the quarterdeck where the sailing master, a dragon of a fellow, schooled the current crop of midshipmen in determining distance and latitude, and shooting the sun with a sextant. Not one of the students had seemed willing to make an acquaintance with Euclid, so it took all of Thomas's discipline to scrub away, but not too fast, while he listened and absorbed sines, cosines, and tangents.

He might well be an able-bodied seaman yet, except that when the midshipmen straggled away, leaving the improvised classroom empty, he had boldly gone up to the blackboard and finished the equation no one had understood. He knew he was in for trouble when the sailing master returned to retrieve his blackboard, found the correct answer, and demanded to know who had done it.

With real trepidation he answered aye. "Then you'll sit in on every class of mine," the man growled. "I'll tell the boatswain that you're mine now."

So began Thomas Jenkins's steady rise to the top of his profession in the Royal Navy. Talent, hard work, and good fortune had kept him employed mainly aboard frigates, which meant a growing one-eighth share of prize money from every enemy vessel captured and sold into the fleet or as salvage. Thanks to the curse of a long war, he was well off.

Now he stood staring at his lathered face in the shaving mirror, wondering just how he could worm his way into a little family of two and make their life better. Suzie warned him about propriety, so he knew that he must be circumspect. When he suggested that *she* do the probing and inquiry, his sister just smiled at him and shook her head.

"*I* am not bored, Tommy," she told him. "In fact, I am becoming excessively diverted."

He felt too grouchy to demand that she explain herself, or perhaps he was too shy, he thought later, wondering when a stable sort of man, which he was, had turned so moody. It was painfully evident that he was missing the sea, and so he told Suzie. She just smiled in the same maddening, big-sister way that used to irritate him no end when he was eight.

After breakfast, Thomas rewrapped the package and allowed himself the luxury of hiring a post chaise for the day. "We'll be driving around Haven is all," he told the manager of the posting house, who provided him a chaise and only one post rider. Who needed two for such a short jaunt?

His first stop was 29 Dinwoody, arriving at a respectable hour to hand over his calling card to the maid, explain himself, and be ushered into the sitting room. Mrs. Myrna Poole entered the room in good time, offered him tea, which he accepted, and expressed her pleasure at being reunited with the ivory-back comb and brush set that had belonged to her mother.

Small talk, small talk, Thomas advised himself as he drank tea, listened to the old lady praise her new house in Haven, the village of her youth, then inquire how he and his sister were settling into her old house in Plymouth. He assured her that all was well, then segued into the part where he explained why he had come in person with the comb and brush.

It was easy enough to describe the younger Mrs. Poole and her charming daughter Beth. The tricky part was to feign merely casual interest in Mrs. Poole's employer, Lady Naismith. He must have done well, because Mrs. Poole launched into a graphic bit of local gossip about the very *common* Lady Naismith, whose husband had clawed and scratched his way to the top of a fishing fleet.

"There is great wealth in herring," Mrs. Myrna Poole told him with a straight face. "And don't you know, he made enough money to attract the attention of our Prince Regent. That led to a loan, which the Prince of Wales paid off with a paltry title," the old lady informed him. "I am told it happens often."

Thomas's heart sank as he heard the woman's tidbits about Lady Naismith's meanness and nipfarthing ways. "My neighbor says she is a martinet and no one wants to work for her," Mrs. Poole continued. "I feel sorry for those who must." She sighed with so much drama that Thomas wondered how she had avoided a life on the wicked stage.

Then came the *coup de grâce*, when Mrs. Poole leaned closer and whispered that her maid had told her that another maid had told *her* that Lady Naismith was sacking her overworked secretary, an upstairs maid, and one of the scullery girls. She leaned closer still to add, "Rumor says that Sir Edwin Naismith is taking too great an interest in those women to suit the old witch." She sat back in triumph, her dose of gossip finished.

"Wait? What?" he had asked, stunned by the news. "Lady Naismith is letting go of her secretary . . . and the others?"

"On Christmas Eve," Mrs. Poole said, almost as if she savored bad news. "I call that heartless, but what can anyone do about it?"

The thought that Mary Ann Poole, lady with a heart of oak herself, must put herself in soul-sucking employment just to survive made Thomas wonder about his nation. It was beyond him that widows and orphans must continue to suffer long after the last signature on the treaty, the congratulatory victory balls, and the departure of kings and rulers for their own countries. And now Mary Ann Poole was soon to be unemployed. No wonder every pence mattered. He thought of her in the stationers' shop and saw her purchases for what they were: a little light illuminating a growing world of darkness.

"These are trying times, are they not?" Mrs. Poole said to him, she who had likely suffered little or not at all.

He agreed that they were, which allowed him to turn the conversation to the poor, and then St. Luke's charity school. That Thomas moved easily from one topic to the other gave him confidence that he was getting better at skullduggery.

"More tea?" Mrs. Poole asked before launching into additional gossip about how little the vicar knew on any subject. "But the poor must take what they can, eh?"

Even the talented ones who exhibit early signs of mathematical genius, he thought, wondering how many promising minds and ideas had been snuffed out by poverty. His might have been numbered among those, had he not taken a chance on the deck of the *Agamemnon*. Young girls had even less chance, and it chafed him.

By the time he left, Thomas's head throbbed. He wanted to snatch Mary Ann and Beth Poole away from Haven and the hand that had been dealt them, just grab them up, hold them close and promise them something much better, even though he had no idea what it was or how he could achieve it. He gave his head a rueful shake—which didn't help the pounding within—and wondered if perhaps boredom was easier than action, and less hard on the heart.

Instead, he directed his post rider to a vague address that included Carmoody Street and a row of four houses close to a shoe factory. Smoke curled up from three of the one-story row houses, telling him that the fourth one must belong to a working woman and her daughter at school.

That bit of detection gave him three doors to knock on. The first was opened by a woman with a nursing baby at her breast who slammed the door in his face. The second attempt introduced him to Sharlto Laidlaw, landlord, and an old Ancient of Days.

This meant more tea, a further trial to his already overloaded plumbing, and more information about the widow and her daughter next door.

Thomas invented some fiction about looking for his distant relative, a Lieutenant Poole survived by a widow and infant child. When Thomas mentioned that he planned to return in a few hours and invite his second cousin's widow and child to dinner, Mr. Laidlaw brightened.

"That will be a rare treat," he said. "You will be the first visitor they have ever had."

With no more encouragement than an inquiring look—my, but he was getting good at effortless detection—Thomas learned that Mrs. Poole's father had been a clerk in a woolens warehouse in Northumberland, where woolens were surely needed.

"She married the youngest son of a vicar, who had a paltry living on the estate of a marquess who spent his days running from creditors." Mr. Laidlaw stared into his teacup as though he were reading his neighbor's destiny. "She came here to watch the lieutenant buried in Plymouth, and then she was taken in child-birth. For all I know, she'd like to return to Northumberland, but that would take money and she has none."

Thomas sipped his tea. "Did the vicar and his wife think to do right by their son's widow and child?"

"Mary Ann said they never looked with much favor on her marriage. They hounded him because he married for love, and not with an eye to finding a lady with enough inheritance to sup-port them both. I hear that army careers aren't cheap."

"Mrs. Poole told me her husband was convinced he was des-tined for greatness in the army," Thomas said. "His parents won't help her?"

"Can't now. Both dead," Laidlaw said.

They sat in silence, each aware how seldom does greatness touch the deserving, but meanness seems to linger forever.

Mr. Laidlaw brightened then, and pointed to a pencil drawing over his mantelpiece. "Mary Ann drew that for me last Christmas. I told her how much I liked a good piece of beef and dripping pudding."

They laughed together.

"She said if she ever got some watercolors, she would steal in here and touch it up." His eyes grew wistful. "I hope she does. That's as close as *this* old body will come to such a feast."

"I beg to differ, Mr. Laidlaw," Thomas said, his mind made up. "When Mrs. Poole finishes work today, I propose to take the three of you to a good restaurant for just such a meal. Do you think she will agree to my scheme?"

"If I assure her that I won't get to go if she doesn't!" the old fellow declared. "I intend to be most persuasive."

Thomas left it at that, bidding the man good day and prom-ising to return at six of the clock, when Mary Ann Poole trudged home from a job where she had to do as Lady Naismith told her without catching the eye of Sir Edwin. And look forward to no employment after Christmas Eve, a worse prospect than her current lot.

Thomas was a man with a good imagination, but he could not begin to grasp how frightened she must be right now. Yet in no way had she indicated her fears. *Well certainly not to you, you simpleton*, he berated himself. *She probably doesn't want to terrify Beth, and it's none of your business.*

Acutely aware of the desperation Mary Ann Poole must be feeling and finding himself powerless to think of a solution, he spent the next few hours back in Plymouth, closeted with the headmaster of St. Clement's School, arguing the merits of accepting as a student the daughter of an army man dead at Corunna.

"It isn't done," the man assured him. "Females, yes, but she must be the poor child of a Royal Navy man."

"Could it be done if I donated a whacking amount of money to St. Clement's?" he asked bluntly, out of patience with nitpicky rules.

"We will see about it," the old priss said quickly, and dismissed him.

And then what? Suppose he succeeded in getting Beth enrolled in a far better school than the one in Haven run by an idiot? He couldn't kidnap Mrs. Poole and drag her to Plymouth to do . . . what with her? He wondered if she would consent to moving into his house under his sister's charge, but that idea strangled itself at birth. Although he planned to be at sea soon, Mary Ann Poole would probably never consent to such an arrangement out of pride, or fear that what might have happened to her in Lady Naismith's employ might be repeated in his own establishment. He knew it would not—he was a man of honor—but society would never countenance such a solution.

He stewed some more, and then got back in the post chaise for the little drive to Haven, an unhappy man.

"I am far from bored," he announced to the world at large, which happened to be a cat slinking down an alley. But was worried any better?

CHAPTER SIX

Although she would not miss her current position as secretary to an ungrateful employer, Mary Ann dreaded Christmas Eve, when she would dot her last *i* for Lady Naismith and close the door on her miniscule income.

Walking slowly past Christmas carolers, she stopped for a moment in appreciation and tugged her muffler tighter. They sang of a baby's birth, shepherds minding their own business on a Judean hillside, and angels with something miraculous to tell the world.

She decided that on Christmas Eve—rather than stay at home and dread what was about to happen to them—she would take Beth and tag along with carolers. They could sing and take away the fear for a few hours.

Christmas Day would bring revelry as Haven's citizens partied and prepared to welcome a new year—1816—fresh with promise and absent war for the first time since the French revolution began. Perhaps if it wasn't too cold, she and Beth could walk through one or two neighborhoods and watch the people inside. Mary Ann was past those days of wishing she were among the company.

As much as she enjoyed being home before Beth, she took a moment to sit on one of the benches for old people and think through the pleasure of Saturday's visit to Thomas Jenkins and his sister in Plymouth. She tried to imagine the sheer delight of sharing her burdens with another adult. Such a novelty was hard to conjure up, because the experience had never been hers. She had gone from daughter in a modest household to bride, with a brief five days in Portsmouth to love her new husband and wave goodbye to him from the dock as the transport pulled away for Portugal and war.

She never saw Bart Poole alive again. From the time he waved goodbye and blew her kisses, she had worked and contrived and struggled to make ends meet by herself. She tried to imagine what it would be like to sit at home, safe and protected by a husband who submitted his body to toil, as Shakespeare put it, so she could welcome him home and ease both their lives. If hard times came, they would share them.

Now what? She had no money to allow her to look for a new position at leisure, no cushion from disaster. She closed her eyes against what she knew was coming. Boxing Day would be followed by a typical working day, only she would have no work. There would be nothing to do but knock on the vicar's door, pour out her troubles, and steel herself for entry into the Plymouth workhouse, she and Beth, who both deserved better.

Better instead to think about Thomas Jenkins, and remember the real pleasure of listening to the lilting voice that marked him as a son of Wales. She admired his confidence, earned in a hard school, no doubt. She liked the ease with which he teased his sister and their casual relationship. His attention to her darling daughter's love of numbers warmed her maternal heart.

Funny that she should even remember the way he smelled, a combination of good honest soap and bay rum, a man's odor, something she realized she missed. She even liked the casual way he was dressed, in ordinary trousers and without a neckcloth. More than likely he had not expected visitors when Beth knocked on his door.

Those were externals. She had no explanation for the way she felt in his presence—a combination of relief, because he seemed to be so in control of things, and the barely remembered pleasure of being in the same room with a man she instinctively liked.

She knew Thomas Jenkins was just an ordinary fellow, retired and not much liking it. He obviously wasn't worried about his next meal or eviction, or any of those terrors that kept her awake at night. She could have envied and hated him, but all she wanted was to see him again.

That was it, plain and simple. She wanted to drift into Thomas Jenkins's generous orbit once more, even though the odds of that happening were less than remote. She had returned his package, he had paid her for the postage, and each had resumed his and her own spheres. End of story.

Beth liked her to make up bedtime tales. Through the years, her stories had been of princes and princesses, and the occasional dragon or villain. Maybe in a few years, if the workhouse didn't separate them, she could tell her daughter of a man with dark hair getting a bit gray around the edges, and dark eyes, and wrinkles around those eyes that probably came from sun, rain, and wind, and the stress of grave national emergency, for all she knew. She couldn't tell such a bedtime story now. Something told her she would cry, an emotion she gave up years ago, because it solved nothing.

She had sat too long woolgathering, and now it was snowing, a rarity this close to the coast. She watched the big flakes settle on her dark cloak and admired their intricacy. Maybe she and Beth could go outside after their bread and milk and study the snowflakes.

She hurried down Carmoody Lane and stopped in surprise to see smoke coming from her chimney. "Beth, you know better than to start a fire," she said out loud. "It isn't that cold yet." She hurried inside her house and stopped in open-mouthed amazement. There was Thomas Jenkins sitting at the table, book open on the table, drawing an angle with a compass while Beth watched.

They looked over at her with uniformly guilty expressions. "I'll get you some more paper," Mr. Jenkins said, while Beth chimed in with, "He wanted some warmth and said he would get us more coal."

Mary Ann wanted to clap her hands at the pleasure of seeing the sailing master again. She had wished for years and not one wish had come true. Yet here he was. She took off her cloak and bonnet and stuffed her mismatched gloves in her reticule.

"I didn't expect to see you again, Mr. Jenkins," she said, which was no way to greet the man, but she hadn't had a lot of practice.

"Here I am anyway," he said simply, and she had to swallow down tears at such an unvarnished comment. Here he was. For just a little while, she could forget her fears because she was back in his orbit again.

Oh dear, it was time for dinner, and she had nothing beyond their usual bread and milk. She opened her mouth to apologize for the paltriness she was about to inflict on him, when he spoke first.

"I delivered the package to Mrs. *Myrna* Poole," he said, emphasizing the Myrna. "I took a moment before Beth returned from school to visit with Mr. Laidlaw next door. I have invited him for dinner in my favorite restaurant in Plymouth—it's not so far—and I extend the invitation to you two ladies, as well. Do say aye."

"Aye," she said with no hesitation, which made the wrinkles around his eyes deepen.

"Good! I've been leading people about for so many years that I probably would have hauled you along anyway, if you had told me nay." He turned to Beth. "We had better clear the table and give your mother a chance to freshen herself before we drag her away."

Mary Ann took the suggestion and went into the bedchamber she shared with Beth. She washed her face in the blessedly cold water she poured from her pitcher, happy to tamp down her high color and warmth. *Did I wish for this?* she asked herself, and marveled.

A glance into her dressing closet assured her that nothing new had materialized since this morning. She had another dress, but it was scorched on the side and she hadn't yet figured out how to hide the narrow burn streak. Her two other dresses were fit for their own burn pile. She found a lace collar that she smoothed out with her fingers. The brooch she used to pin it had been traded to an apothecary for medicine when Beth had the croup last year. She found an ordinary straight pin to tack it together.

The image in her mirror looked back at her with anxious eyes, but at least the straight pin didn't show. She looked every one of her thirty-two years, but she had no more remedy for that than for the scorch on her other good dress. Hopefully, the restaurant wouldn't be too grand.

She returned to the other room and let the sailing master put her cloak around her. He rested his hands on her shoulders for the briefest moment, and she could have died with delight from the simple pleasure that gave her. Beth was ready, her eyes lively. Mr. Jenkins sent her next door to alert Mr. Laidlaw that the excursion was about to begin.

Mr. Jenkins handed over her bonnet. "Mrs. Poole, the Myrna one, told me that Lady Naismith was letting go several of her workers, including you," he said, with no preamble.

She nodded, embarrassed. "I only learned last week, and haven't had time to look for another position. Please don't mention anything to Beth."

"What are the odds of finding work?" he asked.

"Not good, Mr. Jenkins," she said, determined to be as calm as he was, even though ruin stared her in the face. "I could easily do bookkeeping, too, but most employers would rather hire men. Now that the war has ended, there are many men looking for work." She returned his gaze with all the serenity she could summon on short notice. "I'd rather just enjoy dinner tonight, sir, and not worry about something I have little control over."

"Bravo, Mrs. Poole," he said and held the door open for her. He handed her into the waiting post chaise, and kept her hand in his longer than he needed to. He gave it a gentle squeeze and released her to help Beth into the carriage, and then Mr. Laidlaw. He seated them opposite her, then nodded to the post rider and closed the door.

Beth broke the silence with, "I like traveling this way," which led Mr. Jenkins to tell her about riding in rickshaws in China and Siam.

"Have you been *everywhere*?" Beth asked, after he told them about traveling by gondola in Venice.

"I believe I have," he replied.

"What is your favorite place?" Mary Ann asked. The post chaise was a tight fit for four, but she did not mind the pressure of Mr. Jenkins' shoulder against hers. Quite the contrary.

"I was going to say 'the sea,' but do you know, I am enjoying this chaise right now," he said.

"That's no answer," Beth chided.

"Now, Beth," Mary Ann admonished.

"It probably isn't," Mr. Jenkins agreed. "Ask me another day." He shifted slightly. "Mr. Laidlaw assured me this afternoon that he likes the little village in Kent where he was raised. What about you, Mrs. Poole?"

She felt her face grow warm again from such a prosaic question. She couldn't help leaning against Mr. Jenkins's arm as she tried to remember when she had last imagined any place but where bad luck had anchored her. She shook her head, close to tears—she who had resolved never to cry again.

"I'll ask you another day, Mrs. Poole," he said.

CHAPTER SEVEN

Because he knew anything grander than the dining room of the Drake would upset Mrs. Poole, the Drake it was. Mrs. Fillion had already turned over the evening's work to her son, but she had taught him well. David Fillion assured Thomas that there was still a private parlor left and led them to it.

"The other two are full of Christmas revelers," he said as he handed around the menus. "I already have a case of the shudders that might just last until Twelfth Night."

Mrs. Poole smiled at that, so Thomas knew her equanimity had been restored. She sat next to him, looking so lovely that he could only marvel at her composure.

No one had any idea what they wanted, so Thomas ordered beef roast and dripping pudding all around, with bread and cheese. He nodded to Mr. Laidlaw. "This excellent fellow showed me your picture of roast beef, Mrs. Poole."

By gadfreys she had a fine smile. She clasped her hands on the table and gave the old man the full effect of it. Thomas saw the affection in her glance and wondered what such a smile aimed at him would do to his ability to function.

"You're the best landlord, Mr. Laidlaw," she told him.

And then, *mercy*, she turned that smile on him. "And you sir, are a kind friend," she told him. He could have wriggled like a puppy from the pleasure, but he was forty-three and knew better.

Dinner was an unalloyed delight. He thought of all the roast beef and dripping pudding he had eaten through the years in this dining room without overmuch thought, and found himself looking at the tender beef before him through Beth's eyes.

"Mama, have we ever had *anything* like this before?" she had asked her mother after the first bite.

"If we have, I don't remember it," Mrs. Poole replied, which told him more than he ever wanted to know about their meals.

Thomas lightened whatever embarrassment she may have been feeling at such a question by regaling his guests with stories of weevils at sea, and water so thick and long in the kegs that it nearly quivered like pudding. As his guests ate, then ate more when he summoned David Fillion to keep the food coming, Thomas told them stories of rice and mysterious concoctions in the Far East, a memorable dinner of pasta and tomatoes in Naples, and homely corn pudding in South Carolina, washed down with something called apple jack that left him with a two-day headache.

Dessert was cake, which made Beth clap her hands in wonder, and Mrs. Poole mouth *I love cake* as she turned her unmatched smile on him again.

"I am too full to eat this," she told him, and touched her little waist, but she ate it anyway, closing her eyes with each forkful she downed. She ate slower and slower, as if wanting to savor each bite and hold it in memory. Finally, she could eat no more. She shook her head with obvious regret.

A whispered conversation with David Fillion when Thomas went to the front of the house to pay the bill meant that he could present the rest of the cake in a pasteboard box to Beth. She took it with a curtsy, handed it to Mr. Laidlaw, then threw herself into his arms.

"This is going to be *such* a Christmas because we will have cake," she whispered in his ear. "Mr. Jenkins, thank you."

And then she was a well-mannered child again, and it was her mother's turn to struggle, which gave Thomas a little unholy glee. He could do his own struggling later in the quiet of his home.

Mr. Laidlaw assured him that he could easily escort the ladies home in the post chaise, so he would not have to make another round trip, but Thomas wouldn't hear of it.

"My sister will just scold me for eating too much, if I come home now," he said as he loosened the top buttons on his trousers. "Excuse this, but I'm in pain."

Beth laughed and waved the pasteboard box under his nose, which made her mother giggle like a school girl.

They were all so easy to laugh with that he wished he could have signaled to the post rider to slow down so he could savor the moment in much the same way as Mrs. Poole had slowed down to enjoy her cake. He snagged an errant thought out of the cold night air and wondered if this was what it felt like to have a family. If it was, he wondered how *any* man, soldier or sailor, could tear himself away to go to something as stupid and time-consuming as war.

Back in Haven on Carmoody Street, Mr. Laidlaw shook his hand once and shook it again. Mrs. Poole invited him in, which was a fortunate thing, because he wasn't going to leave without a few more minutes of conversation.

Beth set the cake box on the table and just stared at it a moment, before yawning.

"Young lady, you are going to bed," her mother said.

Beth made a face.

"I mean it."

He watched them both, enjoying the loveliness of the moment, even though it was prosaic in the extreme and probably what went on all over the world, even though he had missed it, he and many men like him. *I was cheated*, he thought.

He stared out the window in the sitting room while the ladies of the house went into the bedchamber. He heard muffled laughter, and then a gasp and more laughter, and knew right down to the soles of his feet that he had indeed been fleeced out of much of life's sweetness, courtesy of Napoleon. If he called it unfair, he would sound like a child, but unfair it was.

"Mr. Jenkins?"

"Yes?"

"Beth insists that she say goodnight to you." She gestured and he followed her into the bedchamber, which a quick look around told him that she shared with her daughter. A glance toward the unoccupied side of the bed showed him a miniature sitting on the night table of a man in regimentals. That and a child were all that remained of a marriage cut short. He congratulated himself that he had never taken such a serious step in wartime, then felt like a fool, because he obviously lacked Lt. and Mrs. Poole's courage.

He stood there and smiled down at Beth, decorous in a nightgown that looked like it had been cut down from one of her mother's, and a nightcap tied under her chin. Now what?

"There is a ritual," Mrs. Poole said. "We have already been on our knees praying for poor George and our country. We thanked the Lord for whatever is to come, and prayed for strength to withstand it. Have a seat. She just wants to tell you goodnight."

Charmed, he sat down on the edge of the bed. "Goodnight, Beth. Thank you for coming to dinner," he said.

To his surprise, she sat up and hugged him, then patted his cheek. "Mama always does that to me," she whispered, then lay down again. "Goodnight. I hope your sister doesn't scold you because you ate too much." She yawned. "I think it is fun to eat too much."

He got up, knowing in his heart that his Christmas probably couldn't get much better than this. Mrs. Poole kissed her daughter again then joined him in the sitting room after she closed the door.

What was he there for? His mind—his analytical, careful, scientific mind—felt mushy. He put it down to far too much dripping pudding and cake. Ah, that was it. Might as well lower the boom on his continued meddling in her affairs. He sat at the table and she sat across from him.

"I paid a visit to St. Clement's School today," he said, and continued when he saw her questioning look. "It's a charity school in Plymouth, run by Trinity House." He thought her questioning look would continue and it did. "Trinity House is a sort of red-haired stepchild," he began, which made her smile. "It's an entity governed by a three-hundred-year-old royal charter and some thirty Elder Brothers, as they are called. They oversee lighthouses and harbor and channel buoys, and license navigators. I am licensed through Trinity House, as are some captains—not enough, in my opinion."

He waved his hand. "That's neither here nor there. Trinity House also runs a school in Plymouth and another in Portsmouth for the children of seaman killed in the line of duty."

"That's well and good but—" Mrs. Poole began.

"The school in Plymouth has an extraordinary teacher of mathematics," he said. "I want Beth enrolled there."

He watched Mrs. Poole's face and saw a longing so huge that if let loose could fill a coronation room. "She's bright, isn't she?" she asked, but it was more of a statement.

"So bright," he agreed. "Before you came home this afternoon, I started her on the rudiments of algebra and she had no trouble following me." He laughed, because the atmosphere was charged with Mrs. Poole's interest. "She is either a prodigy, or a miniature lady."

"I've wondered," Mrs. Poole said, sounding wistful now. "I would give the earth to see her enrolled in such a place."

"St. Clement's takes girl, too," he assured her. "The obvious obstacle is—"

"Bart was in the army," she finished. Her brows drew together, and he sensed a change in her, not altogether in his favor. "Why tell me this? Why tease me with something that cannot happen?" She sat back, and took her gaze from his face to her feet. "I am sorry. That was rude of me, but I'm so tired."

He could tell she was tired, her exhaustion more mental than physical. He wanted to pull her close and transfer some of his heart to her heart, but that would just frighten her into throwing him out.

"I intend to make it happen," he said, in his best sailing-master voice. "Don't ask me how, because you would most certainly not approve." There. He would let her wonder. He didn't think she would believe in her wildest imagination that he was planning to put down a sum of money that would demand the Elder Brothers' attention. Mrs. Poole had been reared in her own hard school, one that did not hold out much hope anymore.

She said nothing for a long time, but at least she looked him in the eyes again, her own eyes so pretty and brown and deeper than wells. "I won't ask. I am almost unemployed and there is rent due on New Year's Day that I have no way to pay . . ."

Her voice trailed off, then grew firm again, as he saw the fight in her. "Do your best, sir," she said.

"I will." He took a deep breath. "On a far lighter note, Mrs. P, would you be my guest at a noisy, stuffy, overcrowded dull party on Christmas Eve?"

Ah, relief. She laughed. "You make that endlessly appealing and easy to turn down, Mr. Jenkins."

"I thought so! Every year, the harbormaster throws such a party. I always attend out of obligation. I forgot to add over-cooked food and monumental small talk. Would you care to accompany me?"

She surprised him, as she had been surprising him through-out their acquaintance. "I honestly wish I could, Mr. J! However, I don't have a dress fit for even a dull party, so I must decline."

He relaxed, admiring her . . . her *what* he couldn't say. What a woman. "So you are telling me that if you did have such a dress, you would go with me?"

"Certainly! We could talk to each other and not be bored. I have a prior engagement on Christmas Eve, however. Beth and I are going caroling."

"You will have more fun than I will," he replied, pleased that she would have come. He stood up. "I have kept that poor post rider in the cold for too long. Good night, Mrs. P. Hang it all, Mary Ann."

She laughed at that and did not correct him. She followed him to the door, a far-too-short distance to suit him. "Why are you doing this?" she asked.

An honest question deserved an honest answer. "Mary Ann, a day or two before you knocked on my door, I complained to my sister that I was bored. She told me to do something about it."

"That seems reasonable, Thomas," she replied.

"I am not bored now, because I intend to make things better for you." Might as well unload the whole thing on her, since it wasn't of much consequence to someone with far more troubles than he had. "After I have succeeded, and I will, I will go to the Navy Board in London and grovel and whine until they give me another ship."

Her face fell, which he found unaccountable, but it was late and he knew she was worn out. He was tired, too, and his stomach was starting to object to ill usage. Better to leave right now. He patted her shoulder in lieu of a bow and showed himself out.

He told the post rider to direct the chaise to the posting house instead of Notte Street, knowing that a walk would do his insides good. He strolled along in the cold darkness, thinking of other walks like this up from the harbor. He thought of all the times he consciously tried to correct his sailor's roll and walk with his legs closer together like a landlubber. He had walked that way for months now, but he knew how easily he could readjust to a pitching deck.

Someone bumped his shoulder in the dark and he stepped back, not looking for trouble, but ready for it. The bump was followed by a shoulder slap and then a grin minus two or three teeth. The man was short and Thomas knew him.

"Rob Beazer, you're too old to be out so late," he said, and shook the much shorter man's hand.

"Thomas Jenkins, you're too *careful* to be out so late," the little man declared.

They walked together now, Thomas shortening his gait to match that of one of the kindest victuallers in contract to the Royal Navy. Rob Beazer had been the subject of appreciative ward room chats on days in the doldrums, when the food in kegs was going bad—at least, food *not* furnished by Beazer and Son, Victuallers. Officer and seaman alike generally wondered how someone so pleasant could avoid being cheated by subcontractors, hard-nosed scoundrels to a man. No one ever arrived at any answer, but Beazer had even been toasted aboard grateful ships, or so the rumor went around the fleet.

"You're out late," Thomas said again. "Did Mrs. Beazer toss you over for a younger sailor?"

"Nothing like that," Beazer assured Thomas. "My clerk quit—oh, why quibble? I sacked the drunkard—and I've been pulling the long hours." He poked Thomas in the chest. "The navy still keeps me busy, laddie."

Trust a man aged at least seventy to call a forty-three-year-old a laddie, Thomas thought. "Where away your latest contract?"

"Australia, a frigate shepherding four prisoner transports. Jailbirds have to eat, even though Boney is gone to his own island prison."

"Can't your son take over the late-night entries?" Thomas asked, concerned for the man's health.

Beazer took off his watch cap. "Dead these four months from something I can't spell or pronounce. Meggie is so low and sad."

"I am sorry to hear this," Thomas said, thinking of all the reams and reams of lading bills from Beazer and Son that he had initialed through the years, before having his crew sling the tonnage into the hold so he could balance the burden. "I truly am, Rob."

"I know ye are, lad. Man might be inclined to evil as the sparks fly upward, but sometimes the good ones go, too." Another gusty sigh. "I need a clerk."

Thomas stood still on the sidewalk, his breath coming quicker. He took the old man gently by the shoulders. "Rob Beazer, how much do you trust me?"

If the elderly gent was surprised, he didn't show it. "More than most men."

"I can solve your clerk problem."

"When?"

"Day after Christmas. It's a bit unorthodox, but I can do it. You'll never have a regret."

Rob Beazer regarded him with that shrewd look Thomas remembered from countless visits to the victualling warehouse. He rubbed his chin and never took his eyes from Thomas's. "No Catholics or Irish? No drunkards?" he asked.

"No. I'll bring her and her daughter around on Christmas Day," Thomas said.

The old man slapped his cap back on his head. "What game are you playing, laddie?"

"No game. I am in dead earnest."

They continued looking at each other. Beazer finally nodded. "I can tell ye are."

Thomas knew the matter hung on a thin wire. "Just give her a chance," he said softly. "The same way the navy gave me a chance, and the same way, for all I know, the victualler did who took you in years ago as a common laborer."

"Aye, then, lad. Make it Christmas Day. My warehouse."

CHAPTER EIGHT

Mary Ann's last day of work for Lady Naismith frightened her less than she thought it would. She expected no extra Christmas token, not on this last day when the stingy woman counted out coins into Mary Ann's palm as though they were crown jewels.

She had to write her own letter of character, so she larded on all the skills she possessed, not just a modest few. Even Beth would have told her this was no time to hide her candle under anyone's bushel. She needed employment, and soon.

Lady Naismith barely glanced at the letter, which confirmed Mary Ann's belief that the woman was almost illiterate. Her signature, cramped and crabbed, would indicate such was the case.

Mary Ann put the coins in her reticule, afraid to look at them for fear they would shrink if scrutinized. She put on her cloak, nodded to Lady Naismith, and went to the door.

"You're not even going to wish me Happy Christmas, gel?" the old screw asked.

"It slipped my mind," Mary Ann said, feeling surprisingly serene. "I hope you have the Christmas you deserve."

She left Lady Naismith stewing over that one, and did not look back. As she walked home, she passed sweet shops with proprietors sliding marzipan and candy chews into cone-shaped twists, a poulterer's with forlorn-looking turkeys slung up on hooks, and a linen draper's with handsome swatches of fabric ready for customers with a good deal more money than she had.

She spent a long moment in front of a clothier's bow window, admiring a white rabbit-fur muff that Beth would probably moon over, if she were there. It saddened her that Beth has quit asking for anything, and angered her that Bart Poole's darling, brilliant child had learned to appreciate colored pictures, instead.

But at least there would be colored pictures this year. She cast her cares to the wind and bought a slice of beef for dinner to accompany the cake they had hoarded. They had decided to leave it alone until Christmas Day, to eat with the beef and potatoes, courtesy of Mr. Laidlaw, that would constitute a respectable dinner.

Tonight it would be milk and bread again, but that was no hardship. As soon as it was dark, they would join other carolers at St. Luke's and stroll and sing of new babies and a virgin mother and carpenter father who probably didn't have much between them and ruin, either, if they had to spend the night in a stable. Afterward, the vicar had promised hot chocolate and biscuits, and a little something for his students.

Beth was finishing up her painting when Mary Ann opened the door. She looked over her daughter's shoulder, admiring the bouquet of roses, perfect for some day in January when winter seemed to be hanging on and on. Her own watercolor was finished and dry, so she slid it into a paper sleeve with Happy Christmas on the front and painted holly and ivy sprigs. They could walk to 34 Notte Street tomorrow and deliver them in person as a small token of friendship.

When Beth finished, Mary Ann took her watercolor pans next door and touched up last year's Christmas drawing of beef roast for Mr. Laidlaw, making the beef medium rare, with that tinge of pink he liked. In no time at all she had added dripping pudding, and then in the background, a slice of cake.

"Done! I hope you have a Happy Christmas," she told the landlord as she cleaned her brush and dried it.

He nodded to her from the depths of his ancient, rump-sprung chair, wrapped in a blanket and looking about as content as a man could. "Same to you, missy," he told her. "Let's have a better new year."

He said the same thing every year since Mary Ann had arrived at his doorstep dressed in black, with a tear-stained face and an infant in her arms. She said the same thing she always said. "Let's do."

By the time Mary Ann and Beth finished supper, the sky was black with only a few tinges of light low on the horizon. By the time they reached St. Luke's, snow was falling.

The vicar and his wife were dab hands at organizing caroling parties. In no time they started out, two by two, to sing to anyone in Haven who was kind enough to open their door and listen. One of the older girls, proud and careful, carried the collection box, counting on Christmas generosity to make a little difference in the lives of the poor.

We're not there yet, Mary Ann thought, her hand on Beth's shoulder. Where they would be in a week was anyone's guess, but it was Christmas Eve, and not a time for worry. Feeling like a lion tamer with a whip in one hand and a chair in the other, she forced her fears back into a corner of her mind and told them to stay there through Christmas.

They sang first for the merchants on Haven's modest High Street, which earned a few coins and marzipan for the children. They sang past Haven's great houses, where the doors remained shut. The proverbial butcher, baker, and candlestick makers were more receptive audiences, along with the constable, who shook his cudgel at the bigger boys and made the older girls shriek.

The choir had just finished "A Spotless Rose," when Mary felt a hand on her shoulder. She looked around in surprise, her fist raised, to see Thomas Jenkins.

He gave her fist a shake. "You're ferocious."

"You frightened me," she said honestly, and relaxed when he crooked out his arm and pulled her arm through. She looked at Beth, pleased to see Susan Davis walking alongside her daughter.

She stopped and turned to face him. "You are supposed to be at a boring, crowded party."

"I couldn't even get Suzie to go with me. Whatever charm I ever had must have been shot off in the war."

"Really, Mr. Jenkins," she murmured, happy to be towed along, even happier not to feel alone as she usually did on Christmas Eve, and discouraged and frightened at what the new year would bring.

"In fact, Suzie and I are here to kidnap the two of you and take you back to Plymouth for Christmas Day. We decided to start tonight, didn't we, Suzie?"

"We did," his sister said, "so there will be no disagreement. We have a pretty room for you and Beth, and my 'tween-stairs girl will have a fire lit."

"I daren't protest," Mary Ann said.

"I wouldn't," Suzie told her.

Two more houses and they were back at St. Luke's. While Beth drank her hot chocolate and the grownups enjoyed wassail, Mary Ann smiled to see Thomas clink enough coins in the collection box to make the vicar gasp.

"A naughty lad is Thomas, flaunting his alms before men." Suzie stood beside her. "I must scold him. Do you know, my dear, he bullied me to leave Cardiff and certain ruin and housekeep for him in Plymouth?"

"I'm not surprised," Mary Ann said. "Ruin?"

"I had the merest pittance from my husband and a house in need of repairs I could not afford," she whispered back, her eyes on her brother, who was talking to the vicar now. "He made the repairs, sold my house for a profit, tucked the money into some sort of fund for me, and spirited me away. He's that sort of brother."

He's that sort of friend, she thought.

She was too shy to walk beside Thomas Jenkins on the way home, busying herself with Beth, who didn't need any attention. At the house, it was pointless to argue with either brother or sister. She bundled up their nightgowns into a bandbox the former inhabitant of her three little rooms had left behind and tucked the watercolors under her arm, along with their gifts for each other, wrapped in brown paper.

The cake and beef came along, too.

She sat next to Thomas in the post chaise, too shy to speak, while Suzie and Beth carried on a more animated conversation across the narrow space dividing them.

"Cat got your tongue?" Thomas whispered in her ear as they began the descent into Plymouth.

His face was close to hers and she didn't mind. "Every year I think something might happen," she whispered back. "It finally did. I intend to enjoy tomorrow."

It was his turn to look away, and she wondered if she had offended him. His arm went around her shoulder next, so she didn't think he was too upset. Since the chaise was such a tight fit for four people, she naturally leaned into him, remembering that nice place under a man's arm where a smallish woman fit well. She closed her eyes, determined to remember every single minute of this evening and the next day.

The bedchamber was just as Suzie predicted, the walls painted a crisp white, with lace curtains, a fire in the grate, and a woolen comforter on the bed. Beth stared at Mary Ann and her eyes filled with tears. Mary Ann folded her child in her arms. "Let's just remember everything. It will keep us warm a long time."

Uncertain what to do after Beth slept, she went downstairs and into the sitting room she remembered. Thomas sat on the sofa with his shoes off, stocking feet propped on a hassock, reading his beloved Euclid, and Suzie wound a skein of yarn into a ball. She sat down next to Thomas and looked around at the room, which had been decorated with holly and ivy. A lace-covered table in front of the bow window held presents, so she excused herself, went upstairs, and came down with her few gifts, adding them to the pile.

She looked close at an apple on a tripod of twigs, stuffed with—she leaned closer for a sniff—cloves. Sticking from the top was a green sprig. She turned around to see Thomas watching her, a smile in his eyes and his finger stuck in Euclid.

"Go ahead. Pick it up," he told her, setting the book aside. "We're not so much for Welsh customs, but this one always reminds me of my childhood, what there was of it before the war."

She held up the apple, enjoying the fragrance. "What on earth is it?"

"*Calennig*," Suzie told her. "Little children like Beth take them around to the neighbors, sing, and get small candies in return for *calennig*."

"What is it for?" Mary Ann asked. She took another sniff.

"Fertility," Thomas said, and she set it down quickly as he started to laugh. He patted the sofa. "Join me."

She did as he asked, but not as close, which made him laugh some more. "For heaven's sake," she said finally, and slid closer. She turned her attention to Suzie, who was winding yarn again. "Are there any other Welsh customs I should know about? Your brother is disreputable."

"I know, I know," she soothed. "Nothing here beyond Welsh spoons and a kissing ball." She pointed to the mistletoe tied with red twine and hanging from the ceiling between the sitting room and the dining room. "Our 'tween-stairs girl is already trying to maneuver the constable's son in here for the kissing ball."

Mary Ann's face felt hot, even though the room was a pleasant temperature. There must be a massive change of subject somewhere, but all she saw were a brother and sister comfortable in their house and with each other.

"How did you get to sea?" she asked Thomas.

He put away the Euclid for good, his face serious almost in a night and day sort of way, after his good humor over *calennig*. "I owe it to my mam and Suzie," he said, and passed a hand across his eyes, as though it was a memory tender even now, after probably thirty years. She had no idea how old Thomas was.

"I was ten, and Da said it was time for me to go to the pit. He mined coal in Glamorganshire, like everyone else."

"That's young," she said, tucking her legs under her and leaning back. If they could be casual, so could she. The atmosphere seemed to require it here at 34 Notte Street.

"Not in a coal mine, ten isn't young. I was old enough to pick up the coal my father mined and put it in his numbered basket. Two weeks I was down there from black morning to black evening, and crying in my bed every night. Da was angry." He blew his sister a kiss. "What does Suzie do but conspire with our mam. I played sick one morning. After Da gave me a whipping and left, they scraped together a pound between them and my aunt next door and told me to run away to sea. I did."

"That's young, too," she murmured. "I suppose there is more to this story."

"Aye, lass," he told her, and touched one of her curls that had escaped from her widow's cap before he realized what he was doing. "Oh, sorry. There's more. I'll tell you some day, but look over there. Suzie is yawning."

She turned a little to face him. "Your father was a hard man."

"I thought so at first. I may have hated him for a while. He was a desperate man, my dear, trying to provide for a family. I understand him now, and I certainly don't hate him."

"Did he know of your success?" she asked.

"Aye, right before he died." He touched her hair again. "Your eyes are drooping."

She struggled to sit up and he helped her with his hand on the small of her back.

"Now if this were Wales, I would probably get up at three of the clock, stand in the hallway upstairs and sing hymns and carols. I won't."

"I wouldn't mind if you did," she said, shy again.

"Go to bed, Mary Ann. Think good things."

CHAPTER NINE

It wasn't three a.m., but she woke up to singing. Beth still slept next to her, so Mary Ann got out of bed carefully and opened the door a crack, because her shawl was still in the bandbox.

Brother and sister stood in the hallway, singing, "We Wish You a Merry Christmas." Mary Ann clapped her hands and opened the door wider. In another moment, Beth sat up and rubbed her eyes, then leaped out of bed. Mary Ann grabbed her before she could run downstairs and closed the door, after telling Thomas and Suzie they would dress quickly.

"You're going to like my present," Beth told Mary Ann as she buttoned her dress up the back.

"I always like what you get me," Mary Ann said, then knelt down so Beth could reach the one button in the middle of her back that she could not reach. She turned around and held her daughter close. They rocked back and forth, then Beth patted her cheek.

"It's going to be a good day. I say that every day, but I really mean it today."

Mary Ann kissed her and they went downstairs, hand in hand.

A fire burned in the sitting-room grate and the sky outside was as dark as it had been when she went to bed. Mary Ann thought of what Thomas had said last night about working from dark morning to dark evening. "What time is it?" she asked him.

"It is half five." He nudged his sister. "Suzie couldn't wait."

She nudged back and Mary Ann could have died right then with the loveliness of their camaraderie. "He lies! He was up and singing first." She went to the table of gifts. "I can't wait, Beth. This is for you."

Her eyes wide, her mouth a perfect circle, Beth took the box wrapped in tissue and tied with a red bow. She sat down as though her legs would not hold her, and Mary Ann sat beside her on the carpet. "You can open it," she whispered, when her daughter just sat there staring at the box.

"Pinch me, Mama," she said.

"No need. It's real, child," Thomas told her.

Beth gulped and carefully untied the string that looked like lace filigree. She set it aside and took off the paper. Barely breathing, she lifted the top off the box and took another breath and another.

Mary Ann felt her own breath come in little gasps as she watched her daughter pull a white rabbit fur muff from the box. Not raising her eyes from the lovely thing, Beth put her hands in the muff and leaned back against her mother. In another moment, Beth was in her arms, her face turned into her breast.

"Is it too much?" Suzie asked anxiously.

"A little. She'll be fine," Mary Ann said. She rubbed Beth's back until her daughter was calm again. "See there?"

"I bought her material for a new dress, too," Suzie said, "but this was more important." She reached over and took a smaller package off the table. "For you, Mary Ann Poole."

She felt tears start in her eyes, and wondered what would have happened if she had decided to mail the package back to S.M. Thomas Jenkins, instead of delivering it in person. A week had passed. No more than a week, and here she sat with a present in her lap.

Beth had returned her attention to the muff. Taking off the glittering twine as carefully as Beth had done, Mary Ann set it aside and unwrapped the tissue paper. There lay a copy of *Emma*.

With trembling fingers, she touched the raised lettering of the title, then looked lower to see her own name embossed on the cover. "Thank you from the bottom of my heart," she said, swallowing back more tears.

Beth handed her the brown-wrapped package they had brought from Haven, and Mary Ann opened her daughter's watercolor rendition of the book. She handed her gift of the watercolor muff to Beth, and they put their heads together and laughed.

"Beth, we have something for our hosts," she reminded her daughter.

Mary Ann got up from the floor and sat on the sofa beside Thomas again. "You are so kind to us," she said.

"I have not been bored in a week," he teased.

Beth handed the larger brown-wrapped, flat parcel to Suzie. "Happy Christmas, Mrs. Davis. It isn't so much after your gift, but it's something you can use in January."

Suzie unwrapped Beth's present and sat back, the picture of flowers in a vase in her lap. Her eyes filled with tears as she stared straight ahead at the fire in the grate, crackling away, making more noise than anything else in the room.

"A bouquet in January," she said softly.

Beth was leaning over her shoulder, then leaning against her. "Pansies, and Johnny-jump-ups, and daisies, although Mama says they are common."

"So are we, Beth," Suzie told her. "Roses, too?" She kissed Beth's cheek. "When I get in the doldrums and grouchy from January and February's endless rain, I have flowers."

Mary Ann felt almost too shy to hand her present to Thomas. She had stayed up late two nights ago and pondered it, which meant she had to find the proper scripture, just the right one for a man whose kindness filled her heart.

He took the picture from its holly and ivy sleeve and held it up so his sister could see. He said nothing, but Mary Ann noticed a muscle working in his cheek, and then his lips so tight.

"I . . . I know the River Tamar doesn't look anything like that now, not with the dockyards and shipping lanes," she said, keeping her voice soft because the room seemed almost holy just then. "It's the Tamar flowing into the sound, for when you . . . you go back to sea and you might miss us all just a little."

Suzie sat on the arm of the sofa, her hand on her brother's shoulder. "'He maketh the storm a calm, so that the waves thereof are still,'" she read. "'Then they are glad because they be quiet, so he bringeth them unto their desired haven.'"

He still said nothing. Suzie kissed his head. "It's the perfect gift for a sailing master, Tommy. Think of all the ships you have brought to their desired haven."

"No words, Mary Ann," he said finally, his voice sounding so strangled that Beth looked up from the muff. "No words. You couldn't have done a nicer thing."

"I wanted it to be just right," she said. "A little thank you for roast beef and cake and . . . I'm not certain what else."

She couldn't tell him what she really felt, how he had somehow stuffed the heart back in her chest and made her brave again. She still faced ruin, but she knew she could face it calmly, because somewhere in the wide world and across an ocean or two, someone had done a kind thing. It was too intimate and she had no call or cause to say any such thing. Thomas Jenkins's friendship was something to tuck in her heart and treasure through the rough times she knew were coming.

They ate breakfast in strange silence, but oddly companionable, passing around the dishes, going to the sideboard for more bacon. She poured Thomas more coffee when he held out his cup, and ate until she was full.

Thomas broke the unusual silence. He turned to her. "Get on your cloak, Mary Ann. We have to pay a visit. Beth, you help Suzie and Cook in the kitchen. I believe I smell turkey."

She asked no questions. In a few minutes they were on the street, walking west toward Devonport. He held out his arm for her. "Icy," he said, although there was no ice and she didn't need his help. She took it anyway, her mind a jumble.

They walked toward the docks now, right at the edge of Plymouth, where warehouses began. She looked at him, wondering, and saw his now-familiar smile, which relieved her heart.

He stopped in front of a warehouse with the gate open. She looked inside and saw wagons and carts in front of what looked like loading docks. She had never been anywhere like this. Over the wide gate was a sign. "Beazer and Son, Maritime Victuallers," she said. "Thomas, what is this place?"

"It's a highly successful business run by an old diamond in the rough name of Rob Beazer. The 'and Son' part is difficult, because his son died a few months ago." He pointed to a tidy-looking cottage next to the building. "Rob and Meggie live there. Rob said he would be inside the warehouse."

She wanted to pelt him with questions, but she decided to hold her tongue and trust the man. He had her by the hand now. She gave his hand a squeeze, whether to reassure him or her, she did not know. Startled, he looked down at her and squeezed back.

They went inside the warehouse, which smelled of dried herring, coffee beans, leather, salt pork and other pungent odors she could not identify. Sitting at a tall table midway through the building was a little man who looked up when they came closer. He hopped off the high stool and just stood there. Mostly he looked at her.

"Mrs. Poole, this is Rob Beazer. He has been providing quality victuals through at least one long war," Thomas said. He took a deep breath. "He needs a clerk and I have brought you here. Rob, meet Mrs. Mary Ann Poole."

What have you done, Thomas Jenkins? she thought, dazed with the magnitude of his concern for her. With the fumbled delivery of a package, her life had undergone a sea change.

But here was Rob Beazer, holding out his hand. She was ready to curtsy, but she gave him a firm handshake instead.

"I'm going to stand over here by the window and you two can talk," Thomas said.

Her first instinct was to ask him to stay close by, but this was business and he knew it. So did she. If she entered this man's world, she had to prove herself. Drawing herself up, clasping her hands at her waist so they would not tremble, she told Mr. Robert Beazer what she knew of handling correspondence and filing, and doing rudimentary bookkeeping. She assured him she was never late to work and she could put in whatever hours he required.

"I would imagine yours is a business where flexibility is a virtue," she said. "You probably need to receive goods at all hours, and disburse them in similar fashion, considering tides and all that."

"It was worse during the war," he told her. "There were days when Meggie brought my meals here and I slept on a cot by the loading door. I don't miss those days. You could do that sort of thing, if needed?"

"I could. I have a daughter who is seven, but she is reliable." She glanced at Thomas, whose eyes were on her. "Mr. Jenkins can vouch for her mathematical abilities, too, even though she is young. I would probably like her to check my figures." She smiled then, suddenly at ease. "Perhaps yours, too, sir."

He laughed at that, and then he was silent. He stepped back as though to observe her more carefully. She stood straight and as tall as she could make herself.

"I've never hired a female clerk," he said finally. "No one on the dock has, to my knowledge. Would you be uncomfortable working around men? You're such a pretty lady."

"I am a widow trying to support my daughter," she replied. "My husband died at Corunna and I need this job."

"No drinking? No swearing?" he asked, and she could tell he was teasing her.

"Never," she said, biting off the word. "I write with a bold hand and my penmanship is probably better than any man's."

He turned and walked away, and her heart sank. *I will not cry when he turns me down*, she thought, and put her hands behind her back because they were shaking too much. She would have given the earth just then for Thomas Jenkins to put his arm around her, but this was her interview, her moment.

Beazer stood a moment by the front door. She thought she heard him talking to himself. He turned suddenly and walked back, taking his time, but his step was firm. When he stopped in front of her, he held out his hand again.

"Done and done, Mrs. Poole."

They shook hands. He grinned up at her and put both of his hands around hers. "You're shaking like a leaf, Mrs. Poole."

"I've never been so terrified," she admitted.

Still holding both her hands in his, he told what he would pay weekly. It wasn't any more than what she'd earned before, and she wondered how expensive lodgings were in Plymouth. Maybe he would let her grow a little garden in a corner of the compound, anything to stay here.

"I also need to find a place to live," she told him. "Until I do, I can walk from Haven. It's not that far."

He released her hand and slapped his head. "I'm getting daft in my old age, Mrs. Poole!" He pointed over his head, and then to a door. "Thomas, my knees are creaky. Take Mrs. Poole upstairs and show her the little flat. Two bedchambers, a kitchen and a sitting room, and it comes with the job."

She gasped and put her hands to her mouth, tried to talk and failed.

"You'll start December twenty-seventh? Seven o'clock to six in the evening, Monday through Saturday noon, or whenever you might be needed. I provide your noon meal, too. Meggie loves to cook."

"Aye, sir," she managed to say.

He made a shooing motion. "Take her upstairs, Tommy! Give me your address in Haven, Mrs. Poole, and I'll send one of my carters 'round tomorrow to pick up your effects." He bowed, a funny little bow from a man who would never be mistaken for a gentleman, but who had just changed her life. "I'm going home to my dinner now. Just leave your direction on the desk. That'll be *your* desk, by the way."

He turned around. "I have a big black bruiser of a hound that patrols the compound at night. Between you and me, he is a soft old brute, and your daughter will love him, but he looks like Beelzebub himself. You'll be safe here, and I'm right next door."

She followed Thomas up the flight of stairs, and walked, open-mouthed, through four spacious rooms, already furnished, right down to dishes in the cupboard.

"I suspect that his son lived here until his final illness," Thomas said. "Rugs on the floor, too. What do you think, Mrs. Poole?"

Hang professionalism. Hang serenity. Mary Ann burst into tears and threw herself into his open arms. She sobbed until he picked her up, walked through the connecting rooms as she wailed, and sat down with her on the sofa. She cried until her tears had soaked through his waistcoat to his shirt underneath, but he didn't complain.

He found a handkerchief when her nose started to run, and made her blow it. He folded it over and gave it to her. "Happy Christmas," was all he said, but it set her off again, which made him laugh and hold her closer.

After she had subsided to an occasional sob when she breathed, she sat up and tried to dab at his shirt.

"When was the last time you cried, Mrs. Poole?" he asked gently, taking her hands away.

"When I watched them bury Bart," she said.

"Don't wait so long next time," was all he said, before he held her close again and sat with her in silence.

CHAPTER TEN

Two days later at seven in the morning she started work as victualling clerk for Robert Beazer and Son. Their few clothes and possessions were arranged in the upstairs rooms, and a monstrous geriatric hound possessing few teeth but a fearsome bark already followed Beth everywhere.

When he stopped by to check on them a day later, Thomas told her to keep Beth by her side for a few days, maybe a week. "I'm going to London today, first to the Navy Board, to beg and plead and grovel for a ship's berth. After that—and I intend to be successful—I'm going to Trinity House, where I will not leave until the Elder Brothers agree to install Beth at St. Clements."

"You amaze me," she said. "You did all this because you were bored?"

"Aye, Mary Ann, and a monumental boredom it was," he assured her, sounding more Welsh than usual, which amused her. "Suzie is not at all happy with me running away to the sea again. I have bullied her into keeping my house open, because I'll be in port now and again. By the way, she wants you to come to dinner tonight. She'll probably tell you awful tales about me, but she'll get over it."

He was about to leave, then turned back, reaching for something in his waistcoat pocket. She sucked in her breath when he pulled out her mother's gold chain. "How did you know?" she asked, taking it from him.

"Suzie and I were afraid you were going to spend your money on watercolors and walk back to Haven in the dark," he explained. "I followed you and saw you in the stationery store. Hand it to me."

She did as he said, wordless as he looped it over her head and opened the clasp. She closed her eyes, memorizing the feel of his breath on her neck, hoping she would remember it forever.

"I'll pay you back over time," she said. "It belonged to my mother."

"It's a Christmas gift," he told her. "You can't pay me for it."

She turned around to face him. "Is there any point in arguing with you?"

"None that I know of," he said cheerfully.

She walked him to the door of the warehouse and gave him a kiss on one cheek, and then the other. "From Beth and me," she said simply.

He stared long and hard at her, as though he wished to say something, but he gave a gusty sigh instead. He walked away without looking back, which made her heart crack around the edges just a little.

She had no more time to think about him, because Mr. Beazer kept her busy, showing her how to do double entry bookkeeping, and explaining the details of running such a massive operation. To her relief, Beth watched intently on her other side, so she knew she had an ally, should she forget something important.

She followed Mr. Beazer through the warehouse, tablet in hand, as he pointed out where everything from salt to salt pork was stashed. To her relief, he cast a murderous glare on his warehouse employees and carters, threatening them with transportation to Australia if they so much as looked cross-eyed at the Poole ladies.

Luncheon with Meggie Beazer was pure delight. The food was good, and the woman kept up a constant chatter while Mr. Beazer sat back, puffed on his pipe and watched his wife with no small affection.

Hand in hand, Mary Ann walked with Beth to 34 Notte Street after work and discovered with a pang that the house seemed devoid of furniture, rugs, pictures, and knickknacks because Thomas Jenkins wasn't there.

I don't like this, she thought, distressed at the loneliness that filled her entire body and brain. She had been too busy to think about anything but work, but Thomas was gone.

Suzie didn't look too pleased, either, and she said so. "Little brothers are a trial," she told Beth. "Be grateful you don't have one."

There must be something she could salvage from what had turned into a dismal evening. "We need to be happy that he knows what he wants and is headed to sea again," Mary Ann said, feeling like the last cricket of summer chirping alone on the hearth.

Suzie stood up and paced back and forth. "That's the trouble, my dear. He has no idea what he wants!" She plumped herself down again. "Do you?"

"*Me?*" Mary Ann stared at her and felt heat rush up her body to bloom on her face. "Do I know what he wants, or . . . or . . ." She couldn't even say it. *Do I know what I want?*

By the time they had walked back to the warehouse, she had a headache that threatened to crack her skull open, and the undeniable, uneasy conviction that she loved Thomas Jenkins to complete and utter distraction.

She couldn't even compose her mind to tell Beth one of her patented prince and princess bedtime tales. They said their prayers, then lay side by side, both of them staring at the ceiling.

"I miss him," Beth said finally in a small voice. "Do you?"

Mary Ann nodded, knowing that if she said a word, she would cry again, which would be no fun at all, because Thomas wasn't there to sit her on his lap.

When Beth slept, Mary Ann walked through her lovely flat—employed, well-fed, and discontented beyond all limits. Had she been this miserable when she knew she loved Bart Poole? Surely not. What was different this time?

She was different—Mary Ann Poole, a grown woman, with a grown woman's needs and desires and not a green girl. She had found the most wonderful man in the world for her twice now, and she wanted to thrash this one into February for thinking he needed the stupid old ocean.

I am an idiot, she thought, then said it out loud, to remind herself that he had done her an enormous favor because he was bored. That was it. He was affectionate to her because that was part of his gregarious nature. He was there when she needed him, and he had solved all of her problems and left a bigger one behind.

She loved him.

When Thomas Jenkins, sailing master retired no longer, came out of the Navy Board office after two days of intense discussion, he wondered why he was not so pleased. He looked around, finding no pleasure in London, which surprised him, because he enjoyed the bustle of the metropolis occasionally.

The HMS *Revenge* was a new-built frigate 44, slid off the ways and waiting for sails and sheets in the Portsmouth ship yard. He was to report there in two weeks, orders in hand, and do what he did better than almost any master in the entire Royal Navy.

He should have been leaping like a gibbon from street lamp to street lamp, overjoyed to be reinstated and preparing to sail again. The rigging would take a month, as the ship was victualed and prepared for sea. The shakedown cruise was to the United States and back, carrying a diplomatist to half-burned Washington, DC.

If the *Revenge* proved shipshape, he would consult with Captain Frears, an old friend, and they would set a course for Rio de Janeiro. He'd be gazing up at the Southern Cross again, one of his favorite constellations. The plan was to venture around the Horn and follow the Pacific coastline of the United States, trying to see just how far the reach of that upstart bunch of quarrelsome colonies had advanced. Frears said to plan on a year's voyage, which would be heaven, indeed, since no one would be throwing cannonballs their way or plotting other evils.

He knew he should feel better, but all he could think of was the way Mary Ann Poole, tears and all, had fit so nicely on his lap. And when she leaned against him and soaked his shirt—mercy, but she felt so soft and bendable in all the right places.

He was way too old to be dreaming about Mary Ann like this, wasn't he? And who could sleep thinking about her employment, and was she safe in an empty warehouse at night, and would she maybe write him if he asked her?

The next day he talked to his shaving mirror, his old friend, and reminded the man in the mirror with bags under his eyes that Trinity House was going to bend to his will and let Beth Poole attend St. Clement's School in Plymouth. He had a draft for two hundred pounds from Carter and Brustein Counting House in Plymouth to sweeten the deal and make them somehow overlook that Second Lieutenant Bart Poole, as dead as a man could be in service to his nation, was army.

He did have some satisfying moments at Trinity House, pleased to learn of the expansion of a school for navigators working primarily in the unpredictable waters of the North Atlantic. He had some ideas to contribute that brought pleasant smiles to the faces of men he admired, those Elder Brothers of Trinity House who did their monumental work so quietly and so well, even if most Englishmen were none the wiser about all their unsung achievements.

Maybe he knew just enough of the Elders to grease a wheel or two. After only one day of arguing on Beth Poole's behalf, he was handed a letter allowing her admission to St. Clement's, where he knew she would be taught well, if the mathematics teacher could keep up.

After that day's effort, and even less sleep that night because Mary Ann Poole simply refused to stay out of his dreams, he had achieved precisely what he set out to do in London.

Without question, he was the most miserable happy man of recent acquaintance.

Thomas dragged himself back to his hotel in the pelting rain, ready to growl and snap if anyone on the crowded street bumped into him. He had his orders to report to the *Revenge* in a fortnight and a letter of admission to give to Mary Ann for Beth. True, he was two hundred pounds poorer, but that hardly mattered. Beth was worth that and more. He should have been floating on little fairy wings.

He kicked off his shoes and flopped on his bed, discouraged beyond everything he had ever experienced. This was even worse than peace breaking out. Maybe he was so tired tonight that he wouldn't think of Mary Ann Poole, and her pretty blond hair and dark eyes, and hint of a dimple in her right cheek, and soft skin and little waist, and her courage and virtue and resourcefulness and love of her daughter, her gallantry and kindness to her old landlord and her love of cake and her way of making him laugh.

I could never be so tired that I would not think of Mary Ann, he told himself, and realized his problem, because underneath it all, he was a fairly intelligent man. Mrs. Poole had cured his boredom and then made herself indispensable.

He loved her.

Lying on his back, he reached for his orders to the *Revenge*. He read through the formal, familiar words of "requested and required to join the HMS *Revenge*." He thought of the ships he had sailed straight and true, the battles he had fought, and the exorbitantly high cost of war. He realized with perfect clarity now that he had not been able to move beyond that cost until he saw Mary Ann Poole in his sitting room with an opened package in her hands.

They are not going to be happy when I show up tomorrow morning at the Navy Board, he thought. After one more long look, he put the orders back in the envelope, never to open them or any like them again. He was about to burn his last bridge with the Royal Navy. He waited for the knowledge to cause him pain, but it didn't.

After a breakfast of bacon, eggs, and black pudding, Thomas Jenkins walked to the Admiralty, reneged on those orders, and received a massive reaming out from the Navy Board. The officer in charge tore his orders into little bits of confetti and tossed them out the window, which seemed a bit dramatic to Thomas.

In the privacy of his office, Thomas told his only friend remaining on the Board what had precipitated this decision. The man laughed until he had to loosen his neckcloth. When he calmed down, he told Thomas precisely who to speak to at Chancery Court and wished him well. "Bring her around here when you're next in London," his friend said as he slapped his back and gave him a shove toward the door. "If she is as pretty as you say, the other board members won't lob too many marlinspikes and shells in your direction."

The next matter was accomplished before lunch and left him lighter in the pocket book, but he couldn't help smiling, even though it was raining again. Some Londoners walking by him on the street seemed not to have recovered fully from Twelfth Night. *What a sour bunch*, he thought, then had the honesty to remind himself that he had looked even worse yesterday, before his epiphany.

He planned only to stay a few minutes at Trinity House to pick up the voucher for Beth, but he was collared by a delegation of Elder Brothers who sat him down and made his life complete.

He had to stare a minute and shake his head to make sure he understood what they were proposing. "You want *me* to serve as headmaster for the navigational school?" he asked.

They were patient; they were kind. Yes, that was precisely what they wanted, and named a salary that made him start to sweat. They sweetened it further with a furnished house and servants right here in London. To his query about good schools for a young girl, they just chuckled and assured him he need not fear on that stead.

"Of course, you will take your students out on occasional cruises to the Baltic to test their skills, but that is nothing," the principal Elder Brother said. "Yeah or nay, Master Jenkins?"

He slept the sleep of the reasonably virtuous on the post chaise from London to Plymouth, despite the roll and dip, or maybe because of it. He understood motion better than most men. Mary Ann cavorted through his dreams and bothered him not a whit.

He arrived a day later and had the post riders drop him off at Beazer and Son. Rob Beazer stood at the lading dock, and hurried over to tell him what a jewel Mrs. Poole was. Thomas listened, nodded, and wondered just how long the old fellow would hate him when he spirited Mary Ann away to London. The telling could wait until he knew how the wind blew.

Fully clothed and not in the shift of his dreams, Mary Ann sat at the tall desk. He smiled to see that she had dropped one shoe and the other one was about to come off. She was writing in a ledger and dabbing at her eyes with her apron. He wondered if she had a cold.

"Mary Ann."

She looked up, her eyes huge in her face. She got off the tall stool and didn't bother with her shoes.

"Did . . . did you get a ship?" she asked, her voice barely audible, even though he stood close to her now.

He nodded and she began to sob. He touched her shoulder and she shook him off. "I'm so happy for you," she wailed.

"I turned it down."

She blew her nose on her apron, the only thing handy, and stared at him.

"I couldn't go to sea and leave you behind. I'm forty-three," he added, and felt like a fool. "I absolutely love you."

"I'm thirty-two and I don't care how old you are, Thomas Jenkins. I love you, too."

That tall desk was no place to propose, so he took her hand and towed her to a wooden crate with *dried herring* stenciled on it in large letters. He sat her on it, and himself beside her. He took three documents from his coat pocket, and handed them to her one at a time.

The first was the voucher for Beth to enroll at St. Clement's School. She nodded her head. "She will make us proud."

Us? he thought and felt delight cover him like warm tropical rain, the kind found at about twenty-three degrees and twenty-six minutes in the Tropic of Cancer.

Next he handed her the letter of appointment from Trinity House. She read it, then read it again, her breath coming in little gasps until he told her to breathe deeply.

"I'll be at sea occasionally on training cruises," he explained. He pointed to one of the closing paragraphs. "They already took me by our house. You'll like it."

"I will if you're in it," she told him, which made years of war and disappointment and terror and exhaustion fall right off him like discarded clothing.

He handed her the last document, which made her smile and nod. "We probably can wait for three weeks and cry banns," she said, practical to the end. "I've heard that special licenses are expensive."

"Twenty guineas plus a four-pound stamp," he told her. "I am now an expert."

She gasped.

"I am *not* waiting three weeks. I told you I was forty-three!"

That must have satisfied her because she kissed him. She wasn't any better at it than he was, but they had a lifetime to achieve perfection. What she did excel in was the way she slid her hand inside his waistcoat.

"Will you marry me tomorrow morning, Mary Ann?" he asked. "In romantic January snuggle weather?"

"Will Beth be disappointed about St. Clement's?" he asked when she finished kissing him, getting better already.

"You'll find something equally good in London for her, my love," she said. She was in a position to look over his shoulder. "Oh, dear. Here is who will be disappointed."

He turned around to see Rob Beazer coming toward them, passing a cudgel from one hand to the other. "Perhaps you can find him another clerk," Mary Ann whispered in his ear. "Really soon."

As a man who had also worked his way to success from the bottom, Thomas knew that a man didn't achieve the running of a major business in a competitive town without considerable shrewdness. He also knew that if he were running said corporation and saw his new clerk sitting on a crate of dried herring cuddling with a man, that a fulsome explanation might be in order. He stood up, quite prepared for such an explanation.

Thomas began with no preamble, because he knew Rob Beazer well. After all, a man doesn't spend hours in such a warehouse, going over bills of lading and inspecting cargo without developing a friendship, which in this case was about to be stretched to the limit. "Rob, I have bad news for you."

"You are marrying my new clerk and stealing her away," Rob said. At least he had quit tossing the cudgel from hand to hand.

Might as well brazen it out. "Tomorrow morning. I have a special license. I am, I . . ."

Rob dropped the weapon. With barely suppressed glee, he clapped his hands on Thomas's arms. "I just won five pounds," he declared. "I wagered Meggie that you would not waste a minute in stealing my clerk. She said Mary Ann would make you wait for banns. Shake my hand, Master Jenkins."

They shook hands. "How did you know?" Thomas asked, not certain if he was more amused or more relieved.

"You never saw your face when you brought this lovely lady here on Christmas Day. I watched you while she and I talked and settled the matter."

"My face?"

"In this business, I have learned to read people. I know a liar when I see one, and I know a determined man, too." He glanced at Mary Ann. "I think now that I know what a man looks like when he is in love." He chuckled. "Never thought to see it here among the herring and navy beans, though."

"You amaze me, Rob Beazer," Thomas said. "I thought that all I wanted on Christmas Day was to fulfill an obligation to my sister after complaining about boredom."

Rob shook his head. "T'wasn't what I saw!" He gestured to Mary Ann, who joined them, holding out her hands to both men. "How simple is man," he told her as he grasped her hand. "Mary Ann, I'm going to have to sack you."

She kissed her employer's cheek. "Bless you," she whispered.

"I'll find another clerk." He put her hand in Thomas's. "Take good care of each other."

He turned to Thomas. "As for you . . ."

It was no threat. "Bless you, Rob," Thomas echoed. "Saint Andrews tomorrow morning at eight of the clock, and bring Meggie, of course."

"Thomas, we have until noon, according to the license," Mary Ann said, an efficient secretary to the end, apparently.

"I know, my love. Remember? I am forty-three."

Faithfully Yours

It all started with a letter. No reason it wouldn't end with one.

Nothing much exciting ever happened in Dumfries, Scottish market town in the old kingdom of Galloway. It prospered because of its fishing fleet and English visitors, who came to appreciate its handsome stone houses and tidy businesses, located on the lovely River Nith.

This story begins in 1818 with two young ladies, one the daughter of a local merchant who had become quite comfortable through business dealings, cod, and herring. The merchant may have been actually wealthy, but there is something in the Presbyterian water of Scotland that calls bragging a sin.

The other young lady is Sally Wilson, only child of Dumfries' minister of the Church of Scotland, retired now from the pulpit. Such a man would never be wealthy, but he would be respected. So was his daughter.

Ten years before the beginning of this story, Margaret Patterson, daughter of the wealthy merchant, had informed a young man that she would write to him, as he sailed across the Atlantic to make his fortune in Canada. She had done it as a dare from her equally silly friends.

She shouldn't have teased John McPherson like this. In John's defense, he hadn't thought that any gently reared young lady would ever write to a man not her husband or fiancé. Youngest son of the disreputable, unwelcome McPhersons, John was dubious Margaret would reply. He only agreed to her forward scheme because who doesn't like to get letters?

Margaret confided in Sally Wilson that she had no intention of writing to someone as lowly as John McPherson, which horrified Sally, who did not approve of such casual cruelty. To spare John further humiliation, she agreed to write in Margaret's place, using Margaret's name.

Who understands the minds of young people? Not anyone in Scotland, any more than anyone in England. Maybe things are different in France or Italy, but this is not a story of those people.

That's enough to know as this Christmas tale begins.

On a typical day, Sally Wilson found that from the time she called the village school to order, to the time she bade her little pupils good day, every minute overflowed with arithmetic, penmanship, composition, and improving works.

This day dragged because just before Sally went outside to call her students in, Margaret Patterson dropped off the latest letter from John McPherson.

"I can't stay," Margaret said. "Besides, you are about to call the class to order, and I have so many details yet to work out for my wedding." She waved a ringed hand in Sally's general vicinity. "Sally, you can't imagine everything I have to do!" she tittered behind her glove. "How could you know? You don't have a sweetheart."

Another wave of the ringed hand, and she was gone in the family carriage, probably to track down a pint each of eye of newt and toe of frog for the groom's cake, as Sally's father liked to tease.

Sally took the letter, admiring, as always, John McPherson's impeccable penmanship. For a man who came from a rough family, he had somehow absorbed educational truths as well as life lessons. She remembered him sitting by himself in his poor clothes, seldom washed, in the vicarage school, the one that had become the village school where she taught today. No one ever wanted to sit near him because he reeked. Since her minister father taught the school, he asked her to befriend the lonely lad.

And so Sally had become friends enough with Johnny to know that his mother was dead, leaving no one to see to the washing, ironing. and mending that all the rackety McPherson boys lacked. Sally understood why he smelled so vile, and in the understanding, became a friend.

Had it been ten years since he left Scotland? Sally swept out her classroom and banked the fire. She glanced at the well-traveled letter on her desk, putting off the pleasure of sharing John's glimpse of a new world, and his own efforts surviving in that land of snakes and Indians, and even prospering, if the expensive paper was any indication.

As much as she enjoyed writing to John in Margaret's place, Sally felt a twinge of conscience at duping a well-meaning friend. Ten years older and wiser now, she regretted pretending she was Margaret in the letters she wrote to John. At first, she tried to talk about John's letters to Margaret, but her friend just waved her hand and said she had no time for someone as insignificant as John McPherson.

Hardly anyone in Dumfries received letters, and these were letters from Canada first and the United States now. For a few years she asked herself why Margaret didn't at least read them.

After a decade of writing to John McPherson, pretending to be someone else, Sally had grown in introspection as well as maturity. The Margaret Patterson who had petitioned the more reserved and malleable Sally Wilson to write those letters had become a vain creature, a spoiled one, and a social climber.

Perhaps Margaret had always suffered from those defects, but Sally preferred to give her sometime-friend the benefit of the doubt. She was a generous soul and it *was* Christmas, when one was supposed to overlook pettiness and concentrate on giving, instead of making note of general nastiness.

When she had done everything except put on her cloak and bonnet, Sally sat down, slit the envelope and pulled out a letter that had been sent three months earlier, according to the barely visible postmark. After it had been read several times and answered, this letter would join the others in a pasteboard box labeled Doctor Meacham's Restorative Tonic, and shoved under her bed. She had never thrown out any of John's letters, preferring to read them over and over, and contemplate the writer who had changed mightily in ten years.

In fact, the earliest letters, desperate affairs telling of cold and hunger and ill use as he ventured into Canada's interior to trap beaver, were written on such cheap paper that they needed to be copied onto better paper. The few days' break at Christmas would be a good opportunity to do that. She had worn them out with reading.

She stared at the folded letter, remembering two awful years during those ten when she had heard nothing and finally given him up for dead. Even now, she couldn't help the tears that welled in her eyes, remembering her prayers then her anger that such a nice man should die alone in a strange country. Finally she had resigned herself to the will of God, since the matter was in omnipotent hands anyway—at least that's what Papa said. And besides that, she was writing for Margaret Patterson and not Sally Wilson, who could only anguish in private and pray for John McPherson's safety.

She slid the letter back into the envelope, deciding to read it at home after supper. Since there were usually only three letters a year, she had schooled herself to savor them, because the next one would be a long time coming. Lately she had been writing once a month, telling him Dumfries news, which meant stretching out even the most trivial detail, since Dumfries was a quiet town. She could only assume that when he did get mail, it accumulated in a pile for him to read.

She locked the school door behind her and walked slowly home, pausing as usual at the bridge over River Nith that separated the east side of Dumfries from the west. Accompanied by its usual cloud of seagulls, the fishing fleet was tying up and preparing to sling the day's catch to the wharf, where the poor women who scaled, gutted, and filleted the fish were even now readying their knives.

Several of her students' mothers saw her on the bridge and waved. Sally waved back, happy to teach their children and perhaps, if they were lucky and sharp, school them for something better than gutting fish.

She walked slowly through Dumfries, nodding to her friends, stopping to chat with other parents, and smiling at the students. Released from school only an hour ago, they were working behind counters and helping their families.

Her days were predictable and unerring. She thought of John McPherson, breaking free from the deadly cycle of other McPhersons, who fished a little, ran a few cattle—hopefully their own—smuggled French brandy, and scratched a meager meal or two from exhausted soil, as their fathers before them had done. In spite of family skepticism and a certain amount of disdain from others, John had set out to seek his fortune at eighteen years old, far away from his useless kinfolk.

At least he was a man and at liberty to break away. *Here I remain*, Sally thought, and not for the first time. *Too bad that ladies cannot seek their fortune, too.* She saw no change in her future, not at twenty-four, with only a modest dowry. The story might have been different, were she beautiful enough to allow a man to overlook the deficiency of a skimpy marriage portion.

She was hardworking and ordinary, with no glaring defects, but no soaring beauty beyond kind eyes. On the bright side, she would never lack for employment, and the house would be hers when her father died. *Is that all?* she asked herself there on the bridge. *Tell me that isn't all.*

She put off the letter, deciding to save it for herself alone. She could tell her father over breakfast what John had said. She knew from long experience Papa would advise her to end this deception and send the man a letter explaining just who has written the letters he thought came from Margaret. Ministers were like that.

Better to let her father talk through supper, even though he was retired from the ministry and seldom ventured much before their doorstep now. She knew he had little to tell her, beyond what he had read in Bartell's *Confessions of a Penitent Sinner*, or some other tract or treatise. She would listen through supper, drink a small cup of negus with him in the sitting room later, then make her way to bed, another day done, one much like the day before, except for John's occasional letters.

So it was that she made herself comfortable in bed, cap on her head, warming pan at her feet, and opened the letter.

She couldn't help observing that the stationery was even more expensive this time, too heavy to see through as she held it to the lantern light, and possessing a watermark. On a whim, she reached under her bed, pulled out the Restorative Tonic box and reached for the earliest, most fragile letter, written on scraps, but still signed *Faithfully Yours*.

"You have come so far, my dear," she whispered, even though Papa snored in the bedchamber across the hall and couldn't have heard a black bear trundle through—black bears that John had described in some detail during those first few years in Canada.

She carefully replaced the old letter and hunkered down in bed to read the new one, pretending, as usual, that John McPherson was her fiancé. She knew it was a harmless diversion, but one that she would never divulge to another soul.

She read slowly and with growing delight, relishing the words. John described his promotion to assistant purveyor of furs to John Jacob Astor—a German immigrant, Sally had learned in a previous letter, who had come to American shores with ten dollars and a suitcase of clarinets to sell. This had strangely led to trade in furs, and then real estate, hence the Fifth Avenue address. Apparently there was no end to what even a musician could achieve.

Margaret, I have a place of my own here in New York City, Sally read. *It's been ten long years. I can finally say that the wisest thing I ever did was to leave Dumfries and seek my fortune.*

She settled lower in her bed, reading of his only occasional trips now into America's interior on flatboat and by canoe. Generally, he signed off on great packs of beaver and buffalo robes floated down the Missouri to St. Louis, where they were sorted, then taken overland to New York City. The final destination was the Paris and Frankfort markets, now that the long war had ended and commerce could return safely. *We are even negotiating to sell buffalo robes to Czar Alexander, to make overcoats for his troops,* John wrote.

As always, Sally read between the lines, savoring the confidence that nearly leaped out of the page at her—well, at Margaret. She put down the letter, thinking of her last sight of John McPherson, ragged duffel slung over his shoulder, as he left Dumfries sitting on the back of a hay wain heading toward Carlisle. She had waved to him, and he had smiled back. No one else had seen him off. Even then, through his dirty clothes and hair in need of cutting, she had seen confidence burning in his eyes.

"Good for you, John," she told the words before her.

She picked up the last page of his lengthy letter, gulped, and read it again. "Oh, no," she said. "Oh, no."

Luckily the next day was Saturday and no school. Sally doubted that Margaret ever woke up early, but she didn't care. Letter tight in hand, she marched up the tree-lined lane, bare of leaves now in winter, and right to the front door.

As she waited for the footman to answer her knock, Sally tried to recall the last time she had visited the Patterson home and found she could not. *We were never friends,* she thought in dismay. *I let you use me.*

The footman opened the door, fixing her with a frosty stare. One would think he didn't often see young persons at his doorstep so early, especially someone with hair twisted into a careless knot and left there to languish.

"The servants' entrance is around back," he said, and tried to shut the door.

Fearing just this brush-off, Sally had worn her sturdy shoes, one of which she stuck in the door as it started to close. "I am Sally Wilson, a good friend of Miss Patterson," she said, which meant the door widened a little. "My father was the min—"

"Miss Wilson, I recommend that you come around at a more appropriate ti—"

Another hand flung the door open wide, grabbed Sally, and yanked her inside. "That will do, Reston," Margaret Patterson snapped. "Go away!"

Sally was at least relieved to see that Margaret looked no better than she did. In fact, she looked worse, with dark smudges under her eyes, and a pinched look to her mouth. She couldn't help thinking that the dignified Mr. Mallory, who was going to marry Margaret in a few days, was in for a real surprise the morning after the wedding.

With unexpected strength, Margaret towed Sally up the stairs and dragged her into her bedchamber. Giving Sally no time to catch her breath, she thrust a single sheet of paper under Sally's nose. "I am ruined!" she declared.

Sally held the sheet away from her face so she could read it. "'My dear Margaret,'" she read out loud. "'I'm in Bristol right now and have only to arrange a post chaise to Dumfries. I am eager to see you and talk to your father. Yours faithfully . . .'"

Margaret snatched the sheet back and tore it into tiny bits of confetti. "Don't read it out loud! What are we to do?"

Sally thought about putting John's much-larger letter under Margaret's nose, but changed her mind. Beyond the obvious truth that all this was Margaret's doing, she had a question of her own.

"Margaret, you haven't read a single letter ever," she said. "Why this little note now?"

Margaret was busy in tossing the note out the window, all hundred pieces of it now, maybe thinking that the wind would blow it away and end the dilemma. Sally could have told her that troubles don't vanish like that, but she reckoned it was a little late to inject life lessons into Margaret's woefully slender frame of reference.

"Seriously, Margaret, why now?"

Margaret plumped herself down on her unmade bed. She glared at Sally, then pulled back the coverlets and crawled underneath. The blanket went over her head.

Felling ruthless, Sally yanked off the blanket and posed her question again.

"You'll think I am an idiot," came a small voice somewhere between the sheet and a wool blanket.

I already do, Sally thought. "I'm just curious. I tried to get you to read John's letters and you refused. Why now?"

Silence, then, "Those other letters you pushed at me were so *big*. So many pages! So many words! I was busy, Sally. This was just a little sheet." She pulled the coverlet over her head again. "It came by express last night."

Then, "I was so hoping that cannibals would eat him and no one would know that I had talked the gawky nobody into writing me. What was I thinking?"

Back went the coverlet again. Sally sat down on the bed beside her friend. "Margaret, he was in Canada, and then later in New York City. Cannibals eat people in the South Pacific!"

"How am I to know that?" came a sulky voice.

Paying attention in school wouldn't have hurt, Sally thought. And now John McPherson was coming to see a young lady who hadn't ever written to him. If she hadn't been so disgusted with Margaret and herself, she would have found it funny.

"You have to make a clean breast of it and tell him what you did," Sally said.

"I can't!"

"You had better," Sally told her, pulling back the coverlet again. "Suppose your fiancé gets wind of this?" *Just send John to me*, Sally thought suddenly, and the heart went out of her.

"My fiancé! I had forgotten all about him!" The sheet came away and Sally stared into Margaret's stricken eyes. Her friend grabbed her hand. "Sally, I will tell John McPherson that you had wanted to write to him all along and were too shy. I was being kind to a friend."

Trust Margaret to concoct a scenario favorable to her. "That won't do," Sally said.

"It will if I say so."

Sally sank down beside her friend, wishing she had never agreed to write Margaret's letters, and at the same time, grateful she had been part of John's North American adventure. Without even knowing it, he had opened a window on a wider world she knew existed, but which she never thought to see, except through someone else's eyes. *I can be philosophical*, she told herself, even as she wanted to push Margaret aside and pull the coverlets up, too. She took Margaret's hands in hers.

"He's going to come here, and you are going to tell him the truth," she said, using her teacher voice as though she were advising an eight-year-old, which somehow seemed appropriate. "He'll be humiliated and leave Dumfries as soon as he can. Your fiancé will never know, and we will regret having played such a deception on a good man."

It sounded reasonable. It sounded rational, but oh, the pain in her heart. She knew it had to be impossible to fall in love with someone through a handful of widely spaced letters. Once John heard the worst from Margaret, he wouldn't linger in Dumfries longer than to see his ramshackle relatives—if any still lived—and be grateful he got out with a whole skin.

"It's only John McPherson," Margaret said with a sniff, her expression militant now. "No McPherson has ever amounted to anything."

Tired of Margaret Patterson, Sally rose to go. "You started this and you can settle it."

"You are no friend," Margaret snapped. "Kindly do not bother to show up at my wedding."

"As you wish," Sally murmured. "Do the right thing, Margaret. For once, do the right thing."

John McPherson stayed in Bristol for three days, walking the waterfront, eating in good restaurants, and remembering the lean days when he arrived in Bristol, poor but determined not to remain that way.

This visit to the principal port on the west coast of England was night and day, compared to his unheralded arrival in a rainstorm, cold and trying to stay out of everyone's way. He had been hungry—he was always hungry—and swiped two apples and a pear from a vendor near the waterfront.

He remembered that thievery and walked the waterfront until he located the market with the tables of fruit empty now. He went inside and removed his beaver hat, looking around for the owner.

"Sir? May I help you?" said a man wearing a dingy apron over his work clothes.

He spoke with a deference that startled John, even though he knew he looked the part of a gentleman, from that beaver hat, to a suit of unmistakable American cut, to his well-shined shoes. For a small moment, he had been remembering himself thin and starving, and dressed in shabby clothes that hadn't been washed in months.

"Help me? Yes, you may," he said, recalled to the moment. He reached into his coat pocket for his wallet and drew out a pound note. "Eight years ago, I stole two apples and a pear from you because I hadn't eaten since Carlisle. Please take this and give me no change. I owe you considerable interest on that loan."

The merchant stared at the pound note, but took it. He was a shop owner, after all. Christmas loomed and he had three hopeful children. "This will constitute the first time a beggar boy has done such a thing, so I thank'ee," he told John.

"I've thought about it through the years," John replied. "I didn't mean to be a thief." He replaced his hat and left the market.

His next visit was to a purveyor of Bristol's famous blue beads. He bought a single strand and had it wrapped in pretty paper while he waited.

"For your missus?" the jeweler asked. He motioned for his young shop assistant to press down her finger to make the bow tight.

My missus? John thought. *We shall see.* "Perhaps," he told the man.

A visit to a bookstore consumed more time. He scanned the shelves, still amazed that he could purchase any volume he wanted. He settled on Jedediah Cleishbotham's *The Heart of Midlothian* in four volumes, wondering why Walter Scott still used a pseudonym.

The bookseller recommended a book containing both *Persuasion* and *Northanger Abbey*, "by a respectable lady, sir," the man assured him. Reasoning that all play and no work would make Jack an even duller boy, he bought a new tome, *A History of British India*, probably destined to put him to sleep. It might prove useful if any of the inns he slept in going north had noisy public rooms, making sleep difficult.

Dusk was fading quickly to evening, even though the hour hadn't advanced much beyond four of the clock. He ate a good dinner, popped into the posting house to make certain all was ready for an early departure, and returned to his hotel.

He spent a few minutes in a deep leather chair in the lobby, reading the *Bristol Chronicle*. He had acquired the newspaper habit in New York City. As he read, he heard the inn keep talking to another traveler. He heard whispered "American," and "going north to Scotland," and knew he was the object in question.

So I look like an American, he thought, with quiet pride. *I wonder who Margaret will see, the man of business or the raggedy lad who left?*

He thought of little Sally Wilson, who had seen him off to seek his fortune, sitting on the back of a hay wain, and wondered if she would even recognize him. Of the two young ladies, he thought that Sally would be the least surprised to know of his success, even though he sent his letters to Margaret Patterson. He had a theory about that; time to test it.

Travel by post chaise was far superior to the hay wain. It was certainly a stride in seven league boots from travel in the backwoods of the new United States, which meant days on teeth-rattling corduroy roads made of logs, or horseback for weeks on roads that were barely trails. He preferred the canals of New York State, and even the flatboats on the Ohio River to stagecoach. At least there wasn't much worry from Indians, pushed farther and farther toward the unexplored West near Missouri.

John read and dozed, and then gazed at the alternating rain, drizzle, and snow as they traveled on roads that the Romans had probably laid down years ago, if he remembered aright the lessons from Mr. Wilson, minister of St. George's Church. He thought of Mrs. Agatha Wilson, who had left this vale of tears two years ago, according to one of Margaret's letters. Yes, he would certainly have to pay a visit to Reverend Wilson and Sally.

Evenings in the inns were lonely for such a gregarious man as John McPherson. This trip served to remind him of the great gulf in England separating those served and those serving. Left to his newly acquired American ways, he would have dined with his post riders and played cards with them in the public room.

He had timidly suggested such an evening to one of the riders, who shook his head sorrowfully. "Maybe in America, but not here, sir," the man had said. His following question sounded wistful to John. "Would such a thing happen in the United States?"

"All the time," John replied, missing his new country with surprising longing. The post rider walked away, shaking his head.

They arrived in Dumfries late in the afternoon. The innkeeper at the Garland Hotel—a place he would never have dared enter eight years ago—moved smartly to assure him of a room with dry sheets with a warming pan between them.

"You'll be staying for a few days, sir?" the man asked, again with that deference that John was beginning to find uncomfortable.

"A few days."

"You're here for the wedding, sir?"

"No. Just to visit a few old friends," John replied. "A wedding?"

"Aye, Mr. . . . Mr. . . ." The keep turned around the ledger. "Mr. McPherson. Miss Margaret Patterson is marrying a foreigner from England on Christmas Eve."

Margaret, Margaret, John thought, more amused than surprised, somehow. Funny that she never mentioned such a life-changing event in her letters. Perhaps it was sudden. It occurred to him that even with his little note sent from Bristol, she had not been expecting him, which nearly made him laugh out loud.

Once he had applied a chapter of *History of British India* to his brain, he slept the sleep of the pure in heart. The book had proved surprisingly useful on his trip. Before he drifted off, he wondered what Margaret would say when he knocked on her door in the morning.

He enjoyed a leisurely breakfast at the Garland, then strolled to the Patterson mansion on the edge of Dumfries. A cold mist fell, reminding him there were some things he would never miss about Scotland.

He had never even approached the Patterson manse before, basing all his knowledge of it on a lengthy, tree-lined private road and a mere glimpse of a stone house beyond. Skeletal limbs and a few tired leaves tossed here and there would be his memory now.

He gave a firm knock to a door he never thought to enter, and was let inside, after a brief explanation, by a footman who would have shooed him away ten years ago. He found it gratifying, if a little sad, that no one so far in Dumfries had recognized him. His life here as one of the ramshackle McPhersons had amounted to nothing. Put a man in a good suit, low-crowned beaver hat, and a cloak, and the world opens wide.

I am the same man I was, he thought, as he was shown into a sitting room, after leaving said cloak and hat with the footman. *I am older and wiser, but I am the same man.*

He looked around the lovely room and went to the fireplace, because his hands were cold. No, not just his hands. The room gave off no warmth. A more comforting memory came to mind of the parsonage at St. George's, book-filled and untidy with paper clutter. He had been there a time or two, right after the death of his mother, whom no one lamented except the McPhersons, because no one took the trouble to know her kindness amid squalor. He turned away from the fireplace. Such thoughts were unprofitable. He was here to test a theory.

Someone cleared her throat and he looked up. Margaret Patterson stood in the doorway, as lovely as he remembered her at age fifteen when she approached him and said she wanted to write to him in Canada. Suspicious, he assumed it was a prank, but the hunger to belong had made him agree to her nonsense.

The letters had come to him through the years, kept in the North West Company office in Montreal until a fur trader was heading in his direction, and then in New York City. They had been his lifeline; he had kept every one.

"Margaret Patterson, you have not changed even a little," he said, and gave her a proper bow.

To his amusement, she gawked at him, looking less lovely and self-possessed. Her curtsy was proper, but perfunctory. She looked both put upon and irritated, which he charitably put down to her surprise at actually seeing that man she had corresponded with for a decade. She gestured to the hall.

"Mr. McPherson, my father wants to have a word with you. I'll be here in the sitting room."

Surprised, he followed her gesture and then a footman down the hall to what turned out to be a bookroom. He was now in the presence of the great Mr. Milo Patterson, who could squeeze a penny until it yelped in pain and slunk to a dark corner to nurse its wounds. Patterson had owned that pathetic scrap of land the McPhersons farmed and showed no sympathy when Mam died. *What do you want with me*, he asked himself as he bowed and was left standing in front of the desk like a sorry petitioner.

"What are you doing here?" the big man growled, with no preamble.

No, not a big man. Mr. Patterson's shirt looked too large for him. John smiled at a rather ordinary-looking fellow who appeared to be ill. He was small and the possessor of a pinched, sour expression. John wondered why he had ever feared him. And, come to think of it, his expression mirrored Margaret's.

"I thought merely to visit Miss Patterson," John replied. "I am now situated in New York City and work for Mr. John Astor as a purveyor of furs for the European market. My life has changed significantly since Dumfries."

And then he was asked, in kinder tones, to sit down and say more, which he did, stifling his amusement as Mr. Patterson decided he was worth talking to. He told the man of his own personal fortune, and his growing career with America's largest global corporation.

"I came here to say hello again to Miss Patterson," John concluded. "She was always so kind to me in school, and I never forgot." A little lie in the interest of self-preservation couldn't hurt.

"Do go see her, John . . . Mr. McPherson," the little man said, rising to shake his hand, even bowing a bit. "Please stay for luncheon."

John swallowed down his unholy glee over such an offer and put on his best business face. In dealing firsthand with Iroquois and touchy Hurons in their lodges, he had learned to cover his emotions as he bargained for furs. That same poker face had served him well as he moved up the fur trade ladder and became a middle man. It hadn't hurt that he'd discovered a facility with languages that served him well with Frenchmen, Spaniards, and other tribes on America's frontier.

He politely declined the invitation to luncheon, because he had other plans, and hedged about returning for dinner. He knew he could play Mr. Patterson like a one of Mr. Astor's clarinets, if need be.

As he returned to the sitting room, escorted by the great man himself, John noticed a certain shabbiness to the manor. It was a place going to seed. And why on earth was Margaret only now getting married, and to an Englishman? She had to be nearly twenty-four—no antique, but not the dewy fresh maiden that a man might want to wed.

He returned to the sitting room and waited there, his shoulders shaking with silent laughter, as Mr. Patterson pulled his daughter into the hall for a few whispered words. When she returned, she gave him a brilliant smile, sat him down on the sofa and crowded close to him.

Up close, he found her less beautiful. Her complexion had an unhealthy tinge to it, and her eyes had a hard look.

She placed her hand on his arm. "Do tell me all about your travels, John," she said.

"I did in my letters," he replied. "In considerable detail, I might add."

Oh, he shouldn't do this, but he could not resist. "Surely you have not forgotten my letter about captivity with the Hurons and a near scalping, followed by my escape through a trackless forest?"

"I have not forgotten that incident," she replied, increasing the pressure on his arm. "Poor, poor you!"

His only dealings with the Hurons had been marathon bargaining sessions that left him red-eyed from sitting for hours in a smoky lodge. They had been more than kind, once he spoke to them in their own tongue. The North West Company had declared him king of the Huron trade, which had brought him to the attention of Astor in the brand new United States, and a better career path.

He let her chatter on a few more minutes, because what man doesn't like praise, even the false kind, heaped upon him? As he listened, John began to count himself a fortunate man, indeed, that another of his skills was reading people.

Detaching himself from Margaret Patterson proved to be a challenge, but he was equal to it. He promised a later return, probably no more sincere than all the blather she was heaping upon him. Since Margaret Patterson, that self-absorbed girl, had grown into Miss Patterson, still self-absorbed, he excused his own prevarication.

Once outside, he breathed in the cold air and congratulated himself on his escape. He did turn around for another wave and a bow, because she stood in the doorway, but that was it. He had survived with his whole skin, and a complete confirmation of his decade-long suspicions.

Back in town, he knocked on a more humble door, and was invited in by the Reverend Wilson, retired minister of St. George's and his former village teacher. He spent an edifying hour in the good man's presence. An inquiry about Miss Wilson's address meant another hour to cool his heels and compose himself.

He went back to the inn and wrote a letter, just a short one, to Sally Wilson. He signed it "Faithfully Yours, Hay Wain Lad," and asked the ostler's son to deliver it to the village school. He composed himself for a short nap, and found that all he could do was lie there, shoes off, comfortable, with a huge smile on his face.

He had begun his journey to Scotland wondering if what he thought was true would lead to more disappointment. Somewhere in the middle of the Atlantic, he had reminded himself that his intuition was sound in more than just fur and business. Even better, he believed in himself.

Before he dozed off, he experienced the magnificent epiphany that he had always believed in himself, even when times were at their worst, here in Dumfries, and in the middle of the Canadian wilderness. He thought about his conclusion to every letter of Faithfully Yours, and realized that he truly was a loyal and faithful man, the kind a similarly inclined woman might want.

Still, he felt something remarkably close to fear as he approached the village school. He stood out of the way and watched as the school emptied of children, all of them especially happy because Mr. Wilson had mentioned this was the last day of class until December 28.

When the last child was out of sight, he walked what felt like fifty miles to the door, took a deep breath, and knocked.

"Do come in," he heard. He opened the door.

Sally Wilson sat at her desk with his little note in front of her. She had folded her hands on the desk, her pretty eyes trained on him. He loved how they grew smaller and smaller as her smile increased. He had remembered that about her—little chips of blue glass in the kindest face.

"You're back," she said so softly.

He looked behind her to what must have been spelling words on the blackboard and knew he had been right all along. He knew that handwriting. A decade of work and worry tumbled from his shoulders because he knew he was looking at a friend, at the very least. Under the cloak of another, she had written to him, worried about him, and buoyed him up, whether she knew it or not.

As he came down the aisle toward her, she stood up and walked out from behind her desk. She cocked her head a little to one side in a gesture he remembered from the years she had been his only friend in school.

"I like your hat," she said and then blushed. "What a silly thing for me to say. But I do like it."

And then she was in his arms. He couldn't have said which of them first covered that small distance dividing them; maybe it was a tie. He held her close and then started to chuckle. Just a little laugh, and then a bigger one, which she joined in.

He finally held her off and just looked at her. "All right. Confess. Whose idea was it?"

"Margaret didn't tell you?" she asked. "I didn't think she would."

He kissed her then, because explanation could wait until he did what he had been wanting to do probably since that morning in the rain when she alone saw him off at the beginning of his adventure. It was a long time to wait for a kiss, and he wasn't in the mood to add one more second to his longing.

Another kiss, and another. There might have been another one, but he wasn't counting. He put his hands on her waist and lifted her to her desk. He sat beside her, their feet dangling, their hips touching.

"Margaret wanted to humiliate you," Sally told him finally, after a real effort to bolster her composure. "She thought it would be great fun to leave you thinking that any day now you would get a letter from home."

"You didn't see it that way," he said, when she seemed unable to continue.

"It was an unkindness no one deserved," she said, with a sudden flash of anger. She made no objection when he took her hand in his. "I told her *I* would write you, even though you hadn't asked me to."

"I wanted to, but . . ." John shook his head. "I had enough manners to understand that would have been improper."

She turned slightly to face at him. "If Margaret didn't tell you today, how did you know?"

"I've always thought it was you," he began, then corrected himself. "At least, I hoped it was. Well, I knew for certain after

225

that two-year gap. Margaret—you—had written a pile of letters that stacked up in the company office in Montreal, and finally found me in New York City. You didn't give up."

"I was so afraid you were dead," she whispered, then rested her head on his shoulder. "Then Margaret brought over that letter, the one where you said you were now working for the Astor Company." She put her hand to her mouth, her anguish almost palpable. "This is hard," she whispered, turning her face into his shoulder.

"We have time," he told her.

"Margaret had forgotten to give it to me," Sally said at last. "Six months on top of two years! I started to cry and she just laughed."

He tipped his head toward hers, after sending his beaver hat sailing. "She's a mean-spirited female, Sal. You should keep better company," he teased.

Sally slapped his chest. "Wretch!"

She left her hand on his chest, and he could have lost consciousness with the pure pleasure of her touch. *I am a hopeless case*, he thought, with no regret.

"I went to the Patterson manor first this morning. Mr. Patterson pumped me for information, and I told him that I am one, well off; and two, set on a course to become even wealthier." He chuckled. "He was so pleased! He took Margaret aside and told her, and then she was so pleased, too." He laughed out loud. "What a transformation. She might be hoping that I will return this evening for dinner."

"You won't?" Sally asked.

"Not in a million years." He put his arm around Sally's waist. "I have a fine position with the Astor Company and I live in New York City. I have a well-appointed flat, and am thinking about buying some farmland just south of an area called The Bronx. It's some distance from Manhattan, so I am still undecided."

"You're a businessman, according to your letters," Sally reminded him. "Why a farm?"

"It seems like a good place to raise a family. Someone—you, for instance—could stay there with . . . with . . . children perhaps. Let us consider that."

"We could," she replied, so agreeable.

"I would be home every weekend," he continued.

She pressed against his chest with her hand. "Oh, no! If that someone is I, we'll be together in New York City or not at all. No more letters or long distances." She laughed. "That is, if you are speaking of me."

"I am. Sally Wilson, I have loved you for more than the ten years I was in North America. Will you be my wife? I know it means leaving Scotland and . . ."

She kissed his cheek, and when he turned his head, kissed his mouth, which busied them both for a time.

"That appears to be an aye," he said, when he could talk. "In the interest of honesty and good faith, there is the distinct possibility that Mr. Astor will send me to St. Louis, Missouri, to be his liaison with Pierre Chouteau, his Upper Missouri partner."

"St. Louis? Will I like St. Louis?"

This was not a lily he could gild. "Probably not, at least at first. It's humid and scruffy looking. Pigs in the streets. More taverns than churches. Painted Indians now and then, and fur trappers smellier than I used to be. You'll need to learn French to converse with Chouteau and some of his partners and their wives, but I'll teach you. Is it still aye?"

Her sweet eyes filled with tears. "Aye over and over," she whispered.

He helped her down from the desk, mainly because it was another excuse to put his hands on her waist and pull her close. Arms around her, he asked what she thought about marrying in the next day or two.

She rested her forehead against his chest. "Oh, goodness, the school!"

"I spoke with your father earlier, and he is perfectly willing to take over until the town finds another teacher."

"You already talked to my father?"

"Aye. I am no fool. I told him what I am worth now, and assured him I could take care of you in a style to which you will rapidly become accustomed, since you are a fast learner."

Her face grew solemn. "Can I leave him?"

"I invited him to sail with us, or to come whenever he feels like it. He's considering the matter."

"Well, then," she said. "I have no wedding dress, but I don't care."

"That's my girl," he told her, practically tingling with the opportunity to finally use those words. His girl. His wife. The mother of his children. "Since Scottish churches are much more flexible than those institutions south of the border, what about the day after Christmas?"

She nodded, and wouldn't look at him. In some ways, Sally Wilson was still the shy girl who befriended him so many years ago.

"Did you already ask my father to marry us?"

"Aye, miss. I'm not one to let grass grow underfoot."

Just then he remembered the blue beads in his pocket. He pulled out his little gift and gave the necklace to her. "I bought these in Bristol, of course. No one else can create vivid blue. I wasn't even certain why I bought them. Can I find a wedding ring in this town?"

At the beginning of this story, there was mention of another letter to end it. Margaret sent a note that evening to Sally by way of her lady's maid, who delivered it while Sally and her future husband were cuddling on the sofa and Mr. Wilson was reading and trying not to laugh at their total lack of interest in rational conversation.

The lady's maid looked at Sally and John sitting so close together, blanched, and handed the note to Sally with shaking fingers. Mr. Wilson's housekeeper showed her out and swore later that the poor thing was muttering about the storm and thunder about to descend on the entire Patterson household, and how soon could she find other employment?

Sally opened the note, read it quickly, gasped, and handed it to her beloved, who groaned, and handed it to Mr. Wilson, who shook his head.

He handed it back to Sally, who read it again, as if she couldn't believe her eyes. "She has written to Mr. Mallory calling off their wedding," she said in amazement. " 'I never told John McPherson that I didn't write those letters, so don't say a word, if he should happen to drop by. I have great plans for him.' Oh dear."

So ends this tale of a Christmas in Dumfries. For those who are interested, the McPhersons went to St. Louis, Missouri, where they raised an excellent family of Americans. To the end of her long life, Mrs. McPherson always wore six blue beads on a gold chain—one for her, for John, and for each of their children. She never took it off, her gift from the hay wain lad who remained hers, faithfully.

Lucy's Bang-Up Christmas

CHAPTER ONE

December 5, 1815
Dear Cousin Miles,

Thank you for writing. By all means, dear boy, join us when the Michaelmas Term is done, and after your parents have seen you. Believe me, you are not inviting yourself in vain. I am drowning in paperwork and testy females. I am tempted to bury your cousin Clotilde up to her neck and retrieve her only an hour before the wedding, no matter how illustrious the groom. My sister Aurelia Burbage means well, but she is a wretchedly poor substitute for my dear late wife. She flutters about, making my cook's life miserable with her demands. If Honoré tenders his resignation, I swear I will open my veins.

And Lucy! Lucy mopes about wishing for Christmas in this house, instead of Clotilde's wedding. I tell her that our thoughts must be on her sister's Christmas Eve nuptials this year. I know that Lucy misses her mother and all of my dear wife's holiday traditions. I have promised her a Yule log, Christmas pudding, wassail, and caroling and all the rest next year. "Can't we have both now, Papa?" she asks, *pleading with those big blue eyes. When was the last time you saw Lucy? Contrary miss. Aurelia is preparing her for a come out and Lucy could not care less.*

Your father tells me you are returning to Oxford for more study. I break out in hives just thinking about that much time devoted to books, but to each his own. It is a fact that you Bledsoes come from the brainier side of our mutual family tree!

Join us, cousin. I can't offer you anything but tumult this season, but if you can keep me above water by dealing with correspondence, receipts and milliner's bills, I'll—heaven knows what I'll do. I can't think!

Abandon the hallowed halls of Christ Church College and come soon to the wilds of Kent at your own peril. See if you can jolly Lucy into a better mood. Let us make that your primary task.

Sincerely,

Cousin Roscoe Danforth

Miles Bledsoe tipped his chair back in the confines of his carrel in the Bodleian Library, which meant he banged against the partition separating his space from the one beside him.

"Bledsoe, do that again and you're a dead man," came the voice of the aggrieved scholar whose concentration he had broken.

Miles smiled to himself. Lord Hartley's aggravation would only last until Miles bought him a pint at the Eagle and Child on St. Giles Street.

"I just received good news, Hart," he said, louder than a whisper, but softer than the occasion warranted, since this was even more than good news and deserved to be shouted from a rooftop or two. He waited, knowing that Lord Hartley liked a bit of gossip as well as the next earl.

"Well, tell me," Hart said. "This jaw-me-dead treatise on tenth-century tenants and land rights is calling my name like a diseased harlot."

Miles laughed out loud, which meant a chorus of shushes and foul words from other carrels. He stood up and looked over the partition at Lord Hartley.

"I have a cousin . . . words fail me," he whispered. He waved Roscoe's letter. "I've just been given carte blanche by her father to jolly her out of a bad mood incurred by the approaching marriage of her sister."

"The old green-eyed monster, is it?" Lord Hartley asked.

"Lucy's not jealous that her sister is marrying. She is upset because the wedding is on Christmas Eve, making the usual Christmas traditions null and void this year."

"So you're going to . . . to—"

"Tidwell, Kent, to try my luck. Lucy knows me so well—we're second cousins, after all—but Hart, I think I love her."

Hart leaned back this time. "My first cousins are barely tolerable, my second cousins even worse."

"Lucy is much more than tolerable. I'll have to play this carefully. She has no idea of my feelings. Wish me luck, Hart."

"Very well. Good luck!" Lord Hartley said. "Now leave me alone so I can keep reading this fascinating bit of British history. The entire civilized world is waiting for my paper on the subject."

Miles laughed louder, which earned him several paper missiles lobbed in his direction, plus an apple core. He caught the apple core and threw it back, then sat down to read his cousin's letter again.

Lucinda Danforth, he thought. *Could a fellow even hope for a nicer Christmas gift?*

CHAPTER TWO

"Things are not shaping up well, Miles," Lucinda Danforth announced as she flopped into the chair in her father's book-room, a place Papa avoided at all costs. She knew better than to flutter about with die-away airs for her cousin from the quieter Bledsoe side of the family tree. "Not at all well."

"Nonsense, Lucy," Miles Bledsoe said, after he blew gently on the drying ink. "You cause half of your own problems by bludgeoning about in your graceless fashion. How in the world are you going to convince some hapless rich man with a title to marry you someday?"

She slumped lower in the chair. "Don't remind me that I am coming out in a few months. I call that monumentally unkind." She folded her arms and glared at the disgustingly calm man seated behind her father's desk.

And what did he do but laugh at her? She bore it with what she considered remarkable grace by grimacing at him, rather than sticking out her tongue.

He took out his timepiece and stared at it. "Another fifteen seconds and your face will freeze like that permanently," he told her, which made her laugh.

"That's better. What is wrong now?" he asked.

She had a million retorts and complaints, but Miles had a way of giving her his full attention that reduced them to one fact she had been avoiding since the start of Advent.

"I miss my mother," she said simply.

"I miss her, too," he said, and folded his hands on the paper-strewn desk. "Cousin Penelope would have gone about in her quiet way and organized this whole circus, without any pain to anyone." He took out his handkerchief. "Have a cry, Lucy, and blow your nose."

She took the handkerchief and did as he said. When she finished, she folded the material into squares. "I'll launder it. Thanks, Miles."

"Anytime, cuz." He gave her his patented familiar look, which meant permission to carry on, if she felt like it, and she did.

"All Clotilde does is moon about and cry if anyone looks at her. I thought that being in love and getting married meant a smile or two, at the very least. Doesn't it?"

He shrugged. "What would you do if you were in love, Lucy dear?"

She smiled at that, wondering for a second why some female didn't snatch Miles to her bosom and refuse to let him go. He was tall and handsome and had big brown eyes, round ones that made him look younger than she knew he was. Maybe his black hair made him intimidating. How did she know? He was Miles—the cousin, out of all her relatives, who never failed to make her feel better.

She thought about what he said. "You know, I doubt I would be any different than I am right now."

"I doubt you would be, either," he agreed. "You're sensible and smart."

"Implying that my sister is not?" she asked, wondering what it would take to actually ruffle her cousin's even temperament. No wonder he was considering a career in diplomacy.

"Clotilde is beautiful and pours tea better than you ever will, scamp. I want to be a diplomatist, so that is all I will say. Stop laughing!" He gave her a more serious look. "You know you're going to miss her."

If someone else had told her that, Lucy would have sup-plied an instant denial. Since it was Miles, she gave the matter her attention. He was right, of course. Everything was changing before her eyes and she didn't know how to stop it.

"Whatever her mental acuity, I love her, you wretch. When she comes back to visit, she won't be my big sister anymore," Lucy said finally. "She'll be a married woman. She won't want to crawl in bed with me and laugh about things, or tell me ghost stories, or even go for walks with her shoes off."

"That's the price," he said. "My older brother—you know, Roger—is on occupation duty in Belgium now and commanding his own regiment. We have to let them grow up."

"I suppose we do," Lucy agreed. She stood up and leaned across the desk to kiss her cousin on the top of his head. "Thanks, Miles." Almost at the door, she looked back. "I still want to do something that Mother would have done for Christmas."

"What?"

"I haven't decided. You'll be the first to know, when I do." She opened the door and laughed. "Probably the only one. Everyone else is too busy with the wedding to keep Christmas."

CHAPTER THREE

Lucy suffered considerable penance (for her) by hemming one of Clotilde's new nightgowns and listening to her sister sniff a bit and cry gracefully into a handkerchief more lacey than substantial. Lucy thought of Mile's efficient handkerchief in her pocket and wondered what Cleo would do if she whipped it out and offered the damp thing to her.

"This isn't funny," Clotilde declared. "Lucy, you try me."

And you don't try me? Lucy thought and had the wisdom not to say it. She thought about what her cousin would say, instead. She gazed for a moment at her beloved sister, who had turned into an ogre, and took a page from Miles's book.

"I don't mean to try you. I wish I knew how I could help you." Lucy took a deep breath. "I wish Mama were here to give you a shoulder to cry on. Will I do?"

She did. With a sob, Clotilde was in her arms and crying prettily. Lucy wondered if her far lovelier sister had perfected that talent in a mirror. Tears slid delicately down her face, and her nose neither ran nor turned red.

Now that I have her, what shall I do with her? Lucy asked herself. *Where are you when I need you, Miles?* "Do you wish to talk to me about it?"

"Lord Masterton sent me a list of ways I can improve myself," Clotilde said. She gave a little hiccup. "This is the worst part. I can quote it from memory. 'Miss Danforth, you must remember that you are marrying into one of the first families in the nation, and not another commoner's house in Tidwell.'"

Lucy gasped. "Have you mentioned this to Papa?"

"I wouldn't dare," Clotilde replied. "Think how it would hurt his feelings."

A long silence followed. Lucy toyed with saying exactly what she thought, but didn't think Miles would approve. Still, this was Clotilde, perhaps not the brightest mind in two or three shires, but certainly the kindest.

"Cleo, are you completely certain that you want to marry Lord Masterton?" she asked. "Papa is a gentleman and he is wealthy. We don't need Lord Masterton to give us countenance. We don't require a family title."

"Yes, I am certain," Clotilde said, too quickly to suit Lucy. "All the arrangements are made, my dress is finished, I have a wonderful new wardrobe, and we are bound for a month in Paris, now that Napoleon is gone. Wasn't that the purpose of my London Season?" She sat up and blew her nose. "Besides, I love him."

Do you? Lucy wanted to ask, but had the wisdom to remain silent. Clotilde was older and wiser in the ways of courtship. She had been through a successful London Season, flirted with any number of beaus, both foreign and domestic, and settled on Lord Masterton, a marquess with a Yorkshire estate and a London house. He was older, but Papa had been older than Mama, so that didn't amount to much for an argument. Still . . .

"Cleo, do you call him by his first name? Is that allowed?"

Clotilde shook her head, and her face turned pink. "He says we will only do that in the privacy of my bedchamber."

Lucy felt her face go red, and not in that adorable way that Clotilde pinked up, but bright red. The color would make her cousin Miles hoot and point if he saw her.

"What *is* his name?" she asked, determined to soldier on.

"It is Phillip," Clotilde answered, with some dignity.

"I don't suppose you would ever dare call him Phil."

"I would never consider it."

"So it is to be my lord and my lady?" Lucy asked. She had another question, one more personal. "You say *your* bedchamber. Aren't you going to, well, you know, *share* a bed?"

How did Clotilde manage to rosy up so pink and look so ladylike? Lucy felt her own face go from mere red to *really* red.

Clotilde's sigh was heartfelt. "I suppose that is how people in great houses live."

Lucy thought of the mornings that she and Clotilde had bounded into their parents' bedroom and snuggled down between the two people who loved them best in the world. *I want more than solitary residence in a bed when I marry*, she thought. If that was how great people lived, it was a wonder any of them reproduced.

There wasn't anything else to say. Lucy finished hemming the nightgown after Clotilde left the room for a consultation with Honoré about dinner. She hemmed mostly for penance, because she really wanted to give her sister a good shake, stare at her nose to nose, and order her to find a different fellow.

Even more, she wanted to back out of her own upcoming season—provided for her, like Clotilde's, at the invitation of Papa's sister Willa, who had married an earl with pots of money and had access to a London Season.

"My dratted Season is three months away," she told herself, after looking around to make sure no one was listening. "Perhaps something will happen before then."

Lucy chose the time-honored, familiar path her father would take and decided not to think about it. She started down the stairs, but changed her mind when she heard an awful wailing from the kitchen far below. Aunt Aurelia and Clotilde must have made yet another unreasonable demand to set off Honoré. She chose discretion over valor and retreated upstairs to her bedchamber.

As much as she adored her father, inviting Aunt Aurelia to preside in his late wife's place had been a tactical blunder. She still blushed to think about yesterday's drill in the sitting room, when Aunt Aurelia made her march up and down with a book on her

238

head, simply because she had found Lucy slouched in the library, her legs over the arm of a chair, reading *Emma*.

"How will you ever nab a husband of your own?" Aurelia had scolded, which made Lucy want to scream. The contrast of militant Aunt Aurelia with her own gentle mother was too great. Mama would have scolded her, to be sure, but then she would have sat down with a book of her own, the matter concluded.

And that only led to a bittersweet memory of Mama supervising a parade of dresses for Lucy's spring come out. The modiste from nearby Winchester had been kind enough to bring the dresses to Tidwell, since Mama was unable to travel by early spring.

Even then, the exertion of approving this sleeve, or that shade of yellow, or any number of tiny details had worn Mama to a nub.

"You don't need to supervise so many details, Mama," Lucy pleaded with her that evening, when Mama could barely breathe.

Mama took her hand—such a delicate touch now—and looked deep into Lucy's eyes. "I intend to savor every moment with you, my dearest," she replied. She closed her eyes then. Lucy sat there, sorrowing, until Mama opened her eyes. "I doubt I will live to your wedding. Sh, sh, Lucy! I will oversee your London Season wardrobe. Don't deny me this pleasure."

And so Lucy put a bright face on the dread London Season proceedings, an event that only struck terror in her heart. Mama was putting so much store by the come out. Lucy would have shaved her head bald before she would have denied her mother this last simple pleasure.

She knew she should rescue their chef Honoré from Aunt Aurelia, but she hadn't the heart just then. A faint glow still flickered from her fireplace, so she pulled her favorite chair closer and huddled there, wanting her mother, but grateful at the same time that Mama no longer suffered. Papa had been firm about forbidding deepest mourning after six months, or even semi-mourning, reminding his daughters of one of Mama's final injunctions.

You said we were not to mope about in black, Mama, Lucy thought, pulling her legs close to her chest. In a way, Mama had been right. Black was depressing and a constant reminder of her passing. On the other hand, everyday clothes made Lucy wonder if she would forget Mama faster, when there was no visible sign of their great loss.

Not that she could forget Mama. She thought of Miles's kind encouragement for her to cry, and wished she could return to the bookroom just to sit in silence and know that someone cared. She had already cried all over him once that day; even someone as good-natured as her cousin would probably draw the line at more.

Besides, Miles was busy straightening out Papa's tangled accounts and moving the whole wedding forward. She could sit by herself and think through Christmas.

She knew there would be greenery, because Clotilde had decreed it. The Christmas wreath was already in place. There wasn't Christmas pudding to stir and wish on, because the kitchen staff had to cook and store food for the wedding. Maybe next year.

Caroling was out, as well, because Lord Masterton thought it childish, according to Clotilde. He had specifically stated in a recent letter to his beloved that nothing set his teeth on edge faster than off-key singing, and he wouldn't have it. Presents for each other were a trifling matter and could likely be eliminated. The formal dining room was quickly filling up with presents for the happy couple. Who had time to think of the little gifts of Christmas?

"I do," Lucy said softly.

She couldn't force her London Season far enough away from her mind. The nasty thing kept resurfacing like the bloated carcass of a feral cat she had seen last summer in the fishpond. She wondered if Mama would have forced her to stand still for fittings and practice for too many hours with a dancing master who spent most of his time ogling Clotilde's extravagant beauty.

She glanced at the pier glass in the corner of her room. There was nothing wrong with her looks. She had even received a badly spelled sonnet last summer from a neighboring landowner's son, extolling her general, all-purpose loveliness by rhyming "beauty

fair" with "curly hair," and "dulcet tones" with "sturdy bones."
She and Miles had laughed about it until she had to slap the side
of his head for delivering her a box in person, wrapped in white
paper tied with gold filigree string. When she removed the lid, a
soup bone labeled "Now *this* is a sturdy bone," lay there, cush-
ioned with more exquisite paper.

Even now, she laughed to think of it, grateful to her cousin
for brightening a particularly gloomy day two weeks after
Mama's funeral when she was failing miserably to send notes to
distant friends because Papa couldn't. Together she and Miles
had finished the lot of them, once the bone was returned to the
kitchen.

She saw no need to peacock about London in the hopes of
finding someone to marry her. She knew her marriage portion
was healthy enough to sweeten any proposal, yet not so huge as
to make her a target for vulgar Captain Sharps and swindlers.
There were enough young men in the district to choose from.
Only next door were the two eligible, if shy, sons of Lawrence
and Adabell Petry—one a physician and the other a solicitor.

Clotilde had been a different case altogether, so beautiful
and even tempered that Papa agreed with his sister Aurelia—
for once—and his more sensible sister Willa that only an earl, a
marquess or perhaps a duke would suffice. To her way of thinking, Lucy didn't have that problem. Why go to the bother and
expense?

Eyes closed, she thought through the rest of Mama's
Christmas duties. After a lengthy time considering the matter,
she realized what she should do. She knew she needed an ally,
and Miles was the only one.

CHAPTER FOUR

Miles recognized the knock immediately—two knocks, pause, two knocks. He put down his pen and closed the ledger, grateful for diversion and even more grateful that Lucy was the source of it. She was far more fun than Aunt Aurelia and pathetic Clotilde, who probably should have her brains removed and scrubbed clean for agreeing to marry Lord Masterton. But no one had asked his opinion.

"You again?" he called out. "Have you laundered my hand-kerchief yet?"

She opened the door and gave him that squinty-eyed look that always made the soreness in his neck go away, or the ache in his head, caused by staring overlong at ledgers and receipts. Funny how a visit from his cousin could make him smile inside. She used to drive him to distraction when she was five and he was twelve.

She held out a dry cloth. "I purloined it from Papa's drawer. He will never miss it."

He pocketed the handkerchief and gestured to a chair. To his amusement, she perched on the edge of the desk instead, her foot swinging. *What can it hurt*, he thought, as he sat on the desk next to her. To his delight, she leaned toward him until their shoulders touched.

"We are too late for a Christmas pudding," she began, counting off on her fingers. "Greenery will do, as long as there are no bugs peeking out." She made a face. "That is Lord Masterton's stipulation."

"No bugs, on my honor as a . . . a third son." He tugged the curly hair that rhymed so handily with beauty fair to get her attention. "Do you know what is nice about being the third son? Matthew must set a good example for us and manage Father's estates; Roger gets to bivouac in the rain and fight."

"And you?"

"I have no idea what I want to be yet, except not a nuisance, and no one is pushing me about it. Well, you know I am considering the diplomatic corps." He laughed. "Whitehall doesn't even know *that* yet. What do you think I should be?"

He loved the way the tip her tongue came out as she thought. She had done that since she was a baby.

"You're not devious enough to be a diplomatist," she said, "but you do have excellent manners and vast skill in calming troubled waters. Only consider how well you convinced Aunt Aurelia to let Clotilde make green rosettes for each pew in the church, instead of the white ones *she* wanted."

Since she sat next to him on the desk, she gave his shoulder a nudge. "You even convinced my aunt that green was her idea all along. I withdraw my assessment. You *are* devious enough to be an ambassador."

"Thank you, I think," he teased, nudging her in return.

She sighed then. "I wish I were a man."

Not I, Miles thought. "Now why would you say that?"

"No one is pitchforking you into a London Season. You get to suit yourself."

"I rather think I do," he said. "Don't tell Matthew. Number two brother and I are both receiving a healthy inheritance, with none of the headaches of brother number one. No one seems particularly concerned with what I end up doing."

"Now that you mention it, being a second daughter has roughly the same advantage: a nice marriage portion, and no one clamoring for me to marry a title."

They looked at each other in complete harmony. "What can I do for you, Lucinda?" he asked.

"I have decided to give myself a Christmas gift," his cousin announced. He saw the tenderness in her blue eyes, and wondered, not for the first time, why everyone thought Clotilde was the Danforth beauty.

"And what will that be, scamp?"

"I want to do what Mama would have done for Christmas."

She said the words in a rush, as though lingering over them would be too painful. Miles understood. Marrying gentle Penelope Brewster had been the smartest thing Cousin Roscoe ever did.

"Which is . . ."

"Mama always did something kind for a poor family at Christmas. Usually that amounted to a basket for Christmas dinner, some toys and clothes for the children, and perhaps some money. Let us go to the village school."

"Why not to the vicarage and ask Mr. Portneuf? He will know the charitable cases," Miles asked.

She shook her head. "The vicar is always urging me to read improving tracts and commentaries."

"And you would rather not?"

She gave him a shy look, as if what she was about to say might make him laugh or tease her. "What?" he asked.

"You'll laugh. Clotilde did."

"I am not Clotilde."

She stood up and sat down properly in the chair closest to his desk, so close that he could touch her, if he wanted to. He realized with a little start that he did want to, so he tapped her arm. "Now when have I laughed at you?"

"Any number of times," she replied, "but I am serious. When things are too much to bear, I read the Bible. That's it. Just the Bible. No one's commentary required except my own."

The matter-of-fact way she said it touched his heart. "I should think that would be better than old sermons and improving works," he told her. "The vicar doesn't like that?"

"I heard Mr. Portneuf preach from St. Paul's writings about women not speaking in church," she told him, which impressed him mightily. He couldn't think of the last time he had actually listened to a sermon. Mostly they were to be suffered through. "I don't believe he likes ladies to think."

"Then he is an idiot." He wanted to see her smile, so he leaned closer. "Does your father have any idea what an idiot his vicar is?"

There, she laughed. "You mustn't breathe a word of this to anyone, Miles!"

"That Mr. Portneuf is an idiot?"

"Cousin, you are trying me mightily. That ladies shouldn't think!"

"Ah, that *is* nonsense. Do you have favorite passages?"

"Oh yes," she said.

Her obvious enthusiasm made his heart do a little flip. *You're growing up,* he thought, and felt an odd sort of pleasure at the notion. "Care to share them?" he asked, intrigued with this side of his cousin he had never seen before.

She looked away. "After Mama died, I took her Bible from her nightstand. At first I just put it on my pillow and rested my head on it, because it smelled a little of rose cologne."

"Cousin Pen did enjoy rose cologne," he said, imagining Lucinda finding solace that way, and wishing he had known.

"When I could bear it, I started turning the pages of her Bible." She looked at him, and he saw the unshed tears in her eyes. "I read what she underlined, and then I came to Proverbs 17." She took a deep breath and tightened her lips, which made him take her hand. She gave him a grateful smile.

"What happened then?" he asked, having his own struggle when she gave his hand a squeeze.

"She had written my name above the first part of the verse. *My name,*" she repeated softly, as though even now she could not believe it. "'A merry heart doeth good like a medicine.'"

He nearly stopped breathing when she rested her cheek against his hand. "Miles, when she was suffering and in so much pain, she liked me to sit beside her." Another deep breath, followed by an expression so serious he almost didn't recognize his cousin. "I think *I* was her medicine."

"I don't doubt it for a moment, Lucinda," he said, when he could speak.

She didn't move for the longest moment, which soothed his own heart. He had spent so much time lately worrying about what he would do in life, then wondering about his feelings for his cousin. The depth of Lucinda Danforth was starting to amaze him.

She sat up finally, and flashed him a faintly embarrassed smile. "So sorry! When I feel melancholy, I read Mama's under-lined verses. And lately, I've added some of my own."

"Tell me one," he said.

"It's in Micah." She must have noticed his expression. "Miles, Micah is in the Old Testament. Please tell me you have heard of the Old Testament."

"I have," he said, suddenly not wanting to disappoint this new Lucinda Danforth.

"This part: 'When I fall, I shall arise; when I sit in darkness, the Lord shall be a light unto me.'"

She gave him a sweet look, with no mischief in it. "It really does work."

Then she was all business. "Mr. Cooper is our retired vicar and he teaches the village school. He never minded if I read the Bible and he is the one we should visit."

"You're including me?" he asked, flattered.

"I believe third sons are like second daughters," she told him. "As long as we stay out of the way, we can probably suit ourselves. I intend to have a bang-up Christmas, in spite of everything."

"Such cant!" he exclaimed. "Don't let your aunt hear you."

"Never." She stood up. "Even if there is a wedding and con-fusion, and no one else remembers it is Christmas, I intend to honor Christmas through Mama. Are you in or out?"

"Lucinda, I am in. We will keep Christmas."

CHAPTER FIVE

She would have to ask him sometime why she was suddenly Lucinda instead of Lucy, but it was enough to know that she had an ally in this business of Christmas. "When can you get away?" she asked.

"Right now," he assured her. "I have cleared up a pile of correspondence and set aside receipts awaiting your father's signature. If I do not stand up soon, this chair will grow to my backside, which will mean never finding a suitable career or even a wife someday. Lead on. It's your village, not mine."

She hated to skulk about in her own house, but something told Lucy that Aunt Aurelia wouldn't take too kindly to her disappearance, especially when there was probably a wedding crisis looming, in action, or just finished. Still, it wouldn't hurt to tread lightly down the hall from the bookroom to the front door. Just a few more feet now . . ..

"Stop right there, young lady!"

Lucy winced. She turned around to see Aunt Aurelia coming at her like a frigate sailing into battle.

"If I weren't suddenly so terrified, I would swear," Miles whispered in her ear, which for a small moment proved even more distracting than Aunt Aurelia. Funny how that whisper could make her stomach tingle.

"You are no help, cousin," she whispered back in *his* ear, which made him look a little funny, too. Ah, revenge.

"Yes, Aunt Aurelia?" she said, wishing herself deep in the interior of Canada.

"What is this I hear about you refusing to go to the village to try on a bonnet for your come out?"

"I have better things to do right now," Lucy said, standing her ground, mainly because Miles stood behind her and pressed his hand into her back, where Aurelia couldn't see. "A bonnet can wait."

She said it firmly, enunciating each word. Papa had once warned her about not looking directly into the eyes of growling dogs. Perhaps bullies needed to be stared down and not avoided like dogs.

But what would Mama have done? She put her hand around Miles's hand against her back and pushed him gently away. It took all her courage to move forward, trying to glide as Mama would have done. She held out her arms to her bristling aunt, pulled her close and kissed her cheek.

"Thank you for what you are doing to help us," she murmured. "Weddings are such a trial, are they not? I am going into the village with my cousin to see the vicar about some greenery for the church."

Heavens, lying about church. Lucy hunched her shoulders for a split-second, waiting for lightning to strike. When it did not, she added prevarication to her list of sins to be repented at leisure, preferably after Christmas. Besides, a little fib must be small potatoes to the Almighty, especially since He was probably still trying to recover from all those lies at the Congress of Vienna.

"We won't be long, my dear," she said, and turned on her heel.

Don't look back, don't look back, she thought, as she continued her serene way down the hall that now stretched roughly the distance from Plymouth to Edinburgh.

Nothing happened, except that Miles was by her side, holding her hand. "I think *you* should consider a career in diplomacy, cuz," he whispered, but not in her ear this time, which greatly relieved her. This was no time for impish thoughts, especially about her second cousin.

Milsap asked no questions when she requested her cloak and bonnet. In fact, the butler took advantage of his many years' acquaintance and whispered, "Would that I could run away, too, Miss Lucy."

"You would be welcome," she assured him. "We won't be long. We are going to visit the village school."

"Take good care of her, Mr. Bledsoe," he told her cousin.

"I'll treat her as if she were my cousin," he promised.

Lucy already knew Miles was a good cousin; he became an even better one when he matched his longer stride to her shorter one. Come to think of it, she hadn't been walking with Miles Bledsoe in years. Lately, they met at tedious parties or in stuffy ballrooms. *I like this*, she thought.

"I like this, Lucinda," he said. "Usually we just meet in stuffy ballrooms." He nudged her shoulder. "Are you any better at dancing now than you were at fourteen?"

She stopped in the road and held up her arms. "Try me."

With a grin stretching nearly ear to ear, he held her in the waltz position, and muttered a monotone *one two three* until she started humming an actual waltz and he had leave to stop. Around the road they waltzed, to the amusement of a passing carter and two children, who imitated them with predictable results.

She struck a final note. He bowed and she curtsied and pretended to fan herself, even though her breath came out in cold puffs.

"La, Mr. Bledsoe, you are my hero," she simpered and batted her eyes.

He gave her such a look then, more tender than her silly romp warranted. "I'm calling you Lucinda because I believe you are maturing, but obviously not too fast," he said, a little out of breath. "I am not certain if I approve or not, but I think you are going to grow up, whether I wish it or not."

He crooked out his arm and they continued more sedately down the road. "Country dancing? Polkas?" he teased.

"All the above." She stopped in the road. "Miles, I don't want to go to London for a come out."

He set her in motion again. "It might be a necessary evil. Let me assure you that you will have suitors aplenty."

"How do you know that?" she asked, curious.

"Trust me. I know it," was all he would say.

She gave him her sunniest smile, looked into his eyes and saw surprising depth there.

Children continued passing them as they walked toward the school, which was located next to St. Andrew's. Formerly run by the church, the little school allowed any and all to attend, or nearly all. The people of means sniffed at it as the charity school, but Lucy knew the children were well-served by Mr. Cooper, retired these five years from St. Andrew's pulpit. Some of their own social sphere had thought it strange that her father sent her there, but he knew she would get a sound education.

She tapped on the door and opened it. Mr. Cooper looked up, saw who it was and got to his feet. He straightened out slowly and put both hands on Lucy's arms as she came close.

He smiled when she kissed his cheek, and asked, "Is this your special young man, Miss Lucinda?"

She laughed and shook her head. "He's just my cousin Miles. From the time I was four and able to follow him around, I have been his cross to bear."

"Hardly," Miles said in his own defense. "Was she a good pupil, Mr. Cooper?"

"Aye, generally speaking, except that she had a morbid desire to ask 'why' every time I explained a new approach or theorem."

"Natural curiosity is not to be sneezed at," Lucy said in her own defense.

"Some things just *are*," her former vicar said, "like truth, or law, or even love." He peered closer at her, his good humor evident. "Even you will understand that some day."

He clasped his hands in front of his ample girth. "What brings the two of you here?"

Miles bowed to Lucy. "Your proposition, cuz."

She sat down on the bench Mr. Cooper indicated and smoothed out her skirt. She thought she did a good job of consolidating the whole matter, the tyranny of a wedding versus the annual loveliness of Christmas.

"So you see, Mama always brought a basket of food and clothing for the less fortunate. She did it every year, except last year . . ." her voice trailed off.

"When she couldn't," Miles finished for her.

She gave him a relieved glance, then clapped her hands together, breaking her own spell. "And that is why we are here. I . . ."

"We . . ."

She gave Miles her own smile, the one she thought had earned her the "sturdy bones" and "curly hair" poem. No danger of poetry from her cousin, she knew. "Aye, then, *we* want to do something Mama would have liked to have done, had she had the strength. Isn't that it, Miles?"

He nodded. "Everyone is so busy with Miss Danforth's wedding that we are feeling a tad melancholy. Give us a challenge."

The vicar regarded them both for a length of time that would have grown uncomfortable, if she hadn't know the man so well. He turned back to his desk and rummaged until he found a ledger. He ran his finger down one page, tapped it, and closed the book. In silence, he looked at them, as if measuring their ability, then wrote. He waved the paper dry and handed it to Lucy.

"Mrs. Lonnigan has three children. Her husband died at Salamanca. She is destitute."

Lucy looked down at the names—Mrs. Lonnigan; Edward, thirteen; Michael, twelve; and Mary Rose, eight. She looked up at her old teacher and her vicar before the current one, who always wanted to foist sermons on her. "You want much more than a Christmas basket," she said.

"I do, Lucy. Actually, so did your mother."

"You're saying I only saw the smallest part of what she did."

Mr. Cooper nodded. "She was never one to toot her horn or demand attention. Mrs. Danforth just went about doing far more good than you knew, I think."

"I had no idea," Lucy told him. "What will you have us do for the Lonnigans? What would Mama have done?"

He had a ready answer. "I want you and your cousin to create a better life for this little family. Shame on our nation for not giving more than a paltry pension to those who died in its service. I want you to change their lives. Will you do it?"

Lucy looked at her cousin, who was already watching her. *Does he doubt I can?* she thought. *Does he still see little Lucy, who annoyed him?*

"We will," she told the vicar.

"What should we know about them before we invade their privacy?" Miles asked.

Mr. Cooper opened his class register again, and pointed to Edward's name as they both looked over his shoulder. "These are Edward's arithmetic scores. I believe he could teach the class better than I can."

"And Michael?" Lucy asked.

"He is a scamp. Transportation is a distinct possibility for him." the vicar said, but Lucy saw the laughter in his eyes. "You'll think of something for Michael. Mary Rose loves to read, but there are no books at home." He closed the ledger again. "Here is their biggest handicap: the Lonnigans are Catholic. Lucy, I doubt you are aware of the struggle your dear mama went through to get the children in school."

"I had no idea," she said again, humbled to the dust by the woman she thought she knew. "Mama was such a quiet lady, so calm."

"Are you like her?"

"I want to be."

CHAPTER SIX

As Miles had commented, it may have been her town, but they never would have found the Lonnigans without the little map Mr. Cooper drew.

"I have lived here all my life, but these parts are as foreign to me as the moon," she whispered to Miles as they plunged into a regular rabbit warren of twisting, narrow streets and misery all around them. "You'll keep me safe, won't you?"

"Entirely. Completely," Miles assured her, as he took her hand and tucked her close to him. "If you tell my uncle where I took you today, he'll probably send me away in disgrace. I'd be more surprised if you *did* know this neighborhood."

There is so much I don't know about the world, Lucy thought as the dank walls seemed to lean in closer. She heard children crying—not unusual, of course, except that it was the exhausted crying of little ones already without hope. Hollow-eyed children looked at them from doorways. One little boy held out his hand, as though wanting far more than either of them could provide.

"I have lived a sheltered life," she whispered to Miles.

"That is entirely as it should be," he replied. "We inhabit a completely different world from this one."

"We can do the Lonnigans some good, but what?" she asked. "I don't mind telling you that I am out of ideas."

"That will change, once we get to know them, and not just in an it's-Christmas-have-a-basket-don't-bother-me way. You heard Mr. Cooper say he wants us to change their lives."

She nodded, and clung to his hand. She didn't think she could even change *her* life, and the vicar expected her to change four people's lives. "I'm afraid," she whispered.

He pulled her closer and kissed her cheek. "You wanted Christmas," he reminded her. "As little as you think I know about the Bible, I strongly suspect that Christmas is much, much more than wassail and kissing boughs."

How was it that Miles Bledsoe knew just how to give her heart courage? As they hurried along the alley, she thought of other times he had helped her, mostly without being asked.

Miles kept his eyes on the row of lookalike houses. "This one."

He knocked on the door. After a minute or more, a young lad peeked out of the window next to the door. He looked fearful until Lucy waved at him, and then he looked merely wary.

Miles knocked again. Another long wait, and then a woman opened the door just a crack.

"Mrs. Lonnigan?" Miles asked. "Mr. Cooper from the school sent us to visit with you. May we come in?"

"I . . . I don't have anything you would want," she said, opening the door a crack wider.

"We don't want anything except to meet you and your children." Miles stepped back. "This is my cousin, Lucy Danforth. I believe you knew her mother."

Mrs. Lonnigan opened the door and ushered them inside. She glanced around the alley, and Lucy knew, with a pang in her heart, that the Irish woman was looking for her mother.

"She didn't come with you?" she asked.

"She died six months ago," Lucy said, and not without a quiver of her lips. Here she was trying to seem grown up and capable, and her emotions threatened to betray her again.

"I am sorry to hear that. She was a friend to us," Mrs. Lonnigan said simply.

"So the schoolmaster told me," Lucy replied. "May we sit down?"

She looked around for a place to sit, but there wasn't a chair in sight. She saw four neatly tied bedrolls against the walls and what looked like a blanket on the floor.

"All I have is the floor," Mrs. Lonnigan said and gestured.

Lucy sat on the floor, Miles beside her, not betraying with even a glance that this resting place was somewhat out of the ordinary. The children clustered around, looking interested now, no longer wary.

"I . . . I have some tea," the widow offered.

"That would be divine," Lucy said, feeling suddenly as calm as if she sat on the floor in a hovel every other day. "May I help you?"

"Oh, no. Won't take a minute." Mrs. Lonnigan's face fell. "We use the leaves over and over, so they are well-nigh exhausted."

"That suits me," Miles said. "This way the tea won't keep us up at night."

Mrs. Lonnigan went to a corner of the room to a metal stove that looked almost the size of a replica or a toy. Lucy noticed a pan of something cooking on the hob. It was a small pan, and probably held too little for one person's meal, let along four. No wonder the Lonnigan children looked smaller than the ages Mr. Cooper mentioned. She had never missed a meal in her life. She probably would be painfully thin, herself, if food hadn't been available every day, and in satisfying quantities.

The tea turned out to be just a couple of wilted leaves, but it still warmed Lucy's insides. So did the kind expressions of the children.

She knew she was making Mrs. Lonnigan uncomfortable, sitting there on the floor of a hovel, drinking almost-tea. Lucy glanced at Miles, hoping he would take the lead, but his expression—oh, she knew his expressions—told her that this bit of negotiation was her show. She set down her cup.

"Mrs. Lonnigan, I miss my mother with all my heart," she began. "This Christmas I want to honor her memory. I know she used to deliver baskets of Christmas food. I told Mr. Cooper I wanted to do something more this year, a really bold stroke."

To say that Mrs. Lonnigan looked skeptical would have been an understatement of massive proportions. Lucy did not avoid her glance. Underneath the skepticism, she thought she saw utter life-weariness.

I must not muddle this, Lucy thought. *This is not the time to open my mouth and blather.* She glanced at Miles and saw an encouraging nod.

"I want to do more than just give you a Christmas basket and then forget about you for the rest of the year," she said frankly. "I . . . we will start with food, but we will do more."

"What, for instance?" the widow asked, still not convinced.

"You need work that is both steady and honorable," Miles said. "Let me ask a few questions."

"Ask away."

He turned to Edward. "Mr. Cooper told us you are four-teen, Edward."

"As good as, come January fifteenth."

"Edward, what do you like to do?" Miles asked.

He didn't seem to understand the question, from the quiz-zical look he gave Miles.

"You know, for fun," Miles coaxed.

The boy and his mother exchanged a glance that all but shouted, *These rich people don't understand that life is not fun.* Mortified, Lucy could see that in their faces as clearly as if they had said it in unison.

"What do you wish you could do more of in school?" Lucy asked, amending the question, and earning a look of gratitude from Miles.

This was different. Edward would probably always be of a serious turn, but Lucy saw sudden enthusiasm in his eyes.

"Numbers! Above all, numbers," he exclaimed, sitting up. "I love to add and subtract. I am up to three columns and five rows in my head."

"Goodness. I feel fortunate to add one column three rows high," Lucy said. "Numbers, then, for you?"

Edward nodded. He indicated his younger brother. "Michael doesn't like to talk much, but if he sees something hurt, he mends it. Show her the bird, Mikey."

The younger brother indicated with his head that Lucy follow him to the little stove. She knelt beside him as, with sure fingers, he drew back a clean cloth next to what little warmth there was. She saw a bird with a splint on his wing looking back at her.

"I want him to get well, but I'm not certain just how it's done," he said. "He's alive though, so that is something."

"I can't even keep a plant alive," Lucy told him.

"You add water, miss," Michael told her quite seriously.

Before she knew it, the little girl was in her lap. "What about you, Mary Rose?" Lucy asked.

"I would like to cook, if we had any food," she said.

Lucy thought of Honoré and Aunt Amelia fighting over petit fours and the best icing for a groom's cake and wondered what an always hungry child would make of such silliness. She tightened her arms around Mary Rose, who settled back against her with a sigh. Without words, Lucy rested her cheek against the child's head and hoped Miles would pick up the conversational strain. Another word, and she would cry.

"Mrs. Lonnigan, I know you receive a stupidly small pension," he said. "What else do you do?"

"I am a seamstress, except that most of the people I sew for don't have much more than I do."

"Are you proficient?" he asked, which made Lucy stare at him. Was he being rude?

By the set of her mouth and her serious eyes, Lucy saw that Mrs. Lonnigan understood the question. Lucy began to understand Miles Bledsoe better.

"I can sew a fine seam, make excellent buttonholes, and mend a rip so you wouldn't know it happened, sir," she told him, her head up. "Only give me a chance."

"That's what we will do. Lucy, let us go outside for a moment."

He took her hand without giving her a moment to think about it, and towed her outdoors into the misty dusk. With both hands on her shoulders, his face close to hers, he said, "Here is your task tonight when we return home: convince the housekeeper that Mrs. Lonnigan's services are required to put the finishing touches on Clotilde's trousseau."

"I've never convinced anyone of anything," she said in protest.

"It's time you learned. I'm going back in there to tell Mrs. Lonnigan, who hasn't had a good day since Salamanca five years ago, to be at your house tomorrow morning, ready to work," he told her. "Mary Rose, too, because you're also going to assure Honoré that he needs another girl in his kitchen." He took a deep breath. "One who would like to cook if she had any food."

He gave her shoulders a little shake. "This is *your* work. I have plans for the boys that will require some letters, which I will write tonight while you are busy convincing everyone."

"I don't know if anyone will listen to me," she said again, wanting to feel ill used, but unable to, not if she was going to honor her mother. "Miles, no one listens to me!"

He gentled his tone and touched his forehead to hers. "It's high time they did. You want to make a difference? Make a difference right here and show me." He put both arms around her and drew her closer than she had ever stood with him before, closer even than a waltz. She loved it.

"While you're at it, my girl, get rid of Aunt Aurelia. She's starting to get on my nerves."

CHAPTER SEVEN

Lucy did as he said, telling Mrs. Lonnigan and Mary Rose to be at Number Five Mannering Street at eight of the clock tomorrow morning. Her knees practically knocked together and set her dress rustling as she put on the bravest face she possessed and assured them of work through the wedding, and maybe afterward.

While she talked, Miles took the boys with him into the dark and returned in a few minutes with a greasy bag of pasties from the food cart man. He also handed three roses to Mrs. Lonnigan, who burst into tears and clung to him. He patted her back and told Mary Rose to put the roses in a little jar.

"You'll eat better than this soon," he assured them as they stood at the door. "Lads, be ready for a little journey tomorrow. Bring them with you to Mannering Street, Mrs. Lonnigan."

Miles held her hand as they hurried along through the twilight. "What have we done?" Lucy asked.

"Ask yourself that tomorrow after Mrs. Lonnigan is sewing and Mary Rose is cutting up carrots," he said, sounding un-Miles-like. His voice had lost its teasing quality. He was a man in dead earnest. "I am going to write to the counting house in London where we Bledsoes keep our money. I also have a friend working at the Naval Hospital in Portsmouth who is going to get a letter from me. I'll send them by post rider tonight. We'll leave tomorrow morning."

Slowing down, he put her arm through his and became more the cousin she knew. "Your father wouldn't mind if you came along with me and the boys to London, would he?"

"Probably not," she said. "London? It's so big it scares me."

"I'll be with you. In London, I intend to find an apprenticeship for Edward so he can count money to his heart's content. In Portsmouth, there will be much good for Michael to do."

"Why do you need me?" she asked.

"For company. For courage. I'm not used to all this exertion, either, cousin." He patted her gloved hand. "Just think: you can be out of the house when Lord Masterton arrives."

"Capital notion," she said. "Cousin, you are a genius."

They walked back to Number Five Mannering Street in silence, hand in hand. Lucy's mind was whirling with how she would approach Mrs. Little, the housekeeper, with news that a destitute Irish woman would be showing up for work in the morning. She could only assume that Miles was going through a mental list of things he would write in his letters. All she knew was how grateful she felt that he kept his hand in hers.

Looming even larger was Miles's admonition to get rid of Aunt Aurelia, who was only upsetting Clotilde and turning Honoré into a Frenchman fit for Bedlam.

She didn't know how it was possible, but Milsap met them at the door looking both older and grayer than he had a mere two hours before.

"Miss Danforth is nearly in hysterics because of some new crisis," he said.

"Which one?" she asked, not wanting to know.

"Whatever is the latest disturbance," he replied. "I have quite lost track. I hate to be the bearer of further sad tidings of no joy, but she insists that you come to her room the moment you return."

"I think I will not," Lucy told him.

"A wise choice," the butler said with a slight bow.

"Any such news for me, Milsap?" Miles asked.

"You, sir, are a most fortunate man. No one is requiring your presence."

"Such good news! I think I will remain a perpetual guest throughout my life, which means no one will expect much."

"I thought you had more courage, Mr. Bledsoe," Milsap said, relying on his own clout as a long-time family retainer who had known Miles since he was in leading strings.

"Not I! I am off to the bookroom," Miles said. He kissed Lucy's cheek and turned toward the bookroom.

"I am going belowstairs," Lucy said. "How sits the wind in that direction?"

Milsap waggled his hand. "At least Lady Aurelia has retreated to her room to vent her spleen on whatever poor soul ventures into her orbit, now that dinner, which you wisely missed, is over. Make sure that poor soul isn't you, Lucy."

She gave Milsap her own wave and loped toward the green baize-covered door to the kitchen. She descended the stairs in more dignified fashion, trying to think of something to say to Mrs. Little, a redoubtable housekeeper and something of an ally.

Her timid knock brought a booming, "Enter!" Lucy took a deep breath and began her campaign to make a difference this Christmas.

Good fortune was on her side. Mrs. Little was in the middle of removing her spectacles to rub her eyes. On her lap was yet another petticoat in need of a hem.

Lucy pulled a chair away from Mrs. Little's drop-leaf table and seated herself. "How many more petticoats?" she asked.

"At least five." The housekeeper raised her hands in a helpless gesture. "Ordinarily, Sally Fenn would be doing these, but she is sewing lace around the wedding dress, and complaining that her eyes are too old for such close work. She is also threatening to retire from domestic service and I think she means it." Mrs. Little picked up her needle and thread, stared at it like was an alien being, and stuck it back in the pincushion.

"I can solve your dilemma tomorrow morning," Lucy said. She picked up the needle and thread and pulled the petticoat from Mrs. Little's lap. *Wait for it*, she thought as she began to hem. *Just wait.*

"How will you do that?" Mrs. Little asked finally, her hands folded in her lap.

"I am doing what Mama would have done, had she lived," Lucy began, knowing her mother's great affection for the housekeeper. "There is an Irishwoman, a widow whose husband fought with Wellington and died at Salamanca. She needs work, because her pension is too small for a garden gopher to live on." She kept sewing, deliberately making her stitches wider and more uneven. "I believe she will sew you a fine seam."

"On whose authority is she a seamstress?"

"Her own. I believe her," Lucy said. "She has three children to support. All I ask is that you give her a chance. Please do it for Mama."

Silence. She kept hemming as the clock ticked and Mrs. Little considered the matter. She cleared her throat and Lucy looked up.

"Miss Lucy, what happened to the blue-eyed flibbertigibbet who only this morning was mooning around because nothing was going right? It still isn't, but this is a new Lucy."

Lucy stopped the needle and gave the matter some thought. "I don't know," she admitted. She closed her eyes against the pain of remembering Mama, but she knew that was the issue. For five years she had been going with Mama while she delivered food baskets at Christmas. Mr. Cooper said her gentle mother had fought to get the Lonnigan children enrolled in the village school, even though they were Catholic.

She chose her words carefully. "I just saw Mama and her baskets," she told the housekeeper. "How much more good did she do?"

"Considerable," the housekeeper said. "She rescued the 'tween-stairs maid from a horrible workhouse. She just went in there and dragged her out before the beadle could say boo. And your father's favorite gunbearer?"

"Willie?"

"The very same. Your mama heard that the chimney sweep in town was abusing his climbing boys. And now Willie is here and safe." Mrs. Little spread out her hands. "Those are only the ones I know about. I suspect that she had a great deal to do with finding homes for foundlings, and other things of a similar nature that well-bred ladies don't speak of."

"Why didn't she ever say anything about her good deeds?" Lucy asked, her heart so full that she wanted to run to Miles and rest her head on his knee. The reason why, she couldn't have told judge and jury, but that was her first instinct.

"That was part and parcel of what made her a gracious lady," the housekeeper said. "Come to think of it, she did most of her good deeds at Christmastime. I think they were her gift to herself."

Of course, Lucy thought. "Mrs. Little, when I was old enough, I used to ask her what she wanted me to give her for Christmas. She always said she had everything she wanted."

The two of them looked at each other. "I believe she did," Mrs. Little said.

"And now you want to do what your mother would have done and rescue an Irishwoman and all her children?"

Lucy nodded, unable to speak. Worlds seemed to be hinging on the housekeeper's reply.

"I can think of no higher honor than to call you, Lucinda Danforth, your mother's daughter. Certainly the woman may come." Mrs. Little looked at Lucy's horrible stitches and gasped. "Just in the nick of time, I might add."

"My strengths lie elsewhere," Lucy said with some dignity.

"I expect they do."

"There's someone else," Lucy said, after a moment's pause. "She has a daughter eight years old who would like to cook, if she had any food."

After that declaration, no words necessary. Mrs. Little rummaged in her sewing basket and managed to dab at her eyes without anyone noticing except the only other person in the room, who was busy tugging on her uneven hemming stitches and sniffing.

"Get them both here tomorrow morning," Mrs. Little said finally. "If I have to flog Honoré, there will be room for her in his precious kitchen!"

"Let me go reason with him," Lucy said, feeling flush with victory, but even more, wanting to escape the room to blow her nose and wipe her eyes.

"There is no reasoning with a Frog," Mrs. Little said with finality, "but do try. I'd come along, but . . ."

You want to blow your nose, too, Lucy thought, as she let herself out of the housekeeper's room.

CHAPTER EIGHT

Above all, Lucy knew that for Honoré to allow Mary Rose into his sanctum sanctorum, even to peel potatoes, the little girl needed to be his idea. She stood a moment outside Mrs. Little's closed door, then walked into the servants' hall.

There he sat, Papa's prince of a chef, lured from Lord Elwood's kitchen by a sum of money that Papa never dared disclose to Mama. Honoré leaned forward at the table, his face hidden in his hands. At a loss, Lucy sat beside him.

The chef started at her footsteps, then moved his hands. His was a look of desperation, the sort of expression that usually meant a letter of resignation would be forthcoming.

What would Mama say? Lucy asked herself. "Honoré, I fear you have had a distressing day. May I help?"

The chef waved his arms wildly about as though he were directing an orchestra of two-year-olds. "Lady Burbage will either drive me into an early coffin, or resignation," he said, his voice more mournful than angry. "Everything I suggest, she vetoes. She clears her throat in that irritating way and demands—*demands*— that I change my plans to suit her. And Clotilde just wrings her hands and weeps."

Lucy took his hands in hers, wondering at her effrontery. "And still you soldier onward, Honoré! I have never met a man as brave as you."

Her words, quietly spoken, seemed to sink into the chef's heart, if his expression was any indication. "I do try," he said finally.

"Especially when the honor of France is at state," Lucy told him. "If only other Englishmen had any idea how brave you are to cook during these times of national emergency."

She couldn't think of any current national emergency, now that Napoleon was at his leisure on St. Helena. As she thought, she remembered something she had wanted to tell their cook. In the confusion and distress of Mama's death, she had forgotten. She remembered now.

"I meant to tell you this months ago," she began, and then the familiar tears welled in her eyes. *When* would she ever get over those betrayals of her innermost feelings? She took a deep breath. "Thank you from the bottom of my heart for being so willing to fix Mama those little favorites of hers," she said, not trusting herself to look at him. "I . . . I know it was inconvenient at times, but when she just took a bite of something, it was a bit of a victory. *Merci.*"

"I never met a better woman," he said, when he could speak.

"Nor I."

They sat in silence, until she began to speak of Mama's annual Christmas gifts to the less fortunate in the village. "I want to continue Mama's gift, and here is how: there is a Mrs. Lonnigan, a widow whose husband died at the Battle of Salamanca, defending us from those evil Frenchmen who usurped your own country."

"I remember that battle well," he said, tears forgotten. His voice hardened. "Marmot, Clausel and Foy—three marshals could not defeat Wellington!"

"How sad that men die, even on the winning side," Lucy said. "Mrs. Lonnigan is going to sew for Mrs. Little, and Mary Rose would like to help in your kitchen. Could you allow her, Honoré?" She paused a moment. "I am certain it would have been Mama's wish, too. After all, she worked so hard to get the Lonnigan children, Catholics all, into the village school."

While he thought about the matter, Lucy delivered what she hoped what her coup de grâce. "Honoré, if I ever marry, and I suppose I must, all I want you to do is serve us strawberries dipped in chocolate, if it is summertime."

He smiled at her now, probably well aware of her little subterfuge, but perhaps willing to overlook any manipulation. "That is all? You would perhaps let me serve you sparkling cider to go along with *fraise enrobé de chocolat?*"

"Cider makes me sneeze," she said, "but if you would like to serve it, very well."

"And if you should marry some fine gentleman in the winter?" he asked, more at ease now, because the deep crease between his eyes grew smaller.

"I will hope for a snowstorm so there will be no visitors to bother us," Lucy said after giving the matter some thought. "We will slip and slide our way to the church, and get married. I will toast cheese with my husband and drink your wassail."

"That will never do," he scolded gently. "Wedding parties must be noisy, elaborate affairs, where everyone goes home with a headache and perhaps a few regrets. People expect a party."

"It will do for me," she said, her voice equally gentle. "Until I find such a paragon, you need not worry about Clotilde or my Aunt Aurelia muddying the waters here. Will you have Mary Rose in your kitchen?" she asked.

"*Oui, mademoiselle.* I like your idea. Have her here at eight of the clock, for her first day."

He gave her a sly look next, that exiled son of La Belle France. "And if you can really find a way to keep Lady Aurelia away—"

"I will do my best," she promised. All she knew was plain speaking. Perhaps if it came from her, the least important member of the household, Lady Aurelia would be so surprised she would leave. One could hope, and it was the season of hope and cheer, after all.

Lucy kissed his cheek and darted for the hall, hoping that the Frenchman would not change his mind. She looked around the entryway, which in a few days would be decorated with garlands and bows. Everyone would celebrate such an advantageous match for the daughter of a country gentleman, the daughter who was probably even now crying and wringing out her overtaxed handkerchief. What on earth was the matter with Clotilde?

CHAPTER NINE

"Please have these in the right hands by morning," Miles said to the post rider, in his many-caped riding overcoat.

The man took the letters and money and gave a cheerful salute, opening the bookroom door just as Lucinda was trying to enter from the other side. They bumped into each other, which made Miles's cousin laugh and apologize. The post rider gave her a quick salute and hurried on his way.

"Are you all right, cousin?" Miles asked, imagining how any other young lady of his acquaintance would have shrieked and put on die-away airs.

She nodded, and plumped down in her usual chair. "I admire a man who lets nothing stop him from his appointed rounds. Is he taking your letters?" she asked.

"Aye, miss," he said, trying to sound like the post rider, which made her dimple up in that adorable fashion he relished. "How did you fare in the kitchen?"

She gave him a sunny smile. "Beyond my expectations. I played on Mrs. Little's kind heart, and sewed a terrible seam to make her look forward to Mrs. Lonnigan's arrival in the morning."

"And Honoré?"

"Miles, he is more than happy to employ a little kitchen girl whose father died fighting those dastardly French who drove his beloved royals off the throne of La Belle France." She tucked her legs under her. "I promised him that if I ever get married—"

"Which you most certainly will—"

"That is open to doubt, Miles," she said. "I promised Honoré that if I marry in the summer, all I will require of him are strawberries dipped in chocolate and eaten outside on the lawn. I did agree to champagne."

He laughed at that, remembering how champagne made her sneeze. "And in the winter?"

She gave him a complacent look, the sort that passed between friends and needed little, if any, explanation. And crazily enough, he understood her completely. "All I want to do is shoo everyone home and eat toasted cheese and drink wassail with my darling husband, should I find such a creature. Honoré is convinced I have lost my mind."

Miles marveled how something so simple should sound so right. "You may have hit upon something, Lucinda. Toasted cheese and wassail."

She gave a gusty sigh. "Easy for us to say. We are neither of us in love. Perhaps being in love makes people turn crazy and demand towering cakes with Pisa-like tendencies, flower arrangements, and dresses that itch."

He laughed at that, which made her snatch up a pillow from the sofa close by and throw it at him.

"I ask you, Miles, how would *you* feel with scratchy lace digging into your armpit?" she asked. "That is my unfortunate lot." She sighed again. "I would prefer flannel and bedroom slippers, but no one asked me."

"Nor will they, scamp," he said. "I managed to corner your father when he returned from dinner at your neighbor's, and he was only too happy to let you accompany me to London tomorrow and then to Portsmouth, with our little charges in tow. I have already arranged for a post chaise for the four of us—we'll be crowded but they are small. We haven't the luxury of time to wait for replies. Pack a bandbox and be ready."

She gave him another one of those smiles that was making his heart do strange things. He would have to request some bicarbonate of soda before he went to bed. Perhaps the filet of sole for luncheon was slightly off.

"Oh, please, at least one night in London with your parents," she asked. "I love them."

"Certainly. They would disown me if I were to deny them a visit from you."

"That is the correct answer, Miles," she told him, in all complacency. "I will pack and be ready first thing in the morning."

He wanted to ask her to stay a little longer but there was no particular reason, beyond the reality that he liked her presence. Miles Bledsoe had thought he wasn't a man who required company, particularly since he had spent so much time recently in library carrels. He watched her leave, marveling how she seemed to suck out the air with her. He must be tired; that explained the sudden feeling of loss.

He tried to tell himself that she was warming to him, beyond her own natural affection as his second cousin. He had seen her reaction when he whispered in her ear; it was all a lover could wish. And then she had done the same thing to him, perhaps as a joke.

He knew himself as well as any man his age probably did. From his years at Oxford, he was already well-acquainted with his tendency to over-think matters. Was he trying too hard? Was he not trying hard enough? *Great gobs of monkey meat, what next?*

He went to the window and stared out at the loveliness that was Kent, even in the depths of winter. And if by the smallest chance Lucinda Danforth discovered that she loved him, too, would someone as quiet and dear as she enjoy the life of a diplomatist's wife?

"You're over-thinking, Miles Bledsoe," he scolded his reflection in the mirror. He wished he could talk to his older brother Matthew and ask him what to do. Matt was a husband and father several times over now.

On a whim, he picked up the Bible. He turned first to Proverbs 17, and saw, in his mind's eye, Lucinda as the merry dose of medicine that probably kept Cousin Penelope alive for a few more precious months. He then turned to Micah 7, and read again, "When I sit in darkness, the Lord shall be a light unto me."

They weren't even Christmas verses. As he closed the Bible thoughtfully, Miles knew that if he survived this season, they would always mean Christmas to him. "Try not to over-think Lucinda Patterson," he told himself as he lay down to sleep, sighed, and turned the matter of Lucy over to the Almighty. A man in love can only so do much.

CHAPTER TEN

Her mind a perfect blank, Lucy knocked on her aunt's bedroom door. She opened it when the voice within permitted her and saw her redoubtable aunt just sitting there at her dressing table, hairbrush in hand, shoulders slumping.

She wanted to be angry at this managing lady who was trying to wrest all power into her own hands and organize the dickens out of them, but she found she could not. She saw a tired woman before her, one looking at her now in the mirror's reflection.

"Aunt Aurelia, let me do that for you," she said, coming closer.

Her aunt turned the hairbrush over to her, and Lucy ran its boar's head bristles down Aurelia's beautiful tresses. She brushed and brushed until Aurelia's reflection looked almost at peace.

"We've worn you out here," Lucy said. "That was never our intention, dear aunt."

Then came a litany of scolds and trials that seemed to tumble out of her mouth in a never-ending stream. Shocked at first, Lucy began to listen, and her heart softened further.

Probably not even aware of it, Aurelia had segued from Clotilde's inability to make up her mind about anything, to her brother Roscoe's cowardice or laziness in wanting nothing to do with anything that smacked of exertion, to her own disappointment at Sir Henry Burbage, who was gambling away the family fortune, to her distress at a long-faced daughter who would probably never marry, to another daughter dead in childbirth five years ago, and then to their only son, who seemed to be following in his father's rackety footsteps.

Lucy brushed and listened, thinking of the times she had poured out her troubles to Mama, who probably had troubles enough of her own. She thought suddenly of Miles, who never minded dropping everything to listen to her, when she was melancholic about Mama, or dreading her upcoming London Season. When had she ever listened to him?

What happened as she brushed her aunt's hair was an epiphany Lucy never expected, not when so much was going on, and she felt powerless. *We only want someone to listen to us with love*, she thought. *I am eighteen now. It is time I started listening to others. I wonder if Miles would let me listen to him? I believe I want to.*

When she finished, when Aunt Aurelia's handsome gray hair was an electrical nimbus, Lucy laughed out loud and kissed her aunt's head, wherever it was down there. She pulled her hair and began to braid it as Aurelia sighed and then was silent.

"There you are now, Aunt," she said, after tying each braid with a bit of yarn.

They were both small, so she sat on the narrow bench beside the woman she had been fearing. Looking in the mirror, she saw her own resemblance to Papa's sister, here when she had thought she looked so much like her own mother.

"Look at us," she said softly, unwilling to disturb the moment. "We have the same blue eyes."

Aurelia smiled at their reflections. "I believe we do."

Mama, help me say the right thing now, Lucy thought. "Aunt, we have worn you out. I so wish you would go home tomorrow and rest a bit. Just think: Clotilde's wedding will be on Christmas Eve. You can be back here in four hours, and you will be rested and ready to enjoy it. You've laid the groundwork here, and I can carry on."

Aunt Aurelia stiffened, and Lucy held her breath. With a sigh, her aunt relaxed again. "That would be pleasant. Henry and your cousin are in London right now, probably gambling at White's." She passed her hand in front of her face and then brightened. "I would have the house to myself, wouldn't I? Or nearly so. Maude keeps to her room."

"You could get up when you wanted, eat breakfast when you wanted," Lucy said. "I do like breakfast!"

"I know you do, Lucy," Aurelia said playfully, becoming the energetic but enjoyable person Lucy remembered from years ago, before troubles and challenges turned Papa's sister so brittle. "I remember that time you ate so much bacon in my breakfast room that you had a stomach ache and swore never to eat pork again."

"I didn't keep that vow very long," Lucy said. She took her aunt's hand and tucked it next to her cheek. "Trust me to finish up here what you have begun so admirably. Papa will happily loan you his carriage for a trip home, and we will see you back here on Christmas Eve."

They turned to each other. Aurelia put her arms around Lucy, who felt her own troubles slip away. "This is my Christmas gift to you, dear aunt," she whispered. "You have done so much for us."

Lucy stayed a few minutes longer in her aunt's room, listening as Aurelia talked now of the few remaining things she wanted to do at her home, before Christmas came. Lucy blew her a kiss goodnight and closed the door quietly.

She stood in the darkened hall a long moment. She heard the front door open and close downstairs, and Milsap greet her father, who had taken dinner with a neighbor. Through more mature eyes, she saw Roscoe Danforth for what he was—a troubled man floundering about without his wife to guide him. "Bless you, Papa," she said in the dark. "I pray time will help."

She went to her room, but paused with her hand on the doorknob. It was far too late to bother her cousin, wasn't it? She tiptoed to his door and looked down to see a bit of light coming from inside.

It's just Miles, she told herself. *He won't mind.* She knocked her usual knock: two knocks, a pause and two more.

"Lucinda, what in the world do you want?" she heard.

"You, I think," she said. The door opened more quickly than she would have thought. He must have leaped from his bed.

He was in his nightshirt, a handsome blue-and-white-striped affair that showed off his legs to some advantage. She could tease him about that later.

"Get back in bed," she ordered. "You'll freeze your toes."

He did as she said, and she saw a flash of more Miles than she expected. She sat on the chair by the bed, hopeful that blushes didn't show in near dark.

"I did it, Miles," she told him. "Aunt Aurelia is going home tomorrow."

He had been sitting up. On that news, he flopped back and made her giggle.

"Seriously?" he asked, raising up on one elbow.

"I never joke about liberation," she teased, and then turned sober. "Miles, all she wanted was someone to listen to her and sympathize a bit. I went to her room determined to do that in jest and meanness, just to get rid of her, but I listened instead, I really listened. Life has been hard for her."

"Lonnigan hard?" he asked, his hands behind his head now as he watched her.

"No. She will always have enough to eat and wear, even if Henry Burbage gambles on cards in the winter and horses in the summer. Hard just the same. She has disappointed hopes."

It was absurd in the extreme, but Lucy wanted more than anything to curl up next to Miles and never move until morning. She sat where she was. There would be plenty of time in the new year to work through her own silliness.

Staying there wasn't helping those thoughts go away, so she stood up and went to the door. "I wanted you to know. She will leave in the morning, and I will be ready to go with you to London with the Lonnigan boys."

He nodded, but didn't say anything. He just looked at her with those wonderful deep-brown eyes of his, round like a child's.

She stood in the open doorway a moment more. "Mama listened to people," she said, and closed the door behind her.

CHAPTER ELEVEN

Giving Aunt Aurelia a heartfelt embrace, Lucy waved goodbye to her next morning from the front steps.

After baked eggs, toast and rashers of bacon in the servants' hall that made the Lonnigan brothers' eyes open wide, Mrs. Lonnigan gave her own contented sigh and arranged the first of several petticoats on her lap to hem in Mrs. Little's comfortable sitting room.

Mary Rose, her eyes hopeful now, scraped carrots and chopped them under Honoré's watchful eye.

"She is adept, for one so young," the family chef whispered to Lucy.

"I knew she would do," Lucy whispered back. "Remember to give her bites to sample now and then. She has been hungry for too long."

Honoré drew himself up with pride. "No one leaves this kitchen hungry, mademoiselle," he said. He leaned closer. "Is Lady Burbage truly gone?"

"Truly," Lucy assured him. "She will be back Christmas Eve for the wedding." She gave him her best smile. "If she becomes a bit managing then, you can bear it, Honoré, because it will only be for a few hours."

"I believe I can," he agreed. He kissed his fingers and stretched his hand in her direction. "Miss Lucy, *quelle magnifique!*"

"Indeed she is."

Lucy looked around with a smile to see Miles wearing his many-caped coat and low-crowned beaver hat, two little boys on either side of him. For the tiniest moment, she imagined they were his own children. *Miles, you will be such a father some day*, she thought. *I wonder who their lucky mother will be?*

It was a beguiling thought, but one which did not please her. How in the world would such a wonderful man find a lady good enough?

Lucy shrugged off her unease. She knew she could bully and tease her cousin to her heart's content, but the matter of his finding a wife was patently none of her business. For one moment, she wished them both children again, with few worries. The moment passed, because she knew she could do more good, and do it right now, to make sure this was her best Christmas ever, even with Mama gone.

She couldn't help but admire the Lonnigan boys. Mrs. Lonnigan had turned them out in what Lucy suspected was their best clothing. They were shabby but tidy, faces serious because life was a serious business. She realized with a pang that they knew more about hard times than she ever would. In one respect, they were equal: the boys had lost a father, she a mother.

"Will we do?" Edward asked, the older of the two.

"You will," she assured him. She gave him a pat on the shoulder and straightened his collar. "I am impressed."

"What about me?" Miles asked.

The little boys laughed as Lucy scrutinized Miles, walking around to view him from all angles. Edward chuckled, a child again, when Lucy made a great show of tugging at her cousin's neckcloth, then licked her finger and wiped a smidge of shaving soap off his neck.

Lucy stood so close to him, nothing unusual in itself, except that it was, because she felt herself breathing a little faster, her face warm. *It's just Miles*, she reminded herself, but that admonition did nothing to slow her respirations. She stepped back, irritated with herself.

"Well, uh, let's go outside," Miles said, and she wondered why he should seem so ill at ease.

Without asking, Michael took her grip in hand and started after his older brother. "Thank you, kind sir," she said, which earned her a smile from a boy far too serious.

She realized with a start that what happened to these boys today came close to life or death. A modest career meant a chance. Anything less could spell ruin. *Mama understood*, she thought, and blinked back tears. With great clarity, she remembered Mama's last words to her: "Do all the good you can."

She hadn't said anything like that to Clotilde, and Mama had clung, wordless, to Papa's hand as the final moment approached. "Be sweet," had been her final words to Clotilde, who had sobbed and sobbed. Mama had said nothing to Papa, only looked deep into his eyes, because no words were necessary.

Following behind Miles and watching Edward walking with him, Lucy suddenly understood what Mama meant. *You expect me to do, rather than just be*, she thought, and realized that keeping Christmas this year meant exactly that. Christ hadn't come to earth to be an ornament—he'd come here to *do*. She would have to tell Miles about this, if they had a quiet moment.

"Oh, wait," she said suddenly to Miles. "One more thing. I'll meet you outside."

It wasn't ladylike, even in her own home, but Lucy pulled up her skirts and dashed up the stairs. She burst into Clotilde's room.

Her sister gasped in surprise and stopped her contemplation of her face in the mirror. "What in the world, Lucy!"

Here I go, Lucy thought, as she took her older sister by both arms. "Clotilde, Aunt Aurelia has gone home for a well-deserved rest. I will be in London with Miles for a day or so. Honoré knows what he is doing, and Mrs. Lonnigan is finishing your trousseau."

Clotilde nodded, her lovely eyes open wide.

"I want you to take a serious look at what you are doing," Lucy said, her voice firm. "You're moping about and crying. If I were in love, I would be over the moon with joy and counting every second until I was Mrs. . . . Mrs. . . . oh, I don't know, Mrs. Bledsoe. Whoever."

"It's not that simple," Clotilde replied, striving for dignity.

"I think it is," Lucy said. "It is also never too late to change your mind."

"You are absurd," Clotilde told her.

"Probably." Lucy kissed her sister. "Just promise me you'll think about it. I'll be back soon. I love you."

The post chaise was a tight fit made easier because Michael sat beside her and Edward beside Miles. She smiled inside to see the wonder on the boys' faces, and understood that any previous travels had been on the crowded mail coach.

So she thought. Edward disabused her of that notion when he leaned across the aisle and tapped his younger brother's knee. "Mikey, do you remember those days when we rode on the caisson in Papa's battery?"

"You had better fill us in on your Spanish exploits," Miles said. "I have a strong feeling that you have lived a far more exciting life than we have." He winked at Lucy. "We're boring old sticks, compared to these two."

Lucy wondered how Miles knew the precise way to draw out these solemn children who had seen their fair share of challenge, and then some. Her heart opened up and took in the Lonnigan boys, too, noticing how they sat taller, with a certain quiet pride. She couldn't help but sit taller, too, happy to be in the company of little heroes and a man who had a fine instinct about people. Funny she had never noticed that before.

The miles flew by as the boys took turns telling Lucy and Miles about battles, and heat and dust, and babies born on the march as their father, an artillerist, plied his trade in Wellington's army. The animation on their faces told Lucy everything she wanted to know about the little Lonnigan family, sticking together through war and tumult.

They stopped for luncheon not far from London at a tavern more ordinary than she would have thought necessary, considering how plump in the purse both she and Miles were. She watched the boys as the chaise slowed and then stopped, noting the return of their serious faces, coupled with worry.

The worry vanished when Miles ushered them inside the working man's eating place. It was warm and noisy and full of people exactly like the boys. She couldn't help her amusement to see how the talk died down when Miles found them places, and realized that *they* were the odd ones. They were eating here to keep their little charges comfortable.

"Pasties and cider," Miles said to the man behind the counter. He leaned closer. "We'll take some with us, too. Growing boys, you know."

Lucy never ate anything better.

They arrived in London mid-afternoon, the chaise slowing to a walk as the post rider expertly threaded his way through crowds that had Michael and Edward staring, and Lucy, too. *I really don't want a London Season*, she thought. *Give me a quiet place.*

"You really don't care for London, do you?" Miles asked her.

His evident concern touched her heart, deep down in that place she thought was hers alone. Miles Bledsoe was watching out for her; he listened to her. For the first time in her life, she knew she could share that part of her heart someday—maybe with someone like Miles.

"I don't," she said. "I wish I did, but I don't." She shook her head and stared out the window, embarrassed to be so provincial, and wondering where her heart was taking her. "I like to know my neighbors and walk when and where I want to."

Michael nodded and put his hand in hers, which touched her heart. She squeezed his fingers. "Miles, I do believe Michael and I would rather be at home."

She glanced at Edward, noting the excitement on his face. "You, on the other hand, would be a Londoner," she said to him.

"I would," Edward replied. "This is exciting."

The post rider took them to Half Moon Street, with its row houses two and three stories high, each stoop gleaming white, as though in competition with the house on either side. Lucy saw Miles's mother standing at the first floor window.

"I sent her a quick note that you were coming, too," Miles told her. He leaned across Edward and blew his mother a kiss. Lucy saw her head go back in laughter and then she was gone from the window.

Mrs. Bledsoe opened the door herself and ushered her little guests inside. She pulled Lucy in next, and kissed her. Miles got a hug and a kiss on the cheek.

"Mother, these are Edward and Michael Lonnigan, in London to seek their fortunes."

"You have certainly come to the right place," Mrs. Bledsoe said. "Bolton, show them to their room so they can freshen up before a visit to the counting house."

Lucy watched the boys, seeing the understated elegance of No. 12, Half Moon Street through their eyes—the walls of the foyer a pale green. Instead of the fresh flowers of summer, a Christmas wreath hung above the little table with its silver salver where guests left their calling cards. The boys would have no way of knowing that the charming portrait of a young girl that smiled at them was Vivian Bledsoe at age five, painted by Thomas Gainsborough himself.

Lucy admired the painting now, and saw the resemblance between mother and son, standing close together in the entranceway.

"I'll take them up, Mother," Miles said and kissed her cheek. "You can deal with our cousin."

"Deal with you? My son treats you in a cavalier way," Mrs. Bledsoe said as they mounted the stairs more slowly.

They went first into her private sitting room, where tea and biscuits already waited. Lucy took off her bonnet and fluffed her mashed hair. "Your son has been kind enough to help me keep Christmas as Mama would have, by doing a little good. Thank you, Vivian," she said, accepting a cup of good green tea.

Lucy relished the comfort of the small room, wondering if she could make the Bledsoe home her refuge from the trouble and anxiety of a London Season. In only a few minutes, she spilled out her sorrow at her mother's passing, the unwelcome burden of a come out, and her earnest desire to keep Christmas by helping the less fortunate.

Her cousin Vivian took it all in without comment, edging closer on the sofa until she put her arm around Lucy, which allowed her to rest her head against the woman's shoulder. "Maybe I am the less fortunate," Lucy said. "Edward will be apprenticed to a counting house, and Michael perhaps to a surgeon. I'm the one with no fixed aim and purpose, beyond protecting our cook from Aunt Aurelia."

"Brave girl," Mrs. Bledsoe murmured. "Roscoe tells me that Aurelia can be a trial."

"Less than you would think. I convinced her to go home and rest, and she agreed."

Vivian stared at her. "You have the makings of a diplomatist. I'll tell my son to take lessons from you!"

"Oh, no," Lucy said, embarrassed but pleased. "Miles will manage quite well on his own." She took a turn around the room, teacup in hand. "Clotilde is my cross to bear. She cries and frets and I don't understand why. She claims she is marrying the love of her life." She took a sip. "Cousin, how does a lady know if she is in love?"

Lucy hated to sound so pathetic, but there was no one else to ask. And why she was even asking, she did not know. Thoughts became words, welled up, and escaped. Clotilde seemed to think she was in love, but why so many tears and uncertainty? And why did it even matter? "I am in a muddle," she concluded, vastly dissatisfied with herself. She sat down next to Vivian again.

Mrs. Bledsoe pulled her close. "Lucy, I suspect love is different for different people."

"For you then," she said. "Did you always love Cousin Will amazingly?"

"No! I would be guilty of prevarication if I said I did." She patted Lucy's hand. "I had known him for years. My deeper feelings developed gradually, with no trumpet fanfare or drum roll." Her voice grew a little dreamy, for a woman of matronly proportions and white hair, or so Lucy thought. "One afternoon he came calling and I just looked at him and knew. Bald hair and bad eyes and so tall and thin back then, but I just knew."

"That's no answer," Lucy said.

"Yes it is, you scamp!" her cousin said with a laugh, the spell broken. "And there is this, now that you remind me: I began to feel uncomfortable when he was not nearby. I still do, I suppose."

"I'll just know?"

"You will, Lucinda Danforth, you will."

CHAPTER TWELVE

Miles didn't seem surprised when Lucy insisting on accompanying him and Edward to the Bradfield-Ashby Counting House, which meant Michael came, too. They piled back into the post chaise for the trip to Cornhill Road, a part of London unfamiliar to Lucy.

Miles knew it well enough. "Now we are officially in the City of London," he told them all as they wove through traffic, noise, and bad smells. "Boys like you sled down Cornhill. See there?"

Lucy looked, too, wishing that her sledding days weren't over. Of course, if she married and had a little boy or two, would her inevitable-but-right-now-unknown husband object if she slid downhill, too? She knew Miles wouldn't, but who could say a husband would be as obliging as her cousin?

"This is London's financial district, Edward. Take a good look," Miles was saying. "I can see you doing quite well here." He pointed into the maze of buildings. "Over there on Threadneedle Street—perhaps you can see it—is the Bank of England. Lots of money in there. And here is the Bradfield-Ashby Counting House."

"What will I do here?" Edward asked. "I mean, if they apprentice me?"

"Count money. Tote up long figures. Subtract where needed. Make meticulous entries in ledgers. All those things you enjoy," Miles told him. "If you become really proficient, you might find yourself giving clients advice on what to do with their money."

"That's going to take a while," Edward said, sounding dubious.

"As it should. I have no doubt that you are equal to the task."

Lucy watched Edward's face light up with Miles's praise. The fear left, leaving behind quiet competence.

Lucy couldn't have said if she took Michael's hand or he took hers, so magnificent was the Bradfield-Ashby Counting House. Led by a young man in a dark suit, they passed under chandeliers and down a corridor with a thick carpet and elegant walls to the office of Mr. Solon Bradfield himself.

More dignified than she had ever seen him before, Miles introduced them. Both boys gave a proper bow. Michael seated himself and continued looking around the ornate office, while Edward focused all his attention on the man now seating himself behind a desk carved to a fare thee well.

Edward knows exactly how important this moment is, Lucy thought, impressed with the same little boy that this morning was all eyes over more bacon than he had probably seen in years, if ever.

Miles wasted not a moment in explaining his purpose and offering Edward Lonnigan, son of a dead artillerist in Wellington's Army and a seamstress in Tidwell, as a candidate for an apprenticeship.

"He is skilled in arithmetic and comes here in need of future employment," Miles concluded. "Try him."

The august Mr. Bradfield did precisely that. Lucy watched, holding her breath, as he took a sheet of paper from a drawer, pulled back his cuffs a little, and wrote three numbers each in four lines. He handed the paper to Edward and offered him a writing tool.

"I don't need that, sir," Edward said, as he stared at the paper.

Mr. Bradfield exchanged an amazed glance with Miles. Lucy held her breath.

Edward took his time, then handed the paper back. "Four thousand, two hundred and twenty-five, sir," he said.

Mr. Bradfield took that pencil and toted up the numbers. "Precisely so," he said. He wrote more numbers in five lines, with the same result. Another sheet came out, with two long lines. "Subtract this."

Again Edward shook his head over the offered pencil. Same result. Mr. Bradfield sat back in his chair with a satisfied look on his face.

"You weren't bamming me, were you, Mr. Bledsoe?" he asked, surprising Lucy by using such a cant expression in so dignified a setting. The effect served to relieve the tension in Edward's high-held shoulders. He looked almost like a little boy again. Almost.

"I never tease about money and numbers," Miles said. "No more than you do, Mr. Bradfield. What say you, sir? I am willing to stand as proxy and surety to Edward Lonnigan, if you will apprentice him." He reached inside his coat. "I have a note here from his mother, giving me such permission. Edward's father died under the guns at Salamanca and the boy must make his own way in the world."

Mr. Bradfield turned his attention to Edward, who regarded him seriously, but with no fear in his eyes. "I was an apprentice in a counting house once," the banker said. "I didn't even know my father, so you have the advantage of me, Edward. Someone like Mr. Bledsoe here took a chance on me, too. What say *you*, young man?"

"Aye, sir," Edward said, his voice soft, but with no hint of fear.

Lucy sat back in relief and gratitude as the three men in the room—Edward seemed to grow in stature—drew up apprenticeship papers. Her heart light, she listened as Miles assured both Edward and Mr. Bradfield that either he or a substitute would come by monthly for the six years of the apprenticeship, to confirm that each party was maintaining his end of the agreement.

"If I see anything amiss with his treatment, the apprenticeship ends, and so does Bledsoe money in your counting house," Miles said.

Mr. Bradfield gave a nod of appreciation. Obviously the men knew each other well. "Our apprentices live in a small house a block over on Finch Lane. A respectable widow supervises them and provides meals," Mr. Bradfield said. "The boys have half Saturday and Sunday off. Edward, when the apprenticeship ends, you will either find employment right here, or in another counting house. Our reputation is stellar." He said it with quiet pride, which gave Lucy some inkling of his own hard path. Mr. Bradfield held out the document to Edward. "Would you care to sign this?"

"Aye, sir," Edward said again. He did take a pen this time, signing his name where the banker pointed.

Mr. Bradfield signed, followed by Miles Bledsoe. The banker looked at the page and then at Edward. "Your penmanship is excellent, too."

His head held high, Edward nodded. "My da taught me. He was an artillerist and a dab hand at letters and numbers."

"Just as I would expect from an artillerist. You were more fortunate than most," Mr. Bradfield said. He directed his gaze to Michael, who sat next to Lucy. "And you, lad, are you equally adept at numbers?"

The shy boy cleared his throat. "I like horses."

Everyone laughed. Michael ducked his head into Lucy's side.

"Until something better comes along, we need those, too," Mr. Bradfield told him. He stood up and addressed Lucy this time. "My dear, take these lads around the corner to 15 Finch Lane, if you will," he said. "Mrs. Hodgson will measure our newest apprentice for a suit of clothes. We like the lads to be uniform in appearance." A shadow crossed his face. "I remember my own apprenticeship, Edward. I had but one shirt, pair of knee breeches and torn stockings to my name. No one is laughed at here. Good day to you, Miss Danforth. And you, Edward, I will see two days after Christmas. Be prepared to work hard."

Her heart full, Lucy led the boys from the counting house and around the corner to a neat brick building. A rap on the knocker produced a gray-haired woman in dark dress and apron, who introduced herself as Mrs. Hodgson. In a matter of minutes, the boys were enjoying gingersnaps and milk while the housekeeper went in search of her tape measure.

"Please, miss."

Lucy turned her attention from the sampler on the wall proclaiming, "*God's will be done*," to Michael, gingersnap in one hand and half empty glass in the other. "Yes, my dear?"

"Mama wants me to distinguish myself, too, but I mostly like horses."

A miracle had already happened with Edward. Lucy was ready for another one. "I have no doubt that Mr. Bledsoe will find a way," she assured him.

Michael nodded, but his worried look barely changed. "I also don't want to be far from Edward," he said in a whisper.

She glanced at Edward, who stood with his arms out as Mrs. Hodgson measured him for a suit jacket. "We've always been together," Bradfield-Ashby's newest apprentice said.

In her mind's eye, she saw both boys trudging dusty Spanish roads, following their father as he marched toward his own destiny. She thought of Clotilde, and how her sister's London Season and subsequent engagement had driven a wedge between them, with the gulf growing wider. Soon they would barely know each other. What would Mama have said about these boys?

"Let me talk to Mr. Bledsoe. I'll see what he can do." She moved closer to Mrs. Hodgson. "May I speak to Edward's patron?"

"Certainly you may, Miss Danforth," the housekeeper said. She paused to write Edward's measurement on a tablet. The tape went around his waist next. "After all, we still have a half dozen gingersnaps to go."

She walked back to the counting house just as Miles was shaking hands with Mr. Bradfield at the entrance.

She stood there on the pavement, pleased all out of proportion by the welcoming smile on his face. She thought of all the hours they had spent with each other and felt suddenly as shy as Michael Lonnigan. She knew this cousin of hers so well, but one of them was changing. Whether it was he or she, Lucy did not know.

He took her arm on the sidewalk and shepherded her toward a bench under a counting house window. "Where away, Miss Danforth?" he asked.

She could have just told him what Michael wanted, but she had to say more, had to tell him what was in her full heart. He might think her silly; she hoped not. If she had learned anything in the last few remarkable days, it was that one shouldn't leave things unsaid. And this was Miles, who knew her better than any man alive, even Papa.

"Miles, you're the most magnificent person I know," she said, and felt her face grow warm, even with snow beginning to fall. "At . . . at the beginning of this week, I was just going to take a basket of food to a hungry family." She looked down at the snow settling on her cloak, relieved when his arm tightened around her shoulder, as if he were encouraging her. "Here we are in London, and you have just guaranteed a young lad's future."

"The work is still his to do," he said. "Lucinda, I'll confess to you that I am so happy about what just happened that I want to give you a whacking great kiss and dance a little jig."

"You know you're more dignified than that," she said with a laugh.

He didn't kiss her, but he rested his cheek against hers for an all-too-brief moment. "Kindly do not overlook the good you have done for Mrs. Lonnigan, Mary Rose, and even Aunt Aurelia. Doing good seems to beget more of the same."

"I believe Mama intended that," she said. She took a deep breath. "Michael loves horses, and neither boy wants to be separated from the other. What do we do now?"

He loosened his grip on her shoulder, but did not release her. "I suggest we think about the matter, if you don't mind sitting in the snow."

"Not at all, since you are here, too," she said, which changed his expression from good humor to something more serious. Lately she was seeing more and more of this side of her dear cousin. She wanted to tease him about it, but there was her own shyness to account for, which she could not.

"I started this journey thinking we would go to Portsmouth on the way home to Tidwell. I sent a message by post last night to a surgeon friend of mine at Haslar Royal Navy Hospital," he said. "He is always saying he needs more loblolly boys to do the fetch and carry in the wards."

"Started?" she prompted, when he said nothing more for a long moment, lost in thought.

"A simpler child is Michael," he said finally. "He's young for his age, and I have made myself uneasy with the thought of pitching him into such a place as Haslar." He ran his hand along Lucy's arm, probably not even aware. She wasn't about to say anything, not even in jest, because she loved the feeling. "My friend would watch him, but Michael is a tender little fellow."

"It's probably not the place for him," Lucy agreed. "He likes horses."

He smiled and brushed at her hair. "Snowflakes," he said. "They're quite becoming on you, Miss Curly Hair Beauty Fair."

For the first moment in her lifetime of knowing his cousin of hers, she could not think of anything witty to say in return. She realized she had no wish to break the lovely spell.

The boys did that for her, Michael still a child, but Edward changed. The older boy smiled to see them sitting there, but there was something more in his look now. He had been measured for a suit; he was on the path to adulthood. To Lucy's delight, he wore maturity well.

Dusk had settled over London. Feeling their upcoming separation, the boys wanted to share the same seat in the post chaise, which meant that Lucy was shoehorned in with Miles, his arm around her to make more room. She hadn't really meant to rest her head against his shoulder, but there he was, and so handy.

"You're not wearing bay rum," she said, which only hours ago would have struck her as silly conversation.

"You noticed?" he asked, and sounded pleased. "I tried something new that Roger brought back from Spain on his last visit. You like it?"

"*Sí, señor*," she teased, which suddenly lightened the odd tension she felt.

The butler informed them that dinner would be served in a half hour, so she hurried upstairs to her usual room to dress. The boys went next door and she heard them laughing and talking.

She sat on her bed for the longest time, thinking about Miles Bledsoe, the cousin who had teased her, laughed with her, got her in trouble now and then, shared her silliness, and rescued her from occasional folly. How did he know how desperate she was to never forget her mother, and how unhappy to see Clotilde miserable when she should be over the moon with joy? How did he know?

After her sister's wedding Miles would return to Christ Church College in Oxford. Well aware how he threw himself into his studies, she did not expect to see him, or even get the occasional letter until the end of Hilary Term. Suddenly March seemed so far away. Could she last that long without hearing from her cousin? Worse and worse, she would be in London for her Season, something she knew Miles had no interest in. He disliked ballrooms as much as she did. The hard fact was that she might not see him again for months, a realization which made her uneasy in the extreme.

Reason took over. Certainly she would manage without any word from or news of Miles Bledsoe. He was just her cousin, she reminded herself, and a second cousin at that. She knew she would be forever grateful for his Christmas intervention this year. She would have to thank Papa for inviting Miles to Tidwell; it had proved to be a stroke of genius, a word not generally associated with her fox hunting, pleasure-loving father. Mama had always been his leaven, and without her, Papa floundered. All the more reason to beg off from a London Season this year, and stay home. Papa needed a daughter at home, and Clotilde would be gone.

She resolved to thank her father when they returned to Tidwell. She also told herself to enjoy this evening with the Bledsoes, almost as dear to her heart as her own parents.

She took the boys hand in hand down to dinner, pleased to be joined by her Cousin Vivian, who offered her arm to Edward to escort her to the table. Miles and his father came down the hall from the bookroom, Miles serious, but Cousin Will smiling.

"Lucy, my dear, you grow lovelier by the hour," her cousin proclaimed, to her embarrassment. "No, Miles, it's my turn to see her in to dinner."

Any fears that dinner would overwhelm the Lonnigan brothers proved to be groundless. The footman led them to the breakfast room instead of the dining room.

Even better, the servants had put the entire dinner on the table in serving bowls. There would be no footmen standing about to offer dishes, and embarrass little boys not used to this much grandeur. She smiled at Vivian, communicating her pleasure at the woman's thoughtfulness.

Edward may have been the more astute of the two brothers, but Michael was the storyteller, once he overcame his natural shyness. His face animated, he regaled the Bledsoes with more stories of following the drum through Portugal and Spain.

"Do you miss the life?" Vivian asked, as she filled his plate again with more quail and potatoes.

"I suppose I should," he said finally, "but I don't mind change." He turned his attention to Lucy. "Miss, do you think your housekeeper and that Froggie cook will keep Mama and Mary Rose on?"

"I think it entirely likely," she said, happily perjuring herself, even though she had no idea. "The secret to success is to make yourself indispensable."

"Mama is good at that," Edward said.

"Then do not doubt," Lucy said, touched at the Lonnigan family's mutual devotion. She glanced at Miles, who was looking at her. She swallowed, thinking of her cousin's many kindnesses to her, and his own devotion. All of a sudden, her heart felt too large for her bodice.

The dinner continued with food and small talk, neither of which seemed to register with Lucy. When the boys were starting on their chocolate pudding, Miles stood up and held out his hand to Lucy. "I have something I need to talk to you about." He glanced at his father, as if for reassurance. "It really can't wait."

Lucy stood up, her mind in a whirl. The odd notion that her cousin might declare himself made her breath come faster.

She took his hand, and then his arm as he escorted her from the room.

In silence, he walked her down the hall to the library, a room she particularly enjoyed because she loved to read. He sat her down, but took himself to the fireplace, standing with his back to her as she waited and hoped.

He turned around, looked at her as if already measuring her response, and spoke. "Lucinda, I learned something today."

I believe I did, too, she thought, terrified and overjoyed at the same time. A week ago, she never would have felt this way. *He feels the way I do,* she thought with gratitude.

He sat beside her, but he didn't reach for her hand, even though it lay quite available on her leg. "It's this: Mr. Bradfield let drop an alarming bit of news. He couldn't say much, because he is an ethical man, and this is effectively none of my business."

Suddenly deflated, Lucy did her best to appear interested. "Better tell me," she said, as her heart plummeted into her shoes, probably destined to remain there for the rest of her life, if it was a life without Miles.

"He intimated that Lord Masterton isn't as plump in the pockets as he may have let on."

"*What?*"

He took her hand then, and Lucy gladly let him. "Mr. Bradfield could show me no facts or figures—that would be monumentally unethical—but he cautioned me and suggested in a roundabout way that someone should say something to your father."

Lucy forgot herself and let that unwelcome news sink in. Miles obviously had no intention of declaring himself, or protesting his love, or any other silly scheme she had imagined, but he was still concerned for her family. That was enough. Most girls didn't fall in love with their cousins, anyway. She pushed that thought into a closet in her mind, locked the door, and gave him her attention.

"Will Lord Masterton ruin us?" she asked, suddenly fearful for her ramshackle, dear father, who never met a horse he didn't like, and who had probably depended on her mother for sound decision-making. She felt her heart grow cold with fear.

"He could, Lucinda, and that is what worries me," Miles said. "As matters stand now, your father will pay the Danforth marriage portion to Lord Masterton and Clotilde will marry him. I fear that Cousin Roscoe's new son-in-law will continue to demand money and more money. I fear it greatly."

He released her hand and stood up, walking back to the fireplace to kick at a log. He stopped in front of her and blew out his cheeks in exasperation. "Deuce take it, Lucinda, don't think me a churl if I say that without your mother's calm judgment and wisdom, your father will be pudding in the hands of a practiced sharpster like Lord Masterton."

He sat down beside her again and put his arm around her, pulling her close. "I won't see you and your family ruined, but how can we stop him?"

"You need to tell Papa what you have told me," she said immediately, wanting to leap up and run all the way through London until she was home in Kent. "I must speak to Clotilde." She took his hand. "Miles, I honestly do not know if she has the strength of will to end the engagement at this late date."

He leaned back, tugging her with him. "She must, Lucinda," he said. "There might be repercussions of an embarrassing nature for Clotilde—you know, young lady jilts distinguished marquis." He kissed her hand. "And you might find yourself quite unwelcome in London. I have no doubt that Lord Masterton will spread rumors to soothe his pride."

"You already know how I feel about my London Season," she answered.

"I certainly do." He gave her a hand up to her feet. "We'll be out of here first thing in the morning and ready to do our duty."

Her eyes filled with tears. "Thank you, Miles. We're going to be ever in your debt."

He gave her a hug—the cousinly kind, to her dismay—and started down the hall to the breakfast room, where she heard laughter. He stopped and tapped her nose, something he hadn't done in years, but which he had done to get her attention when she was eight or so.

"Lucinda, there is something even better going on in there. My father may have just made an offer to Michael."

She grasped his elbows. "Please tell me!"

"Nope. Let's just hurry to the breakfast room and see if I'm right."

What she saw made her heart seem too large for her breast. Both Michael and Edward sat close together, nearly on one chair, their arms around each other, both in tears, but with smiles, too.

Vivian dabbed at her own eyes, and Will laughed at them all. "My dears, a man makes a simple request for services, and everyone turns into watering pots!" he said.

Lucy knelt by Michael. "You'd better tell me, my dear," she said. She took a handkerchief from her sleeve. "Here. Blow."

Michael did as she asked. He found a dry spot and handed it to his brother. "Miss, I'm going to stay right here and help in Mr. Bledsoe's stable!"

Lucy bowed her head in relief and gratitude, as she wondered just how many emotions of a startling nature were going to plague her this Christmas.

"Among other matters, Miles and I discussed this before dinner," her cousin said, giving his son a pat on the shoulder. "My stable master is getting a bit creaky. He has been asking for help. I believe Michael here will be just the ticket, eh, Michael?"

The boy nodded and spoke to Lucy. "Miss, he has promised me a room of my own over the stables, and . . . and Edward can stay here on his day off, if he'd like."

"I would like that, above all," Edward said. "Miss, we'll look out for each other in London, and you can look out for our mam and sister in Kent."

"It's a promise," Lucy said.

CHAPTER THIRTEEN

With a full heart, Lucy kissed the Bledsoes goodbye on the morrow, after hearing their assurances that they would be arriving soon for Clotilde's wedding. Miles disappointed her by sending her and the brothers on without him.

"I have a matter of business here in the city," he told her. "It will be done by noon, I am certain. I'll take my horse and meet you in Tidwell by nightfall or sooner."

She nodded, part of her relieved that she wouldn't be sharing close quarters with the man she wanted to kiss, and the other part unhappy for the same reason. In one day she had gone from being a practical, rational female, to someone even sillier than Clotilde, and all because of a cousin she had known for years. She didn't like the feeling.

Occupied with their own plans, the Lonnigan brothers paid no attention to her, which suited Lucy completely. She thought through her uncomfortable dilemma, realizing with a pang that she understood precisely what it felt like to be in love, because she was. She consoled herself that she was young, and someone else might come along someday who would make her laugh, and worry, and want to become the best person she was capable of. Miles was interested in being just a cousin, and not a husband.

Better now that Miles Bledsoe not even return to Tidwell. If she could convince her father and Clotilde of the folly of an alliance with Lord Masterton, there was no need of his comforting presence. Mrs. Little could gather up his clothing and books and ship them to London, or to Christ Church College. He would go his way, and she, hers. They would likely meet now and then at family gatherings, but she would be prepared and calm.

She swallowed her tears and focused on the Lonnigans. With Miles's magnificent help, she had kept Christmas for Mama. One less family was headed toward ruin. She had made a difference in four lives, each life as God-given and important as hers, no matter their difference in station and class. This was charity of the best kind, the charity that mattered. It had been Mama's gift to her, given beyond death.

They ate at the same ordinary tavern. To her delight or chagrin—the matter was in some doubt—Miles joined them just as she was paying the bill. His coat was dirty and mud covered, but his eyes had their same twinkle.

"I'm leaving my nag here, because I rode him hard," he said, after asking the publican for a bag of pasties to tide him over. "You get me in all my dirt in the chaise. My parents will stop here and retrieve my horse when they come for the wedding."

"We're hoping there isn't a wedding," she reminded him as the four of them, veteran travelers now, piled into the chaise again.

"We'll do our best," he said, which struck her as ambiguous in the extreme, and unlike the man she adored. If she hadn't been so miserable, his reply would have made her grumpy.

The boys were asleep when the chaise slowed and the post riders followed Miles's directions to the humble side of Tidwell. Her heart full, Lucy watched as the door opened and Mrs. Lonnigan stood there with open arms. A few words from Miles reduced her to smiles through tears. A few words from Mrs. Lonnigan had him reaching for his own handkerchief.

"Good news. The best news," he told Lucy as he got into the chaise again. "Your housekeeper has found Mrs. Lonnigan indispensable. She has permanent employment. And Mary Rose slices onions better than he does, according to Honoré."

Lucy leaned back in relief.

"You don't mind that I told them all to come to the wedding?" he asked.

"Not at all," Lucy replied, "but we're trying to prevent the wedding, remember?"

"I remember," he said, and nothing more, until they arrived at Number Five Mannering Street.

Finally looking tired—Lucy wondered what fueled his energy—Miles paid off the post riders and wished them Happy Christmas. He picked up his baggage and hers, too, which made her protest. He ignored her objections, but did allow her to go first and open the front door.

All was quiet within, amazingly quiet, too quiet. "Milsap?" she asked finally. "Mrs. Little?"

She looked at Miles, who shrugged, went to the still-open door, and banged on the knocker. She heard a shuffling of feet, and there was Milsap, looking far older than he had only yesterday. He paled noticeably to see her, and then unbent so far as to grasp both her hands, which made Miles stare, open mouthed.

"Miss Lucy! You will not believe what has happened!" he said, sounding more like Clotilde than their old tried and true butler.

"Uh, Napoleon has escaped from St. Helena, too?" Miles asked, which earned him a freezing stare from the Danforth's normally proper butler.

Milsap opened his mouth and nothing came out. He tried again. "Miss Danforth has eloped to Gretna Green."

Lucy gasped and sat down with a thump in one of the spindly hall chairs that seldom were sat upon. It groaned alarmingly, even though she was not heavy.

"Why in the world would Lord Masterton ever do something like that?" she managed to say at last. "A wedding would puff up his pretensions."

"It was not the marquis." Milsap rolled his eyes and sat in the opposite chair, something he had never done in Lucy's memory.

"Who . . . who . . . who?" Miles tried, and then stopped, because he was making himself laugh.

"James Petry," Milsap said, "our next door neighbor!"

Lucy stirred in the chair, which creaked so alarmingly that Miles took her by the hand and walked her to the bottom steps of the hall staircase, where he sat them both down.

Milsap joined them, a shaken man. "You probably passed Lord Masterton in the lane," he said. "He arrived an hour ago. I've never seen someone turn so red, or jump up and down and dump flowers from vases, and just generally make a fool of himself."

Lucy felt a huge laugh welling inside, which she welcomed, after her melancholic thoughts from London to Tidwell. "I wish we had witnessed this," she said, more to herself than anyone else in the room, which now contained a servant or two, in addition to Milsap.

"Aye, miss, he screamed and carried on, breathing out all manner of curses and foul language," the 'tween-stairs maid said. "Your papa just stood there and listened, then handed him his hat, dusted it off, and showed him out."

"Clotilde is well and truly gone?" Lucy asked, still unable to contemplate such a blessed turn of events.

"On her way to Gretna Green, according to this note." Milsap took a much-creased bit of paper from his breast pocket. "Here."

Lucy opened the note and held it so Miles could read it, too. " 'Dear averyone,' " she read, " 'I have aloped with my dearest friend, James Petry . . .' "

"She never could spell," Miles said, looking at the note. His shoulders started to shake. He made strangling noises, which meant Lucy felt duty-bound to loosen his muffler and jerk on his neckcloth. "Oh, my, thank you!" he managed. "Who in the world is—"

"James Petry," Lucy said. "He lives next door. He is a solicitor. In a fit of rare bravery once—perhaps he was mizzled—he told me how much he loved Clotilde, and that he would never have the courage to ask for her hand." She laughed. "And Clotilde told me once what a nice fellow he was, but so shy."

"People confide in you, don't they?" he asked.

"All the time." She stopped and didn't even try not to lean against Miles's shoulder. "People used to do that to Mama." Her face felt wet then, but she didn't mind. She turned to face her cousin. "Miles, when did I turn into my mother?"

He didn't hesitate. "You've always been like her—quiet, calm, a home-body, a problem solver, and so kind."

"That is quite the nicest thing you have ever said to me," she told him, hunkering down to be closer to him.

"I'll say something nicer in a few minutes, but first, we'd better find your father," he told her, just when she was comfortable in that excellent place under his arm, close to his chest. "Up you get. Milsap, go have a drink of something stronger than barley water. You need it. We'll close up here."

The butler gave Miles no argument, which impressed Lucy. She couldn't think of a time when Milsap let anyone else lock the front door. This was turning into a day of surprises.

"Where do you suppose my cousin is?" Miles asked.

"Let's try the library. Papa never reads, but he likes to sit there."

He took her hand and they ambled down the hall, neither in any particular hurry, now that Clotilde and her shy suitor were coursing through the night to Scotland.

"Whatever gave Mr. Petry the nerve to propose to my already engaged sister?" she asked.

"Love does strange things to a man," Miles said, as they walked along, arm in arm.

"Oh, now, how would you know?" she asked. "You told me only a few days ago that neither of us had any idea what it felt like to be in love." She could tease him now. The crisis with Clotilde was over, and he would leave soon. She had all winter to discover how strong she was. With any luck, in ten or twelve years she could see him again and not want to cry. "I remember distinctly that you told me so."

"I now suspect that life can turn on a penny," he said, his voice full of humor. "Only consider Clotilde!"

Sure enough, Papa sat in the library, his stocking feet propped on the ottoman, a glass of something dark in his hand. He gave them an owlish stare, then waved them closer.

Lucy took a sniff. The fumes weren't too strong. He might still be lucid. "Papa, what in the world possessed Clotilde?" she asked.

"There was a note. Ah, you have it, Miles," he said, his words barely slurred.

"I do, and I didn't finish reading it. Let's see: '"my dearest friend . . .' ah, here we are. 'I have been mizzerabul for weeks . . .' I do love how she spells."

"Miles," Lucy said, "must I thrash you?"

"Like to see you try," he teased, all exhaustion gone from his voice. She could tell he was hugely enjoying this bit of Danforth drama. "Here I go. I will finish it. '. . . for weeks. Jemmy just asked me why on earth I was marrying that old toady and not him. I didn't have a good answer." He held the page closer, "'He is a graded tosser!' That can't be. Oh! Oh! 'He is a great kisser!' We'll be home soon. Happy Christmas and love from both of us. Clotilde.'" He folded the note and laid it in Papa's lap. "He simply asked Clotilde. My hat's off to Jemmy Next Door. Better tell me, Lucinda: is he a suitable match?"

"Oh, my yes," she said. "He's steady and hardworking, and worth a bit of money himself. And he's right next door."

Miles was laughing again, except he had his overcoat off now and his neckcloth loosened. He held out his arm to her, and she resumed that comfortable spot where she fit so well.

She closed her eyes, so grateful to Jemmy Petry for working up his nerve. He was the perfect husband for her flibbertigibbet sister who had no more than two or three brain cells, but an ocean of kindness and love to make up for it. Even better, Clotilde would be living right next door to Papa.

Drowsy now, she listened as Miles told her father about the less-than-wealthy Lord Masterton, who was more of a fortune hunter than anyone knew, except his banker. Papa set aside his dark brew.

"This is good news, indeed, Miles. We've probably been saved from ruin by an ugly customer. Heaven knows my dear wife had all the intelligence in the family. She'd have seen him for what he was right away." He shook his head, and his voice broke. "By the eternal, I miss her."

So it turned out that Miles had another arm available for his cousin Roscoe Danforth. Papa sniffed a bit, blew his nose, and managed a watery chuckle. "By George but this will make a good story to tell around the district," he said.

Papa sat up, as reality surfaced. "Lucy, we have to write a lot of letters tomorrow. Clotilde's nonexistent wedding is in two days—Christmas Eve!—and we need to warn everyone away."

"Or we could just have a really fine party," she said. "There's so much food, and a cake, too. I do love cake."

"We could do that," Papa said. "Why not?"

"I have a better idea," Miles said. He tightened his grip on Lucy's shoulder, then moved his arm down her back until his hand rested on her waistband, comforting her and teasing her at the same time. "Lucinda, I can do one of two things. You know I'm headed back to Oxford as soon as the wedding is over."

"Don't remind me," she whispered, her voice small. She took a ragged breath, then decided to try out her future brother-in-law's remedy for cardiac distress. What could it hurt to take a page from Jemmy Petry's book? It would be aye or nay. She could just ask.

"I'm not certain when it happened, Miles, but I love you."

"I know you do," he said, but he sounded unsure of himself.

"Even more than as a cousin," she continued doggedly. Might as well play this out to the end and leave herself no doubt. "So much more. I . . . I wish you would marry me. I know I'm not supposed to ask, but . . ."

She turned to face him, her hand on his chest now, her eyes on his. "I am so happy that Papa invited you to come to Tidwell and help us out."

He smiled then, a smile so huge that she could see it, even in the darkness of the library, lit only by a struggling fire in the hearth. "He didn't invite me, Lucinda." He tapped her nose in that silly way again. "I invited *myself*. I wanted to see you. I *had* to see you." He took her hands then. "Not sure when all this started. I mean, all I was doing the last few weeks of the Michaelmas Term was sitting in my carrel and doodling your name in the margins of expensive books."

She gasped and kissed him.

Or maybe he kissed her. However it happened, she knew she wanted to kiss him lots more, maybe for years. And then she was clasped in his arms, and he was saying silly things that no one at Christ Church College would ever imagine could pass the lips of a double first scholar.

Only a mighty clearing of her father's throat brought them up for air. "Should I sit between you two lovebirds?" he asked, sounding like Papa again.

"Only if you want me to call you out, Cousin, or Father-in-Law, or both, I suppose. What will our marriage—oh, that sounds good—do to future genealogists, I wonder?"

"Nothing, my lad. It's quite legal, as you well know. You could be first cousins, and it would still be legal." Papa sighed. "I just wish Mama were here to savor the moment."

"She probably knows, Papa," Lucy said, from the depths of Miles's generous embrace. "My goodness. She would be way ahead of us and wondering about crying banns . . . Oh, bother! We have to wait three weeks! I can't. I love this man." She giggled. "I'm sounding like Clotilde."

"No, you're not. You sound like a woman in love. We only have to wait until tomorrow," Miles said. He sat up enough to reach inside his coat pocket. "Why did you think I was late this morning? A quick visit to chancery court bought me a special license." He took a deep breath, and suddenly looked so young, even a bit unsure of himself. "I had to take the chance, same as you just did." He grinned at her. "You were just a bit braver than I was."

"Sort of like Jemmy Petry next door?" she asked, teasing him, because he was still going to be Miles, the cousin she had loved and teased for years.

"Jemmy's kind of love must be contagious, Lucinda." Another deep breath. "I intend to take my wife—my, that also sounds good—my *wife* back to Oxford, where I have quite a nice home all ready for her."

"Don't you live on the quad at Christ Church?" she asked.

He kissed the top of her head and must have liked it, because he did it again. "I did until about a month ago, when for some inexplicable reason, I bought a house."

"Miles, you amaze me," she said.

"Me, too." He patted her hip and must have liked that, too, because he did it again.

"In three weeks we'll be starting the Hilary Term, and I can't be late."

Lucy sat up. He tugged her back down. "How long have you been planning this, my love?" she asked, trying out the words and finding them entirely compatible with the way she felt.

"I've known you eighteen years," he said. "This last year, I've noted how greatly improved you have become, over the previous seventeen, up to and including my doodles in the Bodleian. More likely, *I* have improved. I suspect you were always wonderful. What about you?"

She thought the matter through. "Blame your mother. Vivian told me that being in love was almost an uncomfortable feeling, when the man you love was farther away than the next room." She kissed his cheek. "She was right. The idea of you in Oxford and me in Tidwell . . ." She hesitated, barely able to continue. "I couldn't bear it, so I had to . . . propose to you." She laughed, then felt her face go warm. "You have my permission to tell our children someday that you proposed first."

"I'll do it." Miles kissed her, then he cupped her face in his hands, his expression more serious. "My love, I still want to become a diplomatist. That means strange places and bigger cities than little Tidwell. I know you prefer the quiet life."

She kissed his cheek and then his lips, because there they were, and she was never one to waste anything. "If you are by my side, I have no fear."

"I'm not certain I deserve such praise," he said, his voice subdued. "I intend to spend my life, our lives, earning it."

He laughed softly, smoothing over the solemnity because he was Miles. "And a Happy Christmas this has become. With Lord Masterton gone, we are at leave to sing all the loud carols we want, and drink wassail until we're tiddly. What did you tell Honoré you wanted?"

"Toasted cheese, wassail, and you alone," she said promptly. "Will anyone mind?"

Miles looked around elaborately. "Any dissenters? I hear no objections. If there are any, the cheese and wassail will keep until Oxford. I may not have much in the way of cooking utensils yet, but I have a long-handled fork."

They laughed together. Lucy leaned her head against Miles's shoulder. "I have another thought." She sat up, and Miles gently pushed her back. "Miles, do you have a housekeeper yet?"

"I barely have a house, and I already told you about the long-handled fork. That roughly constitutes my domestic property."

"It's this: why not ask Mrs. Lonnigan to do the honors? And Mary Rose could work with the cook."

"When we get a cook," Miles told her. He picked up her hand and kissed it. "You are brilliant, my love. We'll ask them tomorrow." He glanced over at Lucy's father. "Cousin Roscoe, maybe we'll kidnap Honoré."

Papa glared at Miles. "Do it and I will call you out." He giggled, then hiccupped. "Twenty paces with those long-handled forks."

"Oh, Papa," Lucy said. "Miles only has one fork."

"We'll have to take turns killing each other," Miles teased. "Honoré is safe. For a while, anyway. Dear Cousin Roscoe, go to bed."

Papa staggered to his feet. "I'll contact our vicar tomorrow morning early," he told them. "What do you say to a wedding tomorrow at ten of the clock, and the party the day after that on the twenty-fourth, as planned? I doubt you want to wait all the way to Christmas Eve to be married. That's a whole two days!"

"No, Papa, I don't," she agreed, seeking for some dignity, even though Miles thought it funny. "People will be here for the party, and we will already be married."

She looked at Miles, who smiled back. "You'll get your toasted cheese and quiet time with me alone, Lucinda."

Her face fell. "Miles, your parents won't be here if we marry tomorrow morning. We can't do that to them. We'll wait."

In answer, he pulled out his timepiece and studied it elaborately. "They're on their way. I expect them sometime tomorrow morning, quite early." He kissed her cheek. "Believe it or not, my love, I was going to propose to you this evening, and so I told my parents. You were faster, as it happened."

Suddenly shy, she turned her face into his chest, where she felt the steady beat of his generous heart.

Papa was just warming to the subject. "Thank goodness you are Clotilde's size, Lucy. Her dress will look fine on you, and think of the economy for me. Anyone? Yoo hoo. Anyone? Did you hear a word I said?"

"Oh, Papa," Lucy said, her hair a mess because Miles seemed to enjoy running his fingers through it while they kissed. "We are sane and sensible still."

"Hardly," Miles said, after Papa said goodnight and closed the door. "I don't even have a ring for you, let alone a gift."

"Neither do I," she said. She touched his dear face, a face she knew so well. "I'll be your gift and you will be mine. Mama would like that."

He held her close. Together they watched the last of the embers pop and fizzle in the fireplace. In that curious, hallowed way, the benediction of the season spread over them both, because Miles Bledsoe and Lucinda Danforth knew how to keep Christmas.